The Caspian Circle

Donné Raffat

The
Caspian Circle

A Novel

Houghton Mifflin Company
Boston 1978

Library of Congress Cataloging in Publication Data

Raffat, Donné.
    The Caspian circle.

    I. Title.
PZ4.R139Cas [PS3568.A36]   813'.5'4   77-20803
ISBN 0-395-25933-9

Printed in the United States of America

v 10 9 8 7 6 5 4 3 2 1

for
Moreno and Luz Alvarez-Calderón de Levy

Who has once been bitten by a serpent will
be afraid, thereafter, even of a rope.

Nizami, *Leyla and Majnun*

Contents

Principal Characters

at the start of the action: Summer 1948

THE AMUZEGARS

Majid Amuzegar, *a colonel in the Iranian Army*
Nasrin Amuzegar, *his wife, daughter of the Ashrafis*
Parviz, *their son*

THE ASHRAFIS

Amin Ashrafi, *a financier, father of Nasrin Amuzegar*
Mrs. Ashrafi, *his wife*
Bijan, *their son, Nasrin's brother*

HASSAN KARBALAI, *a wealthy industrialist*

THE KARIMZADEHS

Ahmad Karimzadeh, *a businessman settled in Tehran*
Mina Karimzadeh, *his wife*
Farid, *their elder son*
Matin, *their younger son*
Mahin, *their daughter and youngest child*
Abol Karimzadeh, *Ahmad's younger brother and business partner, living in Hamburg*
Zohre, *his daughter*

THE MOMTAZES

Omid Momtaz, *a businessman, friend of the Ashrafis and Karimzadehs*
Simin Momtaz, *his wife*
Firuz (Felix) Momtaz, *their son*

Part i

Ramsar

*M*ichael and I arrived at the Hotel Ramsar around two in the afternoon.

Actually, there are two Hotel Ramsars, the old and the new. They stand side by side, tucked in the mountains: white buildings against a deep, rich background of green. Of the two, I prefer the old building. It is stately and exudes the grandeur of an era gone by. It was built during the reign of the old king, Reza Shah, and I believe he had it constructed with a vision in mind: that Iran should have not just a resort on the Caspian, but a pearl on its shores.

The hotel, as I knew it as a child, stood alone in the mountains: incredibly lofty with its pillars, white masonry, and tall windows. A long, curving driveway led up to its entrance, guarded at its base by two stone lions. On the way up, you passed unending rows of hedges and red flowers.

And going up, you felt giddy: giddiness mingled with anticipation.

When you stepped out of the car, your head was still moving. It was the landscape that stood firmly in place. Behind you was the huge wall of mountain. In front lay the great look down. A long flight of steps — perhaps a hundred or more, I thought then — led down to sea level. Beyond that was the boulevard lined with palm trees. And at the end of the boulevard, up against the beach, was the Casino.

To me the Casino looked like a sea gull sprawled on the sand with its wings outstretched. In the middle was the head and body — the Casino itself — two stories high. On either side were colonnades, extending, on the left to the dining area, on the

right to the changing rooms. And just over the top of this structure, from my view at the hotel, I could see a patch of liquid
blue. This was the swimming pool between the Casino and the
beach. But to me it looked like a blue patch of blood, as though
the bird had been dying or was dead, and in the act of dying had
let out this mysterious fluid, which I call "blood" for want of a
better word.

When Michael and I arrived at the hotel, we parked the car in
the lot beside the new building. My father had loaned us his red
1959 Mercedes 220 for our travels. We had not used it before. On
our trip south, we were pressed for time and had great distances
to cover, going from one ruin to another, and so we had traveled
by plane instead. Nor had we been able to use the car on our trip
to the ruined fortress of Alamut; the roads through the mountains were too rough for a vehicle in such aged, albeit gracefully
aged, condition.

But coming to the Caspian was a different matter altogether.
What was needed here was a smooth running Mercedes. The
roads were good and clear of traffic.

We were well into the first week of September and the tourist
season was practically over — the weekends excepted, when a
few people from Tehran could be expected to show up. Otherwise only a few diehards and latecomers could be seen on the
beaches, small family groups clustered about picnic spreads.

The desertedness of the place came to me as a shock. Driving
up from Tehran, I had expected it, even counted on it insofar as I
had not bothered to make any hotel reservations. But seeing it
burst a tiny myth I had built up over the years: that the Caspian
was always crowded in summer.

Michael found the solitude to his liking. He had had too much
of crowds in Tehran and the south and welcomed the change —
the lack of faces. The scenery, he said, demanded it. Besides, we
were there to soak in as much sun and seawater as we could before returning to Chicago in a week.

Those were Michael's words. And yet, he was not much of a
swimmer. Nor did he like to lie about in the sun: his skin soon
became red and bothered him. It would have maddened him,
however, to come all the way to Iran and not take a dip in the

Caspian. Several dips, in fact — enough to know what the water felt like, and the sand beneath him, so that he could store the experience in his memory.

We allowed ourselves, all in all, five days on the Caspian. The first three we spent at Babolsar, which is on the eastern tip of the sea, before the shoreline curves north. The beach there is reputed to be the best on the coast. The sand is fine and white, the sea floor is smooth and makes a gradual descent. There are no mountains around, no tea plantations, only citrus trees, rice paddies, cotton fields. The land is flat. The air is not overly humid. Compared to Ramsar, it is dry. It is a splendid beach to lie on, but it lacks excitement.

And I must have lain on that beach for a good part of two days, reading, writing letters for the first time in months, and getting a tan, which comes easily to my light olive skin. Michael sat under a beach umbrella, working on his lecture notes, tossing, every once in a while, a postcard-sized filing card full of scribbles into a Pan Am bag.

Otherwise our main preoccupation was eating. Generally, we ate well, but in dismal quarters. Babolsar, too, in emulation of Ramsar, had a Casino. The Casino consisted of a dining room and a lounge, both sparsely filled. The hubbub was missing. You could hear waiters crossing the room. You could hear trays rattling. And when you put your eating utensils down on your plate, you were conscious of doing just that.

I was dejected: something was already brewing inside. We left Babolsar, after an early morning swim on my part, and drove to Ramsar.

Before we got there — around noon — we stopped to walk through a forest. Michael had wanted to see it. I had been there before, but again in the past, as a child. When we were in the thickness of trees, with only a footpath to guide us, he threw out his arms and declared, "The Hyrcanian Woods!"

Of course, he was right. This was the Hyrcanian Woods, which both Greeks and Romans had considered impenetrable. It had gone down in legend as a forest to be feared. To me, however, it was the Herazpi Jungle. The jungle of Hedayat's story, in which the Iranians had sought shelter from invading Mongols.

5

We stayed in the darkness of the forest long enough for Michael to take several pictures of trees at his leisure. He selected the ones with the best gnarls, those draped in Spanish moss, those with branches sticking out horizontally, with offshoots growing out of them directly upward, ninety-degree fashion. Then we drove on to Ramsar.

The scenery changed as we moved westward along the coast. Mountains came into view. The sand on the beach changed color, growing darker. Shingles appeared. The air became sultry. You could sense the moisture in it. Once in the mountains, we were in a thick, green world: from the light green of the rice paddies, we had passed into the darker one of the tea plantations. Finally, the mountains actually bore down on us — dominated our vision — taking our eyes and minds off the sea altogether.

Michael caught sight of the two hotels standing side by side and asked me about them. I explained what I knew; it was the first time I had seen the new building myself.

I was afraid the old building would be closed, boarded up. A negative argument ran through my mind: since the tourist season was over, what sense could there be in keeping it open? Especially when such a functional new piece was standing by its side.

I was unnecessarily pessimistic. When I inquired at the reception desk, I was told that both buildings were open. I still cannot fathom why. There were very few people about. The rooms in the old building, moreover, were cheaper, since air-conditioning was not available. The kitchen, however, was shut, and meals were to be taken in the new dining room.

I returned to Michael with the news. He was in the lounge, standing in front of a window which stretched from wall to wall, looking out on the panorama below.

"That's great," he said with energy. "In these surroundings I would have turned into a miserable tourist."

I looked around as I had when coming in. There were carpets from Kashan and Kerman, potted plants, comfortable gold velvet-covered sofas, marble tabletops. There was the view from the huge wall of glass. It was cool.

I was easily seducible.

To Michael there was something inherently malignant about these trappings. They nettled him. They turned him, as he said, into a "tourist" — something he did not wish to be. Whereas the voice within him, that which had motivated him to come to Iran in the first place, hopping from ruin to ruin, cried out that he was an adventurer.

To me trappings were a part of nature. My nature, if you will. I had grown up with them, and generally I embraced them readily enough. And, frankly, I would not have minded staying at the new hotel, having seen it from the inside. Looking about, I thought I would have preferred it to the old one, but for the pull of the past.

The pull of the past.

I wanted, more than the trappings, to stay in the hotel I had slept in as a child.

Why?

2

*O*n the bed by the window lay Michael Francis Florio. Asleep. Thirty-four years old. American. Single. Associate Professor of English at the University of Chicago. Educated at Holy Cross, graduating summa cum laude, and at Yale, where he was given a prize for his doctoral dissertation. Then Chicago, and another award for excellence in teaching. Published a book on Renaissance literature. Favorably reviewed. Tenured shortly thereafter. Very much settled now in his work.

On this bed by the door was Felix Firuz Momtaz. Very much awake. Puffing on a cigarette. Felix the name adopted in the West, and Firuz his given one. Thirty-two years old. Divorced. Assistant Professor of Comparative Literature at the same university. An Iranian. Educated at various schools in Iran, America, Germany, and England. Attended Harvard, graduating cum laude, then Michigan. No special honors along the way. Professionally very much unsettled.

Unsettled in other ways too. Now growing increasingly aware of the fact. Here on the Caspian. At Ramsar in particular. The old hotel.

I looked at Michael asleep on his bed. It was not his brilliance I envied. That was a quality in him I valued. Our friendship, if anything, rested on mind, on discourse — our mutual ability (and need, I suppose) to turn intellectual matter into emotional content.

Nor did I envy his swift climb to professional eminence. He deserved it. He worked hard and thought well. Had things gone otherwise for him, it would have been a gloomier world to contemplate.

But I did envy him his calm. His ability to sleep in the middle of the day: to adjust so easily to Middle East custom — to nap after lunch. To be in this part of the world and not be agitated. To make lecture notes on the beach.

How many cigarettes had I gone through already? I counted the stubs in the ashtray. Six. Six in a little over an hour, and that is a lot for me. I am generally content to puff on a pipe.

Getting into our room in the old hotel had been a curious ordeal. There was no one behind the reception desk, no one in the halls. We walked about and waited. We ventured into the empty kitchen, tried doorknobs. Eventually we resorted to shouting.

Imagine walking into a hotel and shouting for service! Not just any hotel, but one which defined in your mind a certain sense of style.

I was disconsolate. What, I wondered, had happened to this place?

We went outside and circled the building, in hope of finding someone. When that failed, I ran back to the new hotel — leaving Michael seated on the rim of a huge potted palm — and, breathless, demanded an explanation.

The man behind the desk eyed me coolly. He was applying a fresh carnation to the lapel of his jacket. That done, he spoke a few words into a telephone, then, looking down at his shoes, stated that someone would be over shortly. I waited at the desk until a bellboy in black trousers and white mess coat appeared. He sauntered up to the desk and took a batch of keys from the man behind. Then, without looking back, he walked away, expecting me to follow.

Suddenly, at the door, the idea struck me. I shoved a five-toman note into his hand and told him to get us into a room as quickly as possible. He bowed, transformed into an instrument of my will.

It was as simple as that. Money talked. Word would no doubt get back to the flowered man behind the desk, who would approve: the new arrivals had been housebroken.

But what of the name Momtaz? Had all the magic gone out of that? The man had seen me sign in. Did the name convey nothing at all?

In my father's time it had been otherwise.

We had sandwiches and beer for lunch, and Michael asked for a side order of Beluga caviar, which was served to him in what looked like a parfait glass. He relished this extra bit of luxury. Then we sipped Turkish coffee, outlining briefly what we wanted to do the rest of the day.

Michael wanted a siesta and left the rest up to me. I suggested going down to the Casino afterward and a swim in the pool.

"Why not the sea?" Michael asked.

"We can, if you like," I said. "But the beach isn't good."

We left it at that and returned to our room.

But back in the room, the mood swept over me again, set off this time, perhaps, by a crack in the wall.

Or the thought of going down to the Casino.

Did I really want to go there? Did I really want to swim in the pool, when staying at the hotel was disturbing enough, seeing the place in a state of abandonment and gradual decay?

I thought of the sea gull stretched on the beach — dead or dying — and its mysterious fluid.

Michael was right: why not swim in the sea?

Was it because I had once seen a snake slither along the beach? After which I never dared venture into the seawater, for fear of stepping on a slithering object, or seeing something slithering after me.

The choice lay between swimming in the sea or the pool: the snake's territory or the gull's fluid.

That is how my mind was working when I stepped out into the hall.

I was looking for something familiar: something which was as it had been before — or as I remembered it as being. Grandiose. The walls were yellow. I had thought of them as being white. With brown trim, of all colors! The hall runners were frayed at the edges. The carpets in the lounge were dull compared with those in the new hotel. The furniture was heavy-looking and decidedly of the thirties.

A huge photograph of the old king, Reza Shah, as large as a tableau, standing against a similar background, hung on the wall. That was something. The old king with his bald pate and out-of-date mustache and uniform. That, surely, was the same as before.

I felt a smile come to my lips: the old king was dead — just as dead now as he had been when I had first come here as a child.

3

When I returned to the room, Michael was awake and ready for a swim. We packed our gear in separate bags, got into the car, and drove down the winding driveway and the long boulevard lined with palm trees. The late afternoon air had a mixture of smells: of soil, sea, flowers, and trees. Beneath all was the smell of soil.

When we reached the Casino, I was surprised to see a motel beside it. It was low, flat, innocuous-looking. When we had gazed down from the hotel, it had been hidden from view.

The Casino, by contrast, was glaringly white; conspicuous, as I had remembered. It was of the same architecture and masonry as the old hotel. It stood at the center of things — the long boulevard, the trees flanking the beach, the hedges flanking the colonnades met at its doorway. The mouth. The beak.

We went in. It was dark, hollow. Dank. I had the distinct feeling of coming in from outside, of stepping into an interior world of shadows, like going into a tunnel. Everything had a touch of grayness to it: the walls, the furniture, which was of the same era as that in the old hotel, the carpets even. The windows looked out on the sea, away from the sunlight.

A man appeared, dressed in a bellboy's uniform. He made an experienced bow and asked what we wanted. He was short and balding, middle-aged, and his uniform was too tight for his bulging body. He spoke with a regional accent — and a lisp, his upper front teeth being missing. Unlike the attendants at the hotel, who might well have been brought up from Tehran for the season, this man was local.

I told him we had come to swim in the pool and wanted a place to change. He said we needed tickets and asked if we were staying at the hotel. I said we were. In that case, he replied, the price would be cheaper: three tomans a person. I took out a ten-toman note and told him to pocket the difference, whereupon he grinned and gave a hand-to-heart bow. Then he went to a desk, unlocked it with a huge chain of keys, brought out a wad of pink slips, detached two, laboriously recorded their numbers in a ledger, and asked us to follow him.

As we walked through the colonnades, I looked about for signs of wear — for cracks. The terrace below was smaller than I had thought as a child.

I asked our guide for his name, also how long he had been at his job.

"Qolam Hossein, excellency," he replied. "Fourteen years. But I've lived in these parts all my life." He nodded at Michael. "Is the gentleman English?"

"American," I said, then introduced Michael and myself in return.

At the changing room, the attendant unhooked a key from his chain, opened the door, and put the key in my hand. Then he asked for the pink slips he had given us, which he tore and returned as receipts.

After changing, Michael and I went out on the terrace barefoot. The flagstones were warm from the day's sun. Then we descended the steps to the pool.

11

"You go in first," Michael said. "I was the first one in at Babolsar."

I slung my white robe over a deck chair. Michael sat down on the one across from it. Between them was a small, wrought-iron table, on which I put my bag and towel.

The pool was the same as before: very long, wide, and deep. Deep even at the shallow end. It was made for adults who knew how to swim. Off to the side was a much shallower round pool for children.

There was no one about. Only the attendant on the terrace above, standing and waiting for something to happen. And Michael digging into his Pan Am bag.

I approached the pool's edge and looked straight down. The liquid was brownish green now; it was seawater. Small yellow grains floated about, like dust particles spiraling in a shaft of sunlight. I could not make out the bottom. At the other end of the pool, the liquid's surface had picked up the glow of the sunset.

I walked around to the diving boards: a triangular structure with three levels, the lower boards on either side and the highest in the middle. I decided to dive off the top.

Climbing up the almost vertical ladder, I felt my body pulling me down. When I reached the top, it was as though I were looking down from a three-story building. I approached the edge of the board to test its spring. The liquid below was a sheet of flashing scarlet. Directly beneath, the scarlet faded into a greenish sort of burgundy.

I stepped back, breathed deeply, and took a three-step run, pouncing on the board to get a high, arching dive.

I plunged into the fluid, feeling myself go straight down. I made no attempt to break my dive, as one would in shallower water. I went down deep, until the force of my dive spent itself. Then, slowly, my body turned upward of its own accord, floating at first, then kicking, struggling, as I ran out of air.

I reached the surface with a gasp, my heart beating wildly, then rolled over on my back and swam the length of the pool with leisurely strokes.

Michael lowered himself into the water, using the pool ladder.

"It's warm," he said, treading his way out to the middle.

I made my turn back up the length of the pool, then got out. I went back to our chairs and draped the robe over my shoulders. The attendant had gone. I dried my hair, combed it, and slipped a watch over my wrist. Then I made my way down to the beach.

To walk comfortably, one needed sandals. I passed through the tall grass carefully, stepping lightly on stones. On shingles. Finally, I came to a small stretch of sand that was rough and hard.

I walked up and down this sandy stretch, face down, making a turn every thirty paces or so, then waded into the sea.

The water was cold. The sea floor had a steep, uneven descent. There was a sudden chill in the wind, and I stopped a few yards out. My feet sank into the sea floor, the current pulling them down.

Then I felt a sharp stab in the arch of one foot. So sharp that I yelled and scurried back to the beach, where I fell on the sand and examined my foot. My urge was to reach down and suck it. The movement was awkward. Nothing. My teeth began to chatter. My body trembled. I wanted to get out of there — get back to solid ground, where it was safe to stand.

I got up to run, but felt the stab again. I hobbled away, using my toes for support.

When I came to the pool, Michael was seated on his deck chair, with his lecture cards on his stomach.

"Anything wrong?"

I lowered my heel; the pain had gone.

"Anything the matter?" Michael repeated.

"I've been bitten," I said, sitting down.

"By what?"

"A snake."

Michael lurched forward. "Let's have a look, for Christ's sake!"

He peered at my foot, then leaned back with a look registering the conviction that he had been made the butt of a joke.

"Qolam Hossein!" I shouted.

The attendant appeared from the building, as though he'd been waiting for his name to be called.

"Do you have any cognac?"

"Only Iranian cognac, excellency."

13

"Bring it," I said. "A bottle with two glasses and water."

Then I told Michael what had happened on the beach.

"It was probably a muscle spasm," he said. "Or you just may have stepped on a sharp object which didn't perforate the skin."

I nodded.

"The rest I chalk up to your morbid imagination."

"Is that any better?"

"Would you prefer to be bitten by a real snake?"

"I was," I said. "Years ago. I was playing on the beach, making a fortress out of sand, when I got up and stepped on something sharp. Just then I caught sight of a snake slithering over the shingles into the tall grass. In that split second, I thought I was bitten. A moment later I knew I couldn't have been."

"And now?" Michael asked.

"Now I know I was bitten."

The cognac arrived, and Michael filled both glasses. I took a drink and felt a rush of warmth inside.

"After biting me, do you know what the snake did then? It slithered through the grass and bit everyone else in the Casino — where we sit now. On the terrace. Inside. As a child, looking down from the hotel, the Casino looked to me like a sea gull sprawled on the sand with its wings stretched out. It bit the gull. And as the gull lay dying, the blood flowed out of its body and fell into this pool. The pool we swam in."

4

Thereafter the details were clear in my mind and merged into a pattern. It was rather like seeing the mist suddenly rise from familiar terrain, making things strangely distinct through the haze. Michael asked me to go on, and I did.

I was on the beach, as I said, trying to structure something out of sand. It was the summer of 1948. I was ten years old.

Above, on the terrace, were the mothers and wives, seated in groups, sipping tea and playing canasta for small change. Inside the Casino the men were playing poker at considerably higher stakes.

There were two other boys I knew on the beach: Parviz Amuzegar, who was a year older than I, and Bijan Ashrafi, who was considerably older — I'd say about sixteen.

Parviz and I were temperamentally suited to each other. He was quietly resourceful and easy to get along with, while I was the talkative one who liked to initiate things. It was my idea, for example, to build the sand castle, whereas he was the one who laid out its architecture.

Between us stood Bijan — older, domineering — eyeing us from the water while we piled up sand, swimming, moving about with unleashed energy, forceful in an unpredictable sort of way. He was a terrible bully. He would pounce on us without warning and wrestle us both to the ground, not letting us up until he had both his knees on our chests, one on each. Then he would laugh in disgust and chide us for being weak.

He was dark, slender, and tall — though still not fully grown — and muscular in a wiry sort of way. His hair was black and frizzled, like a helmet about his head.

He resembled no one else in his family. All the Ashrafis were short and light-skinned: Turks from the north of Iran.

To me, he was the opposite of his sister Nasrin, who was decidedly petite and calm in her movements, almost economical: a pale beauty, with a flush of pink in her cheeks, large eyes, and a dense flow of reddish brown hair — like the Doña Isabel Cobos de Porcel of Goya.

One feature, however, they had in common: an open mouth, which refused to close, and full, soft lips. Their source of expression. Expressing what? I don't know. Expectation. Desire. At any rate, it was their mouths you looked at — centered your gaze on — the way you didn't with other people, the other Ashrafis included. It was as though the distinction had been meted out fatelike to brother and sister alone.

15

Nasrin was Parviz's mother, the wife of Colonel Amuzegar. The son had inherited the quiet good looks of his mother: the pale skin, large eyes, and soft, light brown hair. All but the mouth and lips, which were closed and tight, like his father's.

Despite the bullying and daily harassments, Bijan and Parviz were unusually close. Not all that unusual, I suppose, when you consider that they were uncle and nephew, separated by only a few years in age. But unusual in that the relationship had brought out in them a mysterious bond, which is normally glossed over by a much greater difference in years.

They were almost like brothers, but not quite. They were of the same stock — the same tree. But one was a bough unto himself, the other a branch off a separate bough. They did not appeal to the same authority. Bijan could be ruthless with Parviz and get away with it.

I saw him steal up behind Parviz one day and deal him a kidney punch which sent him sprawling into the sand, pulverized, and unable to walk straight for the rest of the day. Mind you, there were tears in Bijan's eyes when he saw what he had done. He was only testing his strength, and who else could he test it on, if not his nephew, who, incidentally, would have swallowed his tongue sooner than tell on him? This was not lost on Bijan, who would help him up, kiss the spot where the blow had landed, and walk him till he was able to stand on his own.

Another day — whack! It would be another part of the body. I marveled at the punishment Parviz could take.

I also writhed with anger; yearned to find a way of getting even with Bijan. I used to lull myself to sleep with thoughts of various medieval tortures I could put him to. The thumbscrew. The rack. But nothing, somehow, matched the thwack of the kidney punch, delivered from behind in broad daylight.

This Bijan also knew. When he had me down with a knee on my chest, he gave it an extra shove to make me understand just where the power lay.

There is more to the story than that, which I will get to later. The point is that, had I been able to, I would have gotten back at him. Parviz wouldn't. He took it all submissively.

He and I were good friends, mind. We appreciated each other's company. We liked doing things together. We were on

16

even terms. Bijan's presence was a pain to him — some kind of torture he put up with. Yet, he was closer to Bijan.

Possibly this was also because I was such a newcomer to Iran. I had just returned from America, more at home with English than my own mother tongue, whereas he and Bijan had grown up in Iran: side by side through the years, except for one brief spell of separation.

All this counts, I suppose, when you consider what makes two people act together, while the third sets himself apart.

When Bijan came out of the water after his swim, he fell on the sand and watched us building quietly. For a while. Then he got up and told us to follow him. He wanted to ride the Colonel's horse and needed our help in diverting the groom's attention.

The Colonel had a dapple gray horse, which he rode all over the countryside. In the summer he brought it up to Ramsar, where he had an estate. In the autumn he took it back to Tehran, where he kept a stable. In spring he entered it in the Jalalieh races, sometimes riding it himself, sometimes giving it over to his Turkoman jockey — the only other person allowed on its back. No one else was to ride it. Those were his orders.

The horse was a champion. It was used to coming in first. As a racer, it had won three gold medals in national competitions, and had done much to propel the Colonel's reputation as a horseman. Now the Colonel was trying to break it in as a jumper.

It was called Marabebus, which means "Kiss me" — the name bestowed upon it at the time of its birth, when the Turkoman jockey had thrown his arms about its neck and planted a kiss on its crest.

This horse, Marabebus, Bijan wanted to mount and ride. Actually, he had done so before — once in Tehran — and had gotten a beating for it. So had the groom, who had been seduced by the boy's talk, only to see him make off with the animal, before taking a tumble. They had had to go after the horse with a jeep.

The Colonel was livid. He dismissed the groom and warned Bijan that if he ever went near the horse again, he would be dealt with in less gentle fashion.

Now Bijan wanted us to go along with him: to be sure, as he

said, to make his task easier, but also, I felt, to have accomplices. If we were caught, there would be three culprits to answer for, rather than one.

I refused, on the grounds that the consequences outmeasured the risks, and that a naked challenge to authority did not interest me.

Parviz vacillated, but went, drawn, I suppose, by the same forces which led him to put up with punishment quietly.

And so, I came to be alone on the beach. At first, I went ahead with our work of construction. But then I stopped. A wave of loneliness swept over me. I felt a chill in the wind. The sand castle ceased to have meaning. Without Parviz, I had lost sight of its planning.

I thought of joining the others with the horse.

I got up, stepped on something sharp, and saw the snake slither into the grass.

Seeing the snake made me change my mind. I ran to the terrace instead. I wanted to tell my mother what I had seen, and, I suppose, to be held.

She was seated at a round table with friends, Mrs. Ashrafi and Nasrin Amuzegar. There was a vacant chair where Mrs. Karim-zadeh had been sitting. They had just finished a round of canasta and were strangely silent.

Nasrin was peeling cucumbers and slicing them into fours for the company. The other two were quietly looking at her, like viewers at a movie.

I didn't know then what was going on. I approached my mother's chair from behind and whispered into her ear — what I thought was a whisper, but came out much louder in my breathlessness.

Nasrin looked up and took me in with those large eyes of hers, her mouth open.

"A snake? Oh, that's nothing." My mother laughed, comforting me in English, and I think she tousled my hair. "Remember the ones we saw in New Jersey?"

Yes, I remembered. That had been two years earlier, and I had been just as petrified then. My mother, dauntless, had gone after them with a long, broom-sized gardening fork, actually forking one at the base of its head. She was very agile, very nimble in her movements. Athletic. Svelte.

She turned to the ladies and explained the New Jersey incident in Turkish.

Mrs. Ashrafi chortled a reply in the same tongue. She almost always spoke Turkish, even with me, who had only a hazy understanding of it. When she lapsed into Persian, it was with a strong Azerbaijani accent.

It was strange to think of her as Nasrin's mother. She was locked into the language in a way her daughter was not. A native of Khoy, like her husband, she had spent her formative years in the provinces. Nasrin, on the other hand, had been born and raised in Tehran; she had attended the Jeanne d'Arc School in the city and was fluent in both Persian and French. Moreover, despite the family resemblances — the light skin, the reddish brown hair — their appearances clashed. Nasrin was compact, fleshier than my mother, what I would call well put together. Nasrin's mother was a strange mixture of emaciation and plumpness, her face rectangular and drawn, her breasts saggy and flat, those of a thin woman. Whereas the rest of her body, from the breasts down, swelled into corpulence. Her hair, too, was a mixture of reddish brown and white, thinning in the middle, where it was parted.

Actually, she was not an unattractive woman. She was grandmotherly. A smile played around her lips all the time. But, unlike my mother, she never broke out into a laugh. She was the type who chuckled inwardly. Her eyes were large and brown, like her daughter's. Her face was without crinkles.

The conversation continued in Turkish, which I grasped in a peculiar sort of way. Peculiar in that I never really knew how much I understood until it was spoken. Also because it had somehow established itself in my mind as the language of adults.

19

How shall I explain it? Children spoke Persian, adults spoke Turkish. But that's too simple.

I was a Turk myself, you understand. We were all of us Turks. Turks from Azerbaijan, therefore an ethnic group within the national framework of Iran. With each other, we allegedly conversed in Turkish; with others in Persian, in various degrees, according to our backgrounds. The older Ashrafis were the most at home in Turkish. The younger ones were equally at home in Persian. As were my parents. As were the Karimzadehs, who had been established in business in Tehran for generations.

The only so-called outsider among us was Colonel Amuzegar, the one full-blooded Iranian, who spoke only in Persian.

And me, too, really, when you think of it linguistically. Brought up in America and recently moved to Iran, I had forgotten just about all the Turkish my parents assured me I had once been fluent in. Persian I had a much firmer grasp of: I could actually speak it. But it was all coming back quickly, and precipitated by moments of consciousness I was barely aware of.

"Omid, how much did you lose?" my mother asked.

My father shook his head and gave a diffident laugh.

"How do you know he lost anything?" I burst out in Persian, giving the filial support I thought the occasion warranted.

"Because," Mrs. Ashrafi answered, not looking at me but at my father with a smile, "he would still be playing if he hadn't."

He sat down and helped himself to the fruit. My mother peeled an apple, giving half to me and half to my father, taking a thin slice from my share for herself.

"How is it in there?" Mrs. Ashrafi asked, with a seriousness scarcely perceptible.

My father shrugged, his mouth full of fruit. He had a habit which drove my mother to distraction of filling his mouth with food, and then chewing long and slowly. It took forever to get an answer out of him at table.

"Ashrafi is doing well," he said finally. "Karimzadeh is about the same as he began with. As for me, I'm down a few hundred tomans."

Which meant around a thousand, possibly more — at that

20

time the equivalent of about three hundred dollars, or roughly half the annual salary of a civil servant.

He paused to fill his mouth again. Another drag of silence.

"Karbalai is doing very well."

That was enough. The fact had been established. Everyone, save myself, understood.

Nasrin Amuzegar rose from her seat, quite pale, and said that she wanted to go for a walk. She took my hand and asked me to show her where I had seen the snake.

We walked together hand in hand — me slightly ahead, pulling her manfully forward. When we got to the tall grass, I looked about carefully, the fear reviving in me. But it came with a different flow: a steady apprehension at coming across the hidden, lurking thing, rather than the sudden rush of being caught by surprise. I pointed out the area the snake had slithered into. Nasrin nodded, her face a blank stare. A very sad look.

Then we walked down to the beach, where I showed her the sand castle, already crumbling as the sand dried. I was afraid she would wonder about Bijan and Parviz. If she asked where they were, what could I tell her?

But she didn't. Not just then. Instead she did a very startling thing.

She raised my hand and pressed it to her breast — right up against the heart, where I felt the pulse beating. With it, my own pulse rose as well.

It was the first time I had felt a woman's breast — or if it wasn't, it was the first time I was conscious of it. I was in rapture: thrilled by its softness and fullness. Then she smiled and kissed my forehead and wrapped her arms around my bare shoulders.

That touch, those movements defined our relationship from that moment on. She was no longer Mrs. Amuzegar, Parviz's mother, but Nasrin. We were no longer separated by years. The gap had been closed with the pressing of a child's hand on her breast. From that point on, there would be different looks between us: a different shaking of hands, of greeting and farewell kisses.

21

And the important thing was that she had initiated it. I could never have conceived of such an action myself, let alone dreamed of such a transformation. It was delicious to be brought into such contact with the adult world.

And it was antidote to the poison in my system — the fear still flowing inside me — the disappointment, too, at seeing the castle half-finished, neglected and crumbling.

We walked along the beach as close to the water as the tide would allow. She looked about for Bijan and Parviz, and asked where they were. I was not about to sunder the new bond between us: I told her.

She stiffened with alarm.

"If he rides that horse and the Colonel finds out," she said, referring to her husband, as we all did, by his rank, "he will kill him!"

It was she now who pulled me by the hand. We walked quickly — in a semi-run — to the other side of the Casino, left of the entrance — where the motel stands now — circumventing the terrace. That was where the Colonel's horse was usually kept. Other people either came by car or walked down from the hotel. The Colonel rode from his estate, a few miles farther down the beach. He came and went, as I remember, always on horseback, riding alone. His batman served in the dual capacity of groom and chauffeur, looking after the horse while the Colonel played cards, and driving Nasrin and Parviz in their green army sedan.

When we came to the spot, groom and horse were gone. The next place to look was the bridle path lining one side of the boulevard — actually, a walkway thinly covered with grass.

We caught sight of them coming toward us from a distance. The groom was walking the horse: the horse in the middle, the groom on one side, and Bijan and Parviz on the other. Nasrin called out. They stopped. The groom cupped his hands behind his ears to catch her words.

What happened from that point on went very quickly — one flow of action without breaks to allow any meaning to register. Bijan snatched the rein from the groom's fingers and made a leap for the saddle. The jump wasn't good. He came down stomach first on the horse's back, one bare foot in the stirrup,

22

the other kicking the air. The horse whinnied and dug its hoofs into the ground, then raised its front legs in a series of small jumps. Parviz fell back into the bushes. Bijan toppled to the ground on his buttocks, but with one hand up, still clutching the rein.

The groom, by now, had recovered his senses. He reached up to grab the rein by the bit, which brought the horse down. Bijan was up again. He made another leap — this time a high one — and glided cleanly into the saddle.

Once mounted, he tried to free the rein from the groom's grasp. The two were at cross-purposes: the groom trying to calm the horse down, Bijan whipping it up into a fury.

The horse lurched forward, and the groom was dragged to his knees. From then on, it was a curious tug of war, with the groom hanging on tenaciously, and Bijan digging his heels into the horse's flanks. The groom was shouting all the time — garbled words I didn't understand.

The Casino door opened, and the Colonel stood behind us on the steps. Tall. Erect. The muscles in his face tight with anger. Then he sprang into action, running past Nasrin and me, and almost, I thought, into the horse.

Bijan saw him coming and gave up the struggle. He slid off the horse, jumped over the bushes, and made a run for the beach.

The Colonel pushed the groom aside, took hold of the rein, and mounted the horse. He turned to Parviz — still in a daze in the bushes — told him sharply to go to his mother, and rode after Bijan.

Nasrin's fingers pressed into my shoulders.

"Majid, don't!" she yelled, her lips quivering. "For God's sake, let him go!"

Parviz was up and running toward us. Nasrin literally pulled him into her arms — the two of us in the same enclosure.

The chase was a spectacle, bizarre and mesmerizing. Bijan running in and out of the trees, barefoot, bare-skinned, except for his swimming trunks. The Colonel chasing after him on horseback — his white shirt blazing in the sunset, in khaki riding trousers and boots.

As he closed in on his prey, the Colonel took off his belt and

23

waved it over his head, buckle flashing, like a Cossack brandishing a saber.

I released myself from Nasrin's hold and ran to the terrace, where the view was better. Everyone was up in his seat, mouth agape, watching Bijan zigzagging in and out of the trees, yelling in fright, and the Colonel bearing down on him, brandishing his belt on horseback.

"He is mad," my father said, aghast, in Turkish.

Mrs. Ashrafi was mute with horror.

Bijan was flushed out of the trees and in the open. He ran for the water. Before he got there, the belt came thrashing down on his back. We heard a sharp yell. The belt came down again. One thrash after another. Whirling in circles — coiling about his neck — the buckle gouging his flesh.

"Mad," my father repeated, but woken now by the word.

It all happened quickly, as I say, in one continuous flow of action, freezing everyone in his place.

But now the spell was broken. My father ran to the beach, shouting at the Colonel to stop. Behind him came Hassan Karbalai and Ahmad Karimzadeh. I hadn't noticed them before. They must have emerged from the Casino.

Before they arrived, however, the Colonel was gone. The beating administered, he turned his horse around and rode along the shore in the direction of his estate.

When I got to Bijan myself, he was lying on the sand, not moving, his face and body spattered with blood and already disfigured and discolored from the beating.

A deep red line ran down his left eye.

6

*B*ijan had to be taken to the hospital in Rasht — the nearest in the area. The damage done to his eye was serious.

He was taken in Hassan Karbalai's car, a 1947 Cadillac, since it was the biggest. He lay stretched out in the back seat, a bloodstained towel over his eye, my father beside him. Ahmad Karimzadeh sat up in front with Karbalai, who did the driving.

It was some kind of custom then — since changed, I suppose — that immediate family and women did not accompany the afflicted on such occasions. They stayed behind, too grieved and in need of attention themselves. That's where friends came in. They simply took over, the men as sort of stretcher-bearers, and the women as comforters. That way, everyone had a hand in what was going on, and everything was seen to.

As soon as the car was gone, the group divided itself, my mother tending to Nasrin, Mrs. Karimzadeh to Mrs. Ashrafi, while Amin Ashrafi paced up and down the terrace, with a grim look on his face.

It was the first time he had emerged from the Casino all day. He had done so just in time to view the beating, like Churchill stepping out of an all-night cabinet session to catch a glimpse of the bombing. I always associated him with Churchill. He had the same rotundity, heavy bearing, and stoop; the same light coloring and lack of hair. Even the same jowly lisp. But he was shorter and had none of the military or aristocratically English aura about him. He was decidedly Turkish: a dealer from Khoy. Interested in money and power. But money first. Money to establish the basis for power, and power to keep it and establish the basis for more. He was shrewd.

His greatest asset, I had heard my father say, was cunning, a natural gift he sharpened by daily use. He knew how to gamble: he didn't count on luck. He lost little and gained over the long run.

Certainly he was not compulsive about it — like Colonel Amuzegar — even though he indulged in it heavily. He gambled as a pastime because in such situations he came to know men — those he was dealing and competing with. He was, in that respect, like a social drinker who went all the way yet managed to hold his liquor.

Another of his assets — again according to my father — was his ability to know his limitations. He rarely put himself into situations he could not get the better of. Which is not to say that he didn't suffer setbacks. He did. He was subject, as we all are, to circumstances. But he knew — as a Turk, as a provincial with limited means and fairly humble origins — how adaptable he was; what he could attach himself to, and what he could not.

His sphere of activity went as far as Tehran. No farther. Outside Iran he was lost. Other countries did not interest him. Other ways of life, other conditions — these were for other people. But within his own defined world he was a shrewd and effective manipulator. More than that, he had a far-reaching understanding of people.

His connections with us actually went back to my mother's side of the family in Khoy. He knew them all well. He had even, at one time, been employed by my mother's father. But the two men had personalities which caused them to move in separate directions. My grandfather's restlessness drove him into import-export — from Khoy to Tehran, to Erzerum, to Istanbul, to Hamburg, where he finally took up residence as a dealer in carpets. Ashrafi, on the other hand, as soon as he came to Tehran, decided to settle down and stabilize his position in the world of finance.

The first thing he did was enter the bazaar — which is to say, he bought, sold, and lent money. But activity of this kind didn't appeal to his imagination, or draw out his instincts as a moneymaker. When the National Bank of Iran was established, he immediately realized the potential that lay there. He entered the bank as an employee and thereby came, as the saying goes, into his own element. He worked hard and advanced steadily.

My father, meanwhile, was being groomed to start a business of his own. The family business was practically defunct. The Momtazes had made the move from Tabriz to Tehran during my grandfather's time. But grandfather Momtaz — according to my father — was an exceptionally lazy man, more concerned with his comforts than their sources. Moreover, the move from Tabriz had drained him of the little energy he had for work. And so the family business, which he had inherited, went steadily downhill.

As a man of leisure, however, he still attracted many people to his house. One of them was Amin Ashrafi.

All Turks who were engaged in business in Tehran knew, if not actually socialized with, each other, in those days.

26

My grandfather, according to the customs of the time, entrusted my father to Ashrafi's care, even though my father was well into his twenties. That way the young man would be provided for without his having to lift a finger.

My father entered the bank as Ashrafi's assistant. Both men were diligent and — surely, they must have been — extremely ambitious. My father claims that they used to spend some fourteen hours a day, each day, six days a week, on banking business.

Ashrafi subsequently became one of the managers. My father took over his position and started building a reputation of his own. When the newly formed National Cotton Board needed a director, my father was offered the job. Ashrafi advised him not to take it, on the grounds that there were too many risks — too many projects of a dubious nature, all needing supervision. If one of them failed, the responsibility would fall on the director's shoulders, and that would mean dismissal and loss of reputation. He counseled him to stay with the bank, where he was doing well.

My father went against his advice and took on the directorship. It was a very lofty position for a man his age — he must have been around thirty-five then — and his salary was higher than Ashrafi's.

But salary wasn't everything. What counted more was the nature of the office held. And Ashrafi was in the more power-wielding position. Which he used to his advantage in acquiring land.

Ashrafi, as I said, was interested in money and power. What brought the two together, however — their common basis — was land. Land, to him, was capital; which increased in value over the years. But more than that, it was the tangible show of fiscal strength, and therefore power; which gave his fiscal position the further support he needed for further acquisition.

Being a man of acquisition, he married his daughter off to a person who had more possessions than he had. And the match was a good one, socially acceptable in every sense.

Nasrin was eighteen at the time, not only a beauty but well-brought up, well-educated, by the standards of the day, and with the financial backing of her father.

Colonel Amuzegar was a captain then. Very dashing. Tall, dark, angular in his features. A much-sought-after bachelor. A sunburned outdoorsman. He had gone through the Officers Training School in Tehran, and was from a well-to-do family. He owned villages — not just land, mind you. Ashrafi owned land. He bought up land in and around the city for later development, as the city expanded. But villages were owned by the aristocracy. And the young Amuzegar had every prospect — all the connections and the personal ability — for a promising career in the army.

Moreover, the couple were in love. That's what everyone said. They were like ripe fruit, ready to fall from a tree. One look at each other and they fell.

When the trouble started is more open to conjecture. Possibly around the time of the birth of Parviz. Amuzegar's gambling, which had been on a small scale before, developed into a mania. He spent all his time away from home. When he wasn't gambling, he went riding.

And he lost. First one estate, then another. Until it became a matter of dire concern to the Ashrafis as to how long the man's fortune would last.

Furthermore, it was rumored that the man was beating his wife.

The war years were a period of catastrophe for the Ashrafis. Not only did they have to contend with the growing problems in the Amuzegar household, but almost overnight Ashrafi lost his position at the bank — a victim of one of the old king's purges. He was jailed and all his land confiscated. Shortly after the old king's abdication, he was released. But the situation was still volatile. He gathered what money he could and went, with his wife and son, to America, where he stayed a brief period at our home, a brooding man in exile.

By contrast, my own family's fortunes were on the rise. My parents got married a few months after the Amuzegars. And though, to be sure, their marriage was arranged, it had none of the social and financial trappings of the previous one. It was a straightforward love match, in the Iranian sense of the term. My father, besides, had a streak of independence in him which almost amounted to pride. If money was needed, then he would earn it himself.

Which he proceeded to do, with a remarkable coming together of good timing, good planning, sheer hard work, and luck.

In two years, as director of the National Cotton Board, he practically doubled the supply of baled cotton put out by the government plants: setting up new ginning plants, installing new equipment in old ones, and reorganizing the labor force. He had a very strong sense of organization — of order in all things. Had he stayed on at his job, he would quite likely have moved into the Ministry of Finance — and, given his particular talents and industry, who knows how far he would have gone in government service? That, at least, is the kind of speculation my parents indulge in, when business takes a turn for the worse.

At any rate, he didn't stay on at his job. When America entered the war, things changed. Another opportunity arose, too tempting not to respond to. America needed all kinds of goods for the war effort, among them cotton. Even the low-grade product. Suddenly Iranian cotton became a potential export item. My father left his job in Tehran to establish a business to meet the demand.

And so in 1942 — with Ashrafi out of prison, but still in very questionable circumstances, with Amuzegar in Azerbaijan, occupied with the military surveillance of supplies going into Russia — we set out for America. My father opened up an office in New York and began importing cotton. All the important ingredients, as I said, came together at once. That's how we made our money.

❖

A year or so later, Ashrafi arrived with his family, leaving Nasrin and Parviz alone in Tehran. We had a house in Mount Vernon by then, and my father used to commute to his office by train. The Ashrafis stayed a few months at our home, before buying a place of their own not far away.

I was at boarding school in Connecticut then, and so got to see very little of them. I haven't the vaguest idea what Ashrafi was doing. It never occurred to me to ask my father. Whatever it was, it couldn't have been much, because he knew very little English and rarely left his house — though visitors were always dropping in. Guests were constantly coming and going, all of them Iranians, some of them Turks. And the kitchen was always astir, filling the house with the smell of food. The furniture was very simple.

My first contact with Bijan came when I returned home for summer vacation. I didn't recall having seen him before, though he said he remembered me. He struck me as a new figure in my life. He was very Iranian — attending a local school and trying to learn English: a task so arduous for him that he was in a constant state of rebellion. I, on the other hand, was rapidly becoming Americanized   fluent in English and already losing my grasp of Persian, so that communication between us was not an easy matter.

Moreover, we soon became wary of each other. We sensed each other's differences. That, in itself, was not so threatening. What was more threatening — for both of us, I think — was the suspicion, the undefined knowledge, that we had different values as well.

That was important. Bijan was a leader who needed a follower. Not just any follower, but one who could carry out his rebellion with him. More than that; one who could share with him the various stages of adolescent experience. Go all the way and not struggle: completely subsumed by his presence, his bearing, his weight, his personality, and ultimately — all in all — his values.

In me he saw a potential follower — a potential ally, a fellow countryman, who might know, might understand, might feel the same way about things as he did. And, at the same time, accept his dominance.

But then, he was also wary of our differences.

The clash between us came one day at his house.

30

He held up a dollar bill and said that I could have it if I would go up to the attic with him — there being guests in the house — lie on the floor, and spread my legs. I didn't know what he was talking about. I was suspicious. But I wanted the dollar. So I took it and went with him.

In the attic, he took my trousers down, had me lie on the floor stomach down, and told me I would experience something so delicious the dollar wouldn't matter anymore. Then I felt him go between my buttocks. My anus contracted, and I wrestled about. I didn't know what it all had to do with, but it felt like having an enema tube pushed inside me. He tried to soothe me. He told me the feeling would give way to immeasurable bliss. He assured me the dollar was mine, if I would just try it for a minute. He took off his watch and laid it on the floor for me to see, then coaxed me down and tried again.

My whole body turned against him. I jerked myself free.

"It hasn't been a minute yet," he said vehemently.

"I don't like it," I said.

"Then put it in your mouth."

I refused. He asked for the dollar back. I refused. He got up and snatched it from my trouser pocket.

I was writhing inside: humiliated, angry, and afraid. The next thing I thought would surely come was a beating.

He told me to put my trousers back on and not say a word to anyone. The last appeal gave me strength.

"I won't," I said, looking into his eyes, "if you give back the dollar."

He threw me a glare that made me cringe, then flung the dollar bill and went down the stairs.

So much for my encounter with Bijan in America. Shortly afterward I went back to boarding school, and he returned to Iran with his parents.

When we saw each other again in Iran, we both remembered the incident, and eyed each other as enemies. I dimly knew then what was associated with sex, though I didn't know the particulars — I must have been late in learning. At any rate, I was afraid of his power. And he too of mine to fight back — in particular, to talk.

31

His knee on my chest gave me the feel of that power. But the knee on my chest was power checked: checked so long as he was afraid of someone — me, anyone — talking.

What I was afraid of in him was the thing let loose: his committing some atrocity, and not caring who talked about it or knew.

When we returned to Iran in the spring of 1948, the overall situation had changed. After three years of excellent business in New York, trade had slackened. America no longer needed the low-grade cotton my father supplied from Iran. Nor was there any particular demand for other items he could come up with, such as carpets. He stayed in New York, trying to set up a new line of import-export, and when that didn't work out, we came back to Iran.

Ashrafi, by this time, had been reinstated in his former position at the bank and his land had been restored to him.

The situation, in fact, was the reverse of what it had been a few years ago. It was my father now who found himself looking for connections in business, and Ashrafi who was in the stable and rising position. If anything, his ability to withstand reverses had bolstered his position.

Amuzegar had done well in the army. He was a colonel: loyal to his superiors and to the new king. As a protégé of the then military governor-general of Tehran, he had participated in putting down anti-government riots. And he had done so, people said, with an admirable show of both force and restraint.

To boot, he was an excellent horseman.

His only flaw — publicly acknowledged — was his gambling. And — not so well acknowledged — his abuse of his wife.

I met the Karimzadehs. How long my parents had known them is another matter. But that's when, for me, they came into view. They were an old business family, established in the bazaar. They had come there, like the Momtazes, from Tabriz, but earlier, before the First World War. After that war, they had begun dealings with Europe, representing various firms in

32

France and Germany. Then they established their own branch in Hamburg. Like my grandfather's on my mother's side, their major line of business there was carpets.

Ahmad Karimzadeh had married into the very well-to-do Bakhtiari family. The Bakhtiaris owned land and villages, the Karimzadehs owned businesses. With the marriage between Ahmad and Mina, the Karimzadehs emerged as one of the leading families in Iran.

Ahmad was the titular and also the acknowledged head of the family. The position was his not only because he was the eldest son, but also because of his judgment — his business acumen and sense of style. He was judicious as I imagine Moses must have been as a prince.

He had married a woman who was not beautiful, but who had character. And that seemed to lead to everything else: to money, to social prominence. What he had done, actually, was to marry his counterpart. In all Iran — I used to think as a child — no two people were more suited to each other than Ahmad and Mina Karimzadeh.

But the point is, he was just as correct in all his other decisions. At least, that was the impression he gave. Also, he made a sharp distinction between business and politics — the way Ashrafi didn't — and he clearly committed himself to business alone.

The family leadership could just as easily have passed into the hands of his younger brother, Abol. But Abol was quite content to play second fiddle, leaving all the really important decisions to his elder brother and taking pleasure in living.

Abol, in contrast to his brother, had married what my mother still refers to as the most beautiful woman she has ever seen. She is used to speaking in superlatives, but there must be something to what she says. I never saw the woman myself, but I did see her picture. She was quite fetching, even in an old photograph.

After his marriage, Abol was sent to Hamburg to manage the European end of the business. The Second World War put an end to all trade with France and Germany. Abol, however, did not return to Iran. Instead, he moved the business to Stockholm — again, like my grandfather — and after the war, brought it back to Hamburg.

The Karimzadehs, then, were a family with fairly strong and long-standing ties with Europe — unlike the Ashrafis, who were decidedly rooted in Iran. Somewhere between the two were the Momtazes — newly arrived from America and trying to see which direction to take.

This was really the down-to-earth reason for our close connections with both families. My father was trying to determine whether or not another venture abroad would be feasible. And if so, who, if anyone, would back him. This time the scheme was to export low-grade cotton to Germany. Germany having lost the war, the potential customer had shifted from America to Europe.

The men behind the scheme were Ahmad Karimzadeh and Amin Ashrafi — and, although I didn't know it at the time, Hassan Karbalai. Whether or not they would act jointly, as shareholders in one corporation, or separately, as independent buyers and sellers, was up in the air. That, apparently, was what all their discussions were about.

At any rate, the only person in their group who was solely concerned with playing at cards — and, furthermore, losing — was Majid Amuzegar.

"Better that he should lose to one of us," I heard Ashrafi comment to my father in Turkish one day, "than have him fleeced by others."

He was not a callous man. Simply practical. He had spoken to the Colonel about his gambling before, but he knew that there was nothing he could say that would change him.

In the final analysis, it was not really the Colonel he was so anxious about. It was his own flesh and blood: Nasrin.

Now, while others were busily engaged in the present — the men looking after his son, the women comforting his wife and daughter — Ashrafi paced up and down the terrace. His face was grim. What he was contemplating, I imagine, was the future.

The marriage couldn't last.

The Colonel was a good solider and came from a good family,

but he was throwing all away with his gambling. Losing went to his head: it brought out the violence in him. And now this latest act of barbarism.

He had lost two of his estates to Karbalai. Two. How long had it taken him to work up the equivalent amount in capital?

Karbalai was no fool. He was something different. Far different from all the rest of them. Not interested in land. No estates. No villages. Not a bazaar merchant, with a background in the usual buying and selling or import-export. Industry. Factories. That's what his vision was fixed on. Already he owned more oil mills — cottonseed oil — than all the country's manufacturers put together. He was making soap. Making margarine.

He remembered the phrase he had come across in America: guns and butter. Karbalai had sold guns during the war, and now he was making substitute butter. He was *making* things. In time, he would put them all out of business. He had to be watched.

Better yet, he ought to be brought into the fold.

Who was he, anyway? Karbalai. The name was Arabic: from Karbala. He was certainly Iranian. But the ethnic heritage behind that? He wasn't a Turk. He wasn't a Fars, like Amuzegar. He didn't have a tribal background, like Karimzadeh's wife. He didn't even have any distinctive features which could place him geographically. He looked vaguely Mediterranean. He had olive skin. Gray curly hair, which was thick, like steel wool. Medium stature. Dark hands with light nails, like those of an Indian. Perhaps he was a nomad.

At any rate, he wasn't a fool. He wouldn't keep both estates. He would keep one and return the other, thereby collecting his winnings from the Colonel on the one hand, and putting him under an obligation on the other. And he would do this for the sake of Nasrin.

Ashrafi wasn't blind.

Possibly the Colonel wasn't either. But he was a fool. He was gambling away more than his inheritance.

"We'll see," Ashrafi said. "If it doesn't turn out one way, it will turn out the other."

He saw me looking at him and asked me to fetch him some soda water. Then he turned to the women and said that they should return to the hotel and wait for the others there. He put his arms around Nasrin's shoulders.

"You'll have supper with us, *qizim*," he said softly in Turkish, meaning "my girl" or "precious one."

There were times when his shrewdness — or perhaps foresight, in this case — provided covert escapes from potentially disastrous situations. The Colonel had offered to put up the whole family at his estate, but Ashrafi had refused, on the grounds that he was going to be at Ramsar only a few days, and that he had business to talk over with friends. Since these friends were staying at the hotel, it would be better to stay there with them, rather than run to and from the estate, which would have been too tiring for a man of his age.

All of which was true. But the fact was, he didn't want to share the same roof as his son-in-law, given the strains in his household. Better to have a roof of his own, in case something erupted.

We drove up to the hotel in Ashrafi's limousine — all in one car — while the Colonel's batman drove back to the estate with a message from Ashrafi.

At the hotel, we showered and changed and had supper in the dining room. It had a tall ceiling, with a chandelier hanging down the middle. The floor was carpeted, and the tables were covered with white cloths, reaching all the way down to the floor. And on the tables were flowers, picked daily from the garden outside. The silverware and china were heavy. Or perhaps I thought them heavy as a child. Anyway, they felt heavier than the ones we had at home. The whole place had massiveness and weight. The drapes were thick and velvety. The windows were open, but screened, and as we ate, we felt the cool air coming in.

Afterward we had coffee in the lounge, and I took sips from Nasrin's and my mother's cups. Parviz was asleep in his grandmother's arms. Neither of us had wanted to go to bed, and our mothers hadn't pressed us to.

It was very late, by my standards, when the car pulled up in the driveway outside. The three men came in, but Karbalai went out again to park the car in the back.

Ahmad Karimzadeh turned to a waiter and ordered supper.

"Where is he?" Nasrin asked.

"Still in the hospital," Karimzadeh said. "The doctor said he should rest there awhile."

"And his condition?" Ashrafi asked from his seat in a very deep armchair. His wife was silent.

Karimzadeh turned to my father, who approached Ashrafi's chair and, bending down, put a hand on his shoulder.

"He is blind in the left eye," he said in a voice scarcely audible.

7

o you know— after all that had happened that day — what was uppermost in my mind, as I lay in bed, trying to fall asleep?

Malaria.

I didn't really even know what it was. It was a disease brought on by mosquitoes — that much I knew. The mosquitoes stood up on their long hind legs and drove their needlelike proboscises vertically into the skin. They sucked blood, which they lived off. And as they did this, they emitted old blood, which had been churning around inside their system, and which had come from other creatures they preyed on. Rather the way an old fountain pen fills up with ink. And this old blood was what carried the malaria.

Malaria was something you never got over. Once you caught it, you either died or put up with fevers and chills the rest of your life. The fever could simply sweep over you at any given moment. And all you could do to fight it was drink gallons of quinine water — which tasted no less awful than seawater.

And all over the Caspian Sea region, these dreaded creatures spawned in millions. The government had tried to fight the spread of malaria by spraying with DDT. Most of the houses you passed along the road had large DDT signs painted in white on the walls, which meant they had been sprayed. But some of them didn't.

And what about the fields with ditches of open stagnant water? The rice paddies?

No, malaria was too large a thing to be brought under control by spraying every so often. There were too many mosquitoes, with too many places to breed in — and people and cattle to live off.

I looked through the window, thankful for the screen. The screen would prevent the mosquitoes from coming inside.

They slept during the day and went about their business at night. What if one had come in during the day and plunked itself down where no one could see it?

All it took was one. Clearly, I had to be careful.

And in between my thoughts of malaria, flashes came to me: of Bijan blinded in one eye, the beating, the chase, my hand on Nasrin's breast, the sand castle, the snake.

Parviz was asleep on the bed beside me — exposed to the potentially lurking mosquito. Although he was a year older than I, he seemed younger. He was asleep when the news came of Bijan's condition. He still didn't know about Bijan's eye, Nasrin having told me not to tell him.

Moreover, I had felt his mother's breast.

I jumped out of bed and pulled a sheet over him — which made him look like a corpse — then jumped back under my own.

I remember having the shivers that night. Darkness had a way of subjecting me to all kinds of terrors I shrugged off in the daytime.

Yet, I didn't dare turn on a bedside lamp. I had the inane conviction that if I did, the mosquito — possibly unaware of my existence till then — would suddenly see me.

Clearly the signs, you might say, of a neurotic child. Possibly. I was afraid of the dark. I was even afraid of dreaming at night.

Dreaming had been blighted for me, when I was at boarding school in America. In class we had read a watered-down account of journeys through Africa. Thereafter, Africa, to me, represented one gigantically overgrown jungle — a place you couldn't even hack and hew your way through. One night I dreamed that I had entered the jungle in good spirits, waving cheerily to friends I was leaving behind. As I walked through the jungle, it got darker. I lost all sense of direction. I panicked and ran into thickets. When I woke up, I was in a sweat, but relieved that the dream had been only that. The next night, to my horror, it continued. I was in the thickets again, struggling to get out. Which I did, but only to get caught up on more vines and snarls. The fact that what I had been through was only a dream was not so comforting anymore. The third night I fought off sleep until my eyelids closed of their own accord. I was in the jungle again, in the same spot where I had left off. But this time I saw light through the trees. I walked toward the light, and to my enormous relief I was out of the jungle. I woke up exhausted. It had been an enormous struggle with the forces of darkness, and I had somehow tottered out alive.

After that marathon, I was afraid for a long time of falling into the same pattern of dreaming. Like the feeling one has after a long bout of hiccups.

And so, lying in the dark, wary of the mosquito, I fought off sleep.

Until I saw a shaft of light under the door which connected my parents' room with mine, and heard their muffled voices.

Then I fell into a very deep sleep.

The next day, at breakfast, I discovered that Nasrin had spent the night at the hotel as well. Ashrafi had taken a room for her, which she and her mother had shared. There had been no mention of that the evening before.

Parviz and I were awakened by my mother, who was fully dressed, and told us to come down for breakfast when we were ready.

The dining room was sparsely filled, which was usual in the mornings. People at Ramsar got up at all hours, and breakfast was served continuously in a leisurely manner until about eleven o'clock, while people sauntered in and out, taking their time, getting used to the day.

Parviz and I found our mothers seated at a large round table at the far end of the room, next to the French windows, which opened out onto the terrace and the garden below. Between them was Mrs. Ashrafi. Evidently, the others hadn't gotten up yet; the places set for them were still untouched.

Nasrin looked as though she hadn't had any sleep. My mother looked tired as well, although she had makeup on, which gave her some degree of camouflage. Nasrin had hardly any makeup at all. She was wearing the same dress as the day before, a white frock with large prints of red roses.

They smiled when we came in and asked how we had slept. We smiled back and said, well — two polite boys — then ate our breakfast in silence. It consisted of sliced melons, buttered toast, and goat's milk cheese — the only kind people eat in the country — and goblets of tea. That was our so-called Continental break-fast in Iran.

Parviz asked about Bijan's condition — the only one who didn't know.

"They say he is doing well," Nasrin said. "We're going to see him today."

"Is he still in the hospital then?"

"Yes."

"May I come with you?"

"No, you had better spend the day with Firuz." She paused. "You can see him when he comes out. It won't be long."

The conversation was conducted in Persian. Mrs. Ashrafi was reclined in her chair, her eyes half-closed, holding a teacup close to her mouth in both hands. No one had said a word about Colonel Amuzegar. There had been a tacit understanding among all of us, since the beating — a common accord reached in silence — that all talk about the Colonel was to be dropped. At least, that's how we children saw it. Parviz and I didn't even mention the matter when we were by ourselves.

In the adult world, no doubt, it was different.

My father came down after we had almost finished eating, looking well-rested and, on the whole, cheerful.

He was the kind of man — he still is, though less so now — who liked to walk into a room with a smile and a hearty hello, regardless of the occasion or the mood of the moment.

I remember reading Dickens' *A Christmas Carol,* the passage describing Scrooge's funeral. I thought of my father. Scrooge's colleagues made light of his death and gorged themselves with food, all of which, I daresay, went to show, from the book's point of view, the callous side of human nature. My father would have fitted into the picture, but not in the way that Dickens intended. He would have burst into the funeral parlor with a cheerful hello and tried — actually brought it upon himself with a conviction amounting almost to a sense of duty — to dispel the wretched gloom. As though people had no business to give themselves over to thoughts of dying. Not when there was someone to come forward with cheerful greetings.

He often encouraged me to do the same. Back at home in Tehran, I would come down to breakfast bleary-eyed with sleep — I was a hard one to arouse in the morning — and there he would be, expecting me to perk everyone up with a cheerful hello.

"Hello," I would say. Actually, "Salaam."

"That's not cheerful enough. Louder."

Louder it would be.

"Now say it with a smile on your face."

It was like taking medicine. But I submitted. Being an only child has certain disadvantages, overtraining being one of them.

My father's cheerful hello didn't quite dispel the gloom, but it made us aware of the day, and the sunlight pouring in through the window. He sat right in the shaft of light, always preferring the sun to the shade. Unlike my mother, who hid from it. He was dressed casually, in an open-neck shirt and beige summer slacks.

The Karimzadehs came in, looking more sober: she in a light skirt and blouse, which puffed up with each blow of air, and he in a very well-tailored summer suit, with a dark shirt open at the neck.

The conversation picked up, and the morning, which had started out subdued, became livelier. Mrs. Ashrafi told Parviz and me to go upstairs and fetch Mr. Ashrafi.

"He is out in the garden with Karbalai," my father put in.

"Fetch both of them, then," Mrs. Ashrafi added. "It's time we got started."

41

The garden was huge, spread over what looked to me then like acres of ground. Behind it, at the back of the hotel, were groves of citrus trees. We sprinted along the paths. Our enthusiasm carried us farther than we needed to have gone. Mr. Ashrafi was not the sort of person to go out on long walks. He paced slowly and took short strides. Walking for him, in fact, was somewhat like the swims he used to take on the beach: going out to knee level, splashing water on his chest, then wading back.

"Let's go back to the hotel," I said.

"Let's ask Musa if he has seen them, first," Parviz replied.

Musa was their chauffeur — an excellent cook and general handyman. He used to come with them every year to the Caspian, where he had a room to himself in the servants' quarters.

We found him on the driveway behind the hotel, washing the Ashrafi limousine, and asked him if he had seen either of the men.

"They're inside having breakfast," he said. "We'll be leaving soon for Rasht to see Bijan Khan." "Khan" was the title of respect usually given to younger male members of households. "Will you two be coming?"

Parviz shook his head. "I'd better go inside to see what's happening," he said.

"I'll wait for you here," I told him.

When he was gone, I turned to Musa. He was bending over the windshield and applying a clean dry cloth to the glass. A moist one hung over his shoulder. He was a burly man, with big hands and large, swollen, but gentle features. He looked like a wrestler who had given up training. His head had been shaved for the summer and had the even texture of a few weeks' growth. His chin had the scruffy makings of a beard. He had a very wide mouth, with gaps between his teeth.

"Musa," I addressed him, as he continued with his work, "do you know what's going on?"

He didn't look up. "That depends on what you mean."

"I mean right under our noses," I said.

"Well, you have a small one, and I have a large one." He laughed.

"All the same," I persisted, "something is happening."

42

"Something is always happening," he shrugged.

"Yes, but what's happening now that is different?"

He stopped his work. "At your age, if you knew, you wouldn't understand. At mine, it doesn't make any difference. What you know and what I know aren't that far apart."

I smiled at the comparison. "What do you know?" I asked.

He laughed at my persistence and looked up to God for assistance. "I know that land is important." He looked down again. "When you have land, you have everything. When you don't, you have your hands and your head, and you work up a sweat."

He scraped his nose and spat into the bushes. He wasn't Ashrafi's man for nothing.

"And that's all you'll tell me?"

"There's one more thing," he said. "The difference between everything and nothing is not so much in the end."

We both laughed at the way I had been diverted.

"I'll let you smoke my pipe one day," he added, by way of consolation. "That way you'll learn all sorts of things you're so impatient to know."

Then the whole company streamed out of the hotel, lining the back door steps, as though a group photograph were about to be taken. My mother called to me and took me aside. She spoke in English.

"I'm going with the Ashrafis to see Bijan in the hospital. I want you to be very nice to Parviz, but don't tell him about Bijan's eye. Mrs. Amuzegar will do that when the right time comes. You boys are to stay here with Mrs. Karimzadeh and Mr. Karbalai. We won't go down to the beach today, but we'll go another time. All right? You'll have lunch together, the four of you, and I'll see you in the evening, before supper."

She kissed my cheek.

"What about Father and Mr. Karimzadeh?" I asked.

"They have some business to attend to and may not be back in time for lunch either. But we'll all be back for supper. All right?"

I nodded, and she kissed me again.

Then the group divided itself; the Ashrafi limousine going west, toward Rasht, and my father's car — a Buick then — in the opposite direction, toward Amuzegar's estate.

The party left behind was an odd one. We gazed blankly at

43

each other for a moment, unused to the novelty of the new foursome.

Then Mrs. Karimzadeh set the wheels in motion again. She held out both hands to Parviz and me and gave a radiant smile, which always elicited a warm response.

"Let's go for a walk in the garden," she said, "Did you know that Mr. Karbalai has a very extensive knowledge of flowers?"

"My dear lady," Karbalai laughed, "you take me aback. If anyone knows about flowers, you do. I merely smell them, love them, and every once in a while pick a few. But I'll tell you what I'll do," he said, turning to Parviz and me. "After Mrs. Karimzadeh gets through telling you about flowers, we'll return to the hotel, and I'll show you a few things about cards."

8

Karbalai was right: Mrs. Karimzadeh had a very good knowledge of flowers. Not only did she name all the ones that we passed, but she knew how to talk about them.

Parviz responded more readily than I did, like a good algebra student going through equations. He had a very keen mind, receptive to the study of natural phenomena. You could tell by the way he fingered the petals, separating the whorls and counting the stamens, that he was storing the knowledge away in his memory.

Karbalai and I looked on passively.

At the bottom of the garden, we sat in a shady nook, on a concrete bench, and the conversation turned to Switzerland. Mrs. Karimzadeh's sons were studying there. She had two boys, Farid and Matin, both older than I, whom I had never seen, and whom my mother talked about in glowing terms. Farid was about Bijan's age, and Matin was two years younger. Both were attending the same school in Geneva, studying languages and basic economics, and preparing for the family business.

She also had a niece, Zohre, the daughter of Abol Karimzadeh and the most beautiful woman my mother had ever seen. They, too, were in Switzerland, but only for a visit.

Mahin, her only daughter, did not come into the conversation. She was some two years younger than I — the same age as Princess Shahnaz, my mother had told me — and vacationing with her mother's side of the family at Ab Ali, a mountain resort.

Later in the summer Farid and Matin were to fly to Iran. Currently they were attending some kind of summer camp for foreign students. They were still relatively new to Switzerland, having been there for a year, and needed to work on their languages.

"All their classes are conducted in French," Mrs. Karimzadeh explained. "But they have to learn English and German as well. It's hard for them, coming from Iran, where they spoke only Persian. But Matin is doing very well. There is no doubt about it: he is the linguist of the family. Did you study French in America, Firuz?"

I laughed inwardly at her conception of American grade school education. "No," I said, "only English."

"Well, you can speak with him in English when he comes. He is studying that as his second language."

Failing that, I thought, there is always Persian — the mother tongue of us all.

"How is Farid doing?" Karbalai asked.

"Farid, poor boy, is trying hard. He has to make more adjustments. He is older and misses Iran very much. But he is working hard, and the summer camp will, we hope, help him. Where did you pick up your languages, Mr. Karbalai?"

"Our generation has a different story." He chuckled. He addressed himself to Parviz and me. "We didn't pick up languages in schools. We picked them up through trade. So I can't say that I know any language, other than Persian, properly. English I picked up in Manchester. German in Hamburg. But what German! Everyone laughs when I open my mouth. French and Italian, to my shame and regret, I have never had occasion to apply myself to. But they lure me, and one of these days I hope to. I'll die an unhappy man if I don't. Your father, Firuz, speaks beautiful French. He picked it up, as I did my English, as a young man living abroad. There is no better way of picking up a language than being in a foreign country as a young man. With your father it was Paris, with me it was Manchester. We both received our training abroad. But we asked for the same things." He laughed and returned his gaze to Mrs. Karimzadeh. "You shouldn't be worried about Farid. He is in a foreign country. He has a good grasp of things. In no time at all, he will surprise us with all the languages he knows."

"You're very kind," Mrs. Karimzadeh said, beaming her characteristically all-embracing smile. "You are probably right. But tell me, don't you also know some Russian and Armenian?"

"Russian, Armenian, Turkish, yes — both kinds of Turkish, Istamboli and Azeri," he acknowledged. "But those are what we refer to in the bazaar as street languages. We know them as we know the people who speak them."

"Do you mean that they're not really so foreign?" she asked.

"Not really. These are the people around us all the time. As a boy, I heard all these languages spoken around me, and so the sounds and words filtered into my ear as parts of my own system of speaking as well. Sometimes when I really get mad and want to call a fellow a rogue, what comes to my tongue is Armenian. It has a roll to it that gets out all the feelings inside. But I never, as a child, heard English or French or German around me." He paused and fixed his gaze on me. "But times have changed. This fellow " — patting my head — " knows English better than all of us put together."

"It's in his blood," Mrs. Karimzadeh laughed. "All the Momtazes are good at languages. You should hear his mother's German."

"I'm aware of that," he said. "Who do you think laughs at me, when I try to sound like *ein echte Hamburger?*"

"Oh, no, Mrs. Momtaz would never do that!"

"Well, she is a *Berlinerin,* and they are very particular about how people speak German. But then, she, too, is in a class by herself. Wasn't she brought up in Germany?" he asked me.

"Yes," I said. "When my grandfather went to Hamburg, he sent for my mother, and she went to school there for a while."

"A *Berlinerin* schooled in Hamburg?"

"Well," I added, not wanting to go into complications, "she actually lived with my grandfather's brother, who had a separate business in Berlin."

"I know your grandfather well," he said. "But not his brother. He is a very astute businessman. But then, you Karimzadehs have a German side to your family as well."

"Yes," Mrs. Karimzadeh replied. "Abol and Simin, whom you've met, and their daughter, Zohre, whom you haven't — a truly beautiful girl. Zohre was born in Iran, but has seen very little of the country. Her German is as good as your mother's, Firuz."

"All these international connections!" Karbalai spread out his arms. "I believe there's only you and me, Parviz, who can claim to be truly native speakers of Persian."

"Oh, no. Me, too!" Mrs. Karimzadeh exclaimed. "If we weren't speaking Persian right now, I'd be as silent as a statue."

Parviz smiled uncomfortably and suddenly shifted his position.

❖

After lunch we went up to our rooms for a nap, although we didn't really need one. Then we gathered in the lobby, where we sat around a low table and drank tea, and Karbalai showed us his card tricks.

My father and Karimzadeh arrived just as we were about to go out for a second walk. Mrs. Karimzadeh suggested that Parviz and I go by ourselves — which we did — while they sat down to talk and drink another round of tea.

What they talked about, I found out much later, was their visit to Amuzegar's estate. My father didn't tell me about it until some five years later, and even then, I think, he did some editing. At any rate, this is more or less the account he gave me.

When he and Karbalai arrived at Amuzegar's estate, they were told that the Colonel was out hunting and wouldn't be back until lunch. They decided to wait for him, drank tea and ate fruit. After a while, they walked down to the beach and walked back up again. They had a late lunch. Afterward they sprawled on the living room sofas and napped until the Colonel arrived.

He threw his hunting gear onto a lounge chair and leaned his rifle against the wall. He didn't say a word by way of greeting, but ordered his batman to bring some refreshments.

My father remembered him as glacial in manner and appearance — like a force under very determined control.

By agreement, my father was the one to make the opening statement.

"We thought you ought to know," he began, "what happened after you left the Casino yesterday. The boy was in very bad shape. We found him unconscious — in a state of shock. His left eye was bleeding profusely. Forgive me for giving you the details so bluntly, but there's no sense in going into them any other way. We only wish to inform you of the facts. We had to take him to Rasht for medical treatment. He is there, in the hospital, now. The belt buckle entered his eye and pierced the sclera. The shock, apparently, took the pain away. But he is under heavy sedation right now, and the doctors fear that the damage done to his eye is permanent. That was the first matter we wanted to inform you about. As for the second, I will be equally brief . . ."

"Please convey my thanks to Mr. Ashrafi," the Colonel interrupted, "for sending word via his chauffeur that my wife would be spending the night at the hotel. As for what you've just told me, he wrote me as much in his letter."

"He didn't say that the damage done to the eye might be permanent," my father added.

"Oh? You saw the letter he sent me?"

"I only know what he himself told me was in it. The rest was from my own observation."

"Please continue with the second point."

"The second point has to do with your wife. She is unspeakably upset at all that has happened. So much so, that she finds it impossible to communicate with you in person . . ."

"So she sent you instead," the Colonel cut in again.

"Not at all."

"Then Ashrafi did."

"My dear Colonel, allow me to finish. We didn't come here on

48

behalf of anyone. We came here as friends — as yours, as well as your wife's and Mr. Ashrafi's. We've seen the harm that's been caused by this incident. We wish to see as much of it undone as possible. What else would you expect us to do, as friends? Sit back and wash our hands of the matter?"

"The point you were going to make about my wife."

"But, my dear sir, first of all I have to establish your confidence."

The Colonel gazed out the window. "You may find that difficult to do."

"Now you're being unfair to Mr. Momtaz," Karimzadeh broke in. "What he has to say can only be said as one friend to another. Otherwise, there is always the danger of being misunderstood."

"I am aware of that."

"In that case, please allow him to proceed, without undermining his position."

"I stand rebuked."

"My dear Colonel . . ."

"Please proceed."

The refreshments arrived on a tray. Amuzegar told the batman to set them down on the table and close the door after leaving the room.

My father picked up the thread again. "As I said, your wife is too upset to see you personally right now. She is under strain. To be more precise, she feels she is being pulled in opposite directions. That's why she is staying at the hotel: to lessen the strain. She has gone to Rasht for the day with my wife and her parents. She loves her brother dearly and is very worried about his condition. Surely, that's understandable. She wants to spend a little time with her family. Afterward perhaps some of the strain will wear off. Perhaps so, perhaps not. I am no judge of these things . . ."

"In the meantime — "

"In the meantime, we think — Mr. Karimzadeh and I — that you should be apprised of the facts. Know what she is going through. See the situation from her point of view. Try to understand. And act accordingly."

"What precisely is that supposed to mean?"

49

"My dear Colonel," Karimzadeh broke in again, "we don't mean to prod you into taking any specific actions — those you must decide for yourself, as you think fit — but rather to urge you to broaden the basis of your own line of reasoning. This is a situation which requires toleration and, as Mr. Momtaz said, understanding. You are a horseman. I myself know very little about horses. But consider this analogy. When the horse you are riding, or about to ride, is acting up — is agitated — don't you give it some rope? Calm it down by letting it give vent to its feelings? Very well, then, that's the point we're getting at. Your wife is extremely disturbed by the recent course of events, and probably wishes to have some time to herself to bring her emotions under control. And the line we ask you to take is to allow her to do this, while trying to be as understanding as possible."

"You are right." The Colonel nodded, with a thin smile. "You don't know much about horses. When a horse acts up, you do not 'give it rope,' as you say, but tighten your hold on it. Bring it under control by making it feel the force of your presence."

"I was mistaken in my analogy." Karimzadeh threw up his hands. "Horses and people are different, after all."

"But I accept your point anyway. You wish me to be sympathetic toward my wife's feelings. Very well, I am sympathetic. I give your horse rope. She is free to come and go as she chooses. I shall remain here until it is necessary for me to return to Tehran. If she wishes to see me, she knows where and how I can be reached. Is there anything more to be said?"

Karimzadeh exchanged glances with my father.

"Well, to be frank, we were hoping that you would show a little more sympathy than that."

"How so?"

"Acknowledging the need for your wife to be apart from you — temporarily, that is — is one side of the matter. But there is another side as well. I'm sure she would like to have some kind of response from you."

"What kind of response?"

"How you feel. About her. About all that has happened. Don't you think she is entitled to that? After all, no response is tantamount to turning one's back. And being sympathetic doesn't mean simply sitting back and allowing one's ill feelings to dominate one."

"Gentlemen, thank you for coming," the Colonel said abruptly. "I have no more to say for the moment. The message to my wife is that she may do as she pleases. If she wishes to see me, I am here."

"We were hoping," my father said, "that you might be inclined to write her a note, or perhaps come with us to the hotel and — without putting pressure on her — explain things for yourself."

"Out of the question. If she wishes to see me, I am here. Now, please, I have no more to say for the moment. Forgive me for not shaking hands, but mine are still soiled from the hunt."

Karimzadeh and my father got up and left. The refreshment tray hadn't been touched.

"He is a beast!" I heard my mother say in Turkish that night, through the door connecting our rooms.

Parviz had been moved to Nasrin's room, and Mrs. Ashrafi had gone back to the one she shared with her husband.

"He refuses to send any word to his wife. He refuses to acknowledge what he has done to his brother-in-law. He doesn't even ask about his son. Instead he behaves as though he were the victim of some terrible injustice. The man is impossible. Insane. What does he expect, after his atrocious behavior? That his wife should run after him to put up with more of the same treatment? No, there's more to this than self-respect — although, God knows, that's important enough. It's a matter of her own personal safety as well. She is not safe with such a person."

"He is a very proud man," my father said quietly. "When his pride is hurt, he becomes difficult to live with."

"Difficult! He turns into an animal! He turns against everything. Didn't you yourself say that he suspected you of being in collusion with Ashrafi?"

51

My father must have nodded.

"Well, then?"

"He had reason to. After all, it was Ashrafi who asked me to go on his behalf."

"But that's no reason to turn against you."

"Well — "

"And you have no idea how upset everyone was at the hospital. I saw the poor boy bandaged up, his face all swollen, and one eye missing beneath all the bandages. I couldn't hold back my tears. And you know I never cry."

"Only when you have to."

"Don't be silly. And what is so amazing is that Nasrin, who always cries, hasn't shed a tear since the incident. She has lost her sleep, her appetite — you saw how little she ate at supper. She didn't have a bite to eat all day. But she doesn't cry. Isn't that strange? She told me how badly she wants to cry, but can't even when she tries to. When she saw the poor boy, she was so bewildered that she simply sat there looking at him, kissing his hands and pressing them to her cheek."

"She's in a state of shock."

"Then, there's Parviz. The poor boy is bound to be taking all this in. But he's so silent, so well-behaved and controlled. He says nothing."

"He is sensitive and intelligent — and controlled, as you say. A remarkable combination for a boy his age. He will shine some day. How far he will go is another matter. But he will shine. It's a good thing that Firuz is here to keep him company."

"Is Firuz asleep?"

The door opened, and light fell into my room. I closed my eyes automatically, as though being caught awake were a vice. My mother pulled back the sheet from over my head, kissed my cheek, and went out, closing the door behind her.

I was beginning now to have a fair idea of what was going on, but was too far removed to have any definite picture. The words I heard in the dark had only flashes of meaning.

"Why does that boy always sleep with a sheet over his head?" my mother asked, speaking more quietly.

"He told me once." My father laughed. "He's convinced it filters the air he breathes."

52

9

*I*t was decided the following day that Bijan should be taken to an eye specialist in Tehran as soon as possible. His eyeball had been literally punctured. The belt buckle having pierced through the sclera, the vitreous body had seeped out, resulting in almost total loss of vision. It was a matter now of determining what little sight remained to be saved.

Plans were drawn up to leave Ramsar the next day. The Ashrafis were to return to Rasht to pick up Bijan and drive on to Tehran the day after. Nasrin and Parviz were to come with us and stay at our house until the Ashrafis arrived. Karbalai decided to go back by himself in a roundabout way, passing through Babol, where he owned a ginning plant.

The only ones to stay behind were the Karimzadehs. Mina thought that Ahmad needed the rest. They saw us off on the driveway.

We had all been at Ramsar less than a week, whereas the original plan had been to spend as much as two or three. My parents could have stayed longer as well, but they clearly felt the pressure of circumstances. Moreover, my father was eager to proceed with his business plans — having apparently reached some kind of decision with the others.

Just before we all left, departing en masse, the luggage packed, climbing into cars, an incident occurred. Not particularly significant, but disconcerting enough. The timing was perfect.

The Colonel's green army sedan appeared on the driveway. The batman stepped out with a white envelope in his hand. For an instant, everyone must have thought it was intended for Nasrin. And if so, how would that affect the group decision to return to the city?

But the batman walked up to Karbalai instead.

"From his excellency, the Colonel," he said, extending the

note. Then he returned to the car, backed up, and drove away.

"What does it say?" Karimzadeh asked, who was standing beside him.

Ashrafi was settled in the back seat of his limousine, but had his head out the window. My father got out of our car.

Karbalai handed the note to Karimzadeh, who passed it on to my father. Ashrafi asked to see it as well. My father went over to him and said a few words, then returned to his position behind the steering wheel.

"What is it?" my mother asked.

"Nothing," he said, releasing the brake. "He says he'll settle accounts with Karbalai when he gets back to Tehran."

It was a small incident. Nevertheless, an ominous sort of intrusion, darkening our departure. And it was an intensely embarrassing moment for Nasrin.

There was only one road then connecting Tehran to the Caspian — the Chalus road. We headed east from Ramsar to Chalus, then drove south, cutting through the whole range of the Alborz Mountains.

It was something of an adventure to drive along that road. It started, from Chalus, below sea level, then wound its way up to heights which made you giddy looking down — over sheer precipices barely a few feet away from you — before descending more placidly to the level of Tehran. It ran alongside rivers, past cataracts, through seeping, dark tunnels. It wasn't paved. It was wide enough — just barely in parts — for two cars to pass. The longer tunnels had guards posted at their entrances to direct the traffic, which was one-way, reversed at intervals by signals from the opposite end. My father drove slowly and cautiously.

And as you made your way south, the scenery changed — from the lush green vegetation of the Caspian area to the dry yellow-gray-brown of the inner mountains. You were in the hollow of earth crust and rock. The humidity dropped. Fresh air ran up your nostrils, and you reached for a sweater. But as the road leveled down to the city, the temperature rose again. A dry heat, which scorched you inside the car, and which brought back precisely the feeling that had driven you north in the first place.

We arrived at our house late in the afternoon, catching our servants by surprise.

Mamad Baqer was watering the flowers, using two huge cans with long spouts, his sleeves and trousers rolled up. Tahibe, his wife, was squatting over a tubful of vegetables, preparing them for pickling — her *chador* wrapped about her waist and a row of jars beside her. Both were barefoot.

Tahibe got up and gave a self-effacing smile and, seeing we had guests, ran off to light the samovar. Mamad Baqer put the watering cans down and helped unload the car — chattering in Turkish all the time, at a loss as to why we had come back so soon.

"Why?" he kept asking my mother, who was directing the unloading. "What's in Tehran? Only heat. And what heat! Believe me, we've had such a drought since you've gone . . ."

"It's only been five days," my mother said. "Don't take out the large things first — you'll rumple the clothes."

"Six, madam. You left last Thursday. And what a sun! It's kept my throat parched no matter how much water I drink." He turned to my father, who was retrieving some papers from the glove compartment. "This is the third time I'm watering the garden today, excellency. If I didn't, you'd come back to a piece of desert."

And so on, until all the luggage and clothes were brought into the house, and tea was set up on a table beside the pool. Tahibe had gone out to buy a cake.

As we sat on the white wrought-iron chairs, drinking tea and eating fruit, Mamad Baqer squatted a little distance away and questioned us about every aspect of our trip. Finally, my father called his attention to the car, which was covered with dust.

"I'll clean it as soon as I finish watering the flowers, excel-

55

lency," he said, loath to get up just then. "Next time take me with you. There are a lot of chores to be done at Ramsar. I know. Mr. Ashrafi takes Musa with him. I've heard about all the work to be done from Musa."

"Who will stay in the house?"

"Tahibe," he said, as though the answer were perfectly obvious.

"Tahibe can't stay by herself," my father remonstrated. "What kind of a husband are you?"

"She has a brother I can vouch for. He can come and stay with her, excellency."

My mother told him to call his wife. Tahibe arrived and was complimented on her choice of the cake. Then my mother explained the sleeping arrangements.

That night, my parents slept in the garden as usual, and a separate bed was set up for Nasrin. All three beds had mosquito nettings.

Parviz and I slept on the roof, with nothing over our heads, since mosquitoes didn't usually fly that high.

I also slept with the top sheet folded over my chest, instead of my head. There was no malaria to fear in Tehran.

August that year was sweltering. It was like being in a kiln. Our house was on Takhte Jamshid Avenue, which, at that time, marked the northern edge of the city. It doesn't now, of course: it's practically a part of the center of town. But it did then. And since Tehran is on a downward slope, the northern part has the distinct advantage of being cooler in summer — cooler, because it is higher and closer to the foothills.

People in the southern part, which is actually the oldest part of the city, fared far worse during these heat waves than we did. These were mostly the low-salaried, the poor, the crippled, or those bazaar families who had settled in the city a long time ago and had not bothered to move.

The bazaar, at this period, was the linking point between the two sectors. It stood decidedly at the center of things.

56

My father had an office in the bazaar, which he went to every morning except Friday, at seven. He stayed there until about one or two in the afternoon, then came back, looking disheveled and soaking with sweat.

In the summer, we practically abandoned the upper two floors of our house and lived in the split-level basement, like fish reaching down to the lowest depths, when the water gets warm. The difference in temperature between the basement and the two floors above it was enormous.

My father would cool off before lunch by flopping down on the sofa in the parlor and lying immobile, while the electric fan created a breeze from the opposite end of the room. Then, when he had the energy to eat, we would all sit down at the table.

My mother insisted that anyone with any sense — and who could afford it — would take a house in Shemran for the summer.

Shemran, at that time, was separated from Tehran by seven miles of desert — nestled right up against the mountains, like a favorite child between the legs of its mother. It was cool. It had houses with huge gardens. Huge walls made of mud and lime, with tall trees reaching over them. Compared to Tehran, it was an oasis of greenery.

Many of our friends had gardens there. Not houses — houses were what people had in Tehran, including the Karimzadehs and Ashrafis. The Ashrafis' garden was the farthest away from Tehran. It was actually located in Niavaran and closer in size to being an estate. I believe the grounds covered something like thirty acres.

At any rate, to get back to my mother's complaint, a move to Shemran that summer would have been impractical for us. We had just returned from America, and my father was too busy with affairs in the city.

As a result, we had to put up with not being able to recuperate from the heat. The evenings in Tehran were as hot as the days in Shemran, and by the end of the summer, we all developed headaches toward the end of the day.

One day, around the end of August, we had a visit, just before lunch, from Colonel Amuzegar. He came unannounced. My father hadn't returned from the office yet, and my mother was completely surprised. He was in full military uniform, with a batch of medals across his left breast and three miniature suns on each shoulder. He apologized for intruding, was ushered into the parlor, and given a glass of *sharbat* — the fruit drink offered to guests in Iran, regardless of whether they like it or not.

When my father came in, he got up and greeted him.

"My dear Colonel, what a pleasure to see you!"

"My apologies for breaking in on you like this."

"No apologies necessary. You will stay for lunch."

"I'm expected at the Officers Club."

"Hang the Officers Club!" My father slapped him on the back. He must have had a good day at the office. "Take off your dazzling uniform and sit down to eat with us."

The Colonel acquiesced.

Mamad Baqer set up another place at the table, then went out to tell the Colonel's batman to take his meal in the kitchen.

After lunch the two men moved into the parlor, which looked out onto the garden, and had coffee. My mother went up to her room, and I stayed behind in the dining room, where I spread a newspaper over the table and made houses by gluing match sticks together.

The voices through the door were muffled. Both men talked softly. After the coffee was drunk, the Colonel got up and took his leave. My mother came down and invited him to come back again, which he agreed to do. Then he shook hands with me and went out into the midafternoon heat, his batman holding the door open for him. My father walked with him through the garden and shook hands again at the door.

When he returned to the house, my mother called to him from the parlor.

"He is a changed person," my father said.

"Perhaps. Or he could be showing his affable side," my mother suggested.

"No. He is different. At Ramsar he was very suspicious, very distant. He didn't want to have anything to do with us. Or his wife, for that matter. His pride was hurt. When his wife didn't come back home, he was stung to the quick. It didn't comply with his sense of duty. So he reacted out of anger. He turned his back on us all. Furthermore, he thought that we were giving her support by asking him to take matters calmly."

"And his whole attitude has changed in six weeks?"

"It's changing. He realizes now how serious things are — that if he wants his wife back, he'll have to do more than just wait."

"So what did he ask you to do?"

"What makes you think he asked me to do anything?" my father smiled.

"Well — " my mother's hands went up — "he came here unannounced. He talked through lunch very politely, but about nothing in particular. He made it very clear that he wasn't going to say anything important until he had you in private . . ."

"He is still very sensitive about going over his marital life, about opening himself up, especially in front of women. Besides, he wanted to apologize to me about his behavior at Ramsar, and he couldn't have done that with you around. I can understand."

"Very well, but what did he actually ask you to do?"

"He wanted me to approach Nasrin privately and arrange a meeting between them."

"Where? Here?"

"Yes. On neutral ground."

"Do you think Nasrin will agree? She was adamant about his having to present himself to the Ashrafis."

"We'll see. But he can't bring himself to see the Ashrafis yet. Not now. Not yet. It's taken him a lot — don't you see — to make himself come here. Let's go after one thing at a time. And the one thing I'm after right now is my nap."

The following Friday we drove north on Pahlavi Avenue to Ashrafi's estate. When we reached Shemran, we turned east and drove for another seven miles over a narrow, curving dirt road, passing pedestrians and donkeys along the way.

At some point, my mother said that we were in Niavaran, although there were no signs or changes in the scenery to indicate it.

The approach to Ashrafi's estate was impressive. The road led right up to the entrance gate, then tapered off to the left, making a detour around the walls — like an inconspicuous stage exit. The grounds were on a downhill slope, which leveled off toward the bottom — surrounded by huge walls made of mud, straw, and pebbles. One could make out the corner walls at the higher end, but the lower ones stretched out of sight. The gate was large and wooden — a faded green.

My father honked the horn, and a saggy-looking man, with shirttails outside his pajamalike trousers, let us through, bowing as we passed.

Inside the grounds, it was like being under a huge canopy of trees. Tall poplars, with branches and leaves that intersected at the top. A coolness and a fragrance of fruits — not flowers — embraced us.

The driveway led us past a pool — the upper pool — which received its water from a mountain stream.

We parked our car under an oak tree, where there were some half dozen others, then entered the house, calling out our arrival. It was just before noon.

Mrs. Ashrafi emerged from the kitchen to greet us. She was not one to distribute kisses. She had an apron over her dress and told us to go into the living room: she was making *khoresht* — or stew — to go over the rice.

It was always a matter of conjecture as to how many people would show up at the Ashrafis for lunch on Fridays. Those of us who were close to them arrived unannounced. But usually there were invited guests as well — people from the bank or businessmen, with their families. Never any foreigners. It was a quiet occasion when we came across less than a dozen. Usually we expected to see as many as twenty or thirty.

The Ashrafis were always casually dressed. Their appearance blended in with the simple furniture and quiet rugs. I don't remember ever seeing anything ornate in their house — either in

60

Niavaran or even in Tehran, where people tend to be more showy in their tastes. Mr. Ashrafi was in a white short-sleeved shirt, open at the neck, his trousers held up by suspenders, which made his stomach bulge all the more prominently. And his wife was always in what my mother referred to as her "cooking clothes."

The guests, on the other hand — and Nasrin, too, in this case — came formally dressed: the women in cool summer outfits, and the men in suits and ties, which they took off as the day wore on.

That's how the visits were paced: formal at first, then more and more casual, until people were slapping each other on the back, with shirt-sleeves rolled up. Lunch was always a very elaborate affair — with huge piles of rice, skewers of *kabab* laid out on flat pancake-thin bread, and side dishes of sauce and stew — all spread out on one long table. Supper was just the opposite: a makeshift affair, which all the women helped in putting together.

Ashrafi was as nonchalant in his greeting as his wife. He was comfortably settled in his armchair and not about to get up until lunch. He waved a hand and bade us sit down, which we did, Iranian fashion, on straight-backed chairs, placed in a circle around the room.

Then there followed the formal greetings with other guests, going around the room: for the men a hand-to-heart bow from their seated positions, for the women smiles and nods — everyone mumbling the very same words of salutation. Somewhat like a chant repeated automatically under one's breath at a religious service.

Nasrin threw out her arms spontaneously and told me to kiss her. She had more color in her face than at Ramsar. I felt her lipstick and makeup on my cheek, which she wiped away with her handkerchief. Then she told me that Bijan was outside in the garden, and that I could swim in the lower pool with Parviz and the other boys before lunch, if I wanted to.

"What about Bijan?" I asked.

"He can't swim for a while," she said. "But you go in anyway."

She told me to change in her room. I went upstairs and

61

slipped into my swimming trunks, then went out the back door to the lower pool.

Both pools were actually pondlike, in that they were rectangular ditches hollowed by shovels. The sides and bottoms were lined with weeds and moss. The upper pool — fed by mountain water, which flowed in one end and out the other — was too cold to swim in. It was under the canopy of trees — oak and mulberry — ever in the shade, and used as a sort of refrigerator, for fruits, especially watermelons. I never saw the pool without heads of watermelon floating in it.

The lower pool, by contrast, was warm. It didn't have an inflow of water. It was smaller, exposed to the sun. It had fish — gold ones and larger, gray ones and other tiny creatures swimming inside.

Bijan wasn't around. There were four or five boys and two or three girls lying in the sun in their bathing suits. Parviz waved me over to the group. They were exchanging stories — about school and their teachers — and laughing often. They had gone mulberry-picking before their swim. One of the girls put some mulberries on a leaf and placed them before me.

I whispered to Parviz about Bijan.

"He's down at the bottom end of the garden," he mumbled. "He'll be back soon."

"What's he doing?"

"He'll tell you himself." Parviz didn't want to go into details in front of the group.

But I still had questions in my mind. "How is he?" I persisted.

"Fine," he muttered, nodding, and returned his attention to the group.

I stretched out on my towel and listened to more stories about school life in Iran.

Then Bijan appeared from the lower end of the garden, climbing over a gully up to our level. He was in the same bathing suit as before — a black one — and sandals. His skin had a burned tint; he was darker than the rest of us. And over his left eye, he had a black patch.

My mind raced back to medieval tortures. I thought of an executioner walking into a cell. Something akin to panic stirred inside me.

Yet I felt like reaching out to him, expressing my grief over the loss of his eye. Whatever our conflicts, I thought, regardless of his actions, he didn't deserve that.

When he reached us, he crouched, smiled, and asked what we were talking about. He took me in with the rest of the group, as though nothing had happened since the last time we had been together. As though I had been with him all the time.

Musa came out and told us that lunch was on the table, and that if we didn't get up right away, all the *tadig* would be gone. *Tadig* was the choicest part of the rice dish — the toasted crust at the bottom of the pot.

We all got up and threw the leftover mulberries in the pool, saving them for the afternoon dip. It was a game we played: opening our mouths as we swam and letting the floating mulberries drift into them. We never actually swam after them. The pleasure was in having the thing done effortlessly.

As we walked into the house, Bijan pulled Parviz and me outside again. He had the open-lipped anticipating look of his sister, a look of concealed excitement.

I had expected, coming up from Tehran, to find him dejected or morose. Ill-tempered. Moody. Whatever else I associated with suddenly finding oneself blinded in one eye. I had thought of him, in a way, I suppose, as a cripple.

But here he was, brimming over with suppressed excitement.

"I've been looking over the gully at the lower end of the garden," he said. "I knew they'd be there. I saw them."

"Saw what?" I asked.

"Scorpions," he answered, his one eye on me. "Parviz knows. But don't tell the others. After lunch we'll go down and catch some. I know how. But don't tell the others. They'll only run back and tell their mothers. Are you with us, Firuz?"

"Yes," I blurted automatically. At that moment I might have agreed to anything. My mind was on something else.

"Good," he said. "Then let's go in."

But this time I stopped him. I couldn't hold back any longer. I wanted to know.

"Did it hurt?" I asked.

He smiled — a very winning and affable smile, which brought out his resemblance to Nasrin.

"A little," he said. "Not enough for you to worry about."

He put an arm around my shoulder, the skins of our bodies touching, then said something peculiar.

"Did you cry for me? Parviz tells me that he cried a lot, and I believe him."

What could I say? No, I hadn't cried. I had felt sorry for him, but not in a way which brings tears to one's eyes. I lowered my head.

"Don't worry," he said, shaking my shoulders. "I rode the horse, as I said I would. I had it in mind a long time. Swimming in the sea, I thought to myself: why not now, while he's caught up with cards? He beats my sister, so I ride his horse. You didn't know that? Oh, yes, he beats my sister. Locks her up, too. Better that he should beat me. He tells me not to ride his horse. I ride it anyway. He beats me up, as he said he would. He gouges my eye out. So much the worse for him. For that he loses my sister. So we're even. I bear him no malice."

He smiled.

10

*L*unch was magnificent. It lasted over an hour. We ate so much of the main dish we had no room for dessert. Dessert, by common consent, was put off till afternoon tea.

Every guest, including myself, complimented Mrs. Ashrafi on the quality of the cooking, some to the point of caricature.

Toward the end of the meal, Musa was asked to come out and receive the plaudits that were his due. He stood at the door, wiping his hands over his trousers, while my father gave a speech on long-grained rice and the difficulty of cooking it just right. Musa, he ended, had mastered the art. Everyone applauded. Musa put a hand to his heart and gave a self-effacing smile, murmuring under his breath: "Your servant . . . your slave . . ."

Other guests got up to make speeches — all about food. When Iranians are satisfied with their meals, rhetoric simply flows out of them. They try to match the taste of the food with displays of verbal skill — which is what usually makes luncheon gatherings such garrulous occasions.

Everything is carried to excess — the eating, the talking — so that the event literally wears one out and prepares one for a nap.

After the meal, while the servants carried the dishes away, the guests dispersed to lie on couches and cots — the women in one part of the house, the men in another. The children were herded off to a room without furniture, where soft mattresses had been unrolled and laid on the carpet side by side, dormitory fashion.

Bijan, Parviz, and I slipped out into the garden. We crouched behind a row of bushes, nibbling apricots and waiting. We had to be sure the servants were sleeping as well. Then Bijan got up and told us to follow him.

We went to the gardening shed, which had mud walls and a low roof, like a chicken hut. He picked out a shovel, a sharp-edged bricklaying trowel, and a gunnysack containing some nails. He emptied the nails into a flowerpot, gave me the sack, handed the trowel to Parviz, and kept the shovel himself.

Then we went to the gully, scampered down its side, and walked along the bottom. The sun was blazing and I felt the need for a hat. I folded the sack and put it over my head.

Near the lower end of the garden, Bijan stopped and gazed along the sides of the gully.

"When it's hot," he said, "they crawl inside their holes. The holes are small — about the width of your finger — and rectangular."

"This one?" Parviz pointed to a spot.

"That's too large," Bijan said. "But let's try it anyway."

He drove the blade of the shovel about three inches under the hole, then pulled it out quickly, shaking it from side to side, so that the earth fell loose to the ground.

"No," he said. "That hole was too large. I'll do the looking."

He tried several other spots, without success. Parviz and I stood behind him.

Then he let out a cry. A spiderlike creature emerged from the heap on the blade, thrashing about. Its tail was almost twice the size of its body — flat, curved, and greenish, with what looked like a hook at the end.

"Give me the trowel," he said.

Parviz extended his arm, then jumped back to watch. Both of us were wide-eyed.

Then, with a very deft stroke, Bijan severed the tail from the body. A greenish liquid oozed out, and the body fell off the shovel and ran about madly over the ground.

Parviz and I pulled back.

"Don't be afraid," Bijan laughed. "It's harmless now. It can't do a thing to you. See?" He scooped up the tailless creature and let it run furiously over and around his arm.

Then he asked for the sack, which I gave him, and tossed it inside.

"Don't let it out." He returned the sack. "Keep the top tightly closed, because these things can slip through the slightest opening."

I held the sack away from me, gripping the open end so hard that I felt the strain in my fingers and arm.

"What are you going to do with the tail?" Parviz asked.

The greenish liquid having oozed out, it had shrunk in size.

"Leave it here for its mate," Bijan replied, overturning the shovel.

Did scorpions have mates? I didn't know whether he was being serious or not.

We caught five that afternoon. I never imagined that so many could be found in one gully alone. One gully in one garden. I looked up at the hills around us, thinking of the great numbers that must have been embedded in this earth.

All five were quickly deposited in the sack. Parviz and I still didn't know what Bijan had in mind to do with them, and he wouldn't tell us.

It was still midafternoon when Bijan declared the hunt closed. He took the sack from my grasp and handed me the shovel. Then he led the way back. There were no signs that the others were up yet.

At the lower pool he stopped and shook out the sack over the water. Four tailless scorpions fell into the liquid — thrashing about. The other escaped.

"For the fish," Bijan said, turning to us. "In no time at all, they'll be eaten. Either that or they'll sink to the bottom."

They struggled frantically between the floating mulberries.

"What about the one that got away?" I asked.

"It won't last the day," he said. "Without its tail, it is useless. It will be torn apart by ants."

Already, as he spoke, one of the scorpions vanished from sight.

We returned our hunting gear to the shed and went back to the house. Parviz and I were silent. Bijan decided he was ready for a nap.

Later the household began to stir, and tea was served. After tea, Nasrin came down from her room in a white bathing suit and cap. Her breasts were full and finely shaped, and there was a hint of the nipples showing through the cloth. Her calves and thighs were full as well. Soft, white, and smooth. "Sepulchral" was the word that came to my lips — even though I didn't quite know what it meant.

As she entered the pool, I felt the urge to shout and stop her. Instead I exchanged a glance with Parviz.

"Come in," she said from the water. "It's beautifully warm."

I hesitated, then dived in, gliding past her legs. Parviz followed. Later so did Bijan, although he was not supposed to.

A few days later — in the middle of the week — we had a second visit from Colonel Amuzegar. He arrived around five in the afternoon, dressed as before in military uniform. He was affable and smiled with his lips. He handed my mother a bouquet of pink roses, then gave me his hat to put away, and said that if I wanted some caviar and fresh figs, I could go to his car and fetch them from his batman.

My mother thanked him profusely and led the way to the parlor, which was decked out for the occasion with flowers, fruits, and pistachio nuts. The windows were open. Mamad Baqer was watering the garden. The room had the full-mixtured smell of a bower.

A waft of jasmine scent blew in from outside. A bee flew in, circled about giddily, striking the windowpane, and buzzed out.

About half an hour later, Nasrin arrived, wearing a blue dress with tiny white polka dots and matching blue leather handbag and shoes. She took off her sunglasses and shook her reddish brown hair, which fell to her shoulders in waves.

She kissed me in the hallway and went into the parlor, not smiling. She looked directly at the Colonel, who avoided her gaze.

She was more distant than I had seen her, but not cold. The look of sorrow was still in her face, but hardened, as though she had arrived at some fixed position, which left her no happier, though determined. There was resolution in her bearing.

The Colonel, who had been uncharacteristically affable up till then, reverted to his formal manner. He spoke in crisp monosyllables. He sat tightly cross-legged, running his thumb over the tips of his fingers.

Tahibe brought in the tea tray and another one of her cakes, which my mother sliced and passed around on small plates.

Nasrin commented on the strong smell of jasmine coming in from the garden.

"Firuz will go and pick a handful for you. Won't you, dear?" my mother said.

I got up to leave.

"No, please don't bother. Not yet," Nasrin remonstrated. "I see Firuz so seldom." She sought me out with her eyes, her mouth open. "Come and sit beside me instead." She patted the sofa cushion beside her. "That is, if you want to."

I crossed the room and took my new place. Nasrin reached into the fruit bowl, put some cherries onto a dish, and placed the dish in front of me.

The Colonel and my parents were nonplussed.

So was I. I was used to leaving the adult world on cue, especially when we had visitors. This visit in particular. All along I had expected to receive the directive to trot off somewhere, so that the battle might begin.

I put the cherries in my mouth and spat the pits into the cup of my fist.

The Colonel leaned over to whisper something to my mother

"There's no need for that," Nasrin said almost blithely. "We can talk openly in front of all. Firuz knows, too, I'm sure. He was present when you delivered the beating." She looked directly into the Colonel's eyes. "There is no need to have him out of the room."

The Colonel was silent. His voice cracked when he spoke.

"What I have to say —" he cleared his throat — "has to do with our marriage."

"Not the beating?" Nasrin's eyebrows went up. Her voice in contrast, had a soft clarity.

"Not just the beating."

"Begin with the beating," Nasrin persisted. "What can you say to justify that?"

The Colonel returned her gaze.

"You might understand, if you considered it in the context of our marriage."

"But what did my brother do to put it in the context of our marriage? If our marriage was at stake, why did you beat him?"

Silence.

"I lost my temper." The Colonel paused. He turned to my father. "If I may trouble you for a cigarette . . ."

"Yes, of course."

My father opened the lid of a silver box and held out a lighter. My mother pushed forward a silver ashtray. The Colonel leaned back and blew out a cloud of smoke.

"He went against my orders. The horse could have killed him. It could have run over Parviz."

"So you blinded him instead. Is that any better?"

"I lost my temper." The Colonel put out the cigarette after two puffs.

"Which is worse, your horse's temper or yours?"

Silence again.

"Tell me, what had Bijan ever done to you? Aside from riding your horse. Has he gotten in the way of our marriage? Has he threatened our lives?"

"Parviz . . ."

"What about Parviz? You beat him as well. You beat all of us. You beat us and go your own way. You ride off on your horse. When have you ever said anything to justify your actions? Tell me, are we expected to take these beatings as a matter of course? Like your perpetual drinking and gambling? For over six weeks now, the boy has been blind in one eye. When are you going to say anything to him? To his parents? Tell me, why have you asked Mr. Momtaz to bring us together at his house? What is wrong with coming to my father's and perhaps directly facing up to what you have done? Why didn't you come to my father's? Is it because you hold my side of the family in such contempt? The boy, after all, is your brother-in-law."

"And you are my wife," the Colonel broke in. "Why didn't you come home at Ramsar?"

"Frankly, I was afraid to come home. I was afraid and disgusted. The next fit of anger and it might have been Parviz or me. I was afraid. There's my answer. Now, tell me why you didn't visit the boy in the hospital. Why you didn't explain yourself while I was still at the hotel. Why you sent your chauffeur with a note — with a note — to Karbalai instead of to me . . ."

"Ashrafi sent me a note," the Colonel erupted. "I had no choice. I sent a note back."

"To Karbalai, and not to my father or me. Why? As a slap at all of us? At me? Because I couldn't bring myself to sleep in the same house with you? I told you, I was afraid. What is your explanation?"

"I . . ." the Colonel hesitated, "was hurt . . . offended."

"Hurt? By what? By whom?"

"Please, Mrs. Amuzegar," my father interceded in a conciliatory tone, "allow him to speak."

"I am waiting," she said. "I didn't come here to get grievances off my chest. I want to hear his explanation. I want you to hear it as well. All of us."

She turned to me and threaded her fingers through mine.

My God, I thought, what if she puts my hand to her breast again now! My heart pounded wildly.

The Colonel looked yellow.

"Nasrin," he started, but stopped. "I love you very much. It doesn't matter now who hears — though, God knows, I'm not used to declaring my sentiments in front of others. I love you very much. But I have this dreadful pride. It dictates all my thoughts and actions. It makes me do what I want to check myself from doing. It pushes me into actions I find hard to justify. When I search for justifications, this same pride drives me into isolation — just when I want and need to break out of myself and turn to others. I tell you, it makes me do some things I scarcely understand, then punishes me for doing them."

"If that is the problem," Nasrin answered coolly, "then do away with your pride. Get rid of it."

"I try to, but I can't."

"Do you?"

"I don't know how to go about it, where to start. It has been so much a part of my makeup — my nature and upbringing — I don't know what parts of myself to weed out. From my childhood right up through the army, I always looked upon pride as a virtue — something to be cultivated. In the army, it *had* to be cultivated. It makes one able to stand one's ground. It makes one's fear of death less terrifying than the loss of self-esteem. It makes one — compels one — to do well. To excel. To make use of one's talents. That is also what I learned from my childhood, when we lived on our estates: to own a village, to own land, and not run it properly was the worst abuse one could do to oneself — and to those one was responsible for."

"And your family? What of that?" Nasrin had almost a glow about her.

"I'm getting to that. What I mean to say is that pride, to me, was always such a public necessity — such a cultivated, functional virtue — that I was never really able to assess its inner workings and value. I was never able to distinguish between its beneficial aspect and what was inherently harmful about it. Actually, this is something I am still unable to fathom: how pride can be simultaneously a virtue and a vice. Do you follow me? I've been doing some thinking these past few weeks — not so much because I set myself to, but because it simply came over me. At first, I brooded. I was hurt and angry. Furious, to be more accurate. But thoughts started coming to me — in the day, at night, through my sleep — of their own accord. It was as though a mirror were being pieced together for me to see myself in. What I saw horrified me."

"And then?" Nasrin asked.

"And then I knew I had to see you. You first, not Bijan. What I did to Bijan was bad enough. What I did to you was worse. I scarcely know how to make up to the boy. The shame of my action overwhelms me right now. In time I hope to see my way to doing the right thing — to make the kind of amends which will be as lasting to him as the loss of his eyesight. But blinding him opened up an awareness in me of my atrocities to you. Those went deeper and had a much more tortuous history. What I did to Bijan — it appalls me to say this — was a manifestation of what I had done to you. Perhaps all along. I don't exactly know since when. But for a long time. Which is why I needed to see you first — alone. To talk about us. And which is why I asked Mr. Momtaz to bring us together at his house. At your father's, the issue would have been clouded over by what I did to Bijan."

"This is all very well," Nasrin said, "and no doubt exonerates all your actions in your eyes. But, unfortunately, now" — she shook her head slightly from side to side — "it's all beside the point."

"No, please, allow me to continue." The Colonel was animated. He was in the throes of self-analysis and conveyed the urge to proceed unchecked to his large conclusion — like a river which had started out as a trickle, gathering momentum and rushing toward the sea.

"My gambling. I want to explain that; I know it disturbs you. It was a manifestation of the same conflict. After the war, try as I did, I couldn't get back into step. Before the war and while it was going on, army life had a pace of its own. I was in keeping with it. We had large duties to perform, and I had mine, which I was trained for. Afterward, when we were stripped of whatever power we had left and given our medals, there was nothing to do but wait. Play the political game. Wait for time and chance to take their own course. I couldn't do that. Not then. The feeling of impotence fairly throttled me. My work had no significance at all — neither my position nor my training. As a nation, we were on the verge of military bankruptcy. We still are. Waiting for something to happen. For the Americans to step in and bolster us up. That's no answer. But that's another matter. At any rate, that's when I began to lash out. To be reckless. My life had no meaning at all. I looked about me. I envied others what they were doing. I envied the architect: he designed houses. I envied the mason who built them. The teacher, the merchant. Your father. At least he was working with his head: running a bank and making money out of buying and selling. I even envied the men who made bread. The peasants on our farm. What was I doing? Nothing. A wasted piece of potential with nothing but time on his hands: trained — as few men are in our country — to perform. Yet held back from performing. Merely going through gestures and motions. All my confidence in myself gradually seeped away. I came to hate myself. I didn't want you to see me the way I saw myself, though. So I turned against you. I did things which were clearly harmful to me — to both of us, to our relationship — and put the blame on you. I always sought ways of fixing my troubles on you. I drank. I gambled. My God, how I gambled! I put you through such misery on that account — you, who did so much to try and stop me. I took up riding. That at least was a release for my pent-up energies. But riding wasn't enough. I gambled. I lost. I tried to make up my losses by gambling more. I continued to lose. I couldn't bear that, because losing — especially to men I regarded as having a firm hold on life — was a confirmation of my own incompetence. It discharged the poison in me. It brought on fits of rage. I took to violence. I lashed out at Bijan. God knows why. Perhaps because he was such a reflection of me. Because in him I saw myself. I went after Bijan in a blind rage of anger. For all I know, I was out after myself. Are you listening? Do you follow me, Nasrin?"

"I am," Nasrin nodded. "I'm glad you're finally beginning to see through some of your difficulties. But as far as our relationship is concerned, it's still beside the point."

"Does all I say have no meaning for you?"

"They are your difficulties. Not mine." She paused. "I'm not your wife anymore."

Those words must have seared his heart. His face appeared to cave in — like a sand castle under the glare of the sun.

"Can't we get back together again by talking things over?" the Colonel said faintly.

"I'm afraid not."

"But I have so much yet to tell you — so much to explain, which I haven't gone into. I tell you, I'm not the same man I was a month ago."

"It's too late for that now."

"Too late?"

"Something happened in me when you blinded Bijan."

"Please, let me explain that incident further . . ."

"No, you would do better to listen. It would make things easier for you. When you blinded Bijan, something inside me broke. The bond between us. All through our marriage, I put up with the strains in our relationship. The beatings, the drinking, the gambling. All that you pointed to. The closed-in life I was forced to lead as your wife. Your getting up and storming off in the middle of the night, then blaming me for driving you away . . ."

"Nasrin, let me explain. It was not that I didn't love you. I did, very much. But, God knows, there were forces in me that wouldn't let me show it. Forces I couldn't cope with. I love you now more than ever before — now that I see what was going on inside me."

"Let me finish," Nasrin said, as though from a considerable distance and height. "For years I lived through the relationship we had, knowing that it was dying by degrees, and yet still clinging to the hope that something would happen to reverse the process — that would take us back to where we started when we got married. Up till the birth of Parviz."

"Parviz," the Colonel muttered limply.

"Your son. Whom you never seem to acknowledge. Whom you claimed, from his birth, to be my child rather than yours. A Turk, you called him. Of Turkish blood, like his mother."

The Colonel lowered his head.

"It's true," she continued, holding him up for show. "This splendid figure of pure Iranian manhood holds us Azeri Turks in such contempt that he dismisses his child as being no part of him. Holds up the greatness of his own cultural heritage against the smallness and meanness of ours. Lumps us together with Arabs and Mongols as having brought about the decline of a glorious civilization. What was it you called us: a race of sheep-trotter eaters?"

"Nasrin . . ." the Colonel muttered, his head still down.

"All right. Enough of that. No doubt there are grievances enough on both sides. No doubt you have complaints of your own you wouldn't mind airing. I'm not arguing that. It's just that it's all beside the point. No amount of talk is going to bring us together. What I was starting to say was that, when you went after Bijan the way you did, something suddenly gave out in me. What had been dying all along died. Even then I held out. I was still susceptible to your influence. Had you come to me while we were at the hotel, I might still have been impelled to go on living with you. The ghost of our marriage then was preferable to the total blank of separation. But you didn't. You sent a note to Karbalai instead. While I was still waiting. That killed the hope. I was no longer your wife." She held up her fingers. "I've taken off the ring."

I hadn't noticed before. I may not have associated rings with marriages then.

"I saw," the Colonel murmured. The crack returned to his voice. "When did you take it off?"

"After we came back from the Caspian. The night I stayed in this house."

The Colonel's lips began to quiver. He pressed them together for control.

"Though that shouldn't make too much difference. You never agreed to wear one yourself — even though I wanted you to. It was too unmanly, you said."

My father nodded in spite of himself. He was sensitive on this point: he didn't wear a ring either. Neither did I, when I was married. Actually, Nasrin's words remained buried in my mind, until my own divorce exhumed them.

At any rate, that was the first inkling I had that cruelty, along with gentleness, resided in her nature. The two blended beatifically as she lifted the ringless finger of one hand and played with mine with the other.

75

"Mrs. Amuzegar," my father said slowly, "are you certain that all this is to your mutual benefit? You have lived together and loved each other a long time." Then he went on to point out the hardships that come with every marriage, and the need to live them through in order to arrive at a deeper mutual understanding and a more rewarding appreciation of life. It was a lecture.

"I understand your intentions and meaning," Nasrin responded, her fingers still intertwined in mine. "I respect what you say. But the point is that my love for him no longer exists. Your comments have that as a basis. In my case, the basis is gone. The love is dead. I no longer love him."

"If that is so, dear lady," my father continued on the Colonel's behalf, since the Colonel was as mute and broken as the pillars at Persepolis, "and without wishing to pry or to exceed the bounds of our friendship, why did you consent to this interview with your husband?"

I'm not being quaint with my diction. Those are the nearest equivalents in English of the words he spoke. He may have been a Turk by blood, but his application of language was innately Persian. The touchier the situation — the more cumbersome to deal with — the more formal his mode of address. As though the ultimate solution could only be reached through diplomacy and tact. Through refinement in the use of the tongue.

"I agreed to see him," Nasrin said, "in order to break off the marriage."

Simple words. Directly spoken.

My father had nowhere to go. He turned to my mother, who gazed down at the carpet.

The Colonel raised both hands to his forehead, shading his eyes. The shaking took possession of his body and hands. Suddenly it was evident that he was having convulsions. That he was sobbing inwardly. Between his convulsions he muttered "Nasrin" — as though that were the only intelligible thing he could utter.

My father reached across and put a hand to his shoulder. The Colonel continued sobbing quietly — almost without sound. Except for an occasional wrenching gasp, when he took a quick, deep swallow of air.

76

Nasrin loosened her fingers from mine and gazed across the room at my mother, who returned her look. Even at that age I grasped this much from their wordless interchange: that this was something which had to be done. And it had to be done this way.

I also sensed — instinctively, I suppose — that the men had no inkling of it. That they were like marionettes having their emotions pulled by sources they scarcely comprehended.

Revolution. The old order toppled, clutching at straws.

"Is it . . . is it," the Colonel gasped through his convulsions, "another man?"

Nasrin exchanged another look with my mother.

"No," she said, lingering on the word. But not assuringly. Emphatically. She didn't leave it at that. "This would have happened in any case."

"Is there another man?" the Colonel fairly bellowed, his hands no longer shielding his eyes, which were bloodshot and glazed.

Nasrin looked back at him as she had when walking into the room — no change in expression.

"I've already told you," she said softly.

"Is it Karbalai?" He almost choked on the name.

Nasrin leaned forward and picked up a plate from the far end of the table.

"There's no sense in going on," she said, without looking up. Then she placed the plate in my hands. "Firuz, will you fill this up with jasmine petals now?"

I was ready to bolt out of the room when the Colonel's words stopped me. It was like hearing someone half out of his mind, radiating optimism in the midst of bitter despair.

"Nasrin, I'll go to your brother. Right now, if you want. I'll go to your father too. I'll have the horse shot. I'll shoot him myself. I'll make it up to you, because I'm a different person now. I know what I've done. I've learned. I won't gamble. I won't ride. I'll love only you. And Parviz too. I'll love only you and Parviz
. . ."

I thought he was going to go on his knees.

I went out the door and ran to the garden. I was in a different world. I literally felt the shorts I was wearing. Conscious of them as being shorts. The open-neck shirt I had brought over from America, with "Cubs" written all over it. Raised in New England, I had chosen, of all teams in baseball, to root for the Chicago Cubs. I still do now.

I was also conscious of my white socks and white sneakers — washed against my will every week or so by Tahibe, on instructions from my mother.

Then I smelled the jasmine. It's scent overpowering as no other flower.

Three shrubs, planted in large clay pots, lined the wall adjacent to the parlor window, grouped together, so that the branches and leaves intersected, making one cluster of foliage, speckled with white blossoms, as wide at the open end as my thumb.

I felt the urge — don't laugh, but I felt this — to leap into the thicket and run my hands through the leaves, like passing one's fingers through hair, thereby shaking the flowers loose and making them fall randomly all over me, perfuming me.

Transforming me — don't laugh — into a bush.

Part ii

Hamburg

11

*A*fter the events of that summer, we stayed on in Tehran for almost a year and a half. Why we stayed so long, after having made the decision to leave, is a complicated matter. It involved business arrangements. Also indecisions. Vacillations.

It was a hectic time for my father.

The stay at Ramsar had brought all the business parties together. All had agreed that the scheme to export cotton to Germany was a good one. The next few months my father worked busily. But then the project hit snags. Questions arose, elements of risk were studied more closely. The parties became more hesitant — more reluctant — to part with their capital.

The first to back down, my father claims, was Ashrafi. Cautious of schemes he was not absolutely sure of — especially ones which involved foreign enterprise — jealous of those not under his own personal supervision, he balked. He advocated a sit-and-wait policy, which was tantamount to crippling the project, the strong point of which was its timing. It marked the beginning of the breach between the two men.

The other two parties had their own business to attend to and so didn't make any determined attempt to see the project through. More and more it seemed that they had entered the scheme in order not to be left out.

As a result, the longer we stayed the clearer it became that if a major move was to be made, my father would have to make it himself, which he proceeded to do, securing the necessary financing and setting up a private firm with his brother, who had worked in the same bank that he had.

But he did this without the zest that had distinguished his earlier efforts. Losing his fresh start and operating independently of the group took some of the wind out of his sails. Moreover, he did not have confidence in his brother's business acumen. His brother was new to the purchase and sale of cotton and was not the type to pick up such things quickly — or willingly, for that matter.

My father began to vacillate. He entertained second thoughts about going. He wondered if staying might not be better. Other ideas came to mind — other commitments unrelated to business.

Politics at that time was getting interesting. The closing years of the forties were a period of rising national sentiment. People were airing views they had previously been careful to hide. During the old king's reign, a blanket of censorship had been thrown over the country. Criticism had stopped. Parliament had been reduced to a rubber-stamp body. Those who spoke out against the regime risked being hauled off to jail. Some were shot

One of my relatives claims that restrictive measures were so stringent then that political thinking came to an end: died in the brain, as it were. Which is stretching the point, since what followed certainly didn't bear out his view.

During the war, the Allies intervened. They wanted to establish and maintain a supply line to Russia, and Iran's neutrality was of little importance. The old king was loath to have foreign troops on his soil, especially since the goal of his reign, and the saving grace of his strong-arm tactics, had been to secure a certain measure of national autonomy. He compromised, however, to the extent that he agreed to allow provisions to pass through, provided that their surveillance was left to his army. This was not a large enough concession for the Russians.

As a result, the Allies forced the old king to abdicate, on the grounds that he supported the Nazis. This changed the internal situation radically. Centralized authority, which had hitherto been concentrated in one man's hands, began to disintegrate. Foreign influence became the dominant factor in politics. The new king was installed on the throne and given the support needed for running the government: Allied support, that is, from the British mainly but also from the Americans, since he had nowhere near the power base his father had built up over the years.

Moreover, the new king was of a different cut. He had attained his position not through a power struggle but by right of succession. He was liberal in his views and more malleable in office. He didn't have the hardness which accrues with tested statesmanship.

The change in regimes led to a different political climate. Political expression came out in the open. There was a return, in essence, to the brief period of constitutional rule, prior to the old king's reign, when Parliament had a voice in running the country.

With Allied troops still occupying the land and Allied power the major factor in domestic affairs, a number of factions sprang up, some resuscitated from their state of hibernation and each seeking foreign support. Most of these advocated constitutional rule, attempting to solidify their positions in Parliament and steer the course of government through legislative action. But these were, by and large, fragmented bands, clustered about leaders who vied with each other over lesser issues.

The most organized of the political groups was the Communist Tudeh — or Masses — party, which received aid from the Russians. This group had been loosely formed in the thirties, but shortly afterward, it had been disbanded by the old regime. Its leaders had been jailed and the rest of the members had gone underground. With the Allied occupation and change in regimes, political prisoners were freed under a general amnesty, and the group assumed its party identity. The party considered itself the most victimized of any political organization and called for a major revision in the country's power structure. It had the capacity, in addition, to draw people out into the streets — much to the alarm of the other factions, which were seeking government reforms through legislative means: seeking, that is, to bolster and not further weaken the powers of Parliament. The other factions thereby came to support, in rather nebulous fashion, the various means the government had of putting down this ostensible threat.

The crucial period of struggle for the Tudeh party came just after the war, when the Russians, still occupying the north of Iran, refused to evacuate their troops, in keeping with the terms agreed upon by the Allies. The Russians had a number of ambitions in Iran. One was to turn Azerbaijan into a separate Communist state. Another was to exert influence over the rest of the country by supporting the Tudeh party; and, more conclusively, once the Tudeh party was established in power, to stage a Communist revolution — the first in the Middle East — thereby bringing the government down and setting up in its place a regime that would bring Iran fully into the Soviet orbit, and finally give the Russians what they always wanted: access to warmwater ports on the Persian Gulf.

That, at any rate, was how the nationalist argument ran. Those were the fears which brought the hitherto dissident factions together in supporting the government's actions against the Tudeh party. In this they were backed by the British, who had their oil interests to protect.

When the rioting started, troops were called in, and the Communist faction was put down a second time. Colonel Amuzegar was commanding a regiment of the Tehran garrison then. And it was the work of this garrison in particular that maintained order for the government. Which was no easy task, considering the volatility of the situation. The Tudeh demonstrations had the makings of a genuine popular movement and could have touched off a large-scale uprising by pulling into their wake the collected ill-will of a frustrated and embittered populace.

For all its ability to bring people out in the streets, however, the Tudeh party had one major drawback: it ran counter to nationalist feeling in Iran. It drew strength from popular grievances — aimed at social inequities and particularly at the British for their exploitation of the country's oil and their constant meddling in internal affairs. But this support eroded when the Russians refused to withdraw from Iranian territory and, further, tried to create a separate party and state in the north.

The final factor in the party's collapse was the breakdown of the Russian position. Pressured by the Western Allies to make a total pull-out or face armed intervention, and censured by the United Nations as a result of Iran's appeal, the Russians reluctantly withdrew.

This was hailed as a major victory for Iranian diplomacy and encouraged nationalist aspirations. With the Russians ousted and the Tudeh threat curtailed, the various factions in Parliament emerged into the prominence they had long been seeking.

And yet, true parliamentary rule faced one major obstacle: the pervasiveness of British influence. Now that the Russians were gone, the next task was to disengage Britain from political and economic dominance. Economically, of course, the major issue affecting the country was Britain's monopolistic control over Iranian oil. Politically, the problem was the administration of these economic interests through government channels: which meant that the British, no less than the Russians, had a bevy of Iranian agents on their payroll — a good many of them in government service and others in Parliament.

During the closing years of the forties, a number of Prime Ministers came and went. Cabinet seats were shuffled. No leader, however, emerged from all the jostling to form a government that had the wholehearted support of the people. Some were accused of crooked dealings, some of being subservient to British interests. What was needed was a national figure of sufficient integrity and stature to win the people's confidence.

Iranians, in their government, are apt to look to individual rather than collective leadership for guidance. This is the mode of thought that stands behind kingship.

The new king, however, was still young, still considered inexperienced. As the titular head of state, he was generally popular. But as a political figurehead, he was vulnerable. The major prop to his kingship — the army — was weak. As an internal security force, it lacked cohesiveness and unqualified authority. Matched against foreign power, it was in no position to hold its own. Militarily, it was taken for granted that Iran relied on the West for its national security. Morale was low.

This had not been the case before. Under the old king, the army had gone through a buildup not experienced in its history since the early days of the Qajars, when the country was preparing to take on Russia in the Napoleonic wars. It had put down internal revolts. It had eradicated dissent from its ranks and created a reputable officer corps. It had brought the tribal chiefs and their private armies under control — making them subservient to the central government in Tehran. It had made the country's borders safe.

With the old king's removal and the entrance of the occupation forces, the army's teeth, you might say, had been pulled. Its power as an effective militia was broken. Political factionalism, which was taking place all over the country, seeped into the officer ranks.

True, the army had taken part in a certain amount of action against the Russians — and even the British. It had also put down rioting. But these were achievements in spite of its weaknesses — ironically showing them up all the more glaringly. If anything, they showed that the country's major recourse was diplomacy.

What was needed now, as political thinking went, was a show of national strength that could stand up to outside power. To the British. The army could not do that, nor could the king. Both had been weakened by interventionist ploys.

The only segment of the country which had not been compromised in that regard — which had, in the minds of many, stood up to the forces of interference — was that amorphous entity "the people."

Iranians, I remember, spoke about "the people" in the most glowing terms. It was "the people" who had the intrinsic sense of Iranianness — not their leaders, who were corrupt, or their soldiers, who were ineffectual. By "the people," mind, I don't mean the same thing that Trotsky meant by "the masses": those, say, who composed something like four fifths of the country, who were illiterate and lucky to get by with enough to live on. I don't mean the other one-fifth either: the ones who were better off and had some sense of the country in relation to the rest of the world, and who could claim to speak on behalf of the majority. I mean those who saw themselves as constituting the body of "the people," those who drew strength from the word. Those who regarded it as much a part of their makeup as the term Iranian. "The people," you could say, was that aspect of Iranian consciousness — the preeminently good side — which refused to see itself as having been touched by centuries of internal corruption and foreign domination.

The voice of the people, therefore, came to reside in Parliament, which emerged as the symbol not only of constitutional rule, but also of national autonomy. Not necessarily the parliament which happened to be in session. But the one in genesis: the entity that existed for the future, when, after much weeding out of undesirable elements, it could function as a truly representative assembly.

If any leader were to arise to lead the nation in its entirety and free it from the domination of foreign rule, it would have to be someone who made his way through Parliament. That is where the country's potential unifying source of strength lay.

The man who emerged to fill this spot was Mohammad Mossadegh.

A wealth landowner. An aristocrat with liberal views. A constitutionalist. A doctor of economics. But, for all that, a self-styled man of the people in his obsessive concern for national autonomy and his ascetic way of life. Moreover, a man of stature, in that he had opposed the old king during his reign and had come through unscathed.

The man had enormous appeal for Iranians.

His physique came to be a sort of national landmark, a caricature of everything that was identifiably Iranian. His pointed bald head, with the furrows above the brows. His huge hooked nose. His beady eyes and hanging lower lip — as though it had been formed from drinking endless glasses of tea from a saucer. His smile, which looked as though something were hurting him. His fondness for casual dress, for lounging about in pajamas, as if he had just waked up from a nap.

And, above all, his love of talk.

He talked with the passionate fervor of one who is totally committed to a cause. With jabs. With thrusts. Shouting. Wheezing. Sighing. Weeping. Clicking his tongue. Modulating his inflections. Never losing hold over his audience. Taking obvious relish in verbal repartee. Varying the length of his sentences. Weaving metaphors around blunt statements of fact. Brushing aside logic. Cutting through his opponents' positions. Never at a loss for words. Never passive. Demanding to be heard. Eloquent.

And all the time whipping up his listeners into an emotional fury. The more intensely he spoke, the more urgently they felt the response to his words. As though he were their nerve center and they the nerve endings.

He was the embodiment of national sentiment. Of obstinate doggedness. Old, bedridden man that he was, he became the country's spokesman.

But not its statesman. That's where the irony and trouble lay.

As a spokesman, he accomplished one very significant task: he united all the hitherto wrangling factions behind him. Somewhat disjointedly at first, then more unequivocally in his National Front movement. The more he talked, and the more speeches he made in Parliament, the more emphatically he opposed the government's half measures and expressed the need for Iran to break off the oil agreement with Britain and push for a new settlement.

He united the country behind him and his movement, in other words, in his outspoken defiance of Britain. No one before him had spoken as he had. Nor did anyone after, for that matter. He spoke as though Iran had all the legal and moral rights on its side — rights which had been abrogated by the British — and that in the consciousness of having those rights lay the power to change the status quo.

At times he was magnificent. Other times his performance bordered on the ludicrous. Those countries with oil interests in the Middle East regarded him, by and large, as a demagogue.

But here, at last, was a national leader who had emerged through the constitutional movement in Iran.

The fact that he later failed and was overthrown was due partly to his own inability to sustain control over the various factions that had united behind his National Front movement, partly to his peculiar brand of overheated idealism, and partly to miscalculations. But it was also due partly to the weaknesses in the very movement out of which his power arose — weaknesses compounded by catastrophes any fledgling constitutional movement is bound to face.

But to regard him as a demagogue pure and simple is to misunderstand what he stood for and the mainstream from which he came.

Basically, the power structure in Iran is tripartite, like a stool with three legs: the army, the government, and the people. During the constitutional period, prior to the old king's reign, the army and government were weak. The people emerged to form the basis for parliamentary rule. Subsequently, the old king assumed control as head of state, relegating Parliament to the background and putting muscle into the army and government. When the new king took over, the army and government were weakened again. Once more the people emerged as powerful through Parliament — disorderly perhaps, at cross-purposes, but nevertheless attempting to have a hand in running the country.

With the emergence of Mossadegh, one might say that Parliament had finally coalesced into one fairly cohesive body. But even then, this is to overstate the effectiveness of this one man and to belittle another factor.

What is closer to the truth is that Mossadegh never did really emerge as the statesman who brought power to Parliament. If he did, he never kept it there long. He, too, was forced in the end to act unilaterally — not through parliamentary sanction, but under the aegis of his own authority as Prime Minister. He came to power through the support of Parliament, but once in power he was concerned, like the old king, with the direct implementation of his own policies.

Overall, the final setback to parliamentary rule in Iran is that no lasting government in its history has put primary emphasis on constitutional law. The tragedy of democracy in Iran is that there are always national emergencies of one sort or another that pull people away from constitutional authority to a more totalitarian form of government.

Hence everyone's dissatisfaction with the present. One is always living in the undesirable present to pave the way for the more desirable future.

"Democracy is something we cannot afford." How often have I heard people say that? "In the future perhaps. When the country is better off — more stable. But not now — not when we're picking a fight with the British. Not when the Russians are breathing down our neck. Not when, as an underdeveloped nation, we've got so much ground to catch up."

It's like this. One day a man wakes up to a clear sky and airs all kinds of optimistic views about the need to strive for a more equitable distribution of power. The next day he sees clouds on the horizon and scurries for shelter under the canopy of authoritarian rule. "When the rain goes away," he says to himself, "provided that it comes, I can step out under fair skies again and resume my speculations."

But, although Mossadegh didn't play out his hand as an advocate of parliamentary rule, he emerged nevertheless from Parliament as the focal point of national consciousness.

In him and his movement the army, the government, and the people came together and presented a consolidated front. That's how a small and relatively helpless country such as Iran in the early fifties came to oust a major — albeit declining — power such as Britain.

The crystallization of this image, as I say, took place over a period of years and against a background of political turmoil and growing hostility toward Britain. Other factors, however, entered as well, creating the impression that here, in Mossadegh, was one person in whom Iranians could place their trust. It had to come at the expense of the king.

The king had recently obtained a divorce from his first wife, Princess Fawzieh of Egypt, on the grounds that she had not borne him a male heir — their only child being Princess Shahnaz. And, given the volatile situation of the moment, a king could well have been deposed for not providing himself with a successor.

But following that, a bizarre incident occurred, which revealed something of a much more fragile nature. In the winter of 1949, an attempt was made on the king's life. He was shot five times as he was walking up the steps to give an address at the Tehran University Law School. The incident was telling. It pointed to the precariousness of the king's existence, to popular unrest, to a kind of sapping of his power, while Parliament was growing ever stronger. It pointed to the need for having a dominant figure, who could bring the various heated factions under control and direct the country's energies more purposefully.

This, by the way, was also the final blow for the Tudeh party. The would-be assassin was thought to be — or, at any rate, branded as — a Communist, and the party was banned for good.

The king survived the assassination attempt, but he had been made to look vulnerable. Furthermore, the following year he made a trip to America, which failed to bring the anticipated military and economic aid needed to bolster his regime.

Mossadegh's star, on the other hand, was rising. He was making speeches in Parliament, rallying the country behind him, defying the once-mighty British. He was wily. He was shrewd. One sensed in him an instinct for survival.

And he was rallying men of all persuasions to his side, among them my father.

My father went to hear Mossadegh at a political gathering in a private home. He was introduced to him by a man named Hossein Fatemi, who was later to become Mossadegh's Foreign Minister.

We had met Fatemi on our way back from America, when we had stopped off in Abadan. He was writing a series of newspaper articles on the Anglo-Iranian Oil Company, and he showed us around the refinery. I remember the incident well. We passed through the British living quarters first — with the gleaming white cottages and even patches of lawn amid the scorching desert — then through the shanty town, where the workers ate and slept. The difference was marked. It gave me my first taste of what all the brewing turmoil was about. At the refinery I saw some workers leaning over the edges of huge vats of oil, scooping up the surface layer of liquid residue with rectangular kerosene tins which had holes in them. I asked Fatemi why the men were using tins with holes. He replied that it was the company's way of discouraging them from stealing ones which *didn't* have holes in them!

The tins were used by laborers as building material for their shacks.

Apparently, Mossadegh and my father chatted quite a while about the economy. He commended my father for his past services to the government and for the part he had played in the manufacture and export of cotton. It was resources such as cotton, he went on, that were needed to build up the economy. Iran had to get away from depending on its oil. My father was asked what future plans he had in mind.

He came home from that meeting a different man: excited. impressed, his spirits raised, the way they hadn't been in a long time.

He started entertaining other thoughts. Should he or shouldn't he remain in Iran and get back into the world of government, this time as a member of Parliament? The notion was extremely appealing. He considered running for a seat from Tabriz.

But then, he didn't belong to any party. And he had been out of the country for some time. Not that these are crippling drawbacks; all the same, there were others who were in better positions. Moreover, running for Parliament required extra capital. Who knows how much? There was a seemingly endless number of pockets to be filled. And who knows to what end? He hadn't been in politics before.

Furthermore, the business would have to be left to his brother. His own going to Germany would have to be put off. Any further delays would kill the project altogether.

The only inducement he had was ideological. If ideology had been enough to make him eligible for Parliament, he might have thrown his hat into the ring — as everyone else, around that time, seemed to be doing. The only talk among men was politics. Newspapers were being founded on a regular basis, one of them by my tutor, a young government worker, who used to come to our house after office hours twice a week to help me with my Persian. He edited a leftist sheet, which earned him a name and later got him into trouble.

Then, almost overnight, the situation changed. The king appointed the army's chief of staff, General Razmara, Prime Minister. Razmara, as a strong-minded reformist and an advocate of a negotiated oil agreement with Britain, was the only viable alternative to Mossadegh. Authority clamped down. A good many newspapers disappeared. My tutor was carted off to jail, never, as far as I know, to be heard of publicly again.

For a while, it seemed as though the spread of militant nationalism had been checked. Ashrafi and Karimzadeh advised my father to leave for Hamburg while the timing was still good, although neither was prepared to back the venture as originally planned, their excuse being that they couldn't act independently while Karbalai was out of the country. He was in London at the time, I believe.

And so it happened that my father got up from lunch one day and, instead of taking his usual nap, went into the parlor with my mother, shutting the double doors behind him. When they emerged for tea, my mother told me, with a zestful smile and a ruffle of my hair, that before long I would be adding German to my growing list of languages.

12

*M*y mother and I preceded my father to Hamburg in the fall of 1950. The purpose of our early departure was to look for a house and enroll me in a school.

We were met at the airport by my grandfather and his German wife, Magdalena. He was a well-groomed man in his sixties, with black dyed hair, naturally gray at the temples, and a trim upturned mustache, wearing a charcoal gray overcoat and suit and a white silk scarf. His wife was a buxom blonde, dressed in blue — which turned out to be her usual color — who laughed easily. I was surprised to find that her Persian, despite a thick accent, was almost as good as mine.

I had been wondering all along about the kind of reception we would have. My mother rarely spoke of her father without letting out some inner resentment. He had married three times.

The first was to my grandmother, as a young man in Khoy.

My grandmother was not a wealthy woman, but she had some means, which he used to start a business. When the business failed, he set out for Tehran, leaving behind his wife and two children — my mother and her eldest brother — to enter a new line of trade. He went into import-export, which took him first to Erzerum and then Istanbul — his intention being to send for his family as soon as he was settled.

In Istanbul, however, he married again and raised another family. Again his business collapsed, forcing him to return to Tehran. He brought his Turkish wife and children with him and set up two separate households; both in Tehran, one for each wife. Apparently, relations between the two families were workable, since he continued to have children by both wives. He ended up having four by each: three sons and a daughter by my grandmother, and three daughters and a son by his Turkish wife — almost as though he had struck a bargain with nature to balance things out.

Sometime after the First World War, he went to Germany. In order to save on living expenses, he brought the two households together. The Turkish wife and her children came to live in my grandmother's house, since it was the larger of the two.

When my grandfather returned from Germany, he had a blond secretary with him — Magdalena. How they all managed to live together under one roof is something I have yet to fathom. Suffice it to say that he subsequently spent his time in Tehran solidifying his position in the import-export business. He had settled on carpets by then as his staple in trade. Eventually, when his shipments were ready, he returned to Hamburg with his secretary and opened a retail store to go with his wholesale business. His Iranian and Turkish wives were left with their brood in Tehran, while he married a third time and settled down to a secluded and more or less peaceful existence — more or less, in that it was interrupted by war, whereupon he moved his business temporarily to Sweden. There he sired his ninth and last child: Cyrus, Magdalena's son, born in Stockholm.

He didn't divorce his former wives. He didn't have to. As a Moslem, he was entitled to four: a sanction his other two wives demurringly put up with. Divorce, for them, would have complicated matters. For one thing, it would have cut off their support.

Besides, Magdalena had come to accept the situation through a canny sort of compromise: so long as she was his only wife in Germany, and he was living with her and her child, what difference did it make what the situation was in Tehran?

It did, however, make a considerable difference: her life in Hamburg was constantly disrupted either by urgent pleas for help or by actual visits from the horde in the East.

Coming to Hamburg, I found it hard not to be predisposed against my grandfather. In Tehran I had been exposed to a barrage of negative propaganda from my maternal relatives: aunts and uncles who had bitter complaints — and all sorts of stories they preferred not to go into — about being left in the lurch and, so they claimed, penniless. Oddly enough, his wives never grumbled. Rather, they retreated into their physical conditions. My grandmother was a sickly person who catered to a malady, broadly diagnosed as *zaf assob*, or neurasthenia, by downing vials of medicine and keeping close to her bed, and my step-grandmother indulged in overeating.

At any rate, it was not Magdalena whom the family blamed. If anything, they looked upon her as a fellow sufferer — as a warm and guileless person, who had fallen into the same trap my grandfather had set for them all; whereas, if anything went wrong in their lives — even my grandmother's taking a turn for the worse — the blame was summarily attributed to my grandfather.

I had gotten accustomed to relatives constantly referring to him as a rogue. He used people, so I was told, mercilessly. He rarely lived up to his obligations. What better proof was there than his neglect of his children? The only one to receive any attention was Cyrus. The others were merely castoffs.

This was not entirely true. Of his eight Middle Eastern children, he had seen to it that the three eldest — my mother, her brother, and her eldest half-sister — had received at least some degree of education in Europe. The others were less fortunate, in that they had been cut off from Europe by the war — in which case he had used his business connections in Iran to get his sons jobs. All but one had turned their backs on him.

On the whole, it was clear that he had left a wide gap in his children's lives, and that nothing he could do would really fill it. All my uncles — even the one who studied in Europe — went to work at an early age. As for my mother and aunts, it was taken for granted that they would marry young — a decree which all but one defied as long as they could; the record being held by my eldest aunt, who turned down suitor after suitor, much to the chagrin of her mother and stepmother and the unmitigated fury of her father, until the outrageous age of twenty-nine. Even then — as another stab at her father — she chose to marry, instead of a respectable businessman, a Pakistani colonel, who, unbeknown to anyone, had attended Sandhurst with Ayub Khan. It wasn't until Ayub Khan became head of state, and the colonel was made his special emissary to Spain, Australia, and finally China, that she was forgiven and brought back — figuratively speaking into the fold. Figuratively speaking, because she never set eyes on her father again, so scathing was her hatred for him.

That was the kind of man he was. He didn't want to have direct, personal contact with his own until they had made their way in the world. Not that he valued the social status they brought. It was much more basic than that. He simply didn't want to have people around who couldn't stand on their own, who relied on him for money and support. Worse yet, who could never take real satisfaction in anything he gave them but always expected and demanded more.

He valued money above anything else. Its acquisition was not an art or a science, but a matter of survival. It was also a touchstone to judge others by. Money was not there to be given; that went against human nature. It was there to be made — through the use of one's head and character. Those who made it deserved respect. Those who didn't were weak. Those who lost it were fools. Those who made appeals for it weren't worth the clothes on their backs.

He had gone through two world wars, two bankruptcies, two wives whose money he had used and amply requited, in his eyes. Now he was married to a third who had been, and still was, his secretary, his German mouthpiece.

I actually wondered whether he had married Magdalena in order to secure his hold over her — retaining her services without having to pay her. If there's any truth to that, the agreement must have been mutual.

I gleaned as much from her manner of devotion to him. It was not so much a spontaneous thing as something practiced and consciously executed. Her devotion was more a tie than anything else. He had provided her with a child and a mode of living which she would not have enjoyed as his mistress.

Not that she was in a position to spend money freely. No, that would have been out of the question. She spent enough merely to look well-groomed and to run an immaculate household, with a maid doubling as governess for her child, a cook whose husband chauffeured the car, and a huge brute of a German shepherd, which needed brushing — by their standards of cleanliness — every day.

She was pretty, without ever having been beautiful or even more than moderately fetching, with a well-kept figure and ample bosoms, but not alluring in a way that would suggest a voluptuous nature. Cheerful, to offset her husband's gloom, chauffeur-driven to her work and back, possessed of a garden overlooking a part of the Alster to satisfy any feelings she might have for nature, she struck me as being like an aging princess shut up in a tower. Not like my mother or Nasrin, who moved about blithely among a circle of friends. Or even like my other two grandmothers, who, whatever their grievances, were the ultimate voices of authority in their homes.

Magdalena was in a category by herself. She had adopted, as a foreigner, the life style of an Iranian woman, to a degree which few Iranians, I think, would have been willing to put up with. Moreover, she had done this in her own country and out of some burning need to live up to the standards which my grandfather imposed.

Which suited him perfectly. As the egoist, which everyone in his family accused him of being, he was the pivotal point in the world of his making. Nor was it an entirely unenviable world: a carpet business, a three-story nineteenth-century white stucco home, overlooking one of the canals of the Alster. His sphere of activity was divided between Gross Bleichenstrasse, where his store was located, and Heilwigstrasse, where he lived. On the outer periphery were the rug dealers who supplied him from Iran and the other outlets to his wholesale business in Bremen and Düsseldorf.

Thanks to Abol Karimzadeh's lackadaisical handling of affairs, my grandfather was now the biggest dealer of Persian carpets in Hamburg, with the only store, in his estimation, which had just claim to being called Haus Teheran.

In a way, he was as much in his element in Hamburg as Ashrafi was in Tehran. The two men had had a wary sort of respect for each other ever since their early days in Khoy. They kept up on each other's activities indirectly, through contact with others — one of these contacts being, of course, my mother.

We drove from the airport to my grandfather's house in his black, chauffeur-driven Kaiser. The chauffeur was fitted out in a gray high-collar jacket and cap and black leather gloves and boots.

When we got to the house, Cyrus met us in the hallway, flanked by the household staff. The dog was, thankfully, kept out of the way, since it didn't take to strangers. He shook hands the German schoolboy way — with a quick downward toss of the head and one strong pump of the hand — then offered his cheek to be kissed. Which made me feel awkward, not knowing whether what looked like standard procedure for adults applied to me as well.

He was dressed in shorts, white shirt and tie, and white stockings pulled up to just below the knees. I had moved up, by then, to trousers.

We were given refreshments, then shown to our rooms for a nap. Cyrus led the way to his, where a bed had been set up for me. One wall was lined with a low bookcase containing encyclopedias, fairy tales, boys' stories, and the like, and a serial edition of Westerns by Karl Mai. An exercise book lay open on his desk. He had been copying out a lesson right up till our arrival, which was why, he said, he couldn't meet us at the airport. We spoke in Persian, although his was weak. Later, when I had a better grasp of it, we switched to German.

On my bed was a gift from my grandfather: a Zeiss-Ikon camera, with a roll of film inside. Cyrus said he was looking forward to getting one on his tenth birthday, which was three years away, after a wrist watch and a set of trapeze swings.

When he left the room, I was able to assess my reactions. I felt myself in a cloistered and closeted world. A world of shorts and maids and chauffeur-driven cars. Of organization in all things. Of scheduled naps and chaperoned outings. Not too different from being in a well-kept dungeon, I thought.

In Iran I had gotten about with a freedom which was beginning to seem enviable by contrast.

I reached for an edition of Karl Mai, glancing over the color illustrations of life in the Far West. They offered a glamorized view of an antithetical existence: with pintos and rawhide and stretches of painted desert. Just the right combination of details to appeal to a boy's sense of adventure, yet a counterprojection of his own limited range of experience.

Oddly enough, dipping into that cameo world gave me a firmer grasp of what was concrete; as though contact with the removed made it easier to face the practical and close.

I sensed, putting the book down, that I would be a captive in my new surroundings only as long as I didn't have a grasp of the language — which made me feel better, knowing how things stood.

I woke up when the maid came into the room. She said that the others were having tea in the sun parlor, and that I was to join them.

After tea we walked in the garden: my grandfather and mother ahead, arm in arm, chatting in Turkish, while Magdalena, Cyrus, and I strolled behind, making do with Persian — the two of them alternating in telling me what I could expect to find in Germany. They never asked about our relatives in Iran.

The garden consisted of a huge rectangular lawn, with a crab apple tree at one end and a flimsy-looking peach tree at another, surrounded by a red dirt pathway. The grass was clean and trim — the type one sees in parks, with signs saying not to walk on it. On either side of the pathway, lengthwise, were rows of flowers and bushes. At the bottom end of the garden was a wrought-iron fence and a gate, which was locked, but which would otherwise have opened onto the canal.

As we reached the bottom, an *Alsterdampfer* steamed through, creating rolls of waves in its wake, mesmerizing to look at.

"You can take the steamer right from that spot," Magdalena said, pointing to a platform on the opposite bank, "to the center of the city — to the Alsterpavilion. There you get off and walk directly across the street, down Gross Bleichenstrasse, and you come to the store."

Later the German shepherd came bounding down the lawn on a leash. The chauffeur, who was pulled along with it, introduced it to us as Axel. My grandfather snapped his fingers to make the dog jump, which it did, in a fearsome way, which made me apprehensive of the distance between us.

Finally, before going inside, we took pictures with my new camera. The sky was a uniform gray, with the imminent threat of a drizzle. I took several snapshots myself, then handed the camera to the chauffeur. He finished the roll of film, while the rest of us posed as a group. Then we all sauntered back to the house; my grandfather and mother ahead, Magdalena, Cyrus, and I behind.

13

*T*he feeling of being in a strange place did not begin to wear away until that evening.

We sat at a dark mahogany table, with a small chandelier casting a dim glow overhead. The maid brought in the soup and laid it down quietly. It was potato soup, which I still remember as being light and tasty. We ate with gusto, in silence.

Then my grandfather threw the table open for talk, his kind of talk, which surprised me for its candor. I never thought to come across such bluntness in that immaculate household.

It was like having a waft of thick, aromatic tobacco smoke drift into an odorless room.

It made my mother uncomfortable.

At home, in Tehran, table talk was invariably evasive and polite. When my parents had things to say to each other, they somehow managed to communicate over my head, behind a cloak of allusions and half utterances, using everyday language in such a way as to create almost a parlance of their own.

My grandfather had no such taste for tact. He talked with no holds barred — as though eating brought out the earthiness in him — bridging two worlds which had hitherto (intentionally, I thought) been kept apart.

"So Ashrafi's daughter has broken off with that husband." He addressed his remarks to my mother in Turkish. The rest of us listened. "What does Ashrafi have to say about that?"

My mother hesitated, unwilling to pursue the subject, but gave in under his gaze. "He is willing to go along with his daughter's decision," she returned, with a slight shrug.

My grandfather let out a skeptical cackle. "He wouldn't be willing, if that were all to the matter. That man has goals in mind."

"What goals?" My mother perked up.

"Not for himself. For his children. Ashrafi can fend for himself. It's his children he worries about."

"How do you know?"

"I know. I have children myself. A disappointment. They waste their time sulking — brooding about what they think I ought to have done for them, instead of thinking for themselves."

My mother was silent.

"Except you, my dear." My grandfather patted her arm. He heaved a sigh, then bellowed, "Helga, come and take these dishes away!" Then he turned to his wife. "The soup was good, *liebchen*. But tell your maid not to make us linger over it."

Magdelena blinked, as though the message had been registered, and called — more softly — for Helga again.

"Where was I?" my grandfather continued. "Oh, yes. Ashrafi's children. How many does he have? Only two? All the more reason to see them properly settled."

What gall, I thought. This coming from a man who had more or less abandoned his own.

"The boy is a mischief-maker, from what I've heard, and hasn't the brains to step into his father's shoes. You'll agree," he said pointedly, "that gives Ashrafi and me something in common. As for the daughter, that seems to be another matter. She didn't do so well in the first marriage." He paused. "So she'll do better in the next."

"What do you mean?" my mother said.

"Ashrafi isn't stupid."

"Well, his own wife wasn't such a treasure to begin with," my mother remonstrated.

"That was different." My grandfather waved a hand, dismissing her point. "He didn't have the advantages his children have. He got the best that was available under the circumstances. It's not his own welfare that's weighing on his mind. He knows he can look after himself. In fact, didn't I tell you — put it in writing — that Omid shouldn't count on his support for shipping cotton here?"

"Yes," my mother countered, with a swallowed-down kind of fury, "but you didn't point out why."

"Why?" my grandfather leaned back, as though the answer were only too obvious. "First of all, because Ashrafi is not the sort of person to depend on. I've known him since he was a boy, and I still wouldn't do any business with him. Secondly, because of what's happening in Germany. I'm selling carpets. Do you know what that means? It means that Germans have money. If they want to buy cotton, why should they go after the low-grade product? Look at this cloth." He held up his sleeve. "Feel it. It's German material. It matches anything that comes out of Manchester. If they want cotton, they'll buy the high-grade Egyptian product. Not ours. If your husband wanted to sell cotton in Germany, he should have come here three, four years ago. Right after the war. I told him as much."

The soup bowls were taken away, and the main dish was brought in.

"Anyway, he has made up his mind, so we'll see what we'll see." He plied his knife to the meat. "There's something else you should know. As you know, Abol Karimzadeh's wife is dead."

She had died of cancer the previous winter. The most beautiful woman my mother had seen.

"Yes, a pity — a great loss for her daughter," she said.

"So I'm told," my grandfather added. "I never see them. But in any case, I hear about them."

Suddenly, in the middle of the conversation, he turned to me, switching to Persian.

"Firuz, help yourself to that cauliflower. You don't find such things in Iran. If you don't like it at first, keep eating. You'll soon develop a taste for it."

I had been avoiding the cauliflower, but saw no way of getting out of it now. I gave myself a modest helping.

"We'll make him grow in this country," my grandfather said, reverting to Turkish. "Last year Abol Karimzadeh took his wife to Zürich. You know about that?"

"Geneva," my mother replied, "to see their nephews."

"They went to Zürich first," my grandfather corrected, "for a checkup on his wife. It was there they found out she had cancer. After that the wife and daughter joined his brother's children in Geneva."

My mind went back to the conversation on the concrete bench in Ramsar with Mrs. Karimzadeh and Karbalai. Farid and Matin were to have returned to Tehran toward the end of that summer, after their studies were over. They never came. Instead Mr. and Mrs. Karimzadeh had flown to Geneva. From there they had gone on to Hamburg, accompanied by Abol's wife and daughter. That much I had gathered from a letter sent by Mrs. Karimzadeh to my mother, which she had read to my father.

"Did you know that Abol Karimzadeh returned to Hamburg while his wife and daughter were still in Geneva?" my grandfather asked.

My mother screwed up her eyes. "I may have known. I don't remember. Is it important? Did he have business to tend to?"

"I don't know about business," my grandfather mouthed through chewing, "but he was seen with someone else."

My mother gave him a look of wary surprise — as if to check him from going further.

"I see you know about that, too."

"No, I don't," my mother shot back, almost as a protest.

"He had been seeing someone else for some time. Ask Magdalena. She has even met the woman. A German. A widow with two children. I haven't. All I know is that it has cut into his business. His affairs are in a mess." He put his knife and fork down on his plate and looked up. "Why do you think that Ahmad Karimzadeh spent such a long time in Hamburg? The man has more than he can cope with in Tehran."

"I was told that Zohre needed tending to. After she found out about her mother."

"No doubt, she did. She may have known more. Who knows? She may have found out about the other woman. At any rate, it didn't need Ahmad Karimzadeh's presence here to settle that kind of problem. Nor to see to funeral arrangements either. Incidentally, Magdalena and I didn't go to the funeral, though we sent our condolences. No, for those arrangements he would have simply flown from Tehran. It was his brother's end of the business he was seeing to. It was weak. Losing ground. It still is. Do you follow me?"

My mother was silent.

"What about Zohre?" she asked. "What is happening to her?"

"You know more about that than I do, from Ahmad's wife." My grandfather shrugged. "All I know is that she is still living with her father and going to school. What else would you expect her to do?"

"She was in hospital for a while," my mother added softly. "Under psychiatric care."

"Yes, that too, of course. Magdalena went to visit her once or twice. But now she is home, as far as I know."

He rephrased the statement in Persian for Magdalena, and she confirmed it.

"You two can talk about that later." My grandfather turned to my mother again. "No doubt, you will both want to see her. But as for this Abol Karimzadeh business, I'm trying to tell you something else, don't you see? It's not just an isolated situation. The affair affects all of us. The Karimzadeh business is not doing so well. Mine is prospering. Mine will continue to prosper so long as the other keeps on the way it's been going. Now Omid is coming to Hamburg. What questions does that raise in your mind?"

He gave her a long, steadfast look.

"What questions?" my mother murmured.

My grandfather pushed his plate away and applied a napkin to his lips and mustache.

"Omid is going into the wrong line of business. Selling low-grade cotton in America was a good enterprise. The timing was right and so was his initiative. It served its purpose. It provided him with capital. Now the situation has changed. In business you have to adapt to changes. I know that he is an expert in his field. But he mustn't let that hamper him. It can, you know. It can hold him back. What's more to the point is that he has a good head on his shoulders. That's ultimately more important than expertise in any field. Look at me. What expertise do I have in anything? I only know how to buy and sell. My business is carpets because I make more money buying and selling those than anything else. In Iran, when I was young — when you were a child — I used to think I knew all about wheat and farm goods. Where do you think I would be if I had kept to that line? Still behind a grocery counter in Khoy. That's where Ashrafi would have been as well. Both of us made changes according to the situation. He switched into the banking business, and I went into carpets. Omid has the same opportunity facing him."

He paused, then proceeded more slowly and emphatically.

"With Omid throwing in his capital with mine, we could take the carpet business out of the Karimzadehs' hands. We could drive them out of the market in Hamburg — and make it worthwhile for you to settle here. I'll mention this to Omid when he gets here, but I want you to be prepared to support what I have to say."

He slapped his palms on the table. "Enough of that talk for

the present. We have delicious fruits in front of us. Magdalena bought them herself."

He stretched out a hand and put a cluster of grapes on my plate. He did the same for his son.

Beaming a private smile at his son, he said, "What do we say after the meal?"

"*Tak för maten,*" Cyrus replied.

The phrase was explained to my mother and me. It was the Swedish expression of thanks for a meal, usually addressed to the host and hostess — a phrase they had picked up in Sweden, and which they had appropriated as a family ritual, in light of Cyrus's birth in that country.

I gathered, from the way they drew attention to it, that in future I would be required to chime in as well.

Just before we got up from the table, Axel was brought in to be given scraps of meat from my grandfather's plate. I thought the occasion a good one to establish rapport with the brute, so I picked up a piece from my plate as well.

I was immediately told to put it down.

The only one allowed to feed the dog at table was my grandfather.

14

Since my German was nowhere near proficient enough for me to be placed in a German school, it was decided, even before we left Tehran, that I should continue studying in English for the time being. As a result, I was enrolled in the British School, Hamburg — referred to by all as BSH. A hard school to get into. It was set up purposely for the children of occupation personnel. A small cadre of students, however, came from various diplomatic backgrounds, and I must have slipped in under that category.

At any rate, BSH gave me my first taste of English schooling.

And before the year was out — I was barely thirteen then — I was to be hankering for more.

My father arrived from Tehran in midautumn. Whereupon my mother and I moved from my grandfather's house to temporary quarters in a *pension*. Housing was not easy to come by in those days — at least, not the kind my parents had in mind. But eventually Magdalena came across something which suited their taste.

It was an apartment in a four-story building on Oberstrasse, between Mittelweg and Rothenbaumchaussee — two major thoroughfares west of the Alster, leading to the center of town. Abol Karimzadeh had a large house not far away, just off Harvesterhüderweg, with a lawn sloping down to the Aussen Alster — overlooking the expanse of the lake.

Our apartment was on the ground floor of the building. The floor above us was occupied by the owner — an old architect and his wife, who had lost a son in the war. The two floors further up were rented to families I scarcely ever saw.

There was very little socializing among residents in that building. The only occasions I remember when people got together were Christmas and New Year's Eve; even then, it was to rub shoulders for what seemed, by Iranian standards, to be an absurdly short time. The owner and his wife would come down to have a glass of cognac with us, after which we would march upstairs — at their invitation — to return the compliment.

It was different with the people below us — the ones who lived in the basement. We had frequent contact with them. The husband was a railroad worker, who supplemented his income by looking after the building. The wife was considerably younger — a woman in her mid-twenties — with a pretty face and soft features, but dreadfully thinning hair, which she made no effort to hide. It made me feel awkward, at first, to look at her, wanting to keep my gaze below her brow, yet constantly catching myself peering up. Her casual bearing, her lack of concern, won me over; made me come to accept her hair, with the skull shining beneath it, as a natural part of her person. As much a part of her, say, as her beautiful hands.

I remember the thrill I got from seeing those hands grooming that hair. Sitting in front of a mirror — looking the thing smack in the eye — and chatting to me behind her back, while I leaned against her bedroom door.

Her name was Gerta. Her husband's was Karl. She worked as a part-time maid for the rest of the residents, whenever extra help was needed.

Also living with them was her father-in-law: a retired railroad worker and veteran of the First World War, who smoked a pipe and enjoyed reading sentimental fiction.

Adjoined to their quarters was a room for our maid, a handsome girl of about nineteen, with a good nature, who picked up Iranian cooking with incredible speed, and who was shy of her speech. Her name was Helga, and she stayed with us several years — until she had enough saved to go back to her village, where, I believe, she got married.

I can't say that the place, as a whole, was exactly sprightly — despite my trips downstairs for card-playing and, later, beer. It was clean. The house had shiny windows. It had white walls. Like my grandfather's house. Like Abol Karimzadeh's. Dazzlingly white in the sunlight. But grayish when the sky was clouded over — as was usually the case in Hamburg — and actually glowering, if walls can be thought of that way, in the rain.

A pall was cast by the immediate surroundings, which fitted in with the wreckage — the ruins of war — I passed daily on my way to and from school in a British military bus.

Behind the house was a paltry yard, not garden, which was poorly kept, and which no one seemed to use, except for hanging out washing. Facing the house, across the street, was a gray concrete block of cement, which looked like a mausoleum, with towering locked doors. It was a synagogue, which had been converted, I was told, into a radio station during Hitler's time. It stood empty all the while I was in Hamburg, ominously dominating the street.

The interior of our apartment had an entirely different atmosphere. In fact, the gaiety I associate with Hamburg life invariably revolves around that and the Alster. My parents furnished the rooms uniformly in the Italian Renaissance style, which they decided would go well with the tall windows and high ceilings.

They had the walls covered with silk paper of floral design — in pastel colors, with a different shade for each room.

My one complaint was that I had no room of my own. Of the five large rooms, I was given the smallest, which was an annex to the living room, with sliding doors partitioning the two. Whenever we had a surplus of guests, I was expected to evacuate it and sleep in my parents' room, on my mother's side of their huge double bed.

In fact, in a way, I evacuated it each day. My own bed was actually a sofa, which Helga made up and unmade every morning and night. A very comfortable piece of furniture — but, still, a sofa. And my desk was a museum piece. In the Renaissance style. Huge. Made of solid oak. With legs carved into figurine hermaphrodites. And my chair the kind of thing I imagined that Richelieu must have sat in. All my books and papers were kept out of sight.

Which felt a little strange, not having my personal effects about. But to offset that was the beauty of the place. My parents had always lived in houses — except for a brief spell in New York. Now they were apartment-living. To make up for the lack of a house, they indulged in the splendor of an exquisite interior. They were catering to guests. Anticipating the future.

It must have been around then — the time we were settling down to our new life in Hamburg — that it began to sink into me consciously that my father had dreams of being a very rich man.

Shortly after we had settled into our apartment, Abol Karim-zadeh held a reception for us. A written invitation was sent to my grandfather and Magdalena. This was a rarity among Iranians in Hamburg, since social occasions were usually arranged by wives over the phone. If anything, written invitations underscored a coolness in a relationship, as though the party doing the inviting were acting only out of a sense of obligation; the only exception to the rule being the invitations mailed for official purposes by the Consul General's office.

My grandfather declined in like fashion. He lived, as I said, in a narrow, private domain, rarely going out on social calls. He left such things to the Karimzadehs of the world.

The Abol Karimzadeh house was large and stood in a row of elaborate edifices, with long sloping lawns lining the lake.

My mother claimed that it had a prewar look. Certainly it didn't appear to have been touched by the war. It belonged to that part of Hamburg which had been cleaned up right after the holocaust, thereby giving it a curiously well-preserved look, as though the war had simply bypassed the area.

Unlike our street, which bore a heavier imprint: drills working into the night at one end and a monument of its own, too huge to uproot or dismantle.

The difference, I suppose, was that whereas the Karimzadeh house was on the lake, ours was inland. As a rule, the farther away you got from the Alster, the more destruction you saw — like a ripple sent out by a drop of water.

The door was opened by Zohre Karimzadeh. She glided into my mother's arms and was kissed on the cheek by my father. Then she acknowledged me with a smile, as I gave her the flowers we had brought.

She was light, airy, very svelte. Willowy. I could say thin, but I wouldn't want to do her an injustice. Some women would give years off their lives to look that way.

Her wrists were slender as well. I remember my attention being drawn to them by the silver bangles, which I thought would fall off. About her waist was a silver chain belt.

She was dressed in black — the required mourning period for immediate family among Iranians being a year.

She had perfectly shaped, long lacquered nails. Not a student's hands at all, I thought. Not even ones you were drawn to feel — like Gerta's, which had flesh about them and movements of a different kind — but ones which appealed to the eye alone, like those in cosmetics ads in magazines.

Her hair was a deep dark brown: the color of mine, but set off more strikingly by the paleness of her skin. Our eyes matched as well. She was taller than I was — about five feet five — and already womanly by my standards, wearing silk stockings, high heels, and lipstick.

110

My mother gave her another squeeze.

They had seen each other before — several times, in fact, since our arrival. And prior to that they had known about each other through friends — who, incidentally, swore that they would make excellent companions, the difference in years notwithstanding.

But they hadn't come together formally before, as hostess and guest. Somehow that encounter between them — greeting each other at the door — brought out things from the woodwork: my mother's desire for a daughter, Zohre's for a mother. And mine, too, I suppose, for a sister as distantly glamorous, almost princesslike, as she was.

The two of them chatted in German, while I hovered about, smiling at whoever happened to glance at me.

Abol Karimzadeh led my father to the center of the room, where the Consul General was sitting — a short, dark man, who jumped to his feet. The two plunged into formal introductions, gregariously effusive and laughing a great deal, my father in a sort of operatic baritone, and the Consul General — his name was Sepenta — in a high-pitched, steady-stream giggle. He had large moles on his cheeks and soft doelike eyes, a low forehead, and black hair sleeked back over his head. His body was trimly pear-shaped. All of which made me think of Rudolph Valentino as he might have been in his decline, no longer the focus of attention, and subject to the vicissitudes of age.

His wife was taller than he was, slightly hunched, but otherwise superbly handsome in her jewels — and exposed in a way no other woman in the room was, in an open-necked gown. She was as silent and expressionless as her husband was boisterous.

Before we arrived, my father had said that he wanted to have a serious talk with the Consul General, but I wondered how serious the talk could be, carried on in that vein. Afterward my father explained that he had tried to steer the conversation to politics, but that Sepenta had backed away, laughter being his form of evasiveness.

Eventually, the person who put my wanderings to an end and guided me to a couch at the far end of the room was Abol Karimzadeh, the man of ill repute. He who was said to have flown back to Hamburg to bounce his mistress, while his wife lay hospitalized in Switzerland.

I thrilled when he took my hand and put his other arm around my shoulder. These hands had groped over the body of a mistress. What erogenous zones they must have felt. Somehow wives didn't come under the same category.

Then I felt a wave of caustic indignation — call it a sense of superiority — well up inside. Imagine a man giving up his all for a mistress. Giving in to his feelings. Letting possessions slip from his grasp. Was he stupid or passionate? Why hadn't he held himself in check, as others had? As I, no doubt, would, when my time would come? Not for me such lascivious abandon. Not I, the Roman Octavius, being led to my seat by the Easternized Antony.

"Thank you, Mr Karimzadeh," I mumbled, as I took my place. The first man I actually knew to have a mistress. In whose footsteps — of all the people in that room — I would follow disbelievingly.

"Are you enjoying your schooling in Germany?" he asked.

"Very much," I said.

He nodded. He was neatly tailored in a gray flannel suit. In his breast pocket was a dull black handkerchief, which matched his tie. His black shoes, though, had a glossy shine. About his wrist was an ebony-dialed watch with a gold band — the same finish of gold as his cuff links. On the back of his fingers were tufts of black hair.

"Is it Germany you like or the school?"

"The school," I replied, without hesitating. I could have said both, but that would have gotten us nowhere.

He paused and looked around the room. His hair was thinning and grayish, with long dark streaks in the middle. My father's was prematurely silver and full. He was a good head taller than my father. His eyelids had a bow-shaped droop, and his lips curved down, almost into a grimace. When he spoke, he looked directly into one's eyes. His voice had the mellow timbre of a heavy smoker.

"It's an odd choice," he continued, "going to an English school in Germany."

It didn't seem particularly odd to me.

"There was nothing else we could do," I responded. "My German is weak. I would have fallen behind in my studies. Besides —" I found it necessary to pause — "I prefer going on with English."

He nodded, as though he could easily see that.

"In Germany or England?"

The conversation was going too quickly for me. I hadn't been in my new school that long. I wasn't even sure that I had begun to think about these things.

"England," I replied, trying to keep up with him.

"That would mean being separated from your parents. Are you prepared for that?"

Prepared for what — separation? Where were we going?

"We were separated before," I said, "when I was in boarding school in America."

"Didn't you find that hard?"

I admitted that I had. "But I didn't have much of a choice then either. It was the best way I could learn English. After two years of boarding school, I returned home and was put into a day school. That was the last time I was away from my parents."

He nodded. "And now that you're growing up, you want to go your own way again."

Growing up? I never thought of myself as anything but a child. I had always been a child, and was therefore fixed in that condition.

"I have to," I said, "because of the language."

At this, he smiled and put a cigarette to his lips. He scrutinized me through a veil of smoke before speaking again. "You're lucky you've found mobility at your age."

What's he talking about, I thought. I'm not even good at languages. All I know is English. Everything else I have to struggle with. Even the Persian I'm conversing in.

Dawn. A breakthrough of light.

How the blazes had we arrived at such a rootless conclusion? I felt piqued. Undermined. I countered silently with my own inquisitive thrusts: where the devil is your mistress? What does she look like? Why isn't she here, so that I can see you slip an arm around her?

113

He must have caught the antagonism in my eyes. Abol Karim-zadeh went on to stage a reconciliation.

"I, too, between you and me," he said softly, "wouldn't mind going away."

"To Iran?" I queried, though sensing that I was missing the point. I was smarting inside and not about to respond to his openness.

He shook his head. "No, there are other places I prefer. During the war, we lived for a while in Sweden — Stockholm. I liked it there very much."

Who was "we," I scoffed inwardly. Your family? Your mistress? Both?

"Isn't it cold up there?" I asked. Another asinine question.

"No colder than your England." He smiled.

His eyes met mine firmly.

So that was it! We were to be two fugitives, seeking refuge abroad. Well, whatever he and his mistress were up to, I was no part of it. The comparison was invidious.

He was the sensuous one. I was not. I was merely wending my way through educational channels. Damn him, what was wrong with that? I was not running away from home, but turning toward an educational system I was beginning to admire.

I got up and walked away, sensing the thrill of delivering a snub.

I sought his daughter Zohre — or rather, wanted her to seek me out — hoping that mutual attraction would draw us together.

But she was still talking to my mother. In a group of women. The center of a feminine world, self-absorbed, like a Madonna to-be.

15

*P*rior to my father's arrival in Hamburg, and before I started school, Cyrus and I would make regular visits to my grandfather's store. At first, we used to go with my mother. But when

I got to know my way around better, we went by ourselves.

My grandfather used to look forward to our coming. When he was in a good mood, he would take change from a tin box and give it to Cyrus for the purchase of a toy and then slip a larger denomination into my hand, presumably for a worthier purpose.

He was always smartly dressed. Businesslike. Both brisk and casual. Brisk with his cadre of gray-frocked assistants, when there was work to be done. But otherwise casual. He waited on each of his customers himself, and if more than one happened to be in the store at one time, he would have tea and cake served, while he tended to each in turn.

Magdalena sat behind the desk in the back room, going over papers and locking and unlocking a safe the size of a small refrigerator.

Occasionally, in the midafternoons, she would put down her pen and announce that she would take Cyrus and me for a walk. Usually we stopped at the bank first, but after that we had seemingly the whole of Hamburg to wander through: the Rathaus, Planten-Blomen, bookstores, the Musikhalle, ending up at different pastry shops each time.

These visits to the store were the only occasions I remember seeing my grandfather outside his home. They were generally brief, since, though he liked to see us, he couldn't abide us for long. Which may have been why, for all I know, Magdalena so readily took off with us.

Though I doubt it. Those outings were breathers for her as well.

The two of them would get up and breakfast together before the rest of us were awake. Then either they would ride to work, or Magdalena would join him later in the morning. It wasn't until supper that all five of us — my grandfather, Magdalena, my mother, Cyrus, and I — came together.

This pattern changed with my father's arrival. It wasn't so much because my mother and I moved out of the house. Rather the two men had different natures. Different dispositions and aspirations. I can't really say that my grandfather ever came to know his son-in-law. They had always been so physically distant from one another that, when the two finally met, it was as though two strangers were expected to throw themselves into each other's arms.

Besides, my grandfather wanted to dominate my father, as he was accustomed to dominating everyone else.

He was given to viewing himself favorably as a self-made man — the way someone would admire his own looks in a mirror. It wasn't that he exactly prided himself on being barely literate, but that he looked upon any form of literacy as being subordinate to business. He knew just enough Persian to communicate orders to his supplier and shipper. That was enough. That was part of what was meant by being truly economical. Likewise his German. He looked upon German as a language of trade.

His own mother tongue had no written alphabet. Azeri Turkish exists purely as a spoken language. So perhaps there was some linguistic logic to his view.

At any rate, it clashed with my father's.

My father was nothing if not sensitive to usage. His ear was attuned to the slightest inflections. His vocabulary was huge in the various languages he spoke, but in Persian particularly, supplemented with a knowledge — though he laughed when he spoke it — of Arabic.

The disparity was cloaked as long as the two men conversed in Turkish — as they usually did — but all too obvious when they switched to other languages.

There were many other points of divergence. Chess, for example. My father was remarkably good at the game, as he was in any activity which required thought and concentration, whereby he had to size up the situation rather than the man making the move.

He didn't have the knack at cards.

My grandfather did. Not only that, but my grandfather had a high regard for card players which he didn't extend to those who played chess. It was as though chess were for altruists, who had nothing better to do with their time than waste it on pointless maneuvers. It had nothing to do with the facts of life.

All this may seem trifling. But it was on points such as these that the two men drifted apart, that they more or less indicated to each other that they were cut out for different lives.

Small contentions which led to larger issues.

The largest, naturally, involved business. How it all started and where things stood, I'll try to relate — even though the story was not made too clear to me at the time. The reasoning being, again — from my parents' point of view, and even my grandfather's — that for a child some things about one's family were best not gone into too deeply.

When my father arrived from Iran, he brought a sizable shipment of carpets with him, which he stored — at my grandfather's suggestion — at my grandfather's warehouse space in Freihaven, the free port in Hamburg. This meant that the carpets were brought into Germany without his having to pay customs. It also meant they could be stored without charge. It was his original intention to bring buyers to the warehouse and sell the shipment wholesale — thereby leaving entry procedures in the buyer's hands.

It was a way of bringing capital into Germany at a tidy, though not exorbitant, profit. My grandfather had proposed the idea to him long ago.

Yet my grandfather also had other ideas in mind. He was hoping that my father, by taking advantage of his proposal and warehouse facilities, would voluntarily add the stock to his own. That way their sale would be left to him, making the two men de facto partners in the shipment. Whatever profits accrued would be shared by both.

Added to that was the boon of taking advantage of Abol Karimzadeh's position. My grandfather would be adding to his stock at a time when Abol Karimzadeh was clearing his out without making replacements.

My father didn't see things that way. He was bringing the shipment to Germany in lieu of capital. He was taking advantage of my grandfather's offer to make as economical a start as possible on his own. From his standpoint, he could, if he wished, sell his goods outright to anyone. To the best buyer available. Which might turn out to be Abol Karimzadeh. What was to stop him? All Karimzadeh had to do was go through

117

Freihaven, where he himself had storage space, look over the goods, and, if he liked them, simply have them transferred from one location to another.

Clearly, any transfer of the kind would have gone against the interests of Haus Teheran. My grandfather wanted a son-in-law who would, if not stand by him in business, at least not get in his way. Certainly not one who would take him on as a competitor.

The issue, to my grandfather, then, was glaringly obvious. My father had two choices before him, both of which could turn in a profit: either he could sell the shipment to him at a fixed price, or, better still, he could enter into the de facto partnership, whereby his capital at sale would be credited toward the purchase of yet another shipment. If the two men found that they could work together, then other such transactions could follow as a matter of course.

In any case, a deal of this kind offered a better prospect than the buying and selling of cotton — which would mean my father would have to obtain his own storage space in Freihaven, his own import license, and set up his own office in the middle of town. All of which would eat into his capital.

Carpets, then, rather than cotton, is what my grandfather counseled. But carpets on his terms.

My father was not the sort to take a back seat in business matters. As director of the National Cotton Board in Iran, he had had a bevy of officials working for him. Later in New York he had managed his affairs successfully as a private businessman. To play second fiddle now to his father-in-law would have been tantamount to acknowledging that his business experience had amounted to naught.

So he handled himself gingerly. He kept my grandfather at bay.

Moreover, since things were not going so well with the Hamburg end of the Karimzadeh business, was it not entirely feasible that he and the Karimzadehs could come to some kind of agreement? Of course, they had not really gone into the matter in Tehran. But then, the situation had been different.

Chances were, I daresay he thought, that Abol Karimzadeh

would be an easier person to do business with than my grandfather. After all, he too was in the market for a better deal.

❈

After the reception at the Karimzadehs', Zohre became a regular visitor to our apartment. She and my mother often shopped together. They had long talks over tea, sometimes joined by my father, while I did my lessons or listened to music in another room. When we had guests, which was about twice or three times a week, she was usually on hand to greet them with my mother.

Yet she and I exchanged hardly more than a few words at a time. To me it seemed as though I didn't really exist for her. Or if I did, I did so, say, as a cat — to someone who isn't particularly fond of cats.

We didn't seem to have anything in common. We were both students, yet she never came across as being a student: she was much too polished for that. I wondered how she got by in her studies. It would have floored me to see her crack a book.

She didn't want to know about Iran. She didn't especially care for music — except for the sweepingly emotional kind sung by Caterina Valente — whereas I was just coming into my Beethoven period. She didn't like to lounge about or play games or go on walks or watch soccer or take in a concert at the Musikhalle. She didn't speak English and backed away from Persian. The only way to communicate with her was in German, which was still a chore for me.

What she did, rather, was to hover around my mother and father.

I wanted to strike some kind of sympathetic chord with her, but she was distant, cold, a brooding German Cinderella, at odds with her father and going about in nightmarish black in devotion to her dead mother.

Which appealed to my mother no end. My father too. Both liked the thought of children expressing all-pervasive filial love.

119

At any rate, the trio they made up left me oddly free to go my own way.

I took to paying visits downstairs, chatting with Gerta, Karl, and his father, and taking furtive sips of beer. We spoke in German, of course, but somehow the language barrier didn't seem to be as formidable with them.

I also went to my grandfather's house, encouraged to do so by my mother, since my parents didn't go there as much as they used to — although my mother dropped in on Magdalena for an occasional chat. In the process, I became a sort of go-between, filling the vacuum. To my grandfather I reported the goings-on in our house, which boiled down to cataloguing the guests who came and went. When I got back home, I reported the goings-on in his, which usually centered around the state of everyone's health and Cyrus and his school work.

One evening after supper, after Cyrus had gone to bed, my grandfather aired his usual complaint that my mother didn't come to see him often enough. The complaint was invariably put in the form of a question, addressed to me, and in a manner which made it plain that no answer would satisfy him. I said something to the effect that she was busy with guests and looking after Zohre.

Couldn't the girl look after herself? "She is almost twenty," he quipped.

"Fifteen," I retorted. Although, given her behavior and looks, twenty might have done just as well.

Magdalena came forward with an explanation, not so much to throw light on the matter — although she could have done that, knowing more about Zohre, through my mother, than I did — as to appease her husband.

Zohre, she pointed out, was going through a trying period. She needed attention. The memory of her mother was very dear to her. Ever since the death in the family, things were different. She was finding it difficult to live with her father.

"You mean, things are in the open now." My grandfather bared his palms to emphasize his point. Cynicism brought out his sense of drama.

Magdalena let him have his theatrical moment before continuing. Clearly, Abol Karimzadeh was not being covert anymore. The woman had been his secretary. Whether or not she was still working for him was beside the point. What counted was that their relationship was changing. He was seeing her in public. She was coming to his house. He had introduced her two young boys to Zohre. Apparently, he was trying to work out an arrangement that would be agreeable to them all. And he was appealing to his daughter for support.

"Which his daughter, naturally, will deny him," my grandfather butted in again, "being the kind of well-brought-up lady she is."

Scoffing gave him satisfaction.

If it was some measure of compassion that Magdalena wanted to elicit from her husband, it was evident that she wasn't going to get any. My grandfather had an inveterate dislike for women he designated as "ladies." Creatures who frittered time and money looking glamorous, for no reason. No, they had their own insidious motives. To uphold some notion of their place in society. Which amounted to nothing more than feeding their vanity. Impressing other people — other women especially — with their façade. Spoiled, useless creatures that they were.

He was about to launch into one of his tirades, which Magdalena managed somehow to avert, though not before he let out a few cannonades, the gist of which was as follows:

The girl was a fool for moping unduly over her mother, when she should be either busying herself with her school work or, better still, thinking about what lay ahead of her in the way of a husband. The father was a fool for involving himself with a woman who had two children by a previous marriage. The man, furthermore, was even more of a fool for letting that aspect of his life interfere with his business. Which brought him around — rather surprisingly — to my parents. My parents, for their part, were not exactly showing the best judgment either. They were letting their ties with the other two parties distract them from more important concerns: my mother with Zohre, when she should be seeing more of her father, and my father with Karimzadeh, when he had much more to benefit by standing by his father-in-law. In fact, the only one who stood to gain anything from all this nonsense was the secretary. There was a person who was using her head. She was attractive, to be sure, but nothing out of the ordinary. She was short, too plump for her height, and evenly blond due to peroxide. She was not young anymore. Yet she had demonstrated a hold over Abol Karimzadeh which others closer to him hadn't been able to match. If things worked out well for her, she would soon be enjoying the kind of comfort and security which his former wife had once relished.

Did we not agree? Did Magdalena not think so?

Magdalena certainly did not. The poor girl had to be pitied. And there was no point in fixing blame on anyone. The woman was sincere, and so was Abol Karimzadeh. The situation was awkward, but by no means nonsensical or unworkable. If people could find their way to happiness, then what was wrong with that?

"And Zohre?" my grandfather threw out as one last poke, his eyebrows well up on his forehead. He got no small charge from seeing his wife's pique.

Magdalena hesitated. Her comeback had been bold and self-assertive — more so than I was accustomed to witnessing. But now the nervousness crept back into her voice.

"Yes, well, with Zohre it's going to be more difficult than with the others," she said softly. But then added: "Which is why she needs someone — an older person, a woman — to look after her."

My grandfather smiled, evidently satisfied with the way things had worked out. Then he turned to me with a suddenness that startled me.

What did I think, he stated — not asked — by way of closing the case.

What did I think? Frankly, I was making patterns on a velvet cushion. I wasn't thinking anything. I was trying to conjure an image. He caught me in the middle of shaping an outline of a plumpish figure — mellow would be more exact — with peroxide blond hair.

When I returned home that night, my parents asked how my visit had been.

"Fine,"I said, louder than I need have.

Was there anything new to report?

"Cyrus is doing well in composition and arithmetic," I replied. "But his teacher is making noises about his posture. Apparently, he slumps over his desk in class."

16

Some time around the early spring of 1951, my parents informed me that they were thinking of sending me to a German boarding school. The one they had in mind was Salem: an institution housed in a *Schloss*, nestled deep in the Black Forest, overlooking the Bodensee and beyond that Switzerland. Salem was the sister school of Gordonstoun in Scotland, they said, both of which Prince Philip, the Duke of Edinburgh, had attended.

I was stricken with panic. Such a move would mean my adapting to yet another educational system — worse still, having to switch languages, the very thought of which appalled me. I was getting along perfectly well in the British system and loath to give it up. Besides, I had already set my sights on going to Britain — nothing concrete in the way of how or when, simply flights of fancy. Now I felt an urgent need to defend my position: convince my parents that another radical change at that stage of my life — still thirteen — would be disastrous.

My parents were surprised at my heated reaction, but, much to their credit, handled things calmly. They took me to see an educational counselor, who tried to reason with me. He informed me about Kurt Hahn and his methods at Salem, pointing out that they were modeled on the British public school system. But nothing he said could sway me. Going to England by then had become an imminent necessity: school systems aside, that was the surest means I saw of safeguarding English as my principal language.

Finally, my father gave in with a laugh. There was something admirable, after all, he acknowledged, about such doggedness in one so young. If I were so set on going to Britain, then so it would be. He left the choice of a school up to me.

The relief I felt, mingled with gratitude, was enormous and lasting.

After that my mother and I conferred with the headmaster of BSH — a man named Towel, who pronounced it like hole — who gave me several prospectuses to take home. Whereupon I retired to the seclusion of my sofa-bedroom, sat in my Richelieu chair, and pored over the descriptions and pictures.

It didn't take me long to decide. Because I liked the look of the place, because I liked the expressions on the faces of boys my age — clustered around a swimming pool — I chose St. George's School, Harpenden.

Toward the end of that summer, as my departure drew nigh, my father decided to accompany me to England. He wanted to look over the school and become personally acquainted with the headmaster. But there was more to it than that: he felt the need to spend some time with me by himself — to show me around London and the sites of his youth. His stay there had been brief, but his memory of the place, he claimed, was still fresh. The two of us had never taken a trip by ourselves. We decided to stretch out the journey and go by train.

My mother didn't shed tears at the station, and so neither did I. Besides, Zohre was there to see us off. Had she not been, the leave-taking might have been different.

In the train, I walked up and down the corridors, taking in deep breaths of cold air. I was susceptible, at that age, to all forms of travel sickness. I had been seasick, airsick, trainsick, and carsick. In fact, once I got in a car, any moderate distance presented a hazard. Slow-ups, traffic lights, unsteady driving, gasoline fumes were all potential factors to turn my stomach on end.

There were ways, of course, of fighting off travel sickness. Sleep, for example. The best way to counter the feeling of nausea was to lull oneself into a state of oblivion, before the rocking motion developed gyrations inside. Another was a steady inflow of air.

Pills were a preventive measure — not a remedy — which couldn't always be relied on.

In the train, the pills taken, the antidote was to walk up and down the corridors — which worked out well enough, until we came to the Channel, where I got sick on the ferry.

When we arrived in London, it turned out that I knew the city better than my father did. One year at a British school, taking history and literature alone, is enough to imprint in your mind the map of London forever.

We didn't look up the major tourist attractions. We had only two days there and spent most of that time seeking my father's old haunts.

On the morning of the third day, we took a train from St. Pancras Station and forty minutes later stepped off in Harpenden. My father checked his bags at the inn. Then we got into a taxi — my heart pounding — and drove up a hill to the school.

Uniformed boys and girls were milling about. The school was coeducational. The boys were in dark green blazers, with the white rose of Yorkshire on their breast pockets, gray shirts, trousers, and socks, black shoes, and green ties. The girls had on their summer outfits: light cotton dresses, with vertical pale green stripes and waistbands of the same material.

An older boy — a prefect, it turned out (and a probing eye could have discerned as much from the thin diagonal red stripes in his tie) — helped us with my luggage and showed us the way to the headmaster's study.

Over the main entrance, chiseled in stone, was the school motto: "aim higher." Along with the figure of a loinclothed archer on one knee, pointing a bow and arrow straight up. It struck me as being ironic that the motto of my school in Connecticut had been "aim high."

We waited in the office of the headmaster's secretary — an attractive, largish woman, with whom I do believe my father actually flirted — until the adjoining door opened, and the headmaster extended his hand.

I had visualized him in advance as being awesome in stature — a sort of projection of Dr. Arnold stepping out of the pages of *Tom Brown's Schooldays*. Headmasters, after all, were people apart. They were giants among a race of schoolboy pygmies. Even the benevolent "Hole," as he was called at BSH, had the aura of greatness about him.

But my imagination had not gone far enough in capturing the particulars. Here was a British Zeus, as he waved us into his study, shook hands, and delivered a terse directive to his secretary. Those were his thunderbolts lined up against the wall.

I was asked to sit in a straight-backed chair, directly in front of his desk, while my father was offered the more comfortable one with a cushion on it, somewhat off to the side.

The desk stood squarely in the middle of the room, on a small oriental carpet. Around the walls were books (though not that many), photographs (in plenty), and trophy cups (shining like armor). A large window, with ivy creeping in at the edges, looked onto a lawn, beyond which were hedges and trees.

Then came the questioning: had we had a good trip?

The headmaster kept shifting his gaze between my father and me, so that I couldn't tell who he wanted to answer.

Yes, we had, I replied.

A very good trip, my father added, smiling.

Was this our first time in England?

The first for me, but not for my father.

Oh, really? His eyebrows went up, and he turned to my father to find out the details.

For a while, I thought, I was out of the range of his scrutiny.

I needn't have worried. It was my father he wanted to interview, not me. He had a letter about me from my previous headmaster — besides which, there was plenty of time and a lot of other ways for him to come to know me better. In my father's case, however, it was a matter of determining his position from a single interview.

Not that I was capable of making such a lucid deduction at the time. I was expecting the headmaster to turn his attention on me at any moment — and not a little mesmerized by the incongruousness of the encounter before me:

My father with his Continental-cut suit, his silver hair brushed straight back Continental fashion, radiating good will in his keen regard to form.

The headmaster with a solid, grim head and massive shoulders, his dark hair parted just to one side of the middle, and tufts of hair over his eyes, wearing a dark blue blazer, with a King's College, Cambridge, badge, and God knows what tie — a regimental one, no doubt — placing concisely worded, well-enunciated questions (he was talking to a foreigner, you know), then resting those huge shoulders of his against the back of his chair, as he listened impassively to my father's replies — replies rendered even more eloquent than normal by his attempts to convey native constructions in English.

I felt as though this sturdy Englishman would ask my father, in his quiet, offhand way: "And you sell oriental carpets, Mr. Momtaz?"

He wasn't English, as it turned out — he was Scottish. In fact, he had fenced for Scotland, played rugby for Scotland, and been shot in the leg for the whole British empire — making it necessary for him to wear a leg brace, which clinked as he walked.

There was a knock at the door — not the side one we had come in through, but the front one, which led to the hallway.

"Enter!" the headmaster bellowed. He had what was known — I later found out — as "a splendid chapel voice."

A boy my own age stepped into the room.

"Mumford, this is Momtaz," the headmaster said, then turned to my father. "Do I pronounce the name properly?"

"Perfectly," my father acquiesced with a laugh.

I was told to report to the housemaster and come back.

Outside, Mumford stopped at the section of the hallway directly across from the main entrance.

"This is the Venus Alcove," he said, with a slight cockney accent. His parents owned a pub in Potter's Bar.

"Why is it called that?" I asked.

"Because a statue of Venus used to be here." He paused —

presumably to allow the fact to sink in. "That's the first thing we show all new boys."

Ah, England, bastion of tradition! Was there any point in applying logic to the issue?

We climbed a flight of stone steps, then knocked at another door.

Another firm "Enter!"

The air was gray with cigarette smoke. In the middle of the room, once again, was a working table — not a desk — large enough to seat eight at a meal. Piled on top were sheaves of paper, notebooks, and books, all in disarray.

The housemaster eyed us with a squint, blinking rapidly to ward off the smoke from his cigarette, which dangled from his lips. The ashes fell wherever they did.

Decidedly not as imposing a figure as the headmaster. But awesome, nonetheless, with his austere black gown, yellowish coloring, hollow cheeks, protruding cheekbones — all in all, projecting an emaciated coldness. My future history master, it turned out. His health had broken down in India, where he had been a major in the British Army. He had contracted malaria there, and was forever wiping his forehead and pate with a handkerchief.

The housemaster bade me turn over whatever money I had — which he summarily deposited in a drawer — adding that I could look forward to sixpence a week pocket money.

Downstairs, Mumford became more affable.

"What kind of name is Momtaz?"

"Iranian," I said.

"Oh." He paused. "What are your others?"

I hesitated between Felix and Firuz, then decided to stick with Felix. It was simpler that way.

When we returned to the headmaster's office, the two men were ready to part.

"I'm glad I finally know where that carpet comes from," the headmaster said.

The carpet had belonged to his wife's mother and was thought to have been a Sarouk, until my father determined it to be a Nain.

At the door, my father couldn't resist quoting a line from Sadi, which he translated roughly as follows:

"Pick at his flesh as much as you please, but when you are done with him, pray leave the poor father the bones."

The two men laughed and shook hands.

After which we collected my bags and rode with Mumford in another taxi to the boys' dormitory, a half-mile away. There my father kissed me goodbye and said that he would see me the next day, before leaving.

I cried that night — silently, under the blankets, because there were at least nine other boys in the room.

The next morning I ate a gigantic breakfast, examined my schedule, and attended chapel with the rest of the school. By the time the morning's business was over and the initial introductions were made in class, I was in surprisingly good spirits. So much so that when my father arrived to make his final farewell — just before lunch — I shook hands, instead of kissing him. At which he cupped my cheeks in his palms.

17

*J*had left Hamburg in a russet-flecked tweed suit with a Continental cut, wide lapels, and crimson tie. Autumn colors, chosen by my mother. I returned the following Christmas vacation in school uniform: black cap, green blazer and tie, and the rest a sort of standard drab gray.

My mother laughed when she saw me at the airport. I would have to change into something more suitable, she said, since we were going to have guests.

On the plane, I had imagined a long conversation with my parents about school life in England. There was a good deal to tell them which hadn't gone into my letters. But even before we stepped into our car, my mother exploded the news that the Ahmad Karimzadehs were in Hamburg — children included —

which seemed to shove everything else into the background.

Then, as soon as we entered the apartment, the telephone rang. After which Helga, wearing a starched see-through apron, gave my mother a sheet of messages, which kept her busy on the line.

My father and I, meanwhile, sipped tea in the living room, helped ourselves to one of Helga's delicious *Apfelkuchen*, and tried chatting — but with ears half-cocked to what my mother was saying. Hardly the sort of *mise en scène* I had anticipated for launching into my narrative.

When my mother breezed into the room, it was to whisk me off for a bath and change of clothing. The guests, she said, would be arriving any minute — her way of emphasizing the need for instant action.

It is an Iranian custom that, when someone arrives from abroad, close family and friends show up to celebrate the occasion as soon as possible. Usually the person is met on arrival and borne home, where others come to greet him.

Had we been in Iran, the first ones to meet me would have undoubtedly been relatives, then friends of long standing. Being no more than a lad, I could hardly have expected a larger crowd.

But in Hamburg, where one was away from such ties, lesser intimates stepped in to fill the breach. It was another one of those unwritten rules — never articulated, but tacitly understood and accepted by all those who considered themselves a part of a social set — that every arrival was to be met with an *éclat*, reflecting the kind of response one would normally expect to receive in Iran. As though home fires had to be kept burning at all costs.

There was always the same profusion of phone calls, flowers, and impromptu visits.

Now, it might seem, from all this, that one's personality was bound to be submerged by the tidal wave of convention: that personality, actually, had very little to do with the matter. If the guests were coming ostensibly to see me, they were, in fact, merely bowing to form, in deference to my parents, which, in itself, could be regarded as a pretext for socializing.

But the fact is, the dynamics of social intercourse involved a different process: not a submerging of one's personality, but a drawing of it out into a web of ritual. There it lay preserved — but also entangled in a vaster meshwork.

I'll try to illustrate.

The Karimzadehs were family friends. As such, they genuinely — I never doubted it — looked forward to seeing me. As I did them. The point is, did they have to see me on the heels of my arrival? The answer to which simply had to be yes. As family friends, they had to go through the ritual of being, if not the first, then certainly among the first to arrive. Otherwise, how else could they demonstrate their closeness to us?

As for others more distant, the Sepentas, say, the same held true, though with slight variations. And herein lay a rather curious twist. If the Consul General, say, didn't show up sometime during the week (as it turned out, he and his beautifully bare-necked wife came that very evening), my mother would have been offended — but on my account, rather than hers. "The Sepentas," she would have said, "didn't do the right thing by you" — which would have put me right in the spotlight of the snub, as though I were the one who should have felt slighted.

On such threads, one's personality came to be engaged in, rather than submerged by, the ritual.

Not that any of this made it easier for me to budge from my spot.

"What about Grandfather?" I asked, from my reclining position.

I looked at my father. He didn't answer.

"Have your bath first," my mother said, piling up the used dishes and teacups, then called for Helga.

Helga ran the water in the tub, while I changed, then returned to the kitchen to prepare an improvised meal for fourteen or more. Gerta was summoned from below to lend a hand — a quick greeting in German and a wave, on my part, from the bathroom. And my father — everyone else being occupied — went out to buy bottles of *Steinhäger.*

My bath was steaming hot, and I lowered myself into it slowly. Normally, I didn't have the patience to stay in long, yet I felt the urge all the same. There was commotion outside, and I had the antithetical desire for solitude — the kind that massages the mind — with a lot of bustle around.

My mother asked, from the other side of the door, if I wanted my back scrubbed.

Decidedly not! I sat up. A boy of fourteen, with pubic hair and public school views!

I got out and dried myself.

Before I was finished, though, my mother strode in, waving away the steam, and applied a fresh towel to my hair.

Another Iranian fixation: to dry oneself as thoroughly as possible before emerging from a bath. Wrapped up to ward off the chill.

She kissed my cheek.

"I've laid out your clothes in the bedroom," she said in English, by which she meant their bedroom.

"What about Grandfather?" I repeated.

She went on, regardless, that she had selected one of my father's ties for me, along with matching socks, then added: "Your father and he have had an argument. But you should call him tomorrow anyway. I'll tell you about it later."

"Why not now?" I queried.

"The guests will be arriving any moment."

The doorbell rang.

❖

The Karimzadehs were the first to arrive — all but Abol, who promised to come later. Gerta popped into the bedroom as I was putting on my jacket and held up the flowers they had brought. Red carnations.

Stepping into the living room, I was conscious of making an entrance.

Mrs. Karimzadeh let out an "ah" and spread her arms to embrace me. She smiled with the whole of her face. Her hair was swept up now, and redder than I had remembered.

I crossed the room to the armchair she was sitting in and planted a kiss on either cheek.

132

"What a man you've grown into, Firuz!" she beamed. I was as tall as my mother, who, in turn, was noticeably taller than she.

"Height is not everything," my father laughed, from his seat. "The mind must grow as well."

If it was the business of a guest to make a compliment, it was that of a host to turn it down as congenially as possible. Like refusing tea or candy, on the guest's part, the first time it was offered.

"As far as the mind goes," my father continued, "our man" — emphasizing the word *aqa*, which Mrs. Karimzadeh had used — "is still green."

Then he turned to me and quoted an aphorism which went something like this:

"Aqa shodi qabl az in ke adam shodi."

Everyone laughed, while I stood still with a planted smile. Such verbal gambits were the usual way for a son in the family to be thrust into a group.

The meaning of the statement is roughly as follows: "You've turned into a mister before becoming a man." Which is not really a full translation. *Aqa* means more than just "mister"; it also means "lord" or "man" in the social context, such as, say, "gentleman," whereas *adam* means "man" in the broader category, embracing mankind. So that another way of conveying the statement would be: "You have become a man outwardly, but you have not yet developed the inner potential."

You are, in other words, "still green," as my father put it.

"Green" was his overall term for anything unripe or undeveloped. Every now and then he would squeeze my head with the palms of his hands — as though he were testing a melon — and declare that the insides were still "green."

Which, oddly enough, made me associate my brain with the color of my school blazer.

I turned to Zohre — who was seated on the sofa, between Mrs. Karimzadeh and my mother — no longer dressed in black, but now stunningly chic in dark colors. A daring mixture of brown and blue, with a purple satin scarf about her throat. But darkest of all was her hair — luxuriantly beautiful against her pale skin.

She offered her hand, with the finely manicured nails, but limply, pulling it back just as I got hold of her fingertips — which made the whole act of handshaking seem ludicrously gross and irrational.

Ahmad Karimzadeh stood up and introduced me to his sons, Farid and Matin, who stood up with him. We shook hands and mumbled the usual introductions in Persian.

"Your servant."

"Your slave."

"And this is Mahin," my mother announced, placing both hands on the shoulders of a girl too young to be expected to say or do anything of her own accord in a gathering of older people.

I had been in the same position in Iran.

"She is the sweetest, most adorable creature in the world," she continued, pressing her cheek against that of the girl. "And now that I've got hold of her, I won't let her go."

Clever woman that she was, my mother had placed the picture of this girl — taken in Iran, when she still had baby fat in her cheeks — in a silver frame, which was now conspicuously ensconced in the place of honor, on the middle shelf of the glass-cased cabinet against the wall, between the area where the guests were sitting and the door. Anyone walking into the room could no more miss seeing that picture than the Dresden dolls on the same shelf: figurines, about six inches high, of a woman at the piano and a man leaning over it, dressed in the style of Mozart's time. Or the Iranian flag, which stood between them on the shelf above.

(Incidentally, the other display areas for photographs were the dining room cabinet, which was reserved for family snapshots — including one of me as a baby, lying naked on my stomach on a leopard skin rug — and the desk in my sofa-bedroom: on top of which was a picture of Ashrafi glowering, taken in New York, seated behind a desk, and looking as though he had just looked up from work — a favorite pose of Iranian officials.)

Mahin reacted to my mother's remarks with a smile. Not a giggle — the way some children do, when singled out as a favorite. She allowed herself to be coddled, without squirming or looking down.

134

Another wondrous thing: she looked me right in the eye. Her smile broadened, breaking open her lips and showing a set of small, even, white teeth — as fragile as the porcelain work in the Dresden dolls.

Her coloring, by contrast, was ruddy — the result of her stay in Switzerland, it turned out, when the topic turned to complexions.

Standing back to look me up and down, Mr. Karimzadeh remarked that "Firuz looks pale."

It would not have done to say that I had been sick on the plane, and so England's climate came under fire.

It was generally agreed that I should switch schools to Switzerland.

"Mahin was pale, too, before we went to Genève," Mrs. Karimzadeh said. "But three months there made all the difference. See how red her cheeks are now?"

"Like apples." My father winked.

My mother stroked the back of her hair, which had a page-boy cut.

"Why don't you let your hair grow long?" she asked softly. "It would look beautiful on you."

"She refuses," her mother put in quickly. "She says that long hair gets in her way, and she doesn't like pigtails."

"It makes me sweat when I go horseback riding," Mahin added, by way of making her objection more explicit. "Then I have to wash it."

More laughter around the room.

"Don't you wash it anyway?" my mother continued her playful questioning.

"Yes, but this way it's easier."

My mother pressed her nose to her hair.

"Well, it smells like a rose now."

Mahin smiled. "Zohre gave me a rinse."

At which Zohre started — the sudden mention of her name bringing her out of a trance.

As endearing as such talk was to the men — hearing their loved ones going on about each other — as soon as the tea was brought in, Mr. Karimzadeh and my father moved to the far end of the room, by the windows, and chatted in Turkish about the state of affairs in Iran.

The remaining group then further divided itself: the women sitting around the coffee table — Mahin pressed as close to my mother as physically possible — and the three of us boys forming a triangle in our straight-backed chairs, unable, really, to hear ourselves talk until we got up and moved toward the door.

The boys told me that they had arrived in Hamburg only a few days before. Their parents had flown from Tehran to Zürich, picked them up at their schools in Geneva — Mahin having been put in a school near her brothers — and together they had made the trip to Germany. They were staying in their uncle Abol's house for the duration of their visit.

They dispensed the information as a twosome — the way close brothers do — taking turns filling in the gaps. Yet they were also opposites — like their uncle and father — as though some law of nature governed their species. Matin's eyes darted around the room, while Farid's stayed fixed on mine.

Both Farid and Matin were older than I. In height, I stood midway between them.

Of the two, Matin, the younger, displayed the sharper intellect. He was the lively, talkative one, with the animated gestures and restless eyes — and a head somewhat large for his body. Before long, he drifted off to the group around the coffee table, only to drift back again. As though one line of conversation weren't sufficient to sustain him for long. Like an impulsive chess player, moving between two boards.

Later in the evening, he spoke French with my father at an incredible clip, which impressed my father enormously. He put an arm around his shoulders and pronounced him "brilliant."

"Oh, yes," someone then said, "and he has written a charming book of verse in French as well."

The "book of verse," it turned out, was a notebook, which he showed me on a later visit to the Karimzadehs, when he confessed — somewhat tiredly, in the privacy of his room, with his legs dangling over the arm of a chair, and a cigarette between his fingers — that, actually, he was more interested in prose and had written several stories too bawdy to show anyone in his family, other than his brother.

Farid, by contrast, was demure and passive. He exuded a quiet charm, which came of his being both genuinely modest and unsure of himself. He preferred to listen rather than talk. He spoke with a crack, in wavering tones — as though his voice were still breaking, and the process had been an unduly long one, like a miserable cold one never got over.

He was handsome, though, and well-proportioned, as his father was. He looked dapper in his three-piece suit. His facial features were those of his mother: a low forehead, topped with a thick wave of hair, an angled nose, close-set eyes, and a mouth shaped for smiling.

With Matin, it was the other way round: he had the broad, downward cast of his father (and uncle) — the same pale Turkish coloring — and the pert compactness of his mother's physique.

It was hard to tell which of these family traits were shared by their sister and to what degree. Mahin, if anything, seemed to be physically set apart from her brothers by the process of growing up — though, curiously, not so much from her parents. She was as yet undefined, with her long legs, small torso, and flat chest: not quite the beauty my mother made her out to be.

Soon other guests arrived, with snow on their shoes and the look of cold on their faces. These included the Sepentas and Kemalis — another business family of fairly long standing in Hamburg — and with them a woman I hadn't seen before. She worked at the consulate. They came as a group, each couple bringing flowers.

With these fresh arrivals, the noise in the apartment swelled to a din: the grownups laughing and talking at once, vying to help each other off with their coats, only to be put off by Farid, Matin, and me — who rushed to our tasks like efficient stewards — while Gerta took the flowers.

"I shall die of the cold!" fairly bellowed the woman who worked at the consulate. Her name was Mrs. Habibi. A divorcée, it turned out, in her late thirties or thereabouts, with a husky voice which drew attention not so much by its loudness as by its resonance. "I came from a warm climate to die here in the cold!"

She went on nonstop, as I raised my hands to help her out of her coat. It was mink.

Farid, lucky fellow, was in the process of practically undressing the Consul General's wife, who outdid all other feminine competition in her low-cut dress.

"Is this Firuz?" Mrs. Habibi turned to my mother. She had a down of dark hair on her upper lip.

My mother introduced us.

"My luck is changing. I expected a boy, but now I have a man to escort me around Hamburg."

She cupped her gloved hands over mine, gave it a squeeze, flashing a toothy smile, then swung around to allow the coat to fall off her shoulders.

As she stepped into the living room, she held out her arms to Zohre and pleaded: "Come and warm me, my dear. I'm frozen to the bone!"

They embraced, each planting a hardly tangible kiss on the other's cheek, and talked arm in arm — Zohre finally showing signs of life, even laughing — until Mrs. Habibi noticed Mahin eyeing them and beckoned her into their fold.

I was surprised at how squarely — for a woman who was new to our group — she stood at the center of things. Zohre so taken with her — it was odd.

After the initial hubbub died down, the men congregated around the window area, Farid and I joining them. Matin, as before, wandered.

Mr. Karimzadeh, being the latest to arrive from Iran, was asked for his assessment of the country's state of affairs. He described the goings-on in terms of who was newly appointed to office, but refrained from passing judgment.

"It's too early to tell," he ended his account, with a shake of the head and a frown.

Which brought out an energetic nod of approval from the Consul General.

"That's what I keep telling our dear friend, Mr. Momtaz. But he won't hear of it and insists that action be taken now."

"What kind of action?" Mr. Karimzadeh raised his eyebrows.

"Well, my dear sir, that's a long story," the Consul General laughed. "You've only just gotten here, whereas we've been at this for over a year."

"And I still haven't succeeded in bringing his excellency around to my viewpoint," my father laughed in return.

"What it all boils down to," Mr. Kemali said — he had a long, thin mustache extending to the corners of his lips, and thin strands of hair brushed back over his shining skull, which made him look like Igor Stravinsky — "is that Mr. Momtaz has set up a shadow cabinet, in case all goes wrong over the oil issue."

"Not a shadow cabinet at all," my father corrected him, "but basically the same one, with a few significant changes."

"Those significant changes," Mr. Kemali went on, "involving those of us here who gather to play cards."

My mind flashed back to our stay in Ramsar.

"Well, there's no denying it." The Consul General waved a hand debonairly, "Mr. Momtaz would make an exceptionally capable cabinet minister. I'm thinking specifically of the Minister of Finance."

"Yes, of course," Mr. Kemali bowed, "but as for the rest of us, well . . ."

"I can't disagree with Mr. Momtaz's choice of talent," Mr. Karimzadeh smiled. "But what does this group have in common that could stimulate the aims of the present government?"

"Sound business sense." My father smiled in return. "Coupled with a sense of national purpose. A group of businessmen, who see eye to eye on major economic issues and support one another, could turn the country around and soon make it economically viable."

"How so?" Mr. Karimzadeh asked, radiating benevolent sympathy.

"By making the country economically self-sufficient. By developing, as the Prime Minister said, local industry and agriculture, while the conflict goes on over the oil issue."

"You mean, by cutting out oil revenues altogether." Mr. Kemali wanted to bring the conversation around to the gist of the matter.

"Not altogether. Temporarily," my father corrected him again. "The oil settlement with Britain is not going to come about in a month or a year. It may not come about for several years. Meanwhile, the country has to survive. How is it to survive, unless the economy is put right in its fundamentals?"

"Is oil not a fundamental, my dear sir?" The Consul General smiled.

"With all due respects, your excellency, no." My father shook his head. "It has been a chain around our neck and a source, as you well know, of political corruption. As long as our country is dependent mainly on oil revenues, we are subject to control from outside."

"But how is a program of economic reform — no, let us go further than that and say economic reconstruction — going to be put into practice?" Mr. Kemali asked, in spite of himself.

"Through laws," my father said unequivocally. "Through laws enforced by the government and businessmen fully cooperating with the government — for their own benefit, let me add."

"I doubt that such an impetus can come from the government," Mr. Karimzadeh countered softly.

"Why not?" My father beamed. "It has done so before. I myself was a part of such a reconstruction program years ago."

"That's true," the Consul General added generously. "The service you performed is remembered to this day — and will be for a long time. But tell me," he sniffed, "does this mean that you give your wholehearted support to Mossadegh's economic policies?"

"You are a representative of the government he serves," my father retaliated. "Do you?"

"My dear sir!" the Consul General's hands went up, as he looked around laughingly at the others. "Why do friends have to talk like this?"

"Because neither do I. Politically, the man is sincere. He wishes what you and I and all of us wish: to relieve the country of foreign control and total dependence on oil. But that's a political objective, not an economic one. Economically, his policies need reassessment and direction. By businessmen — those who are economically minded — rather than those who hold strictly political views. That's the tragedy of his cabinet: it is made up of men who have political ideals and don't know how to work out, let alone implement, an economic program. Do you disagree with me?"

"It's pointless to disagree with you." Mr. Kemali sighed. "You may be our future Minister of Finance. Instead, why don't you implement something else and set up the card table?" he laughed.

"Who's going to set up the card table?" Mrs. Habibi remonstrated from the other end of the room. "What, again? So soon?" She addressed her complaint to the women around her, though clearly she had the attention of all. "As soon as those men get together, they have the card table out. What would happen if they didn't play cards for a change? If they talked to us for once? Do you think that's likely to happen? Never. That's what I like about German men. They're so attentive to their women. Isn't that right, Mrs. Momtaz? Aren't they more sociable?"

Her protest made everyone laugh, even — quite needlessly — me, who reacted out of a sense of social obligation. Though I can't say as much for Mahin, whom I caught looking bored and twirling the end of her hair.

The men apologized profusely and suggested, by way of a compromise, since they couldn't very well be asked to give up their cards, that the ladies sit down with them.

Which didn't impress Mrs. Habibi one bit.

"Very clever of you" — she eyed them with theatrical scorn — "when you know perfectly well that you gamble and we don't."

Before I knew it, Mahin was standing beside me and whispering into my ear.

"Your mother says she wants a group photograph taken before everyone sits down to cards. She asked me to tell you to ask the man downstairs if he would come up to take the pictures."

I nodded and turned to leave, when she asked if she could come along.

Downstairs we interrupted Karl and his father in the middle of their supper. Hearty greetings in German passed back and forth. They put out an extra dish and glass and asked us to join them. Mahin eyed the room inquisitively from the doorway.

I asked her if she wouldn't mind staying down for a bit. She shook her head and sat at the table, silent and upright — not a girl anymore, but transformed into a little lady.

I forked a sausage from a steaming pot, put it on the plate, and extended it to her.

She shook her head.

Karl poured beer into the glass until the head ran over the brim. I drank it without waiting for the head to die down.

"I'll have only half," Mahin changed her mind.

I cut the sausage, forked one half, and gave it to her on the plate, eating the other with my fingers and dipping it into the pot of mustard.

"Do you eat here often?" Mahin asked, as though we were at a restaurant.

The immediate effect of the beer — and the change in atmosphere, too, I suppose — made me feel cavalier. " As often as time allows," I beamed at her. I offered her a sip from my glass.

She shook her head. "Wine, yes. Beer, no."

Which took me aback.

"What did the *Fräulein* say?" Karl asked, knowing that he had missed something.

And so the four of us chatted brokenly, until Karl finished downing no less than five long sausages — to the astonishment of Mahin, who kept eyeing me after each one was dispatched — and polished off his glass of beer.

On our way out, I asked his father what new novel he was reading.

He held up a book with a cover illustration of a woman — voluptuously clad in a bathing suit — seated on a rocky beach, with her back to the viewer, looking out on a crash of waves, and the title inscribed in the turbulent sky: *Die Liebe ohne Ruhe.*

"Good?" I asked, in my pithy German.

"Like all the others," he said. "I don't like stories to change."

Upstairs the smell of cooked rice and various side dishes had crept through the apartment and made a sort of familiar counterbalance with the noise.

I gave Karl my camera, and he adjusted the flash.

"But where is Abol?" someone asked. "We can't take a picture without him."

Mr. Karimzadeh explained that he was driving up from Bremen, and that there was no telling when he would arrive. He suggested that we go ahead without him.

Mrs. Habibi rolled her eyes. "If that man isn't in Bremen, he is somewhere else. No, I'm very happy that I've got Firuz as my escort now. Firuz, come and sit by me for the picture. You're our man of honor this evening."

And so it came about that I was the only male figure seated in that photograph (which takes up a full leaf in my parents' album): the men standing behind the sofa against the wall, the women clustered around the sofa, my mother clutching Mahin, Zohre on the other side of Mrs. Habibi — who was positioned slap in the middle — and the other two boys squatting on the floor.

When the picture came out, I was surprised at the contrast I made with the others: sitting with legs tightly crossed, arms folded, and a blank expression on my face — as though I had posed for a team photograph.

The picture-taking over, Karl was offered a shot glass of *Steinhäger*, and the rest of us drifted into the dining room and ate standing.

My father carried on the conversation in French with Matin that I referred to earlier, while Mr. Karimzadeh queried me about school life in England. He listened attentively as I touched on a range of subjects.

"What you say is very interesting," he nodded, by way of rounding off my summary. "Did you know that Parviz is thinking of going to school in England as well?"

My mind blanked. Parviz who? Then it dawned on me that he was referring to Parviz Amuzegar. He seemed so remote then. I had thought of him strictly in terms of my past in Iran.

"Yes," Mr. Karimzadeh continued, "he is almost finished with high school, and he wants to get his *baccalauréat* in England or America. He hasn't decided which. In any case, he wants to pursue his studies in English. Did your mother tell you about that?"

"I haven't had time." My mother's voice surprised me from behind. "My poor boy has only just arrived."

Mr. Karimzadeh smiled, then returned his gaze to me. "Parviz is a very good student. Particularly in the sciences."

"Why do you say simply 'good'?" Mrs. Karimzadeh joined us. "They say he is at the top of his class."

143

We were getting to be the center of attention — always an uncomfortable feeling for me in Iranian circles.

"They also say his English is perfect," his wife pressed on. "And he hasn't even been out of the country."

"He used to attend Alborz," Mr. Karimzadeh explained. "But then he switched to your American school. You really ought to write to him, Firuz, and give him your views about England. His mother is coming to Hamburg as well."

"When?" I asked, then felt myself blush.

"In a few months. The summer perhaps. You could talk things over with her. She would appreciate that very much. She herself prefers England to America — because of its closeness to Iran. But then, he seems pleased with the American system. So he is trying to make up his mind. You've been to both places — you're familiar with the two systems of education — so you should have a solid basis for comparison."

I was about to qualify that view, when the doorbell rang and the long-awaited Abol Karimzadeh arrived.

I met him in the hallway, as Gerta was opening the door. He looked vaguely tired and apologetic. His eyes were beady and his clothes were wrinkled. I was better able now to discern the contrast between him and his brother. He was the frailer — not just the shorter — of the two. More refined in his features, but not as distinguished looking. Not as well preserved. Distinctions such as these hadn't been so apparent before.

He apologized for being late.

"Am I right in thinking that sweets are still rationed in England?" he said, with a rasp, as though his voice were tired, too.

I said they were.

"In that case" — he pulled out a long, thin box from his coat pocket, unwrapped and unribboned — "I thought you might prefer chocolates to flowers. At least you'll have the satisfaction of eating them." He winked.

Which I didn't. They were portioned out among the guests after dinner, as they played cards.

Meanwhile, my parents ushered him into the dining room, and as I hung up his coat, I heard Mrs. Habibi's voice declare mockingly, almost belligerently, "At last! At last!"

144

The following morning I woke up late and was surprised to find my father still sitting at the breakfast table in his pajamas and bathrobe. His face bore a scowl, and he had a faraway look in his eyes.

"Good morning!" I said, in the usual hearty manner expected of me.

He responded to form, and his expression changed — but not the look in his eyes.

My mother had heard me get up and called from the kitchen. All the plates had been used except mine, which had a slice of cantaloupe on it, and the newspaper was crumpled.

"Go ahead with your fruit," my father said. "After you finish eating, I want you to come to the office with me. There are some things you ought to know, and we can have a talk by ourselves."

Then he got up and handed me the paper, adding that if I read a page of newsprint every day, I would never forget my German. He left to shower and change.

I skimmed through *Die Welt*, while eating my cantaloupe — finally settling on the sports page.

My mother came in with my breakfast, a pot of tea, plus — a new feature to our table — a creamer of milk for my tea. She, too, was in her dressing gown.

"Did you sleep well?" She kissed my temple.

I said that I had.

She sat down and poured tea into two glasses with silver holders. (We rarely drank tea from cups.)

"Did you like Farid and Matin?" She added a dash of milk to mine and stirred it.

I said yes.

"And Mahin as well?"

I nodded.

"Zohre is getting more beautiful, isn't she?"

There was no denying that.

"What about Grandfather?" I asked. "Do I call him this morning?"

My mother let out a startled laugh and leaned back to observe me — as though to acknowledge objectively that, when one really got down to it, her son, basically, had a one-track mind.

Then she frowned. "Your father and I have had a long talk about it, and I think, after all, you should hear him first. He'll tell you about it at the office."

Since there was only one bathroom in the apartment, I waited until my father got out. As I was getting dressed, I heard my parents talk about money. My mother needed cash for groceries. My father made a fuss. What about the money he had given her only a few days ago?

That was almost a week, my mother argued.

But that was a hundred marks, my father remonstrated. It had been meant to last her longer than that.

My mother itemized her expenses. Still my father was adamant. We were spending too fast and freely.

Then why did he insist on throwing so many dinner parties, my mother countered.

At which my father flared up.

From this point on, it was to be ever thus: costly evenings followed by mornings of retribution. We were extending our hospitality beyond our means. Yet hospitable we had to be, or face the bleaker prospect of dropping out of society.

My father and I drove to the office, across from which was Gross Bleichenstrasse. It was strange to see Haus Teheran without dropping in on my grandfather.

My father's office was on the fifth floor of a large building with rotating elevators. As we walked in the office, our two employees got up. One was Herr Köhler, a man in his seventies who looked much younger: impeccable in dress and habits. He had come out of retirement to be our secretary and bookkeeper. The other was a tall lad named Poggendorff, the office boy, a few years older than I, whose father had been killed in the war.

My father gave me some letters to type, while he attended to business with Herr Köhler.

Around one-thirty or so, he said he would treat me to lunch at

146

the Rathaus. But a phone call detained him. Instead, I went out and brought back a bag of sandwiches. After eating, my father told me to look over our carpets in the storeroom and asked Poggendorff to show me around. It wasn't until late in the gray December dusk that he came into the storeroom and asked Poggendorff to put on the tea.

When we were alone, he walked around between the piles of carpets. "I want to teach you a lesson in business," he said. "What do you think is the value of these?"

I said I didn't know.

"Let's say two hundred thousand marks." He gazed at the ceiling, that sum being equivalent to roughly $50,000 at the time. "This represents about half the shipment I brought here. Do you know in whose hands the other half is?"

"Grandfather's?" I suggested.

"They're in his hands." He stopped. "He won't give them up. Do you know why he won't give them up?"

I shook my head.

"Because he claims they are his. When I came from Iran, I brought a shipment of carpets to exchange for German currency. Karimzadeh agreed to sell them for me at a very small commission. But the carpets were stored in your grandfather's warehouse. When I asked for their delivery, I found that he had already sold a few pieces on his own and pocketed the money. When I asked him for the money, he said that the ones he had sold had been from his own stock. When I questioned him further, he changed his story and insisted that the pieces had been bought on his account. This was a matter of several thousand marks — almost ten. So I thought I would let the issue rest, take delivery of the others, and settle that part of the business with him later. When he delivered the goods to this office, do you know what I found? He had taken the choicest pieces for himself and substituted pieces like this."

He kicked over the corner of a carpet and let out a laugh.

"In return for a Kashan, I get a Heriz."

He shook his head. "The man is a crook. He is a millionaire, who steals from his family."

A pause and another shake of the head. "But he is also a busi-

147

nessman. Not the kind of businessman I am. If I take him to court, he will countersue me. He has fixed his books to show enough so-called evidence on his side to make for a lengthy, costly investigation. You must bear in mind that I'm new to this country. I am still not familiar with all the procedures. If I take legal action, my business will suffer, and my name will be tossed about as a man who brings suits against his own relatives."

He gazed out the window, into the dying light, then turned to me.

"But that's not the worst of it." He smiled bitterly. "If you can believe it, my dear son, he has tried to step between your mother and me. When we were in England, he confronted her and actually advised her to divorce me. He claimed that I wasn't strong enough in business to support her. Can you believe that — coming from a man who has cut off his own children? What is more, he wanted to take you as well. He wanted you and your mother to live with him, and bring you up to step into his business with Cyrus."

I felt a huge wave of protectiveness well up inside. There was a lump in my throat.

"What are you going to do about it?" I asked.

"Cut off all ties with him. Not have you or your mother see him again." He spoke emphatically. "To have you see him again would be to have you contaminated by him. As far as money goes, what's lost is lost, and the word is out that his dealings are crooked — so his business won't exactly prosper from this theft. No, we shall cut him off like a snake. When you see a poisonous snake, what do you do to it? You crush it. If you don't crush it immediately, it will strike you and spread venom throughout your whole system. He is a snake that has to be crushed — avoided at all costs. All ties cut. Do you follow me?"

18

*T*hat winter the rift between my father and grandfather cast a pall over everything. One was conscious of it all the time. Occasionally, my mother and I tried discussing it. But, invariably, my father got angry and cut us off. And to have carried on by ourselves would have been too close to dissembling.

As a result, I never did get in touch with my grandfather — even though I was approached rather surreptitiously one day by Poggendorff. Apparently, he had been spoken to by one of my grandfather's staff, who told him to convey the message that he wanted to see me. I said no, fearing to incur my father's wrath.

Meanwhile, the Karimzadehs kept us socially busy; their family seemed so characteristically strong, while ours was breaking up into feuding factions. Hardly a day went by without our seeing them.

Also there was Mrs. Habibi, the newcomer to our group who was now so much the center of attention. It was hard to think of her simply as an employee of the consulate. She was evidently so much more. Not because of her work, but in her capacity as a social figure. In the drawing room, let us say, she was on a par with the Consul General himself, or with anyone else, for that matter. My mother said that she had wealth and came from a large landowning family.

Which explains, I suppose, a great deal. But not her charisma — or "wonderful charm," as my parents put it. Some people reacted to her by climbing out of their shells, while others crawled back deeper inside.

The difference between Zohre and me.

Under Mrs. Habibi's influence, Zohre became increasingly a different person. She chattered and laughed. She mingled with adults, soliciting attention, instead of sitting back passively. She even exuded a playful seductiveness — as the unattached beauty — which made some of the wives think of her as having reached the marriageable age.

My mother's explanation for her change was that she was imitating Mrs. Habibi, that she needed the example of someone who was the complete opposite of herself in order to bring out her sociable side, and that in Mrs. Habibi she had found the right person.

A view which gave much credit to Mrs. Habibi's influence. But which was also a neat — and somewhat evasive — way of looking at things: considering that Zohre had been just as much influenced by my mother before, though then she had followed the path of demure femininity.

It also glossed over what was increasingly, though vaguely, apprehended by all: namely, a possible romantic connection between Mrs. Habibi and Abol Karimzadeh. This was more a hope than anything else. Still, even as that, the coupling of the two had the unspoken blessing of our group as a whole — and the more open support of his daughter.

At any rate, our day-to-day contact with the Karimzadehs and Mrs. Habibi came as a welcome relief to my parents. It lifted, for them, the pall in our apartment. With me, I confess, Mrs. Habibi's presence — the Karimzadehs' bustling as one big, happy family — drew me deeper into the gloom.

On Christmas Eve, I thought I would seek some form of sanctuary. Ahmad Karimzadeh had booked a table for us at Haus Vaterland — a sort of family nightclub, with harmless, circus-style entertainment, along with the usual singing and dancing. I backed out on the grounds that I had made a previous arrangement with friends to attend midnight mass at St. Petrikirche. Which was a lie. Still, I knew I couldn't get by if I said I wanted to be by myself. Mrs. Habibi clapped her hands, claiming that it was a very novel idea, and rallied the whole group to go along. Since our table had been booked, Mr. Karimzadeh suggested that some of us go, while the others stayed behind, and that we could all join up at the nightclub afterward. The party that went to the church — the "pilgrims," as we came to the called — consisted of Mrs. Habibi, my parents, Zohre, Mahin, and me. My "friends," I was assured, could join us as well, if they wished.

A phone call, on my part, put an end to that matter: my "friends," I announced — two brothers of my concoction — had come down simultaneously with the *grippe* and were bedridden.

We were late getting off to the church, which was packed when we arrived. There, too, Mrs. Habibi made her presence felt. She complained that she couldn't hear a thing. We pushed our way forward. Then she hit upon other complaints. When was the singing to begin? How long did we have to listen to that old buzzard moaning? My mother and Zohre started giggling. My father was infected as well. They bit their lips and forced themselves to be still.

"Let's leave," Mrs. Habibi whispered suddenly.

My parents and Zohre imploded anew.

"We can't." My mother tried to control her voice. "We've just arrived, and everyone will look at us."

Another word from Mrs. Habibi at that point and she would have collapsed.

They tried to focus hard on the service.

Then Mrs.Habibi turned to my father with eyes closed. She breathed huskily: "I'm going to be sick."

"What?"

She nodded vigorously. "These fumes are making me sick. I shall throw up all over the floor."

"You're not serious!" He didn't know whether to believe her.

"On the tomb of my father — as God is my witness — Omid, I'm suffering."

We made a sober exit: my father propping up a drooping Mrs. Habibi, eyes closed, mouth open, while the rest of us followed, trying to make ourselves inconspicuous.

Outside, Mrs. Habibi took in several deep breaths of cold air, then opened her eyes. "I feel better. Now, let's go to Haus Vaterland before I get sick again!"

My parents and Zohre doubled over with laughter — while Mahin and I exchanged glances, our hands in our pockets.

The story made the rounds in Hamburg for years to come.

What surprised me was that I heard a version of it much later in Tehran, with a different cast of characters, except for Zohre and Mrs. Habibi — who, by then, was one of the three women members of Parliament.

I was glad to get back to St. George's. Three weeks of idleness and socializing — along with the oppressive gloom in our apartment — made me impatient for the simpler, more routined, open-air existence of a schoolboy. I also took to my books with zest.

Sometime around the end of the school year, I was approached by the secretary of the Debating Society (a Sixth-Former and prefect by tradition) to take up Iran's position on the oil issue — that is, if I felt up to it.

There had been a basis for this lofty invitation. I had argued earlier in the Remove vs. Fifth Form debate. The Fifth Form, traditionally, as the senior class, represented the Conservative party. Remove had to do the best that it could in advocating Labour. I argued the point, as the designated Labourite and underdog, that, given the prevailing attitudes and policies of British management, the position of the British working man was basically untenable in the world market: hoping thereby to cut into the national sentiment of both forms. I used one of my father's business ventures as a case in point, though not mentioning him by name. Germany (my father) was selling screws to Burma. Germany was able to do this — that is, capture a hitherto British market — because of strikes in Britain (a naked lie). Germany had lost the war, whereas Britain had won, and Burma had always favored Britain in trade. What was to be done about this? Let the British working man have a more equitable share of the profits and strikes would disappear.

I lost by a handy margin. But then, Remove always lost to the Fifth. It was like St. George killing the dragon. The point was, I had made a fairly respectable case — so I was told — for Labour.

And so, I was on for the Debating Society, which was small, clannish, composed mostly of Sixth-Formers, met once a month, and was always desirous of fresh topics. Not that the

Anglo-Iranian oil issue was particularly "fresh" at the time. It had been in the papers for years. The British public had made up its mind on the matter long ago. Britain, as usual, was in the right, and Iran flagrantly in error. Mossadegh was obviously a rogue and a rascal, who refused to deal with people on a rational basis. Why, after all, would he still refuse to negotiate?

The best chance I had of making an inroad into such an attitude was to reconstruct the events in a manner that would allow for an alternate view.

The outline of my argument ran as follows — and I have used it since on other occasions:

First of all, Iran's position on the oil issue had not been a hard-and-fast one to begin with. After the Second World War, Iran had sought to negotiate a new, more equitable agreement with the Anglo-Iranian Oil Company. It had not intended to liquidate the oil company's holdings and set up a nationalized industry in its place. To do so would have run counter to the country's economic interests, besides which, it lacked the strength to make such a move.

The rift between Iran and the oil company occurred when Britain refused to acknowledge that Iran had any legal justification for seeking a new agreement. British argument posited that a negotiation had already been worked out during the reign of Reza Shah, and that both sides were bound by the contract to keep to the specified terms for the stipulated period of sixty years.

Iran countered by disputing the validity of an agreement that distributed profits so unevenly. As far as national sentiment went, the contract had never been popular. It was unanimously regarded as a British imposition — as a blight on the country's politics, as well as a drain of its resources.

As attempts at negotiation failed, pressure mounted until, finally, the extremist position solidified in Parliament and won the support of the people.

That was more or less the gist of half my argument. The other half explained how Mossadegh had come into power, and why the government had taken the drastic measures it had.

Just prior to my coming to England, the Mossadegh government had not only nationalized the oil industry, but had broken off diplomatic relations with Britain, and expelled all British personnel from Iran.

For this part of my argument, I had largely my father to thank.

In June 1950 (shortly before my mother and I arrived in Hamburg), the oil issue was still open for negotiation. The king appointed General Ali Razmara as Prime Minister, in a move to establish a strong national government from above. The country, by now, was threatened by turmoil. Razmara was charged with rectifying the situation by bringing about long-awaited internal reforms and settling the oil issue. His appointment, by and large, was received with a sense of relief and approval. In Razmara, the British too saw at least a powerful figure with whom they could deal.

In March of the following year, however, Razmara was assassinated by a member of the Fedayane Islam — a fanatic religious organization. The king was then put in the awkward position of having to choose between continuing the policies of his former government, or giving in to majority pressure from Parliament. He chose to do the first and appointed as the next Prime Minister his former Minister of Court.

Parliament, at this juncture, passed a bill, by unanimous vote, providing for the nationalizing of the oil industry, and called on the new government to put the bill into action. The Prime Minister backed down and offered to resign. Within less than two months after the death of Razmara, the interim government had been toppled.

This time the king had no alternative but to appoint Mossadegh as the new Prime Minister.

The appointment touched off a national celebration. Whereas less than a year before, the public had responded favorably to Razmara's more moderate measures concerning oil, now national sentiment stood firmly behind Mossadegh's hard-line policy.

From this point on, power shifted from Parliament to the government. And Mossadegh's method of keeping things that way was a rather novel one for that part of the world: he put into effect a policy of opposition to the British that revealed itself as a surprise at each step.

This was the basis of his popular support: he put an end to British control over internal affairs and reasserted, in its place, a sense of national self-determination.

I reminded my audience of Churchill's dogged stand during the war — which didn't go down too well with my listeners; Britain being linked, by analogy, with Germany.

But that, at any rate, I went on, was what Britain was up against in the oil issue: not just one man's or one government's opposition, but the opposition of a whole people.

Given, then, that the issue cut deeply into national sensibilities, how was Britain to deal with a government and people that had ousted it from its former position of authority?

By adopting an understanding and flexible attitude. By listening to the case of the man who was most responsible for bringing about the predicament they were in, instead of trying to shout him down.

The fact was, although Mossadegh was espousing a hard-line policy toward Britain, there were others in his National Front movement who wanted him to go much further than that and align himself with Russia.

Britain had fought two world wars with Iranian oil. If that oil were to pass into Russian hands, then Britain's position would be weakened indeed.

Mossadegh, as a nationalist, had no intention of allowing one foreign power to take over the place of another he had just ousted. All the same, further political crises could take matters out of his control. It was best, then, for Britain to hear him out and negotiate, while negotiations were still possible.

I was applauded for my effort, but voted down 11 to 1. The one person who voted for me was my opponent, who, as custom dictated, had to vote for the other side anyway.

After the debate, the secretary congratulated me in a rather singular way: he invited me then and there to be the Communist party candidate in the school's mock elections. St. George's, he said, had never had, in his time, an advocate for Communism, and in me he saw a fairly plausible spokesman.

I pointed out that the case I had made had very little to do with Communism.

That was all right, he assured me. To argue the Communist

155

line, one didn't have to be a Communist oneself. One had simply to continue going down the path I was going.

That spring, I received two pieces of news that came as a surprise. The first one — after the initial jolt — elicited a smile.

As a rule, my parents wrote protectively. They wrote joint letters, with one of them starting out and the other coming in around the middle or end. Neither delved into personal matters.

Then came a letter in which the subject could hardly be avoided. My mother wrote separately, explaining that my father was too busy to add a few words just then.

Abol Karimzadeh had run off with a German woman to Sweden. He had done this suddenly, just before the Now Ruz celebrations, without saying a word to anyone. The only way they knew of what had happened was through a terse letter he had written from Stockholm.

The German woman, it turned out — and my mother didn't mention this — was the notorious mistress whom no one talked about. Apparently, they had married secretly in Germany and taken her children with them.

Zohre, my mother added, was crushed. The poor girl was so unnerved by the incident that she had to be taken to a doctor (a psychiatrist, it turned out). My mother was busy taking care of her.

What was equally shameful, the letter went on, was that Abol Karimzadeh had absconded with some of the firm's money, claiming that that was his share of the business.

In plain, the Karimzadeh family, whom I had thought of as representing one big, staunchly united clan, had been presented with a coup d'état.

Ahmad Karimzadeh had flown from Tehran to Stockholm to set matters right, but had gone on shortly afterward to Hamburg, without, apparently, having made much headway. He was thinking now of taking over the Hamburg end of the business himself — until, at least, Farid was old enough to step into the picture. My father had offered his services.

At any rate, all was up in the air for the time being.

There was no mention at all in the letter of Mrs. Habibi's reaction. Later, my mother wrote that she had been transferred to the Iranian embassy in Rome. When I got back to Hamburg that summer, she was gone.

The second piece of news stirred up other feelings. Nasrin Amuzegar had remarried. She was now the wife of Hassan Karbalai. He had, apparently, been pursuing her for years. Both my parents were ecstatic about it. The marriage had taken place in Tehran, with the Ashrafis present, but very few others.

I remember walking over the grounds, letter in hand, very much conscious of treading on grass, as I mulled over the name, Nasrin Karbalai. It didn't sound as right as Nasrin Amuzegar.

For a while after that, my parents kept mentioning the possibility of her coming to England with her husband.

There was also the business of finding a good English school for Parviz. St. George's was one which they, naturally, wished to consider, having heard about it through my parents. I was asked to take up the matter with my headmaster. Which I did. He said that references and grades were necessary, as well as an interview. I wrote back as much, but never got an answer.

Nasrin and her husband didn't come to England. Not together, at any rate. Karbalai, I later found out, had come over by himself. Instead, they traveled through Europe, spending time in Paris, on the Côte d'Azur, and, when the weather got warmer, in Germany.

My mother informed me that the newlyweds would be in Hamburg by the time I arrived home for the summer.

What followed thereafter was another turning point. This one, too, I happened to witness, just as I had the last time I was with Nasrin. Only this time the part Nasrin played was very different — if you can call it a part at all.

It had to do with Zohre.

But Nasrin was there. And so was I. And so was the sea.

It all came about as result of a group outing to Travemünde.

157

19

When I returned to Hamburg that summer, I found that the Ahmad Karimzadehs had moved into Abol's house. Zohre was living with them. Their children, however, were still in Switzerland.

Nasrin and Hassan Karbalai arrived for a visit around the end of July.

They had been touring in Europe ever since their wedding in March During that period, Hassan Karbalai had made several trips on his own for business reasons, one of them being the one I mentioned, to England.

On this, his latest round of excursions, he had left his wife in Nice, flown back to Tehran, then joined her again in Geneva. From there they had proceeded to Hamburg, where he spent no more than a day or two before taking off for England again.

It was almost as though he had stopped over only to drop off his wife.

Nasrin — it had all been worked out beforehand — was to stay with the Karimzadehs until Karbalai's return, after which the couple were to move into a hotel.

It wasn't until considerably later that I learned that at least some of Karbalai's trips to England had been made for the purpose of negotiating with Britain over the oil issue. Though which party on the Iranian side he represented, I'm not sure. He might have been sent as an unpublicized government agent, or as an even more unpublicized envoy of the court. It's hard to unravel what exactly was going on in those days, and which sides people were taking. The political ground kept shifting.

Just before the Karbalais arrived, we had received some important news from Iran. Mossadegh had taken over as Minister of National Defense, on top of his position as Prime Minister. Previously, the king had made his own appointment to this post. Following that — we had heard — some generals had been jailed. There was no report of Amuzegar, who was still, at that time, a colonel.

My father questioned Karbalai about these matters, but all he got was veiled answers. Karbalai claimed that he had not been in Iran long enough to find out what exactly was happening. Mossadegh had clearly whittled down the king's power. But whether this was only a temporary measure or an attempt to change the overall structure of government remained to be seen. As far as he himself was concerned, he had spent most of his time overseeing the affairs of his ginning plants and cottonseed mills.

Karbalai projected the image of a businessman concerned, basically, with the management of his private industry. He had done very well by staying out of politics. What reason would there be for delving into it now, especially when things were so uncertain?

Yet, it was difficult to overlook the well-known fact that the first fortune he had made had come through the sale of arms. Surely, his affairs could not have been so far removed from politics.

At any rate, his departure left Nasrin as a guest of the Karimzadehs.

She was radiant that summer. Lively, petite, warm, and beautiful. Her hair was a deep, burning auburn, her eyes large and sensitive — her lips full. She had lost the pale, anemic cast of four summers ago. Her body was trimmer. All these made her seem younger than before. I was inclined to think of her as still in her twenties. She was thirty-two.

People said that she and Karbalai were perfectly matched. Karbalai looked the same as before — physically, he never changed. His skin was taut and sunburned; his hair had the same steel-gray color and wiry fullness. The only notable difference in his appearance was his clothing. Whereas before there had been a somewhat rakish look about him, now he was stylishly chic. Both he and Nasrin dressed expensively.

One had missed that side of her when she had been the wife of Colonel Amuzegar. There was nothing hidden about her beauty anymore.

What gave her the radiance, though, was that she was happy

and showed it. She was the center of attention as the comely bride.

My mother claimed that she was so moved by the change in Nasrin's fortune that she wanted to cry.

Nasrin was constantly surrounded. And, given the heavy socializing touched off by her arrival, it was impossible, at first, to have any privacy with her — which I wanted, and which I thought she did as well, if reading eyes meant anything.

Our chance came when my mother spoke up about my involvement with music. Immediately, Nasrin turned to me and asked if I would take her to a concert. I suggested an open-air series at Planten-Blomen. She agreed and told me to fix a date.

Naturally, when the time came, we went as a group. Before the program got under way, though, she stood up and asked me to go for a walk. She slipped her hand through my arm — I being the taller one now — and as we strolled between the flower beds, I was conscious of smells: floral scent mingling with perfume.

We talked about me first, then about Parviz. She had mentioned before that he wouldn't be coming to England. I asked for the details.

"He has decided to study in America. I wanted him to study in England — to go to your school. That would have been nice, no?" She smiled. "Anyway, he has made up his mind, and he should do what he chooses. He wants to be a scientist, and he says that the sciences are more advanced in America than in England. Is that right?"

I said I didn't know. "Is he going straight to college?"

"No. He has one more year of high school. So he has decided to spend that year in America, preparing for college. It was the principal of your school in Tehran who suggested it. As of September, he'll be attending Andover Academy in Massachusetts. Have you heard of it?"

She meant Phillips Academy in Andover — the name seemed vaguely familiar.

She smiled again, wistfully, missing him already. "I'll have only two weeks with him in Iran before he leaves."

"Why doesn't he join you here?"

160

"Well," she sighed, "he spent four years with me, without seeing much of his father. Now he wants to see something of him before leaving."

This was the first time she had referred to her former husband. I wanted to go one step further and ask about Parviz's reaction to her remarriage. But I balked, and she went on.

"Besides" — Nasrin gave my biceps a squeeze — "we didn't know that he would be going to America. When we left Iran, we thought there was a very good chance he would be joining you in England."

We turned around to head back to our seats.

"What about Bijan?" I asked.

At this she laughed and tossed her hair. "The boy is impossible! He gets into more scrapes than anyone I know. The truth is, I have no idea what we're going to do with him. My father has tried to get him into business, but he is too wild for that. He is not cut out for a desk job. As it was, he just barely made it through high school."

She gave me a quizzical look. "Have you heard stories about him?"

I said no.

"It's just as well. People like to exaggerate. It's not that he is bad — it's that he is a . . . problem. No, he is impulsive." She smiled. "But otherwise he has grown up quite nicely, you know. Girls find him very attractive. Women, too." She was almost bragging. Then she sighed. "But that, too, has its problems."

She paused, becoming pensive. "It's odd: the only one who has any real influence over him is Parviz's father. Isn't that odd? He is closer to that boy than he is to his own son."

She drifted into a mood, then blinked out of it. "Anyway, if nothing else works, he could always go into the army. Though you know how my father would react to that!"

Just before we reached the rows of seats, she pulled my arm. "Tell me," she added quickly, as though the thought had just occurred to her, "how is Zohre? I know what others say about her, but what do you think?"

What could I tell her? Apart from the little I gleaned from my mother's letters and my own distant observation, there wasn't much I could add. She was depressed, uncommunicative — more so now than before. Which wasn't surprising, considering the recent events in her life. But what she was going through inside was buried matter.

"I'm worried about her," Nasrin said. "Has she been more depressed since my arrival?"

"I don't think so. I don't know."

"I think she has." She nudged my elbow to proceed. "Keep an eye on her, Firuz. She needs to be close to people."

Her words surprised me.

"But I'm no closer to her than you are!"

"I know," she nodded. "It's sad. She turns away from those she needs to be close to."

We got to our seats just as the orchestra was striking up von Suppé's overture, "Morning, Noon, and Night in Vienna."

When Karbalai returned from England, a week or so after his departure, the wives planned an outing to Travemünde. It was the obvious resort area for our group to go to, since it was only a few hours by car from Hamburg. The women wanted to get out into nature, and the men wanted to "feel the pulse," as they put it, of the Casino.

My mother, I recall, tried to book us rooms for a weekend, but since nothing was available, we made it a Sunday excursion instead.

The kitchens were busy the night before, the wives and their help preparing the elaborate food we were to eat on the way: assortments of rice, meat, vegetables, and sauce — all heated in the morning in pots with towels around the lids to seal in the warmth.

Our party consisted of the Karbalais, the Karimzadehs, Zohre, the Sepentas, the Kemalis, and us. We went in three cars, the spouses splitting up so as to make the drive more "sociable."

I was herded into the Sepentas' limousine — a Mercedes 300, which belonged to the consulate. On the way, Karbalai entertained us with humorous stories, told in a blasé manner, which made Sepenta, who was driving, laugh uproariously. I sat in the back with Mrs. Kemali; a thin, sickly woman, with rheumatism in her legs, who had spent many years in Germany, and who — unlike her husband — was fluent in the language.

As usual, I was asked to comment on my school life in England. Once the subject of studies was raised, the tone of the conversation became appropriately earnest. Sepenta expounded his views on education. When he was finished, the laughter resumed.

Just before we reached Travemünde, all three cars pulled off the road. My father got out of the car in front and consulted the others as to where we should eat.

My mother suggested a place further ahead which had trees and cut grass and overlooked the sea. My parents had been there before with Magdalena and my grandfather. My father wasn't sure where it was, so my mother got out of the Kemalis' car — another Mercedes, like ours — and joined him.

When we arrived at the location, we all got out and stretched. Sepenta wanted to wrestle with me. Kemali opened his backgammon set and engaged my father in a game before he had so much as finished taking things out of the trunk. Mrs. Kemali spread a blanket on the ground for them.

"Where's the samovar?" Sepenta shouted, releasing me from a hold he said he had picked up at the *zurkhaneh* in Tehran. "What kind of an Iranian picnic is this without a samovar?"

Mrs. Karimzadeh laughed and said that she had brought one in the Kemalis' car, at which she was applauded for her forethought.

My father alternately cast dice in Turkish and quoted verse in Persian. Sepenta responded with more verse. Kemali begged my father to keep his mind on the game, otherwise he couldn't take his money with a clear conscience.

Mr. Karimzadeh and Karbalai had wandered off with Nasrin, Zohre, and my mother in search of a choice spot where we could eat. They came back, announcing that they had found one, and asked us to move.

"What's wrong with staying here?" Kemali grumbled. "It's

near the cars. We won't have to go back and forth so much."

Sepenta laughed and quoted a line, which he attributed to Sadi, about the virtues of moving.

We carried our equipment down an incline, near the edge of a cliff, with trees and bushes behind. After we had all settled down to eat, a sea breeze came up, creating a chill, and we ate our lunch in jackets and sweaters.

Through it all, the playing of backgammon went on: Sepenta taking over from my father, then Karbalai changing places with Sepenta.

After lunch, Sepenta and Kemali went back to the cars for a nap. The other men took turns at backgammon, while the women made tea and chatted.

I felt restless and bored. I got up and asked if anyone cared to go for a walk — a concession to form, which I didn't expect to be taken up.

"Why don't you go along, dear?" Nasrin turned to Zohre.

"Yes, do go along," her aunt urged. "The exercise will be good for you."

"I don't want to," Zohre mumbled.

But the others were adamant. I didn't like the position I was in. Reluctantly, Zohre got up and followed me.

When we were out of earshot, I wanted to apologize. Instead, I asked if she wanted to walk along the cliffs.

She shrugged and eyed the ground.

I tried striking up a conversation — which turned into a vapid monologue.

We reached a point where the ground leveled down to the beach. I asked if she cared to walk on the sand.

She shook her head. The wind wrapped her long hair about her face. "I can't in these shoes. You go ahead. I'll wait for you here." She sat down decisively.

I was annoyed at the rebuff, but also restless for action. I scampered down the slope, exhilarated by the release of physical energy and being close to the waves. I turned around and shouted at her to take off her shoes and come down barefoot.

I couldn't tell whether she responded or not.

I took off my shoes and socks and waded into the cold water, wishing I had brought my bathing suit. I stood there, until it seemed senseless to be just standing there — neither fully in or out — then went back up the cliff.

Zohre had her head down over her knees. She didn't acknowledge my approach.

Odd, I thought, how a person in the throes of a mood can dominate another.

I was breathing heavily from the climb. Suddenly, I felt impelled to act. I put my arm about her waist and caressed the lower part of her breast.

She drew back, startled.

"No, don't. What are you doing?" Her face was locked into a grimace.

I felt abashed — exposed as a lecher — but pursued my course anyway. "Tell me what you're thinking right now, otherwise I'll feel like a fool."

Her features softened. "You feel like a fool?"

I nodded.

Her lips trembled. "Well, I feel like a fool, too."

Her eyes were glowing and bulbous. She gazed at the grass and stroked it with her fingers. I noticed the nails had lost their polish, and the thumbs were gnawed.

"I never wanted to come."

"We'll go back, then," I said. "They shouldn't have forced you."

"I don't mean on this walk. I mean on this trip. I mean Germany. The whole thing." She started breathing spasmodically. She was going to cry. "She made me do it."

"Who?"

"Mrs. Karbalai."

She tugged at the grass, uprooting it.

"Nasrin?" I failed to see the connection. "How does she affect your being in Germany?"

"No, on this trip. This outing. She made me come." She was talking through tears now. "Who does she think she is, telling me to come like that — and then ordering me to go off with you? She's not my aunt. She's not my mother. Who does she think she is? She's . . . horrible! She's . . . full of herself and conceited!"

The floodgates having been raised, the rest came out in a torrent.

"She marries one man, then runs off and leaves him for another. Then comes over here to tell me to do this and that. And pities me. And laughs at me."

"She doesn't laugh at you."

She flashed an angry look through red eyes.

"Yes, she does. You all do. Even my aunt. Even your mother. But she's worse than the rest. Ever since she came here, my life has been hell. Worse than hell."

She grimed her face with the dirt on her hands. I offered the clean end of a used handkerchief, but she was oblivious.

"The only one who . . . only one who" — she couldn't get out her words now — "had any feeling for me . . . who knew what I go through . . . was Mrs. Habibi . . . and she's gone . . . because my father . . . like Mrs. Karbalai . . . couldn't stand to be with . . . my mother and Mrs. Habibi and . . . me!"

She broke into such violent sobs that I thought she would spit blood.

Unfortunately, just then, we were intruded on. Nasrin, Karbalai, and my parents had set out on our tracks to join us. They arrived at the worst possible moment.

Zohre jumped up and screamed.

It's impossible to try to convey her incoherence, as they tried to soothe her. She lashed out at everything. Car, trip, Germany, walk, her mother, that horrible man, that woman, children, all of us children.

Then she reached into her quiver of arrows, selected the sharpest, and let it fly at Nasrin.

Parviz. What about him? Where was Parviz? What was he feeling, now that his mother was enjoying herself with another man?

She ran off somewhere in the direction of the cars, waking up Sepenta and Kemali.

Nasrin sat dumbstruck.

Now it was she who needed tending to. Karbalai and my mother bent over her, while my father went after Zohre.

Then my mother turned to me angrily and demanded an explanation, insinuating that I was in some way to blame for it all.

Which made me nearly choke with indignation.

"It's all right," Nasrin assured her. "He only tried to do what I asked him."

Which also surprised me. Had that been my motivation, after all?

Somehow they managed to calm Zohre down with goblets of tea.

But calming her down didn't put an end to the crying. She carried on in a low wail in Mrs. Sepenta's arms — separated from the rest of the group, in the Sepentas' limousine.

Nasrin cried, too, and so did my mother.

It then became necessary to decide what ought to be done next. The Karimzadehs insisted that the rest of the group go ahead to Travemünde, while the three of them returned to Hamburg. My father offered to drive. The others objected. If the Karimzadehs were going to go back, then so would they.

Sepenta stepped in to officiate: the man of reason in the midst of emotional upheaval. What harm had been done? Zohre had gotten upset. She had said some things that she would be sorry for later — that she was, undoubtedly, sorry for now. Why not give her some leeway — leave her in the capable hands of his wife — and go about matters as normally as possible? We could all proceed to the Casino, as planned, and let the affair work itself out in due course.

Karbalai was inclined to agree. There was no sense in maximizing the problem.

Nasrin objected. The girl was suffering. She needed attention.

Zohre had all the attention she needed, Sepenta countered, from his wife. He himself would speak to her later. What was best for her now was to be with people she hadn't offended. Given a little patience and comfort, she would soon be ready to face the others.

His reasoning triumphed. We proceeded to Travemünde. The men gambled in the Casino. My mother went for a walk with Nasrin and Mrs. Karimzadeh. Mrs. Kemali joined Mrs. Sepenta and Zohre in the car. I was left to wander about on my own, but given definitely to understand that I had incurred my mother's displeasure and would have to answer to her later.

When we were ready to go back, Sepenta claimed, in the

darkness of the parking lot, that Zohre was asleep in his car. She had asked his wife if she could spend the night with them, and he insisted that she should; arguing that she needed the distance to regain her equilibrium.

Mrs. Karimzadeh objected. But Sepenta now was clearly the voice of authority. His suggestions had prevailed: the rest of the day had gone well. The crisis seemed to be under control.

We drove back to Hamburg, with Zohre taking my place in the Sepenta's limousine, her head nestled against the shapely bosom of Mrs. Sepenta.

The following evening, Gerta came to our door and handed me the afternoon paper. She thought that an item would interest us, even though no names were mentioned.

A girl had fallen out of a fourth-floor window of the apartment belonging to the Iranian Consul General into a canal directly below. Luckily, a man had seen her and jumped in to save her. The incident was described as an accident.

When I showed my mother the item, she leaped to her feet and was on the phone in an instant.

She called the Sepentas and the Karimzadehs. Both parties confirmed the report, but wanted the matter hushed up — which is why they hadn't called even us. Had the man who had rescued her not given the story to the press, the incident would have never been made public.

My parents reacted with shock.

I wondered what Sepenta's face must have looked like.

Nor could I resist the temptation of raising a point with my mother: if I had been responsible for all hell breaking loose at Travemünde, then what did she have to say about Sepenta's part in what appeared only too plainly to be her suicide attempt?

My parents didn't think my argument funny.

Zohre was taken to a hospital, where she spent several days undergoing treatment for shock. She was diagnosed as having suffered a nervous breakdown, for which the suggested cure was a complete rest and change of environment.

Everyone seemed to have a pet theory as to what that entailed. It was rather like planning an ideal vacation for her, without any limitations on time or money.

The one thing humorous about the whole incident was Sepenta's part in it and his attempts at exonerating himself. To hear his side of the story, he was the innocent victim of a terrible breach of faith.

Even my parents had to laugh.

The Sepentas had done everything that night to see to Zohre's comfort and needs. Sepenta had offered to sleep in the guest room, so that Zohre could be with his wife. Since they slept in separate beds, Zohre would have been assured of a good night's rest. But she had been adamant: she wanted to be alone. After drinking a glass of hot milk — which Mrs. Sepenta herself had prepared for her — she had gone straight to bed, thanking them calmly and cordially. He himself had looked in on her before retiring, believing her to be asleep.

The next thing they heard was the splash outside. He looked out the window, then dashed out of the apartment in his bathrobe. Happily, when he got to the embankment, she was already out of the water.

The man who had pulled her out had been handsomely rewarded.

There were other versions of what had happened. According to another account, the Sepentas were blissfully asleep through it all, until they were awakened by knocks at the door.

Still another version had it that Sepenta had gone to Zohre's bed and tried to seduce her, whereupon Zohre had panicked and jumped out the window. That was the one I came across in Tehran.

At any rate, the incident turned out to be a source of embarrassment for Sepenta. Rather than make a clear-cut admission of the matter — beyond our own tight little circle, that is — the course he took, for official purposes, was to deny that the whole thing had happened at all. Anyone who claimed that a Miss Such-and-such had leaped out the window of his building was either a liar or worse.

As a result, the incident became a rumor, and the accounts that circulated were much more damaging than the circumstances warranted.

Someone even told me once that his wife took drugs and, on one occasion, had mistaken a window for a door.

The most remarkable thing about the episode, though, was its outcome. And who could have predicted it? Nasrin went to visit Zohre in the hospital. Suddenly, a bond of affection sprang up between them. They cried, they talked, they kissed and made up. And after Zohre got out, they were bosom companions.

The upshot of it all was that when the Karbalais returned to Tehran, they made plans to have Zohre come and stay with them. Now that Parviz was about to leave for America, there was a gap to be filled in their lives.

Everyone agreed that Zohre was long overdue for a return to Iran. Her last four years in Germany had been tragic and tension-ridden. Now it was time for her to make a fresh start in her country — to seek new bonds. To think about marriage.

Zohre, for her part, was anxious to go. She left Hamburg for Tehran shortly after I went back to school.

The city she returned to, which she barely remembered from her childhood, had just gone through a round of political turmoil. Within a year, another would follow, with shattering results.

Mossadegh had survived the summer ordeals with remarkable success. He had reduced the king's power, as I mentioned, by appointing himself Minister of National Defense — thereby securing control over the army and the other armed forces during that crucial period of confrontation. He had also quelled an increasingly rebellious faction in Parliament. He no longer had the unanimous support of that body: opposition was growing to his unilateral emergency moves. A national election had been scheduled for the middle of July. He canceled the election on the grounds of widespread political corruption. When Parliament protested, he submitted his resignation, and the king appointed a new Prime Minister. Four days later, due to rioting in the streets and bloody shows of support on his behalf, he was back in office, stronger than ever. In fact, Parliament, thereafter, reversed its position and gave him plenary powers for six months.

This gave him the authority to go ahead with more stringent measures: he dissolved the Senate — which had been the focal point of resistance against him — proposed further acts to limit the power of the court, and broke off diplomatic relations with Britain.

For a year or so after October, my passport had to be handled through the Swiss embassy in London.

But Mossadegh's political successes were also countered by mounting economic problems. The road having been cleared for his unilateral actions, his overall policy was leading the country into a state of bankruptcy. He had mistakenly assumed that Britain, in order to survive, would ultimately have to negotiate on his terms. What happened instead was that oil production was raised in other Middle Eastern countries: namely, Iraq, Saudi Arabia, and Kuwait.

He was also thwarted in his efforts at getting economic aid from America to outlast the period of confrontation with Britain. It became only too clear that America was not about to give any financial assistance until Iran was ready to settle with Britain.

Factions within his own government accused the two countries of working hand in glove. Furthermore, they accused the court of being opposed to the government's reforms and sympathetic to foreign interests.

The Tudeh party, which was still officially banned, but which had been largely responsible for his support in the streets, now sought a more active role in guiding the affairs of state.

This brought matters to a head. Mossadegh's government was

accused of being sympathetic to Communism — both by xenophobic elements in the West and by splinter groups in Iran that had become disenchanted with him.

All this resulted in another round of opposition, more arrests, and the imposition of martial law — and that from an army which could no longer be totally relied on.

Mossadegh decided to consolidate his position by concentrating on reforms. Those opposed to his measures were more or less counted out of active service and defined as antigovernment elements.

Ashrafi, once again, lost his position at the bank. He submitted his resignation before having to answer some charges, and flew to Hamburg for medical treatment.

He arrived with his wife sometime in April 1953, and didn't leave till the end of that summer. I never got to see him. By the time I came home for the summer vacation, he was laid up in a hospital — so I was told — just north of Hamburg, in need of total rest and isolation.

Apparently, before going there, though, he had met with my grandfather. The two men had had a long talk. It was the first time that they had set eyes on each other since their parting in Tehran years ago — before my grandfather's marriage to Magdalena. Before the age of electricity and plumbing, as the phrase goes in Persian. I wondered what they talked about.

At any rate, around the time of Ashrafi's arrival in Hamburg, Mossadegh's supporters in Parliament began calling for the dissolution of Parliament altogether. With Parliament closed — it was argued — the government would be given emergency powers to enact legislation hitherto opposed. Once the period of crisis was over and new reforms were in effect, a national election could be held — a legitimate one this time — and a more representative body could be voted into power.

Naturally, such a proposition raised a hue and cry both in and out of Parliament. The Tudeh element — or those broadly associated with it — not only supported the move, but demonstrated in favor of the removal of the king. When pro-Mossadegh rioting got out of hand, forces within his own government counseled that Mossadegh dissociate himself from such an extremist position. The army and police moved in to quell the demonstrations — but with restraints as to how far they could go.

As a result, both sides became disenchanted: the rioters, because Mossadegh had turned against the very segment of the populace that had supported him in times of need, and the army and police because they had been checked from coping with the situation as they saw fit.

I remember coming across a *Time* magazine article, which described the mood of the army then as that of "a sullen eunuch."

In any case, what all this led up to was the stormy period of confrontation in August 1953. A period which marked a change of course in the nation's history. Like a landslide, altering the slope of a mountain. A great burial — huge and, at the same time, infinitesimal.

The month began with Mossadegh getting his way in dissolving Parliament by way of a referendum. In doing this, however, he had openly violated constitutional authority, which required that any dissolution of Parliament be approved by the king. This the king refused to do. Instead, he issued a decree, dismissing Mossadegh as Prime Minister and appointing, in his place, General Zahedi. Zahedi had been a former friend and supporter of Mossadegh, and had served as his Minister of National Defense. After his removal from office, Zahedi had voiced his opposition to Mossadegh's government from the Senate. When the Senate was dissolved, he had gone into hiding.

The king's Imperial Guard moved swiftly and silently to put the decree into effect. They arrested, by night, three of Mossadegh's cabinet ministers — including Hossein Fatemi, who had taken my mother and me on a tour of the oil refinery, and who was then the Foreign Minister. Next, at dawn, they were to have taken custody of Mossadegh himself at his house — the colonel of the guards handing him the king's note of dismissal.

Instead, they ran into a wall of tanks and troops loyal to Mossadegh. The guards were disarmed, and the colonel was put under arrest. More government troops then surrounded the royal palace and parliament building.

173

The king and queen were vacationing, at the time, in Ramsar. When they received word of the coup d'état, they fled by private plane to Rome.

All this took place around the third week of August. I remember the time well: we were all agog at the news, scraping for every bit of information we could get through the press and the radio.

Mossadegh, it seemed, had succeeded in removing all obstacles from his path. The king was out of power. Parliament was closed. The army had moved to support his position. The whole country now was seemingly behind him.

We didn't know whether to feel joy or concern. The way was now paved, apparently, for a revolutionary government. We heard reports about mobs taking to the streets, in wild celebration. The Tudeh faction, we also heard, had declared the country a democratic republic.

But there was an ironic touch to all this. Confined, as he was, to his house — a sick and bedridden man — Mossadegh had little, if any, actual control over what went on in the streets. It was almost as though, in reaching the height of his power, he had exposed his fatal weakness.

Within four days of his successful coup d'état — which had been brought about, it was said, without the firing of a shot — a counteroffensive was mounted by loyalists in the army to topple his regime.

The army had now been given the task of restoring order in the streets — especially of turning back the enthusiastic Tudeh element.

The loyalist faction took matters into its own hands. Pro-monarchy demonstrations and parades were staged without hindrance. The loyalist army and mob then joined forces to assault government-held positions.

The man pinpointed as the spearhead of this drive was Colonel Amuzegar. He had led a column of tanks into the streets, then armed the loyalist mob with rifles. Whereupon they had assaulted the radio station. Along with that, his men had occupied other government strongholds: police headquarters, the offices of the pro-Mossadegh and Tudeh parties.

Finally, battalions of tanks confronted each other. Mossadegh's forces ran out of ammunition first, and it was all over. The losing commander was torn apart by the loyalist mob. And so, it was said, was Hossein Fatemi.

My mother wept at the news.

Mossadegh was taken into custody. The king returned from Rome to assume full power. Soon afterward, Amuzegar was made a general. Later he became chief of staff, then Minister of War.

Part iii

Cambridge-Tehran

Cambridge

21

The political changes in Iran affected all of us, though in ways that were different and not wholly discernible for a number of years. Life in Hamburg continued as before, with business for the Karimzadehs and my family going on as usual. But for those in Iran, the changes were more immediate.

Ashrafi's position took a sharp turn for the better. After leaving Germany and the hospital, he returned to Iran via Switzerland. Shortly afterward he was elected president of the Chamber of Commerce, a post he retained — or "sat on," as my father put it — for a decade or so.

He opened an insurance company: the first in Iran to be fully subsidized by Iranian capital. He had done this, so it was claimed, to provide for his son, who became its first manager. But Bijan was unruly — not the sort to be happy, as Nasrin had said, with a desk job. Furthermore, he was — in his early twenties — notoriously unreliable. And this attempt at saddling him with responsibilities not only failed, but backfired. Bijan ran off with some 50,000 tomans — or roughly $8000 — of the company's money and spent it all on a week's spree in Rome. He returned to Tehran — with an Alfa Romeo — ordered back by his father, who admonished him severely and turned him out of his job. Ashrafi made up the money himself and installed one of his former associates at the bank in Bijan's place. The affair was hushed up, and, from that point on, the insurance business became a success.

This venture aside, as the price of land in and around Tehran skyrocketed, Amin Ashrafi's wealth multiplied. Between the time of Mossadegh's overthrow and the early sixties, my father calculated, his investments in land increased at least twelvefold.

He also made annual visits to Europe and Hamburg on behalf of the Chamber of Commerce — until his health took a turn for the worse, and he was forced to cut down on his activities.

But despite these steady improvements in Amin Ashrafi's financial and social status, it wasn't *his* life that altered so visibly; it was his daughter's. After all, when one saw him, one didn't really take in what was going on behind the scene: he looked the same as ever.

In Nasrin's case, her marriage to Karbalai had made her not only conspicuously wealthy, but socially prominent — bringing out her well-groomed and immaculate side. Which made one think of a resplendent butterfly, freshly emerged from a cocoon. In her twenties, she had been a woman unhappily confined. In her thirties, she was the opposite: entertaining lavishly, entertained in kind, and making frequent trips to Europe with her husband and her father.

In the process, she formed close ties with the court. When the king built his summer palace in Niavaran, Amin Ashrafi had to sell a portion of his estate there, so as not to own a larger piece of land than his royal neighbor.

As I looked through our family albums, I suppose the period I fancied her to be at her very peak was when she was visiting Hamburg in the company of the king's daughter, Princess Shahnaz. The princess had just married the son of the former (and some say the king's favorite) Prime Minister. Both women were dazzling in those photographs. The princess in her black coat and white ermine collar, and Nasrin with her hair up, face thinner, cheekbones defined, and mouth open.

That was back in 1958. The photographs were taken in my parents' apartment, shortly before their return to Iran. And at which time I was in my third year of college.

Getting into college, like my going off to England, was a wrenching experience.

"College," at my school, meant basically Oxford or Cambridge, and I had long since settled on going to Cambridge. The British system, however, is geared essentially to turning out specialists through a lengthy process of examinations, and in taking these, I had fallen precariously between the arts and the sciences. My major subject was biology, and my other two — which should have been in related fields — were English literature and French. As such, I was no more than an all-round dilettante.

Some way had to be found of dealing with this problem.

Back in Hamburg, my parents had only the broadest notion of what was going on. To them, the English system of education was as complicated as its currency, and they left the details to me. They simply wanted me to "do well" in my studies. Beyond that, my mother entertained thoughts about my going into medicine or the diplomatic service. My father, on the other hand, had no doubt whatsoever that once my schooling was over, I would return to Hamburg to take a doctorate — not just a bachelor's degree, mind: with him, it was a matter of going straight to the top — in economics.

Now this melee of conflicting issues had somehow to sort itself out by the end of my last year in school.

I saw a way out in returning to America.

Which may not seem all that novel an idea — especially since I had been schooled there before. But the notion simply went against years of indoctrination and training. I had by then come not only to speak with an English accent, but to think English thoughts, accept English values, particularly in matters relating to education.

I applied to Harvard rather surreptitiously from Hamburg. Later, in spring, I took an absence from school to take the college entrance exams in London. Within weeks I received a letter of acceptance.

Thereafter, the thought of returning to America became increasingly attractive — and, furthermore, feasible.

All the same, this did not prevent me from applying to various colleges in Cambridge. It simply prolonged my indecision. I wrote to the Dean of Freshmen at Harvard that my coming was still tentative, then plunged into a slew of Cambridge entrance exams.

The last month of school was the traditional period of idleness: idyllic in the sense that those of us leaving had nothing to do but amuse ourselves, but otherwise hell in that we were awaiting results.

I delivered my final oration before the Debating Society on the downfall of the British Empire, which was both applauded and booed: applauded because I was the society's outgoing secretary, and booed for its content.

Then the rejections came in — from every college save one. A letter from the Master of Emmanuel — the great Welbourne himself — announced that a spot might be found for me in biology, although the matter was still pursuant to further considera tion.

I was ecstatic — though more torn now than ever. I decided to stay on in England that summer and await further word from the Master.

I was scheduled to do so anyway. My parents, after almost six years in Germany, had decided to visit Iran. The trip was business, but personal reasons entered as well. For one, my grandmother was ailing — more so than usual. So they planned a long stay, traveling by car and coming back around the beginning of September.

Eventually, another letter from Emmanuel informed me that my admission had been granted, but two years in advance — that whereas my work in biology had been found satisfactory, in other areas (chemistry, I suppose) I lacked readiness. The letter concluded by suggesting that I fill in the time by doing a stint in the army.

Which army, I thought: the British, the Iranian?

Not that my parents would have ever stomached such a thought. Two years away from schooling, and I would have been rooted to my father's business for life.

The matter was settled. It was well into August now. I cabled the Dean of Freshmen at Harvard that my coming was definite. Then I made plans to get back to Hamburg as quickly as possible. There was much work to be done in the few weeks ahead.

22

I returned to Hamburg around the beginning of September. My parents were due back from their auto trip shortly afterward.

Helga was off on vacation, and Gerta let me into our apartment. She also gave me a letter from my grandfather. It was written in Persian and said that I was to call him as soon as I arrived.

I hesitated, having had no counsel from my parents. When I phoned, however, Magdalena informed me that my mother had written them of my coming from Tehran.

I hadn't spoken with her for years. Yet she was warm and cheerful — chatting as though the passage of time and the family quarrel didn't matter.

She reiterated the point about my grandfather's wanting to see me right away — which I gathered to mean, before my parents' arrival. I went to their house for supper the following night.

Cyrus was away at summer camp. Magdalena was still prettyish, with her almost orange colored hair and dark blue dress. She had the same friendly laugh and warm feel of hands, with the well-manicured nails — which made her seem perennially unaging.

My grandfather took my hand in both of his and kissed me on either cheek. He was wearing a dark, pin-striped suit, with an Iranian flag in the lapel. His hair and mustache were immaculately dyed and groomed.

With an arm around me — we were the same height now, both five feet eight — he led me into the living room and had me sit in an armchair facing the long sofa, the two ends of which he and Magdalena occupied. He offered me *gaz* — an Iranian candy, made from crushed tamarisk roots — and pistachio nuts. Both, he said, were from Kerman.

Then he told me to give him an account of my schooling.

He listened attentively, as I spoke. Occasionally, Magdalena wanted to ask a question, but he held up his hand.

I continued talking through supper. Magdalena had made a point of having potato soup, which she knew to be my favorite. We had dessert afterward in the living room, with a cup of Turkish coffee for me. Then my grandfather left the room and came back with a gold wrist watch.

"Do you realize, Firuz," he said, "that you are the first person in our family to have a real education?"

He didn't say this as a compliment, but rather as a matter of fact. As such, no, I couldn't really say that I had considered the matter from that standpoint.

"And now you're going to go on to get an even better one. You've done that on your own. No one can ever take that away from you. What you will have in the end is a mind of your own. Ultimately, that's more important than gold. That's why you get this watch for your work. Such things as watches always come afterward. First comes the work."

He threw up his hands. "As for your uncles — even your mother and aunts — I wish I could say as much for them. They want the rewards to come first, before all the work. And so they end up being subservient to both status and money."

He smiled at this and went on. "Without having either. Am I correct in my thinking? Do we see eye to eye on this issue?"

I could hardly tell. It was almost as though I were reduced to a child again. My gratitude aside, I was still suspicious of him. Was this an attempt at putting a rift between my parents and me? Between the rest of our family and me — thereby isolating me, so that I had no one to turn to but him?

I glanced at Magdalena. She looked particularly content, with her knitting — but then, she was more isolated than anyone. She had no one to turn to but my grandfather. After he was gone, there would be only his money, and Cyrus was too young to be any support.

"I see what you mean." I nodded.

"I hope you do." My grandfather smiled. "Because I only mean to encourage you — to tell you to go on. In spite of the others. In spite of what they may say or how they may pressure you. Always remember this: you have your own life to lead, and that life comes first. With it, of course, comes responsibility to others, but not at the cost of oneself. Therein lies your strength: the true value of yourself. If you don't understand this," he concluded with a wink, "you're not a Turk."

Or a Greek, I thought, elaborating on his point. What about Ajax in Hades, still resentful of Odysseus for winning the armor of Achilles? Was that not what the notion of Hades was all about — that shadowy underworld, where spirits suffered throughout eternity for not having achieved to the fullest what had been meted out in a lifetime?

Was my grandfather driven by the same fears that had plagued the ancient Greeks: of going through life without living it totally — for himself?

At the door, he shook my hand sturdily, then held it. He told me to write him. That if he ever went to America, he would visit me. That I shouldn't forget Magdalena and Cyrus. That when I was finished with college, he would give me something better than a watch. That we had my future yet to talk about.

Then he kissed me on both cheeks again.

"Be firm. As long as you are firm, all will be well in the end. God go with you."

Magdalena slipped a soft package under my arm, with a ribbon around it. It was a blue sweater she had knitted for me. Then my grandfather's chauffeur drove me home — not in a Kaiser this time, but a Cadillac. The same color: black.

My parents showed up several days later, tired from their road trip, but with many stories to tell — interrupted constantly by telephone calls.

With their arrival, I became aware of the fact that they knew almost nothing at all of my going to Harvard. I had written them about it from England. They had even acknowledged as much, by congratulating me on my getting into "college." But somehow they had never actually digested the news. It floored me now to see that they didn't really make a distinction between Harvard and Cambridge.

My first impulse was to get agitated, as before. But that, I soon surmised, wouldn't help matters, since my parents were even more agitated than I was. My mother didn't wish me to be so far from them, and my father felt the pangs of my slipping away — not only that, but turning into an entirely different being from the one he had bargained for.

My only recourse was to stand fast and try to reason with them.

My father wasn't content with that. He argued angrily when I gave him a rundown of the expenses involved. The figures for Harvard were three times as high as those I had given him for Cambridge. The matter of my going came to turn around money. That provided an outlet. I offered to apply for a tuition scholarship, as well as an Iranian government grant: that would cut down the costs by half.

My father balked, but eventually agreed. He would give me a one-year trial, he said with finality. If I didn't get both awards by then, I would have to return to Hamburg — either to go into his business or take up studies in Europe.

I accepted his terms, and we kissed as friends. He said he was proud of me.

The cold thought crept over me: if he hadn't backed me up then, would I have turned to my grandfather?

In any case, for once throughout our stay in Germany, I saw a useful purpose to all our socializing. The pressures and bustle of social life diverted my parents' attention from my going. The matter, for me, was finally settled when I heard my mother excitedly chatting over the phone about her son being bound for college in America.

There were social gatherings every night, right up till the eve of my departure.

My last night in Hamburg, in fact, I left early from a dinner party at the Karimzadehs', in order to finish packing.

Even then, while packing, I wondered whether or not I was doing the right thing in going away again. Wasn't this, in a way, akin to insanity?

I felt lonely and wanted to cry.

Then the doorbell rang. I opened the door, and there in the hallway stood our old landlord, holding up two glasses of cognac — as though Christmas had come early that year. He came in and offered a toast.

After that he pressed my hand and offered a bit of solid advice:

"Firuz, du must fest sein!"

First, my grandfather. Then our old landlord. Both within a fortnight, counseling me to be "firm" — *"fest."*

Both had gone through wars and upheavals and managed to come through with something indomitable about them.

But what was there, I then wondered, to be "firm" or *"fest"* about?

23

I arrived at Harvard on a Sunday afternoon, the day before orientation was to begin. The cab pulled into the Yard and stopped in front of University Hall, the administration building — across from the statue of John Harvard, in fact. The driver and I had settled upon that as my destination, since I didn't know where to report to.

I paid the fare and got out. The building was closed, and the Yard practically deserted. Eventually, a janitor directed me to the basement of a building nearby.

I carried my bags, sweating, down the steps and through a hallway, where I met a man who turned out to be my future supervisor in Dorm Crew — the outfit charged with cleaning up rooms. He was an unsmiling, hefty fellow, who spoke — when he spoke at all — in a thick Bostonian accent, and looked, in his suit, like the young Edmond O'Brien in one of his gangster roles.

He glanced over the list of incoming freshmen for the room assigned to me. My name wasn't listed. I felt a surge of panic. Was it possible that the college had summarily dropped me? I gave him the letter from the Dean of Freshmen. He nodded and turned to another sheet of paper, found my name, crossed it off, and marked it down on the regular list.

"You haven't been given a room yet," he said. "I'll put you down for Wigglesworth. You can stay there till you get your regular assignment. The buildings won't open till tomorrow. Come back in the morning, and I'll give you your room number and key."

The way he spoke made it seem as though he looked upon all such dealings with disgust. I thanked him and picked up my bags. He asked where I was staying.

I told him I didn't know.

"Wait outside." He cocked his head. "I'll drive you over to the International Student Center. They can put you up for the night."

Now, normally, my reaction would have been to refuse this offer — allowing the man either to retract it or press it more firmly. But such a reaction seemed ludicrously out of place. Rococo even.

At the International Student Center, a friendly graduate student — clad in a gray Harvard sweat shirt, chino slacks, white socks and sneakers — led me up to a room with three beds. He offered me one for $2.50. Then he mentioned that there was going to be a spaghetti dinner downstairs at 50¢ a plate, and that I was "free to join in" — which confused me semantically. Did that mean the meal came with the room or not? In any case, I wasn't hungry.

I washed up and went downstairs to phone the only person in the area I knew.

Parviz Amuzegar had had a remarkable career as a student. He had graduated from prep school two years before, having spent his last year at Andover. He was now a junior at MIT, working toward a degree in chemical engineering. That much I had gathered from Nasrin and my mother.

What had amazed me, though, when I heard about all this, was how he had managed to move ahead so quickly, while adjusting to changes. He had switched from an Iranian to an American school — going from Persian to English — and picked up a year in the process, before proceeding to Andover. That, to me, was amazing by any standard. If my grandfather had thought of me as a worker, then what would he have thought of Parviz?

Actually, I had been longing to see him. The bond we had had in the past nurtured pleasant thoughts about our meeting again. I had imagined several ways of our reestablishing old ties.

But there was no answer. I called again later that evening.

I skipped supper and went out for a walk, taking along a map of the campus. The sky, though overcast, was still light. I passed Radcliffe Yard, then ambled through the Common, and caught sight of Memorial Hall — which struck me as a monstrosity: neither a church nor a fortress, but something in between — then turned up streets such as Sumner, Kirkland, and Irving.

The red bricks contrasted sharply with the other Cambridge I had in mind — the one with gray, Gothic architecture, and buildings alternately squeezed tightly together and spaced apart by huge green lawns. The meadow behind King's. The Cam.

In the middle of my walk, it began to rain. I took shelter in the doorway of a walk-up apartment building. Looking out the door, with its large plate of glass, I felt a searing sense of loneliness.

Yet, it would not be fair to say that I would have given anything to return to familiar surroundings. I accepted the fact that I was there to stay, and going back before I had finished what I had set out to do was unthinkable.

But it was also delicious to give in to one's feelings. I let the tears run down my cheeks, not wiping them. There was no indication that the rain was going to stop. I stepped outside and walked back, getting drenched.

In the process, my disposition changed. The sound of tires and the glare of lights on wet asphalt gave the place a new presence.

When I got back, there was a largish crowd in the living room.

Cups and cookies were set on a table. The friendly graduate student bade me join the circle.

I did so, without bothering to dry or change. A girl asked me if I wanted coffee or cocoa.

"Cocoa," I said, helping myself to a biscuit.

"You're English, aren't you?" She handed me a cup.

Then I went into what later became a routine for me: no, I was Iranian, but had been educated in England, though I had come to America to continue my studies. In the process, however, I found myself sounding more English than usual.

It was a strange phenomenon and, linguistically, one which I could never quite fathom.

Over the years that followed, my accent became increasingly Americanized. But any reminder of England — a reference to my school, say, or a moment of nostalgia, or the desire to phrase things a certain way — had the innate potential to bring out my linguistic *alter ego.*

So much may have been natural. But once that happened, it was a matter of sounding not just English, but English to the hilt. Of being English even to the point of caricature.

A group gathered around the table with the cups. The conversation turned from national backgrounds to politics. I held forth as usual, dipping freely into the plate of cookies, and made a defense — of all things — of British policies in the Middle East!

I tried to get through to Parviz for a week — still without success. He was living not in a dormitory, but in a place of his own on Memorial Drive. My mother had given me his address.

The weekend after my arrival, I walked along the banks of the Charles, looked up his apartment, and slipped a note in Persian into his mailbox.

Meanwhile, I had moved into my temporary quarters in Wigglesworth Hall — a two-bedroom suite allocated for three. It was smallish, comfortable, but barren.

I had found, to my surprise (I was always surprised in those days), that the college provided rooms with only the most basic furnishings: a bed with a mattress, a desk, and two chairs — plus a weekly change of sheets. The rest was up to the students.

My roommates, it turned out, were as transient as I was. One was a last-minute arrival from upstate New York, who had been bound for Cornell before suddenly hearing from Harvard. The other was a silent, expressionless youth, who rarely went out, and who was forever borrowing things — stationery, stamps, toothpaste, soap — as though he had come without a stitch and expected to be gone any moment: the heir to a fortune named Angus.

It was Angus who informed me one day that Parviz had called.

I called back and finally got hold of him. His voice sounded alien and distant. I couldn't connect it with the Parviz I had known. He spoke calmly, maturely — in a deep register which lacked emotion. All of which checked my impulse to be effusive. I found myself sounding unnaturally English again. Our opening and closing remarks were in Persian, but the rest of the conversation — which didn't amount to much more than a series of questions and answers — was conducted in English. He had an Iranian accent, though not a heavy one.

I mentioned that I had tried to reach him a number of times. He replied that he had been late getting back, but didn't go into details. Despite the steadiness of his diction, he conveyed the sense that he was in a rush. He suggested that we meet over coffee at the "Hayes-Bick on Mass. Ave."

I had rather been hoping that he would ask me over to his apartment. The conversation put a damper on me.

We met at the Hayes-Bickford as planned. He was there ahead of me, seated at a table with a blonde in a pink blouse — her hair tied back in a bun.

He had said nothing about another person over the phone, and I had expected our get-together to be a private occasion.

We recognized each other instantly. His facial features were the same as before: the thin lips, the delicate lines to his nose and jaw. But his eyes seemed smaller, sharper, behind horn-rimmed glasses. His hairline peaked above the temples, and the hair itself — which was a darker brown than his mother's — had lost its boyish texture. It was thick and wavy, and gave his face, which narrowed at the chin, a somewhat triangular shape.

He was handsome in a distinctive way, which was underscored — oddly enough — by his clothing. He had on a white shirt, a blue and white ascot, and a brown tweed sports jacket with an English cut and a matching handkerchief in his breast pocket, all of which set him off as being both distinguished and casual.

Also, although he was only a year older than I was, he seemed well into his twenties — not a boy anymore, but decidedly a young man.

He got up and shook my hand. He was slightly taller than I was and slimmer — almost frail, with his narrow waist and hips. Not athletic. I was surprised to see mocassins on his feet.

"Meet Gloria." He waved a hand at the blonde. "She's a sophomore at Lesley."

"I'm happy to meet you." I made an Iranian bow.

"So am I." She grinned broadly and blinked. "I've heard so much about you. Parviz tells me that you knew each other as kids in Iran."

She pronounced "Parviz" and "Iran" without an American accent.

I was about to sit down, when Parviz told me that the place was self-service.

"Why don't you get your coffee first, then we can talk for a bit." He consulted his watch. "I have to be off pretty soon."

I asked if either cared for another cup. Parviz shook his head, but Gloria held hers up.

"Plenty of cream, please," she said, blinking again.

When I returned with the coffee, the two were in private session.

"Well," said Parviz, breaking the mood, as I sat down, "tell us what brings you to this part of the world."

Actually, I had already gone over the matter briefly on the phone. I delved into the details of my course of studies in England — covering more ground than necessary. Parviz encouraged me to talk, not knowing much about the English system of education. He detected that I had some doubts about my decision to come to America.

"Never mind," he said, at the end of what amounted to a monologue on my part. "You made the right choice. The place will seem different to you, once you get used to things."

Odd, I thought. Here was Parviz giving me moral support about schooling in America, whereas the last time I had seen him, I had been the one who had just returned from the country. He hadn't even known English then.

"What do you plan on majoring in?" he asked.

"I don't know," I replied. "Perhaps I'll go into English."

"You're bound to do well in that." Gloria placed her fingers on the back of my hand. "Your English is perfect. And so is your accent. I just love it. Don't lose that while you're over here."

I noticed that her nails were bitten. Not down to the quick, but far enough to lose their oval shape.

"Are you majoring in anything?" I retorted clumsily.

"Psychology." She nodded. "Though I wish I'd gone to Radcliffe for that." She glanced at Parviz. "They have so many better courses than we do."

"Gloria," Parviz said with a firmness in his voice, "all you have to do is sit in on them. It's not going to kill you to do a little extra work on your own."

Had that been what they had been talking about?

Gloria nodded and looked down at the table.

Parviz glanced at his watch again.

"What about you?" I turned to him, not wanting him to leave without saying something about himself. "I spoke with your mother, but I never did understand at what point you decided to change to the American system."

Parviz eyed me and smiled. He had not really looked at me directly before.

"We'll save that for another time," he said. "I've got to get back for an eleven o'clock class."

He got up.

Well, I thought, as far as that goes, I've got an eleven o'clock class myself. But I was quite willing to forego it. After all, how often did such meetings occur — spaced apart by so many changes and years?

It was an unsatisfactory end to our encounter. I didn't feel as though the ice had been broken — notwithstanding my long, personalized account, which had been intended, I suppose, to do that. Parviz had responded as an interested listener, rather than, shall I say, a participant in the same life history.

That aside, between us sat Gloria. It was evident — just from that meeting — that the two of them had a life of their own. One which made my arrival on the scene seem somewhat of an intrusion.

When was the barrier between us ever to go down? There was always a third party to our friendship which took priority. In Iran it had been Bijan. Here it was Gloria.

I walked them to Parviz's car, which was parked on a side street. The two got into a green Lotus convertible. Parviz started the engine and rolled down the window.

"We'll have to see each other again soon," he said, putting on his prescription sunglasses. "I've got your phone number, and you've got mine. So let's keep in touch."

Then he drove off with a rattling sound — and I returned to the Yard to start a course on the Epic Tradition.

24

*G*loria Anne Brady was the eldest daughter of Colonel Edmund Brady, U.S. Army, and his wife, Edna, both residents then of Alexandria, Virginia. Colonel Brady had been stationed — along with his family — for three years in Iran, as military attaché at the American embassy. Both Gloria and her sister had attended the American Community School in Tehran. There she had met and "gone steady" with Parviz. She had been in the tenth grade and Parviz in the eleventh. The year after that, her father had been transferred to Washington, D.C., and the family returned to America. That was the year Parviz had gone to Andover. She had finished high school in Alexandria. Since Parviz, by then, was attending MIT, she decided to come to Lesley. She had applied to Radcliffe, but hadn't been accepted. Actually, she would rather have gone to Briarcliff or Swarthmore, but the fact that Parviz was in Cambridge more or less eliminated them as possibilities.

So much I learned from Gloria, while she was cooking supper for us in Parviz's apartment, some two weeks later. Parviz had called to say that he would be late, on account of a "chem lab."

And I had arrived with a letter in my pocket, informing me, finally, of my room change. That night was to be my last in Wigglesworth.

After the phone call, while I was making the salad, the conversation became surprisingly intimate.

About a year or so after her arrival in Iran, Gloria had had an affair with an Iranian of Greek origin at the school. The school then had a large enrollment of students with different backgrounds — many whose families had left Europe during the Second World War. This student, an accordion player who had a band of his own, apparently had pressed her to marry him, with the intention of emigrating to America. Colonel Brady found out and intervened. The boy was paid off, and the affair was brought to an end. Gloria, as a result, suffered miserably — both wanting her lover, yet disgusted by his imposture. She turned to Parviz "as a friend."

Listening to Gloria's account, I began to surmise why Parviz had put off explaining his reasons for coming to America. Mingled with educational considerations were ulterior motives.

It was a tribute to my kind of naiveté then that I thought of my educational background as being more complex than those of others. It wasn't really. Complications abound — especially for those who study abroad. Though why limit it to that?

Gloria, in any case, didn't touch upon any of that. What she went into instead was her growing attachment to Parviz. Both, she said, derived a sense of support from each other. Both had felt "isolated" in Iran. Parviz had witnessed his mother's second marriage. That had affected him more deeply than his parents' divorce. The divorce had stimulated him to become more intellectually self-reliant — his father having always been alien to him anyway. But the marriage had made him more keenly aware of his emotional needs — and those of others as well. He was understanding of her in a way that was difficult to qualify.

As for her, she saw something quite special in him. His refinement, no doubt, had something to do with it. But more than that, it had to do with the honesty with which he applied his intellect. His will. His brain power. It was Parviz, really, who had shown her what to do with herself. Up till she met him, she had been merely vacillating — seeking approval wherever it was to be found. With him she felt stable, grounded — self-aware. More than that, on a course of her own, supporting him, emotionally, the way he supported her.

She laughed bashfully at her unrestrained account.

"We're quite happy, you know. He's grumpy at times and puts a lot of pressure on himself. But it's worth it to have the communication we do."

It made eminent sense to me. And it wasn't just because of the sherry we were drinking, which rushed to my head and made me feel benevolent toward the whole human race. I was grateful for her openness.

She looked prettier, too, in that kitchen, than the time we had met. Her hair, for one thing, which had been gathered into a bun, fell freely down to her shoulders. It was a lovely mixture of uneven blond — light on the outside and dark within, as though a distinction were drawn between exterior and interior.

Moreover, she had soft, pale skin and blue eyes, which I hadn't gazed into before. Nor noted her shape. Her skirt swayed as she walked — as did her hands, which she held close to her breasts. Full breasts. Narrow waist. White legs.

None of which I had previously taken in. Possibly because of the frumpish outfit she'd had on — a reflection of the style of the fifties. But also because my attention had been focused on Parviz.

We took our sherry into the living room — Gloria next to the floor lamp. She pulled up her legs, exposing a thigh. I immediately pictured her naked.

Before us, on the coffee table, was an ivory chess set, with large pieces lined up for combat.

The apartment didn't look at all like that of a college student. The building was modern, with air conditioning and wall-to-wall carpeting. The window, which overlooked the Charles, took up half a wall and had ceiling-to-floor drapes. In front of it was an antique bench, with a row of potted plants. In the middle of the room, between the coffee table and the two armchairs facing the sofa, was a lively red and black Turkoman carpet. Behind the armchairs were bookcases and an array of record-playing equipment. Across the room from the window, next to the kitchen, was a cocktail tray on rollers: with bottles, glasses, ice bucket, shaker — the lot.

The whole ensemble projected the life style of a man who was holding down a steady position.

Or that of a young married couple.

I noticed, later that evening, on my way to the bathroom, the double bed. There were cosmetics and cream jars on the shelves over the toilet. And the kitchen itself was organized the way a woman would want it: with a spice rack, matching pots, dishes, and utensils, and a row of cook books.

The whole place, in fact, had a domestic and settled aura about it, which contrasted sharply with my own barren, temporary quarters.

Parviz came in with a carton of ice cream — our dessert, it turned out. He took off his jacket and fixed himself a drink: a martini on the rocks without the olive or onion. Gloria put the ice cream away and tended to the supper.

"What are you having — sherry?" he said over his shoulder. "How about a refill?"

I declined — I was already feeling the effect of what I had drunk — then I changed my mind. Why not another? I was thankful for being slightly inebriated anyway. The drinking had changed my mood.

I had come predisposed to be somewhat cool toward Parviz — having felt snubbed by his distance over the phone and the lack of rapport at our meeting. Which feeling grew into resentment, at not finding him present on my arrival. It was as though a statement were being made about our new relationship: that I was no longer of any central concern to him, but existed merely as a figure peripheral to his stay in America.

It was so clearly evident that he had a life of his own — his schedule, his apartment, his closeness to Gloria. All these punctuated the gap between us.

But the sherry — and listening to Gloria — had dissipated the bitterness. I was mellow. In the mood for another try.

Parviz plumped into an armchair and nodded at the chess set.

"Do you play?" he asked in Persian.

"Not well."

"Never mind." He bolted down his drink. "I'll give you a game before supper. Gloria," he called out in English, "is there time for another drink and a game before supper?"

"Go ahead," Gloria said from the kitchen. "It's only pot roast." She added, "Firuz made the salad."

"You take the white," Parviz beckoned, getting up to mix another drink. Then he sat on the floor, across from me.

He mated me in an embarrassingly quick series of moves.

"I told you I wasn't good," I apologized.

"You weren't ready," he said, setting up the pieces again. "Next time you'll do better."

I played the second game more cautiously. All the same, I was being soundly beaten by the time Gloria rejoined us. She sat in the same seat, under the light, and tucked up her legs.

"I give in." I threw up my hands.

Parviz smiled. "We'll reverse the board."

"I'm afraid that won't help."

Parviz — for the first time — let out a laugh.

"Don't let that bother you," Gloria addressed me. "He plays on the chess team and doesn't want anyone to know until he has thoroughly trounced him. I don't agree with his tactics, but there it is."

"That's not true," Parviz laughed again. He, too, was beginning to feel his liquor. "The point is, I like to play chess — regardless of whether it's serious or not. Any game is a challenge. So were these, Firuz."

He actually leaned over and patted my shoulder. "Tell me,

would you still have played, if you had known I was on the chess team?"

"Why not?" I made an elaborate gesture. Actually, my head was reeling.

"There, you see?" Parviz cast a glance at Gloria. "I'm not the ogre you make me out to be."

Gloria rolled her eyes and said that supper was ready.

Parviz was jovial. The two martinis — along with his demonstration of prowess at chess — had taken effect. He opened a bottle of red wine, and we sat down to the pot roast.

Gloria wanted to hear about our childhood in Iran. Parviz laughed and made a few allusions to our past. Then he launched into a narrative of the horse-riding incident — the one in which Bijan had lost his eye. The way he went over it was such that all the horrifying details were left out. There was no mention of Bijan's losing an eye, or of the beating, or the separation which had come about between his parents. Rather the episode reflected a boyhood escapade: Bijan, Parviz, and I getting into just another one of our scrapes.

After supper, which we ate in the kitchen, we moved back into the living room. Parviz lit up a pipe. Gloria, after clearing the dishes, poured out cordials. We resumed our places — Gloria under the lamp, with a bag of knitting by her side.

I asked Parviz how he had come to decide to study in America.

"Well, you can't get a good background in physics or chemistry in Iranian schools." He spoke through his pipe. "So I would have had to make the switch sooner or later. I decided on the sooner."

"But why to America?" I asked.

"My best subject was math, so there was no problem with that. Iranian schools are good in that field. It was a matter of defining one's position in the sciences. Not that math is strictly a science, I admit." He waved a hand at Gloria and smiled. "But the sciences are what I was interested in. And America offers the best in that area."

"What about England?" I was conscious of sounding English.

"Weren't you intending to go there? At least, that was what I gathered from your mother."

"No, not England," he shook his head. "It may have been something she wanted — possibly because she liked the idea of your being there. That might have set a precedent. But it wouldn't have worked out for me."

"Why not?"

"The language, for one thing. In Iran I had tutoring in English — which was enough to get me into Community School, but not enough to prepare me for England. In England I would have fallen behind in my studies — whereas I was already ahead in the sciences."

I nodded.

"You see, in your case, you started with English at a very early age — before you had found any direction in your studies. With me, it was the other way round. I took up English primarily because of the education that went with it. I could just as well have thought in terms of studying in France or Germany. But America, from my standpoint, offered the best possibilities. There is no better place, really, for studying engineering. MIT is a case in point."

He glanced at Gloria.

"Though, I admit, there is something to be said for Cal Tech."

"Are you going to go on for a doctorate?" I asked.

To Iranians the doctorate was more than just a degree: it was the status symbol of the elite.

He shrugged. "It's too early to say."

"Oh, no, it isn't." Gloria shook her head. She spoke louder in his presence than when we had been by ourselves. "That was no casual reference to Cal Tech."

Parviz smiled. "In any case, I'd have to return to Iran before going on to do graduate work. I couldn't just jump into a field, with only a theoretical background. I'd have to consider the applied side as well. It's no use pursuing a particular line of research in America which has little or no application in Iran."

He got up and reached for the bottle of cordial.

"Another round for everyone?"

He filled all three glasses and sank back into his chair.

"Actually, Firuz," he continued, refilling his pipe, then lighting it, "I'll have to modify a part of what I said about my reasoning for taking up English. My motivation wasn't entirely academic."

He smiled. "Do you remember the time in Ramsar, when you and I went for a walk with Mrs. Karimzadeh and my stepfather?"

My mind rushed back to the scene in the garden. Yet it also stopped at the reference to his stepfather. It was true, of course, that Karbalai was his stepfather. But how he was going to refer to him was something which I had been vaguely wondering about. The term "stepfather" seemed, somehow, to indicate a degree of closeness — bridging the gap between different family names.

Parviz, after all, was still an Amuzegar.

"The three of you talked about languages," he went on. "You probably don't remember. But it was then that I started thinking seriously about picking up another language — not just casually at school, but to use as you did. With only Persian behind me, I lacked the mobility you had."

Mobility and languages. The same association Abol Karimzadeh had made several years ago.

"I do remember," I put in hastily. Then I said something I wished I hadn't. "You weren't jealous of us, were you?"

It was the wrong thing to say. A woozy blunder which rolled off my tongue.

"Of course not." Parviz's smile vanished. "I merely noted a lack in myself."

He crossed his legs — his sudden aloofness making it clear that I had insulted him.

Then I saw a character trait in him that had been there all along — cloaked in childhood, but discernible now. Parviz lacked a sense of humor.

Like his father, perhaps, as I had come to think of him.

The recognition — the comparison — made me even more awkward. I, too, reacted the way my father would have done. With joviality, to cover up the discomfort.

201

"Well, things have certainly changed since then." I laughed.

Oh, no, I thought, as soon as the statement was out. He'll think I'm referring to the circumstances in his life: his parents' divorce and his mother's remarriage. I was alluding, in fact, to his grasp of another language. Intentions and words were pulling in opposite directions. I forged ahead anyway — relying on words for their sound, rather than any concrete meaning.

"It's really very strange, going over the past the way we're doing. It makes things seem different from the way one normally thinks of them. I mean, the process is somewhat like seeing a head attached to a pair of legs, with no torso in between. Which I haven't, but still. What I mean is, the past, I daresay, would have seemed more alike to both of us, had we grown up together — instead of having just the past and the present, as we have now, divided by an interim I'm not making any sense."

"Yes, you are." Gloria nodded over her knitting. "I know what you mean. I experienced the same thing when I got back from Iran."

I waited for her to go on, but she didn't. Then I saw a way out of my dilemma and turned back to Parviz.

"I mean, take Bijan, for example. He is fixed in my mind as the person I knew. But, surely, he must be different to you, who have known him all along."

"Oh, I don't know about that!" Gloria put down her knitting. "He's just as impossible now as ever."

The comment took me aback. It indicated a degree of familiarity with Parviz's family which I hadn't expected.

"He's in trouble all the time. He won't settle down to any work. He lives it up with his cronies. Gets people into trouble. Gets women into trouble — all the time. He's busted up one marriage already. He's made a mess of his father's business."

"Gloria," Parviz intervened.

"Well, it's true." Gloria eyed him. "What would he do if your grandfather didn't bail him out all the time? Now your father has gotten into the act."

She looked at me. "Parviz's father has gotten him into the army. Not that that's going to do any good. He's going through

202

the Officers Training School. I can just see what's going to come of that."

"Gloria tends to exaggerate." Parviz knocked the ashes out of his pipe.

"Gloria doesn't exaggerate, my pet," she said in a lower key.

She was a mystery to me. Quiet, soft-spoken, and warm in the kitchen, before Parviz's arrival. Then loud — even to the point of being abrasive — in his presence. Now softer again, in arguing with him. I wondered what the exact nature of the attraction between them was.

At any rate, they were at cross-purposes. Parviz wanting to cover up, and Gloria to expose. The former sitting rigidly still, while the latter shifted her position on the sofa.

"I mean, the guy has done all sorts of things. You wouldn't believe it, Firuz." She blinked at me. "He's been shot in the back by a policeman, jumping over a wall, while he was breaking into a house — for the fun of it. The house of the Swedish ambassador. The affair was hushed up — though I'm sure you've heard of it."

Which came across as a contradiction: her asking me to believe something which I was already supposed to have known. I hadn't.

"Everyone has," she continued. "He's gotten away with other burglaries — also for fun. He goes down Pahlavi Avenue, standing on a motorcycle. I've seen him do it! He's crazy. He's a case study. And what burns me is that everyone makes him out to be normal."

She shook her head. "I don't know. It bothers me. It bothers Parviz as well, only he covers up for him — like the rest."

There was silence.

"Have you finished?" Parviz said from a distance.

Gloria glared at him.

"Because if you have, I'd better drive Firuz home. It's getting late."

It was an unsatisfactory close to our evening. Parviz and I had failed to hit it off. Parviz and Gloria had embarked on a quarrel. Parviz was distant. Gloria was pouting. And I was feeling queasy.

Not at all how I'd hoped the occasion would be.

Parviz drove me home in the Lotus. The conversation in the car was forced and uncomfortable. All the more so for me, because of a recurrence of my damnable motion sickness.

I said good night in a flash and rushed up in time to throw up into the toilet bowl.

I threw up twice — disgorging all that I had eaten and drunk. I dropped my clothes on the floor and climbed into bed in my underwear. My legs felt supportless, but my brain was teeming with clarity.

Parviz had driven me home in his Lotus. I was a long way off from having a Lotus myself. I was a scholarship applicant.

Parviz was the grandson of Ashrafi — the self-made millionaire whose fortunes were ever growing. The son of Amuzegar — the landowner and now one of the heads of the army. And the stepson of Karbalai — the industrialist. As such, he was the scion of one of the wealthiest collections of families in Iran.

No wonder, then, that he had been all along cool to me. The distance between us had been measured not only by time, but by money.

25

Parviz and I didn't see much of each other in college.

After my room change, I fell in with a new set of friends — a garrulous pack of scholarship students who studied and worked part time during the day and spent the night talking. We remained a clique throughout college.

Then there was my own scholarship to think of. Getting one came to be the preoccupation of my first semester — keeping it, my main business thereafter. As a result, I fell into the kind of academic groove that cuts one off from the outside world.

Still, Parviz and I did have occasional contact during my

freshman year. We went to the Harvard-Yale football game, took in a musical show in Boston which he had extra tickets to, and, in spring, we picnicked at Walden Pond with some of his friends. We were always in the company of others. Always with Gloria. Never by ourselves.

At the end of that year, he and Gloria returned to Iran for the summer.

When they got back in the fall, they had a gift for me from Nasrin: a silver cigarette case, engraved on both sides. On one side was a floral pattern; on the other was a medieval hunting scene: an archer on horseback, caught in the act of shooting a leaping doe.

The gift struck me as being singularly beautiful — especially since it wasn't the sort of thing I expected to be given me.

I wasn't smoking then, though I had thought of doing so. The question was, how to begin? I needed reasons. Prompting. Why? Because it was also fixed in my mind that smoking was a vice. My parents, all along, had been firmly against it — ever since my father had resolutely given it up years ago in Iran. I had seen them usher guests politely to the door, then rush back to the living room to throw open the windows and empty ashtrays with unspoken disgust.

The cigarette case made the difference. I liked the feel of its weight in the breast pocket of my jacket. I carried it with me on special occasions. During the intermissions of concerts or plays, I would open it and take out a cigarette. Then I would close the lid and tap the cigarette on both ends, before putting it to my lips.

I tried writing Nasrin a letter of thanks in Persian — which turned out to be difficult. I was too conscious of my shaky grammar and penmanship. And so the task was put off until it became a guilty omission.

After returning from Iran, Parviz buried himself in his course work. He spent most of his time in his lab. Gloria phoned me once to break off a tentative dinner engagement. We were supposed to have eaten out at a restaurant in my area, but Gloria canceled for Parviz on account of an upcoming test. Parviz, she went on, was finding his last year the hardest. He was taking all the courses he wanted, but these were also the toughest, and he was determined to do well in them all.

She also let it out — though I don't think she intended to — that he was trying to make Phi Beta Kappa.

In any case, I didn't hear from them again until the following spring, when I received an announcement of their wedding. Parviz and Gloria had gotten married at the home of her parents in Alexandria.

The news jolted me. Not because I hadn't expected them to marry — in fact, I thought of them as practically married already — but because, here they were, friends, a few miles away, and they hadn't breathed a word about it.

Questions came to mind: was the whole thing done in haste and secrecy? If so, why? Were they wary somehow of word getting out before the event? Again, why? Why the private wedding, with notices sent out afterward?

I called Parviz's number several times, before finally getting hold of Gloria. She sounded flustered, but happy — too busy to go into details properly and promising to do so another time. As a result, I received a quasi-logical account.

Parviz and she had decided to get married in May rather than June, because, for one thing, her parents had to go off to the Philippines. (For a vacation? Another tour of duty abroad? We never got to that.) For another, Parviz wanted to get back to Iran to start work on a project with his stepfather. Yet they also wanted to have time for a honeymoon in Europe.

Did that mean, I interjected, that they weren't going to be returning to America?

Not for a while, she replied. In a few years perhaps, since Parviz was quite serious about going on to graduate school. At any rate, they were also in a rush to set out on their honeymoon — which was more important, they thought, than an elaborate wedding in the States. A larger wedding would have brought in friends and relatives from all over. A small, quiet one in Virginia served the purpose just as well, since her side of the family — grandparents included — had been present.

Had Parviz's parents been present, too?

No, they hadn't. Parviz had explicitly asked them not to come, because there was going to be another ceremony to go through in Iran anyway. A Moslem ceremony, she tittered. Gloria was going to be a Moslem.

I said something facetious about the material pleasures of an Islamic paradise.

Whereupon she retorted with conviction, "Oh, it's fascinating, Firuz!" I didn't know whether to take her seriously or not. "Don't knock your faith. It's got some better things to offer than Christianity has."

I asked where things stood regarding her own graduation.

Well, she sighed, she still had a year to go and some units to make up, owing to her switch into sociology. (The first I'd heard about that.) But she could always finish her degree requirements, when Parviz went on to do graduate work.

She apologized for rushing: there was so much to take care of before going to Europe. She rounded off the conversation by insisting that I not send them a wedding gift. It would only mean more packing for her.

"What would really be nice," she concluded, "what would really please me, Firuz, would be for you to come and see us in Iran. I'll need friends there, whom I can talk to — like you."

I hung up dissatisfied. I hated the telephone for being such a convenience — such an easy substitute for personal contact. The trouble with it was that it led to other substitutes. Gloria and I saying goodbye without seeing each other made it all the more feasible somehow for Parviz to bow out altogether.

It was shortly thereafter, I gather, that Parviz learned that he hadn't been elected to Phi Beta Kappa. They set off for Europe before his graduation. His diploma was forwarded to Iran by mail.

That same summer — in July 1958 — my grandfather died. I received the news from my mother in a short, typewritten letter — which was rather like being apprised of the facts through an obituary column.

My grandfather had died of a heart attack, she wrote, in his sleep, leaving everyone stunned, since his health had been considered sound. My parents had attended the funeral. I was asked to write a note of condolence to Magdalena and Cyrus in German.

Even these facts — bare as they were — were not strictly accurate.

My grandfather, I later found out, had been ill for a year after a bout of pneumonia. He had been ordered to rest at home and leave his business to others — a directive he must have found hard to follow. As for the stunned response to his death, Magdalena had woken up one morning to find him dead beside her: that was the real shocker.

Why could I not have been told as much in the letter? When I posed the question to my mother, she replied simply that she wanted to spare me the details. Which I took to mean that death, like sex, was not a subject for open discussion. Especially between parents and children.

Yet there was a difference.

Attitudes about sex one could chalk up to the mores of society. Reactions toward death went deeper. They involved the world of superstition: to dwell on its particulars — to linger over its details, as my mother put it — was tantamount to tendering it an invitation.

At any rate, after my grandfather's death, my parents and Magdalena resumed their old ties. More than that: they became closer to each other. Even my father. Magdalena was alone — the sole person in charge of my grandfather's business. He was eager to help her.

So my parents took to having supper at her house — just as they had upon their arrival in Hamburg. And, for a brief while, their lives seemed to intersect at every key point.

Then came the disclosure of my grandfather's will, which caused another major cleavage in the family.

The will settled his property and business in Hamburg jointly on Magdalena and Cyrus. The other wives and children were meted out equal amounts of cash, which some went through in a year, and the more affluent invested. The grandchildren — myself included — received nothing at all.

This, my mother still claims, had not been my grandfather's original intention: he having, apparently, confided in her, at some point, about another form of distribution.

The will was eventually contested in court. It was challenged on the ground that it deviated from Islamic practice, and that my grandfather had been an Iranian and a Moslem. Wives, according to Islamic laws of inheritance, are entitled to equal shares of one eighth of the husband's estate, while children receive the rest: the sons getting twice as much as the daughters. The court, however, ruled that since my grandfather had also been an *Inlander* — or German resident — his legal affairs in the country came under the jurisdiction of German law. The will was upheld.

All this didn't come about until later. By which time, feelings and circumstances had coalesced into an embittered, drawn-out family feud. Meanwhile, another revelation caused immediate sparks to fly.

A favorite had emerged from my grandfather's will: his son by his Turkish wife — the one who had followed his advice and gone into business with him, supplying him with carpets from Tehran. This son, my half-uncle, was designated as Cyrus's guardian and my grandfather's successor in taking over the management of Haus Teheran. Not ownership, mind. That was to remain in the hands of Magdalena and Cyrus. But the actual running of the business.

My mother was greatly put out by this. It brought into the picture a half-brother she didn't trust — and who had very little knowledge of German, let alone running a business in Germany. And it deprived her of being Cyrus's guardian herself — which was something she had all along looked forward to.

Evidently, my grandfather had talked to her one way and acted another.

In any case, as matters stood after the will — with managerial powers given over to one son and most of the wealth passed on to two principal beneficiaries — clearly the Turkish and German sides of the family had profited at the expense of the original, the Iranian.

Magdalena, let me add — and I can only surmise as much from my parents' accounts — wasn't in the least bit disturbed by any of this. She was quite happy to have a family member look after the day-to-day end of the business: it freed her to lead a life of her own. As for my half-uncle's guardianship of Cyrus, that meant next to nothing at the time: it was tantamount to giving her total control. And that is precisely what she had: total control over domestic affairs. Over her home and her child. Her only contact with my half-uncle was at the office.

A strange twosome they must have made: he, newly arrived from Tehran — with a Turkish wife acquired on the way — speaking Turkish all the time. No German. She, a German in her own country, having to communicate with him — and through him to buyers in Iran — in Persian!

Anyway, whatever the oddities of their relationship, a new Magdalena emerged from the shell of the old one. Henceforward, she went to the office only when necessary. (She soon had a secretary take her place in the back room.) She attended concerts and plays, cultivated friendships with people — Germans — she had known only slightly before. She indulged in a little overeating. In clothing, she experimented with colors.

I like to picture her as raising the hems of her skirts a fashionable inch or two.

And she had that awful dog put away! (It had gone mad after the death of its master.)

In fact, she had a phrase for herself which she laughingly divulged to my mother, and which gave a sort of vivid focus to her self-image: *"die lustige Witwe!"* she called herself.

My mother, too, had to laugh when she remembered that.

My mother had a distinctly twofold response to the change in Magdalena: one as a relative, whose fortunes and feelings had been hurt; the other as a friend, who was sincerely glad to see her break through constraints. As my grandfather's daughter, she couldn't help feeling jealous and resentful at having been cast aside so spuriously — so connivingly, she claimed. But as a onetime confidante — as a woman — she was moved to feel sympathy: even satisfaction. Possibly also — despite being locked in a quarrel — a newfound admiration.

And so she could lash out and laugh at once.

With my father, it was different. His reaction was more un-equivocal.

From his standpoint, he had offered Magdalena — at a trying point in her life — as much help as was possible. He had further suggested that they join forces and go into business together — which, after all, was what my grandfather had wanted all along. But all these gestures and offers of support had been gently but firmly turned down. Finally, with my half-uncle's arrival, it became evident that she had interests of her own — interests which she was well aware of, and which, given the circumstances, conflicted with his.

So my father changed his tune and made one last attempt at recovering his losses: namely, the carpets my grandfather had embezzled from him. Magdalena and my half-uncle stood fast and united, refusing to acknowledge any misdealings in the past.

And thus the lawsuit was instigated.

The Iranian side of the family supported my parents in challenging the will: the spearhead of that challenge being my mother.

It was, as I say, a bitter period in my family's history — with factions being split for almost a decade.

The story, though, had a much grimmer ending.

Shortly after the court's decision, Magdalena found she had cancer of the breast. The cancer then spread. Within one year of my grandfather's death, *die lustige Witwe* was laid to rest by his grave.

Cyrus was no more than a schoolboy then. My half-uncle became his guardian in fact as well as in name. Cyrus was then put into a boarding school in Switzerland. My half-uncle assumed full control of the business as the head of the family.

Some say that he was out to steal Cyrus's inheritance; others that he was waiting for the day when Cyrus would finish his studies and come into business with him — taking over the management of Haus Teheran — so that he could return to Iran and his beloved nook in the bazaar, supplying Cyrus with carpets, as he had their father before.

(The truth was that my mother's instincts were right: my

211

half-uncle never did adjust to Germany. He lacked, one could say, the crucial ingredient: a subservient Magdalena to help him.)

At any rate, the issue is moot. For, after finishing his schooling, Cyrus, at the age of eighteen, was given a car. Driving through Scandinavia — ironically, as he was passing through his native Sweden — he was killed in a crash.

With the death of Cyrus, the German side of my family came to an end. (My grandfather's brother, by then, had moved with his family to Nice.) And Haus Teheran passed into the sole hands — temporarily — of my half-uncle. Whose wife never did learn to speak a word of German.

These setbacks aside, business in Hamburg had not gone well for my father. His income from the sale of cotton had fallen so far below expectation that he had moved into another line of import-export.

Ever since their car trip to Iran, in fact, my parents had been ruminating about another move back. Their letters reflected as much: my father complaining about the slowness of pace at the office, and my mother wistfully passing on news from Tehran.

On the whole, it was an uncomfortable situation for both of them — neither profitable nor satisfying. Yet it was also the kind of existence which was easy to prolong. Something was needed to prod them out of their static ambivalence.

The death of my grandfather, of course, was one such factor. With his death, my parents had thought, at first, of definitely staying: of joining forces — in some magic way — with Magdalena. (Helping her with Cyrus. The business. Becoming partners in Haus Teheran. God knows what else. Possibly even bringing the two households together.)

When that bubble burst — followed by litigation and loss of face — the response was to move in the opposite direction: to leave. To start anew in their own country.

But this was reacting negatively. My parents — my father

especially — needed positive incentives. Being an optimist, he was ever looking for support and advice from someone around him. This time that someone, I think, was Ahmad Karimzadeh.

Around the middle of September — the start of my junior year, and about the time relations between Magdalena and my parents had begun to sour — I received a letter from my mother, giving a detailed account of a party they had attended at the Karimzadehs'. They wouldn't have gone, she qualified, in deference to my grandfather's death, except that the party was thrown in honor of Farid's and Mahin's graduations: Farid's from college and Mahin's from school. Up till then, the whole family — barring Ahmad — had been in Switzerland.

In contrast to my family, the summer of 1958 was a particularly revitalizing period for the Karimzadehs.

Farid, at twenty-five, had earned his degree in economics from the University of Lausanne. Perhaps a late age to be finishing college, but not all that late considering the results. He had picked up English and German, as well as French — which is not bad for a person who once stuttered and struggled with languages. Moreover, with his theoretical training behind him, he was ready to step into his father's business.

Matin, at twenty-three, was to follow suit a year behind him. He would have finished at the same time as his brother, except for a lingering illness — hepatitis — which had forced him to rest. But he was cured now, though forbidden to drink alcohol.

Their sister, Mahin — who my mother gleefully claimed to be the smartest of them all — had finished her girls' school "at the top of her class," and had just been admitted to the prestigious Polytechnikum in Zürich. She, unlike her brothers, had decided to pursue her higher education in mathematics and exclusively in German.

The only apparent problem in that family was Mina Karimzadeh's chronic backache. She had taken to seeing doctors regularly and putting on and taking off a back support.

But even that was temporarily under control, when my parents went to see them.

Mina Karimzadeh, my mother wrote, was all smiles, though putting on weight. Mahin was not only bright but beautiful —

clearly the focal point of the family's attention. Moreover — again, as opposed to her brothers — she was athletic. She skied and played field hockey. And still went riding, of course.

My parents — my mother especially — practically idolized Farid and Mahin. Farid was a prince — an heir apparent — and Mahin a princess. Those are the words we use in Persian to describe not just nobility (since nobility isn't quite the same in Iran as in Europe, being short-lived and not as blood-conscious), but anyone to whom the terms seem to apply: that is, anyone with the combined assets of good looks, good breeding, personality, conviviality, money, and youth — the sum total of which adds up to a promising future.

Farid and Mahin were *shah pesar* and *shazdeh khanum* — "regal offsprings" masculine and feminine. Mahin was furthermore *mah* — "moonlike" — in tribute to her mature beauty (just as Nasrin, say, had been a decade before). Whereas, as a child — at the time of her first visit to Hamburg — she had been *gul*: "flower." That is, beauty which is young, fleeting. The kind to be picked.

Matin my mother wasn't so sure of: and so he passed mention without these lordly titles. He had remained short and had exhibited a tendency, even in public (which isn't the thing to do) to be moody. She went so far as to suggest that he had lost the glitter of his adolescent brilliance. She didn't actually put it this way; rather she quoted my father's remark that he had found him disappointing. Not quite the end product one expected of a child prodigy. The once quick-witted conversationalist.

The change in him was attributed strangely — and perhaps wisely — to his long illness: as though the hepatitis had scarred not only his liver, but his soul.

At any rate, Mahin had taken over as the brains of the family. The lustrous Athena of the shining eyes. And as for business, Farid — the tall, good-looking *shah pesar,* the courtly Adonis — was coming into his own as his father's successor. "Matured," as my mother put it.

It was at this gathering that Ahmad Karimzadeh announced that Farid was to take charge of the Hamburg end of the family business. As such, he was duly given two sets of keys: one to a new Mercedes 180, and the other to the house. Thereafter, the house by the Alster was to be his residence.

With Farid at the helm in Hamburg, Ahmad Karimzadeh was free to return to his affairs in Tehran — which included the management of a new agency. He had secured for his firm the representation of a large German company, which manufactured heavy machinery: compressors, cranes, construction equipment, and the like. To boot, Ashrafi had asked him to fill a vacancy on the Chamber of Commerce.

How did all this affect my father? As I say, he was amenable to counseling.

Ahmad Karimzadeh suggested that he return to Iran as well, since nothing was being gained by his staying in Hamburg. Iran was making money off its oil — expanding its economy. Foreign companies were interested in coming into the country. The time was ripe for going after agencies. German. Japanese. American.

Especially, in my father's case, American, because of all his past contacts.

My father listened, and in an astonishingly short time, he liquidated his business, sold and shipped the household goods, and was off to Iran with my mother.

From hindsight, whatever the merits of Karimzadeh's proposal, his sense of timing couldn't have been worse. For during the late fifties and early sixties, it was not Iran where the businessman's dream was being realized, but Germany. The German economy boomed in a way that made other countries seem at a standstill.

Karimzadeh, of course, continued to prosper in spite of his leaving, since part of his business remained in Hamburg. But my father, once he pulled up stakes, like the desert Bedouin, left no traces behind.

It was a decision he never stopped regretting, especially in light of what was to follow — by which I mean events in Iran.

My parents were back to Tehran in time to celebrate the Iranian New Year, 1338.

215

I remember the date because they sent me a card, and I was reading Chaucer at the time and using the card as a bookmark. Switch calendars, I fancied, and Chaucer and I are practically contemporaries!

My parents moved into a house on Farvardin Avenue — opting to rent, for the time being, rather than buy. The house was located about half a block south of Shah Reza Avenue and the southern perimeter of Tehran University — next to a tea house.

My father went back to his old office in the bazaar — which had been used by his brother during his absence. His brother, meanwhile, had moved out of the district into newer, plusher quarters.

Thus settled once again, my father reopened correspondence with a company in Texas which manufactured cotton-ginning machinery. With whose executives he had been on good terms from long ago. As director of the National Cotton Board, prior to the war, he had negotiated the purchase of ginning plants and related equipment for the Iranian government. As a result, when he returned from America after the war, this same company had asked him to be its exclusive sales representative in Iran.

My father had accepted, setting up an agency in partnership with his brother.

With his departure for Germany, however, the management of this agency had passed into the hands of his brother. Who was not about to give it up upon my father's return.

This posed a problem.

My father had been the former head of not only their firm, but also their family. He was not one to play a submissive role to a younger brother who had made a habit of coming to him for assistance.

Moreover, the company in Texas had long been dissatisfied with my uncle's handling of their business. The fact was my uncle, as a businessman — regardless of his plushy, new office — belonged to the old school. He didn't specialize in any one line of goods, or pursue an aggressive sales policy. Rather he sat back and waited, as it were, for business to walk in. Along with im-

216

porting cotton-ginning machinery, he also sold carpets, bought promissory notes, took over abandoned shipments — among them, for example, several crates of low-grade powdered ink from England, which he subsequently had bottled and distributed to stationery shops near schools to be sold on consignment.

That's how his mind worked, my father complained: he couldn't distinguish between pennies and dollars. He had no idea of the potentials that lay in running the agency properly.

Ultimately, if one had to pin him down, my uncle's real desire was to be a lazy landlord: to own property and have money pouring in without his having to invest any further energy or capital. Penny merchant or not, this wish was fulfilled.

Why, then, should he have been particularly concerned about not turning back the management of the agency to his brother?

Because of his son. He was saving that position for my younger cousin, who was also in college.

The manufacturers in Texas, however, were not inclined to wait. They responded favorably to my father's queries — glad to have him back in Iran. Certainly they did not want to get involved in any family dispute. On the other hand, they agreed that a change in management was in order.

How all this was to be worked out was the subject of their correspondence with my father. That is, before setting down any new conditions to my uncle, their authorized agent, they negotiated behind his back.

Naturally, when my uncle got wind of this — and he was notified rather crisply and suddenly by letter from Texas — he got furious. Accusing his principals of double-dealing (which didn't help), and his older brother of many worse crimes. From his standpoint, he had been the one who had kept the agency going: the poor younger brother, ever taken advantage of — always forced to stay at home, minding the business, while the elder one pranced about Europe, the world, doing as he wished.

In a way, it was an ancient, almost Biblical feud: that between two brothers — one who had roamed abroad and returned home cosmopolitan, and the other who had stayed behind, a provincial.

Their subsequent clash, however, was luridly Iranian.

There are several different versions of what happened — depending on who tells the story and what the occasion. The following is a condensed account:

My father was riding in my uncle's car. My uncle was driving — my father beside him. One of them said something that offended the other, whereupon the two men started slapping each other. Then my uncle tried to shove my father out of the car. The door was flung open and my father hung out, then, swung back in and landed a punch on my uncle's nose. The car went haywire and ran into the gutter — the open door slamming into a cyclist, sending him flying. Later they saw a stream of blood flowing under the car and discovered that they had run over a chicken. The cyclist got up and threatened to take action. At least five people, according to my father, laid claim to owning the chicken. Each had to be paid, along with the cyclist. As well as the policeman, who had come to officiate.

The car was abandoned in the gutter — its axle broken — with the policeman on guard. While my father and uncle hailed two taxis and drove off in opposite directions.

This episode settled matters decisively. The agency would have to go to one man or the other. My father pulled out of their firm — at some loss to himself. The company in Texas sent a special agent to Tehran to talk to each party separately. After a formal review, the agreement with my uncle's firm was terminated and negotiations were begun with my father.

This is where I stepped into the picture.

After graduation, I flew to Dallas and met with the company's executives as my father's representative. I then went through a brief training period as the prospective spare-parts manager of our then soon-to-be appointed agency.

My father never asked me whether I was interested in joining his business. Nor did the question ever crop up between us as one of those unresolved issues. The fact was, he needed me — and under those circumstances, there was only one way to respond.

Not that I had any burning alternatives in mind. I had emerged from college with a B.A. in English and not much more in the way of a sense of direction.

Quite the opposite of Farid at Lausanne, and I was well aware of it. There he was, fortunate fellow, stepping into his father's shoes and loving it! Cut out for business from skin to core.

In my case, I was responding to my father's instructions. And beyond that, vaguely, to another pull: an urge to return to Iran.

The company in Texas, by the way, didn't give us the agency until well into September. During the interim between the termination of my uncle's contract and the signing of ours — when they had been without any local sales representative — they had sold four ginning plants in Iran, thereby saving the agent's commission on all of them.

They were loath to enter a family dispute, yet they were not averse to making money out of it.

Ethics be damned. Business is business, and each party had its own interest.

The CIA had acted in the same detached fashion in hauling down one government and setting up another in its place to cater to American and European oil concerns.

Tehran

26

J arrived at Tehran's Mehrabad Airport in the middle of August 1960 — a sweltering month.

The plane landed around midnight. Even at that hour, the heat hadn't abated. I remember stepping out on the platform and feeling a gust of ovenlike air not just hit, but engulf me.

I was back in Iran.

I caught a glimpse of my parents, waving from the terrace above. Whatever the time, that terrace — the whole airport, for that matter — was teeming with people. As though Mehrabad — literally, "the province of light" — was the one section of the city that never saw sleep.

After going through customs, I fell into the arms of relatives: my uncles — those on my mother's side — their wives, whom I had seen only in photographs, and their children, who held out flowers and waited shyly to be kissed.

All told, there were about a dozen on hand to greet me. Not many, considering the occasion. Certainly, a far cry from the large group that had seen my mother and me off the last time to Germany.

A poignant reflection of the rifts in our family.

My uncles carried my bags to where the cars were parked, insisting on accompanying my parents and me home, regardless of the hour and their having to work early in the morning.

We crammed into two cars: a low, flat Citroën (which one of them had borrowed), and the bright, new Mercedes my father had driven the year before from Hamburg.

On the way, my parents proudly called attention to the new features lining the road: buildings, bottling and packaging plants, young trees, and overhead lights. None of these had existed a decade ago. Between the western edge of the city and the airport, there had been only a stretch of desert.

All the same, as we veered off the highway into what turned out to be our street, I was once again under a familiar canopy of darkness. The street lights — if there at all — were not lit. As we pulled up to our house, I noticed people sleeping in front of the tea house — some on cots and others rolled up on the pavement.

My father got out and opened the large double gate. A man then rushed out to help him, bolting one side back and holding the other, as we drove past into the courtyard.

My mother introduced me to our servants: another Azeri couple, a cook and his wife. Before I could check him, the husband clasped my hand and kissed it. His wife tried to follow, and I said no. But my mother told me not to hold back, since that was the custom. Later she said I would have to give them some money.

When the others arrived, we all filed into the house — the servants taking the bags from my uncles, and my mother going into the kitchen to set up the flowers.

In the living room, the atmosphere became suddenly formal.

We sat in a circle, waiting for tea and looking each other over with self-conscious smiles. I was introduced again to the children, who were coaxed into uttering my name, and who, in the process, became shyer than ever, hiding behind chairs.

Then my mother came in with the flowers, followed by the servant with the tea, and the spell was broken. My uncles wanted to compare heights. So we stood back to back. My middle uncle was the tallest by an inch or so, and I came next.

Not enough for my mother, who had wanted me to grow magically by that much — spreading her fingers. She was also concerned about my receding hairline.

She herself was beginning to look matronly. No longer the svelte figurine she used to be. My father, on the other hand, was more distinctive than ever — with his hair fully white.

After our relatives left, I pulled out my pipe and asked for some Scotch — which came as another jolt to my parents. Though my father laughed and said he would join me.

We talked briefly about my trip, then dispersed for bed.

My mother showed me my room and opened my suitcases — one of which was practically given over to gifts. Most of these she had written me to buy for relatives, to be distributed on return visits.

I then climbed into the bed prepared for me. On the balcony now, instead of the roof. But still under the stars. In the cool, which had finally set in, I fell asleep immediately.

✵

When I awoke, the neighbors were doing their laundry. The high walls of the balcony had shielded me from the sun — otherwise I would have woken up much earlier.

I went downstairs for breakfast.

We rarely ate, I found out, in the dining room — that room being too dark and formal. Rather we used the small table in the hallway, where it was light and breezy, and the windows and door opened out on the courtyard.

My parents had eaten, but were still in their nightclothes.

221

After the usual cheerful greetings, my father handed me the paper — this time in Persian — and went upstairs to bathe and change. My mother brought my breakfast, which consisted of the standard melon, cheese, and bread — the *barbari* kind, which is manna itself, when crisp and freshly baked — along with tea in a glass with a hot, silver holder.

All this was familiar and to be expected. What caught me by surprise was the centerpiece: a bowl full of jasmine, floating in water.

I, too, then went up to my room to change — my clothes having already been unpacked for me. I didn't bother wearing a jacket.

Downstairs, my father was in a light summer suit, going through papers in a briefcase. The cook was applying a cloth to the gleaming, red Mercedes.

My father and I then got into the car and backed out of the courtyard. It was fairly late in the morning, and the clear blue sky had acquired a whitish haze. That, in itself, was a sign of another scorching day.

As we drove south, toward the bazaar, my father asked me to name the streets. I remembered only a few, since the area wasn't one I had been too familiar with. On the other hand, it had remained much the same.

Actually, it was not the route itself that created the confusion, but the traffic. The people. The masses of pedestrians — thrown in with donkeys and horse-drawn carts, peddlers toting their wares, bicycles and cars. So that the farther south we drove, the less precise became the distinction between pavement and street.

My father parked his car several blocks from his office, and we got out and walked, passing, along the way, rows of carts laden with fruit, piled up in pyramids.

My father's office was on the corner of Buzarjomehri Avenue, which is on the northwestern tip of the bazaar. Each section of the bazaar has its own name, which is known only to those who frequent the area. Our section was called *chahar-rahe galubandak* — or the Galubandak Crossroad. And that designation may well have preceded the naming of streets.

The building itself was outwardly modern and stood out in contrast to the ones around it. It had four stories, a concrete facade, and the plain, flat, architecturally *nouveau* look of the thirties. The ones beside it were flimsy structures, half as high, made of a motley assemblage of wooden beams, bricks, and dried mud.

The inside, on the other hand, was distinctly prototypical of the bazaar. Of the old world. With dark, narrow passages and brick floors. Plaster walls, which rubbed off on your hands and clothes, and which had finger marks all over them. Thin, wooden doors, which creaked in their frames, and through which voices could be heard. (Hence, I suppose, the practice of speaking in undertones when negotiations were conducted.)

Also, there was the ever-present latrine stench, which came from the end of each corridor.

I say "latrine" rather than "bathroom," because that was literally what a *mostara* was — without a bowl or flushing system. Only foot props for squatting and a funnel-shaped aperture — the sides of which were usually lined with feces. And a copper jug and faucet with which to do one's washing.

The building itself was called a *seray*, or an "inn." As opposed to an *emarat*, which is the term applied to newer constructions going up all over the city, and which means simply "a large building." A linguistic dissociation, dividing the old from the new.

In any case, the offices were by and large lavishly carpeted, the furnishings heavy and simple.

As we walked into our office, a young man jumped up, as though conditioned to respond to the door. The desk behind him had nothing on it, nor had he been engaged in doing anything other than sitting and waiting.

This was our office boy, Golayat. He was about my age, short, with a thick shock of stiff, black hair, which stood out on all sides like a brush, an equally stiff, trim mustache, and strong, white teeth.

I thought of him as being older than me — as a man — because, at twenty-two, he already had a wife and three children.

223

All five of whom lived in one room, without any private toilet facilities.

His name, which is rather unusual, though distinctly Islamic, means "the Flower of Life," referring to the other one, the Afterlife. He was illiterate and devoutly religious, observing the fasts and praying the requisite five times a day.

He was also a Turk from Gilan and spoke Persian with difficulty and a thick, though not Azeri, accent. He always smiled. He had only good things to say. He never criticized. He always accepted.

Bending down to kiss my hand, he told me that he was my slave.

I never learned his last name.

My father gave me a quick tour of the office, then went to his room and tended to some affairs. There were three rooms in all: my father's on one side, mine in the middle — which was also the reception room — and the other, which was the storage area or *ambar*. Every office in the *seray* had an *ambar*. Ours contained only a few carpets and office equipment brought over from Germany. Later it would be packed with crates of cotton-ginning machinery.

My first task, as the designated spare-parts manager, was to open a file on each of our prospective customers. But I was in no mood to get to work right away. So I chatted with Golayat instead — no easy thing, since he was awkward with Persian and shy — then drank tea and gazed out the window.

Our office was on the third floor and offered a fairly extensive view of the bazaar. One could see the minarets of a mosque and the tops of a few gigantic, elderly trees, over a patchwork of arched and flat roofs. The mosque itself was hidden. Directly below was the courtyard of the *seray*, which was parched to the point of barrenness and reflected the glare of sunlight. With square, inlaid bricks the color of dust, a small pool in the middle — with not a trickle of water — and an outhouse in the corner.

Precisely at noon, the call to prayer was sounded from one of the distant minarets. My father did a cheerful imitation from his desk, while Golayat excused himself and went into the *ambar* to pray.

Later, while I was leafing through the handbook on cotton-ginning machinery — glancing over the illustrations with the kind of removed captivation one has, say, when viewing the ads in *The New Yorker* — my father called me into his office. He told Golayat to fetch more tea, screwed the lid of his fountain pen, and significantly set it down.

The moment had come for talk. I chose the comfortable armchair across from him. Golayat brought in the tea — with the prescribed two lumps of sugar on each saucer — and we switched from Persian to English.

First, my father wanted to know about my stay in Dallas: my impressions of the people I had met, and so on. I noticed that my air letters were laid out in front of him.

Then he leaned back and launched into a narrative of his own. It was one which he had carefully prepared — and which had an intrinsically dramatic structure. He said he wanted to bring me up to date — to give me "the details." By which he meant all that pertained to our current position in business: how we had gotten where we were — the whys and the wherefores.

He went over each of our reverses chronologically, one by one. The conflict with Magdalena and my half-uncle. The loss of the carpets. The losses incurred in moving to Tehran. The conflict with his brother over the agency.

Their historic fight in the car.

Each of these segments had its own climax, yet led up to the larger one he was coming to.

When he got to the present, I thought he had finished — having done with the past and looking now to the future. But he gazed out the window and let out a sad chuckle. There was more to follow. One searing episode he had saved for the last, to top it all off.

"My dear son." He turned around. "There are people one should trust, and there are people one shouldn't. How does one draw the line between the two? I thought I had a friend — someone whose advice I could follow. I was wrong. When your mother and I returned to Tehran, we wanted to buy a house. I went to Ashrafi's bank to see if I could muster some capital.

225

Financing conditions in Iran are different from those in America. Here one has to come up with most of the money. The bank advances the rest — or whatever it's willing to negotiate. I didn't want to part with a sizable sum. The past few years had put a strain on our resources, and I didn't have any income at the time. So I asked Ashrafi what he could do to help me. Do you know what he said?"

Another pause.

"He told me that it was the wrong time to buy land. That the cost of housing was too high. That interest rates were at their peak."

He chuckled again, this time with a smile.

"Here is one of the biggest landowners in Tehran telling me that land is not worth investing in — that he himself is trying to cash in on some profits. Isn't that a joke? The fact is, as we sit here, the price of land is soaring. Soaring!"

He clapped his hands and got a genuine laugh out of this. It was almost as though he were talking about another person's folly.

"So what did he advise you to do?" I was loath to hear about any more setbacks.

He threw up his hands in a gesture of disgust.

"That's where this cursed dilemma of friendship confounds one. What are friends for, if not to be trusted? But it is dangerous to think that way. He advised me to invest in a consignment of logs. This consignment belonged to a merchant who had been financed by the bank, but who had run out of money. The merchant was willing to take his losses and sign the goods over to someone else, provided the bank note was off his hands. Do you follow me? In other words, I was to refinance a deal that the bank had made. And Ashrafi presented the case to me as a real opportunity. For 30,000 tomans, I could take delivery of the logs in Zanjan and ship them to Tehran, where they were worth well over three times their original value. It was a good short-term investment. And, naturally, one which he himself could not profit from, since he represented the bank. He also told me that, before I came along, he had been thinking of contacting my brother, since he knew my brother to be interested in such short-term arrangements. Oh, the man is a rogue! Do you know where Zanjan is?"

I nodded.

"It's up in the mountains. I went there to investigate. I wrote you as much."

I nodded again. He had written about going to Zanjan, but hadn't mentioned the details.

"The logs were good. They were high-grade walnut. I made a study of their value and saw that it was worth the investment. Besides, I had the word of a friend. Do you know where the deal went wrong?"

He tapped two spots on his desk with his forefinger and drew a line connecting them.

"There was no problem in getting the logs from Zanjan to Tehran."

Then he tapped a third spot, slightly behind the first, and started to push his finger forward, but stopped, as though an invisible force were resisting it.

"The problem was in getting them from the village to Zanjan. From the valley where they lay to the town. There isn't a road. The only possible way of getting them out of that valley is to lay down a road oneself, which is out of the question. And which is what the other merchant would have had to do as well. Meanwhile, the logs lie up there, being eaten into by worms. All this Ashrafi knew. He was the one who had arranged the original financing. When he saw how the deal was going, he sought a way of getting himself off the hook by hooking someone else. That's the kind of man he is. And it isn't as though we are talking about money out of his pocket. No. It was simply his reputation he wanted to save — as a bank manager. What do you say about that?"

The question was rhetorical. I was fuming inside. More money down the drain. Another ally turned into an enemy. Another rupture in our relations with others. Where was all this leading?

I got up and paced about.

But my father hadn't finished: there was still the concluding twist of irony.

227

"And do you know where that man is headed for now?" My father eyed me placidly, then leaned forward and whispered. "The Senate. His appointment was announced recently in the papers."

He let out one final laugh, which capsulated his reaction.

His viewpoint was fixed: as long as Ashrafi was totally, unadulteratedly the villain — the blackguard — there was some satisfaction to be gleaned in being on the other side. But this was also the satisfaction of the gulled: the victimized.

Small comfort, I thought, to be gotten out of that. Or maybe not so small, after all. At least he hadn't lost his sense of humor.

He dismissed the whole past with a Chaplinesque wave of the hand.

"But never mind that Ashrafi goes to the Senate. May God continue to shower blessings on him. But sooner or later he will have to step down as president of the Chamber of Commerce. And when he goes, it looks as though Ahmad Karimzadeh will take over his place. Another position has to be filled."

He nodded and winked.

"We still have friends in high places. Karimzadeh has encouraged me to make a bid. With Karimzadeh's support — and now this agency — I can come in strong!"

He thrust his arm forward, then clapped his hands.

That Friday my parents and I stayed at home to receive visitors. These were coming, my mother made it clear, expressly to see me.

That made the occasion official. Which meant wearing ties and suits, in spite of the heat, and — for me — being at the mercy of the doorbell. If people were good enough to venture out into the sun and greet me with flowers, then I was the one to meet them at the door, not the servants — whose task it was to revive them, almost immediately upon arrival, with icy glasses of *sharbat*. They, too, poor devils, were made to put on extra clothing and shoes. Along with having to endure the heat of the kitchen, which had been a sort of blazing furnace ever since breakfast.

Naturally, anyone coming was automatically invited to lunch. And there was no telling how large that number would be. As a result, one had to prepare for an approximate maximum. If one's predictions were off, one had an inordinate supply of leftovers to cope with. Sundry dishes to be distributed among servants and neighbors.

That, by the way, was one means of paying off extra help: not just with money, but food.

The smart visitors came early — before their faces were lined with sweat. (How often some of the women had to redo their makeup!)

My uncles and their families were the first to arrive. They stayed the whole day — for supper as well — the wives helping out with the serving. These were followed by friends — some of whom I had to be introduced to. They all knew each other in one way or another. And they all stayed for lunch — a few leaving shortly afterward, while others remained to play backgammon and cards.

After tea, a fresh batch arrived. Among them, Lieutenant General Amuzegar. And with him — odd to see them together — Zohre Karimzadeh.

This was not entirely a surprise. The surprise had come earlier — that morning — when he had phoned and talked to my mother. He had heard about my return from the Karimzadehs and wanted to know when he could see me. My mother invited him to our gathering, and he said that he would be over with Zohre around five.

They had all been vacationing at Ramsar: the Karimzadehs staying at the hotel, as usual, and the General at his estate, until work had forced him to come back to the city — along with Zohre, who had wanted the ride.

"He is a very kind man," my mother declared happily to the company, returning to the living room. "Always considerate of others and interested in what they are doing."

Up till then, the very same words had been said of a certain Dr. Safarzadeh — a senator and a former teacher of my mother, who was due to join us late in the day.

Then she turned to me. "Every time we see him, Firuz, he asks about you. You know, of course, that he is chief of staff now."

The guests joined in the accolade. Not only was he a fine officer, but an honest person. Which was not easy to find in Iran in those days. Moreover, he had the confidence of the king. In the next cabinet reshuffle, no doubt, he would be named the Minister of War.

All the same, a few left before his arrival, though others stayed expressly to see him.

In the afternoon, my father accompanied me to the door each time the bell rang, until the General — or *timsar* in Persian — showed up with Zohre.

I said that it was odd seeing them together. This wasn't just because I associated them with different worlds: Zohre with Germany and the General with Iran. But rather because together they created a certain impression.

The last time I had seen the General, he had been struck down by his wife — whimpering and broken. Here he was, twelve years later, a man well into his fifties, and who looked it. With graying hair, which was thinning. A small paunch, where there had been only muscle before. And a somewhat smaller physique than I had imagined. Had he shrunk, or had I simply grown?

In any case, he had aged, but the woman had not. I don't mean Zohre. But the one of yore. The one who had downed him.

As I opened the door, I was astonished, for a split second, by the blue dress and dark glasses.

My father greeted Amuzegar with all the decorum of a medieval steward welcoming a knight into a castle. Amuzegar, for his part, was energetically jovial.

"Firuz." He clasped my shoulders. "How nice to have you back! How could you stand to be away for so long? Do you not love your parents? Your people?" Then he laughed and pinched my cheek — not what I expected of a general. "It's good to see you again. You've turned out well. Hasn't he turned out well?" He glanced at Zohre who had shaken hands with my father, without saying a word. Now she gave me a smile. A madonnalike beauty. With suntanned skin — fresh from the Caspian —

230

dark hair in an immaculate wave, and a pearl necklace about her throat. But cold, limp fingers. And the same reluctance to touch.

As with the General, the last time we had met, the circumstances had been explosive. But whereas the General had broken out of his mold, she had stayed within hers: the same cold beauty of the past. Only more beautifully the same. Like the bust of Nefertiti.

There was one conspicuous difference, though, which I didn't pick up until after she talked. She could speak Persian fluently. Afterward, in fact, she claimed that she had actually forgotten the German she had once been so conversant with. I couldn't quite accept that — or reconcile myself to the phenomenon — until I later came across another person: a woman from East Germany who had emigrated to France after the war, and who had so thoroughly buried her past that she had emerged, as though reincarnated, *une Parisienne.*

Everyone stood up when the General and Zohre entered the living room — the women, too. My mother, as hostess, introduced both around, then seated Zohre among the women.

The usual two circles then started to function: the smaller, quieter one of the women — with Zohre at the center, silent and brooding, an object to be gazed at — and the larger, louder one of the men, dominated (whether he liked it or not) by the General. Whatever he said was taken as an official statement. All eyes were reveringly riveted on him. No voice challenged his. Only my father's revealed a trace of intimacy — and even that was obviously coated with respect.

When I started to cross my legs, my father shook his finger across the room, as though to say, "Not in such company."

And there was good reason for all this. Once a ranking officer stepped into a room, one was automatically reminded of being a subject of the king. And here was no ordinary ranking officer, but the man at the top of the echelon.

What magic there was when he casually threw out, "His Majesty said to me . . ."

Here was a man who was rubbing shoulders — on a daily basis almost — with the sovereign! And evidently he was quite fond of the phrase, too, since he used it often enough.

231

Beyond this, there was the General's presence itself, which gave a sort of vibrant, physical quality to what was otherwise abstract. Namely, the photograph behind him: that of the king in regal attire (one couldn't really call it military since no one else came close to dressing that way) — with massive epaulets, broods of medals across the chest, and medallions pinned to a sash — gazing stone-faced across the room at yet another photograph. That of his daughter, Princess Shahnaz, caught smiling in a mink coat and hat.

The picture had been taken in our apartment in Hamburg — and by none other than Karl, the basement dweller. It expressed no patriotic feeling at all, but rather was up there for personal reasons: because Princess Shahnaz had visited our apartment, along with Nasrin — and because Nasrin was known to be even closer to her than her former husband was to the king.

The General and Zohre paid the shortest visit of all. They stayed for about an hour, then got up to leave — forced away, the General apologized, by a dinner engagement.

Outside, in the hallway, while Zohre was talking to my parents, Amuzegar took me aside.

"I suppose, Firuz, that you are going to take advantage of your exemption from the draft."

I said yes. As an only child with a father over sixty, I was not required to do military service.

"That is fine." He nodded, talking confidentially. "That is as it should be. That is the law of the country. And I suppose — judging from what your father says — that you intend to go into his business."

I said yes again, though not as emphatically as I could have done. My eyes were on his rows of medals, and I couldn't tear them away. He noticed this and smiled.

"Well, that is as it should be, too. A son owes much to his father. But he also owes something to himself, which he comes to learn about in time. But if it should turn out . . ." He turned his back to the others and whispered. "If it should happen some day that you get tired of business, or find that business does not suit you — that could happen, you know — then come and see me, and we'll talk things over. I could be of help to you. I hope you follow me. My intention is not to meddle in family affairs — what goes on between father and son. No, that's between the two of you. But only to assist, in case you need me. Remember, I am your friend, as well as your father's."

He slapped my back and spoke more volubly.

"When *are* you going to come and see me?"

He went ahead before I could answer. "What a pity you didn't come home earlier. You could have joined us in Ramsar with your parents. My son is up there now with his wife. So is Bijan. They are all at my estate. Why don't you go up and join them? There is plenty of room, and I am sure they would be happy to see you. You could go horse riding with Bijan. Do you ride?"

"A little," I lied.

"Well, Bijan can give you some pointers. He is a very good horseman. He could be even better, if only he applied himself." The General laughed. "But he has other interests. Prettier ones, too."

He glanced at Zohre.

My father heard the General and approached us.

"What's that about horses?"

"I was telling Firuz" — Amuzegar put a hand on both our shoulders, making us a threesome — "that he should go up to my estate and have some fun with Bijan, Parviz, and the others. It's too hot to stay in Tehran."

"Your excellency is too kind," my father bowed. "Yes, it is certainly hot."

"The Karimzadehs are up there as well, along with their daughter from Switzerland. Does Firuz know her?"

"Oh, yes." My father laughed. "They're old friends from Hamburg."

"Then so much the cozier." The General smiled, releasing his hand from my shoulder and holding it out to Zohre.

When she saw this, she broke away to join us.

"If Firuz goes," he added, "he can take Zohre with him."

"Take me where?" Zohre asked.

"Ramsar," the General said in a puckish manner.

"No!" she walked right past us. "I've had enough of that place!"

All of a sudden, there was the teen-age bitch of Travemünde.

The General eyed her silently, then shrugged.

"In that case, stay here in the heat." He turned back to me. "As for you, Firuz, go up whenever you wish. I'll put a car and driver at your disposal, if you need transportation." He held out a hand to my father. "I hope you can spare the boy a week or so, Omid — before he gets all tangled up in our bazaar."

"As your excellency wishes." My father laughed.

The exit into the street was awkward. The General and Zohre bumped into a startled Dr. Safarzadeh, who was gazing questioningly at the limousine parked in front of the gate, with three silver stars on its license plate. Turning around, he stepped on Zohre's shoe. Which left a black splotch on the white leather.

Safarzadeh — in contrast to the General — was a quiet man, who exuded hardly any aura at all. A bald, thin, scholarly type, in his "youngish seventies," as he put it, he had been a teacher of my mother at Robert College in Istanbul, and was now "enjoying life," to quote him again, "as a senator." Which meant, in his case, that he received a government stipend for services rendered in the past as an educator and a prominent man of letters. He had been president (briefly) of the newly established Pahlavi University in Shiraz, before stepping down in favor of the Senate appointment — because, as he claimed, of "the politics involved," which were "alien to a poet's disposition." And also because that would have meant leaving Tehran and his beloved new house. He had married recently — for the first time — a woman half his age said to have been his former housekeeper ("I always told myself that I'd have to do it before reaching seventy, otherwise I wouldn't do it at all!"), and, in the process, had unexpectedly sired a daughter of whom he was so unabashedly proud that he had just published a volume of verse in her name.

No one seemed overly impressed with him.

Naturally, there was a letdown after the General's departure. A release of tension — as though one could breathe again. But even after my mother's grandiloquent introduction, the mood had shifted to small talk. And so the two of us — Safarzadeh and I — came to occupy a corner by ourselves.

Which turned out to be the most enjoyable part of the whole

day. We talked about literature and schools. Writers he had known. Then, gingerly, he spoke about politics and his past.

In his youth he had been a revolutionary, taking part in the uprisings in Azerbaijan: a fiery constitutionalist, who had gone through imprisonment and hiding.

He, too, by the way, was an Azeri Turk. One of the few I knew who wasn't a merchant.

When he got up to leave, he offered — in his quiet, offhand way — to introduce me to the head of the English Department at Tehran University. Would I be interested in teaching there on a part-time basis?

Of course, I would, my parents broke in. To have any member of the family — let alone one's son — teach at the university was a gigantic feather in one's cap.

Was this something I wanted?

I said yes, too, for all sorts of reasons — the prospect of payment being one. (As yet I had no indication of receiving a salary from my father.) There were others as well, too blurry to get hold of. I hadn't given much thought to teaching before.

The doctor went home to his wife and small daughter, both of whom had provided more stimulus for talk than any of his own prestigious accomplishments.

When the others were gone, too, my parents cleared away a few things and straightened the furniture, before giving over to the servants. It had been an exhausting day for all of us, but especially for the servants, who were still operating at a mechanical pace.

"That Zohre is a sulky creature," my father sighed, as the three of us sat with our feet up in the living room. It was after eleven.

With that simple statement, my parents got into an argument.

As it turned out, I never did go to Ramsar that summer — I got "tangled up" in the bazaar instead. The following week, a representative of the company in Texas flew out to finalize the terms of our agency contract. Then the next Friday, my parents and I paid a return visit to Dr. Safarzadeh, who informed me that he had arranged a meeting with the head of the English Department.

The week after that, we went to Shemran. My parents wanted to look over some houses, and then stop by the Karimzadehs', who had returned from the Caspian. Mahin was due to go back to Switzerland soon.

After an early lunch, we drove — with a broker — up Pahlavi Avenue. The vast stretch of open land between city and suburb had diminished, filled in by new side streets and buildings going up. Halfway, a new restaurant had just opened, specializing in hamburgers — the latest rage in Tehran.

Pepsi-Cola had made its impact years ago.

We walked through several houses — none to my parents' liking, but all expensive. In Shemran, the broker kept saying, one didn't just pay for the dwelling, but also the land value. He urged us to invest, before prices went higher.

To my parents, though, they had gone high enough already. The same sum which, a decade ago, could have purchased a mansion with a huge garden attached, was now barely sufficient for a modest two-story house with a yard hardly worth mentioning. To invest under such circumstances meant more than a huge outlay of money. It entailed a loss in self-esteem, a decline in social status.

We dropped the broker off at a bus stop, and drove on to the Karimzadehs'.

To get to their house — which my parents referred to as a "villa" — one had to go down a narrow, winding dirt road, past mud walls and shabby huts, bumping along at a pace which was only slightly faster than walking to avoid the rough spots and the ditch to the side. Just before the house, the road broadened. A tall poplar stood at the entrance. The building itself was larger than any around, as were the garden walls and the trees inside.

Under the poplar, two cars were randomly parked: a Mercedes and a large American model — with an attendant keeping watch. My parents had expected to see more, and wondered whether we had come too early.

A servant led us through the house to the terrace. Several tables, with white covers, were set up in front of the pool. On top of two were bowls of fruit.

Ahmad Karimzadeh got up to greet us. The gathering was almost familial. There was only one other party of guests — and those my parents knew. My father shook hands with a Mr. Kemali. Not the one we had known in Hamburg — the card-playing enthusiast who had gone with us to Travemünde — but his brother, who was in business in Tehran. My mother exchanged kisses with Mina and Mahin Karimzadeh, then acknowledged Mrs. Kemali and her daughter with the customary nod and smile.

Mrs. Kemali was heavy and dark. She sat with her legs spread apart at the knees and crossed at the ankles; her fingers intertwined, palm upward, below the abdomen — a posture she maintained, breathing audibly, all afternoon. Her daughter, by contrast, was pixyish. Her name was Monireh — or Moni, for short. A girl of about eighteen, with laughing eyes, moon-faced, and lips waiting to be kissed.

Next to her was Mahin: only two years or so older, but clearly a woman. With a slim figure and face, legs beautifully crossed, and dark brown hair, which curled up at her shoulders. One could see now the resemblance between father and daughter: the straight nose, the firm chin. The same lines when they laughed. Even more, the inclination to laugh at the same things.

Mr. Karimzadeh had changed hardly at all. His wife, though, was stouter, and her face, which had always been smiling before, showed signs of fatigue: of having to put up with pain.

As for Mr. Kemali, he was just as bald as his brother in Hamburg. Another facet of Igor Stravinsky — though without the mustache.

They had all been up at Ramsar and were bronzed alike — except for Mrs. Karimzadeh, who (like my mother) made a point now of staying out of the sun.

Three more chairs were placed between the two tables, and we sat in a semicircle, facing the pool, with the parents on one side, and the children on the other. I was sandwiched between Mahin and a huge potted geranium.

My mother looked about and asked for Zohre. She had expected to see her.

Mrs. Karimzadeh smiled uncomfortably, and replied that she was staying at the Karbalais'. She went on to explain: since the Karbalais were in Europe, and Parviz was away on business, Zohre had decided to keep Gloria company.

The conversation then quickly turned to me: how had I done in college, and what were my reactions on coming back? I was congratulated on not having forgotten my Persian and handed a glass of *sharbat* by Mrs. Karimzadeh, who took the tray from the servant.

My parents, in return, asked about Farid and Matin.

They were well, Mr. Karimzadeh acknowledged. He heard from them regularly. Matin was turning out to be a great help to Farid. He had finished his studies and entered the business in Hamburg.

"And when will Mahin be leaving for Switzerland?" My mother turned to his daughter.

Suddenly, one was aware of a stillness — one which had been there all along, disguised by restraint. But more than that: a reluctance to communicate — which was brought out in the pause between question and answer. In the looking about to see who would respond.

"I'll be leaving in ten days," Mahin replied.

"So soon?"

"I've had a long and eventful vacation." Mahin threw a glance at her father. "And I would like to see my brothers in Hamburg, before returning to Zürich."

"Well, we wish you the best in your studies," my father chimed in. "And to show that we mean it, we'll come to the airport to wish you *bon voyage*."

"Oh, please, there is no need for that!" Mrs. Karimzadeh remonstrated.

"But that would give us the greatest pleasure," my father magnanimously countered.

Mr. Karimzadeh seemed to be deliberating a point.

Reaching for his glass of *sharbat*, he said softly, "My wife and I have an announcement to make."

He stirred the glass, with the ice in it, then put the spoon down. My parents were waiting with smiles.

"We have promised Mahin to Bijan Ashrafi."

My mother's hand went up to her lips.

The Kemalis evidently knew already, judging from their lack of response. My father and I were completely surprised.

"Is that so? But how . . ." My mother was at a loss for words. ". . . wonderful." She completed the statement.

My father opened his arms and gave a jowly laugh.

"But you can't do this to us." He beamed at Mahin. "We've hardly seen you at all. You're our daughter, too. It's too soon for us to be losing a daughter. Just because a son has come back is no reason to give up a daughter."

Mahin smiled back. One could see that she liked him, but she was also composed.

As for me, I had this throbbing sensation all over my chest, accompanied by a numbness of the fingers. Sometimes it isn't until you hear such news that you begin to recognize your feelings about a person.

Not toward, but about.

And not specific ones either — but generally. Which is worse.

Without really knowing Mahin — and my father had dropped the word — I had "lost" her. Had there been, at some point, a vague expectation — wishful thinking — that perhaps, some-day, the two of us . . . ? And hence the need to tread on the matter so lightly?

My mother was full of questions, but also nervously hesitant. She didn't quite know whom to address. Mrs. Karimzadeh was sitting beside her.

"Have you . . . settled on a date . . . a time for the betrothal?"

"Not yet." Her old friend put it almost kindly.

"We have agreed to *promise* her," Mr. Karimzadeh bore down on the distinction, "but we haven't agreed on making a formal engagement."

He said this in a manner which was rather reflective of our talks, the week before, with the representative from Texas.

"We agree to give you the agency, Mr. Momtaz, but with the stipulation that Mr. Karbalai buys from us, without going through you."

"Why?"

A shrug. "Because that's the way Mr. Karbalai wants it. That's the way he's been doing business with us for years."

"He buys from you, without your agent receiving a commission?"

A nod. "That's right. He has his own agent in New York. So, technically, we're not selling to you in Iran, but to him in New York."

"No, I can't agree to that."

Another kind of shrug. "You'll have to. Your brother did. It's all perfectly legal. Karbalai may have ginning plants in Iran. But when we sell to him, we sell to New York. The rest is his business."

And so, here we were, listening to another kind of distinction: the subtle difference — which evaded me at the time — between being "promised" and "engaged."

If one was "engaged," then one was practically married. One went through a *namzadi* — or an elaborate ceremony, in which everyone of significance known to both parties was invited and usually showed up with a gift.

The "promise" of an engagement, on the other hand, was a sort of declaration of intent: henceforward, neither party was considered eligible for marriage to anyone else. Both were put on ice, as it were, until the marriage terms had been worked out.

The two stages, as far as I know, having nothing to do with religious practice. Rather they derived, I tend to think, from the procedures of bargaining. They might have even been a businessman's invention.

At any rate, Karimzadeh, the businessman, unwound the love story.

"When we were at Ramsar, my daughter saw a good deal of Bijan. He came to our hotel and offered to take her riding. They went every day — accompanied by Moni. After a while, we saw that they had come to be fond of each other. But she had her studies, and he had his duties. And so we thought it best that they be temporarily separated. If they are truly fond of one another, they can have their *namzadi* next year. By then, Mahin will have finished her studies. And in a year —" He tapered off. "We can find out what kind of a young man Bijan really is. Whether or not he is ready for marriage. This is our opinion, and Mahin agrees."

She didn't move.

"A very wise decision," my father rejoined, then turned to Mahin. "May I wish you the best for the future in the way of happiness and good fortune. A year is not a long time to wait, when such important matters as one's education and future partner in life are at stake. Yes, indeed, it's a very good decision!"

He was voicing a general feeling of apprehension. Translated that meant: we are surprised by all this. We don't know what kind of person Bijan really is. But we do know that he has been a bit of a rogue. Now, it is possible for people to change — and the prospect of marriage is as good a point in one's life as any. If, within a year, a rogue can demonstrate that he can lead the life of a saint, then, by all means, young love, or romance — or whatever it is — should be given its due.

"My congratulations as well." I nodded at Mahin. "The last time I saw you —"

"I was only a girl, is that right?" she smiled, anticipating me wrongly. "Come, I'll show you the garden," she stood up abruptly. "Moni, you come, too. Our parents want to talk."

The three of us walked in silence — Mahin in the middle — until we rounded the pool and came to a path. I wanted to say something but didn't know what.

"Your garden is huge," I commented.

"It looks large from here, because you can't see the walls. But when we get to the end, you'll have a better view of its size."

Our footsteps were noisy on the gravel.

"The trees are magnificent," I added, out of some native Iranian instinct, I suppose, which places trees, aesthetically, on the same level as flowers.

"Yes, they are." Mahin looked about. "That's what I like most about this garden. It has a green to it which you don't find in Europe."

"Not as deep?"

241

"Yes, very deep — if, by deep, we mean the same thing. I mean intense. The intensity of the green here is different. It is lighter. Look up there."

She pointed to a quivering aspen. "That green is almost silver. And the one over there is almost blue. That's why we have no autumn colors. All our colors come and go in one spell. Our green lasts the summer, then dies."

She reminded me of the way her mother once talked about flowers.

I was about to say that the Greeks, too, saw colors in terms of intensity rather than shade, when she touched my shoulder.

"You've known Bijan longer than I have."

"I haven't seen him since I was a child."

"All the same, you've known him since then — which is important. Until three weeks ago, he was only a name to me."

Moni laughed.

"Does that bother you?" I asked.

"No, no. It's not that. When something like this happens, it doesn't make any difference how long you've known a person. Things happen in a way they simply haven't before. It's like finding a new being within you. Someone you've always wanted to know. Yet that being is there because of someone else. All of a sudden, you are a new creation — but also part of another. A beginning. Do I make myself clear?"

I said yes.

"Well, in any case, no, it's not the speed with which things have happened that bothers me. I have an excellent father, who talks sense into me all the time. We've had a very long talk, and we've come to a mutual agreement. No, it's something else."

She picked a daisy and put it absently to her nose.

"It's that my own happiness is based, in a way, on someone else's sorrow. Can any good come out of that?"

The question was directed at me, yet seemed rhetorical.

"I don't follow you."

"I'm not the only woman in his life. Before I came along, Zohre was in love with him. She still is. Did you know that?"

I shook my head. But that, at least, explained Zohre's reaction at our house.

"Well, that is the bad side of this situation. I knew that Zohre

242

was in love with him a long time ago. In fact, that's how I associated him in my mind: as her future husband. Otherwise, as I say, he was just a name to me. Someone my parents talked about. Then we met at Ramsar. He wanted to go riding, and Zohre wouldn't go with him. So he took me instead. We rode along the beach. We had a race — which I won. But afterward I saw the kind of horseman he was. He took my scarf and placed it on a stick, which he drove into the sand. Then he went after it, galloping at full speed. Each time he snatched it, he drove the stick deeper. Until, finally, he fell off his horse. When I went to help him up we kissed. It was as sudden as that. Both of us knew what was happening. When we got back to the hotel, Zohre knew as well. It was eerie. It was almost as though she had been watching us all along. She went to her room and didn't come out, until the General came to fetch her."

Mahin twisted the stem of the daisy around her finger, causing some petals to drop.

"What happened then?"

"Then, to put it bluntly, with Zohre away, Bijan and I no longer felt so guilty. Every day Moni and I would go to the General's estate, where he and I could be alone. We talked — endlessly. He uncovered his whole past — all his escapades and affairs. He wanted us to get married immediately. But he knew that his reputation would stand in the way, and didn't want me to learn about him through others." She smiled. "He was right. When my father found out about us, he tried to warn me about him. But, by then, it was too late. I already knew much more about Bijan than he did. Including his involvement with Zohre."

We reached the end of the garden and turned back.

"What is Zohre doing now?"

Mahin shrugged. "She is staying at the Karbalais' until I go back to Switzerland. Then I hope she will return to our house. I feel very sorry about her. As you know, other than ours, she really has no home of her own. You know about her father?"

I nodded.

"Well, he is living in Nice now, with his second wife and her children."

"Not Stockholm?"

"No, they have moved. Anyway, he has cut himself off from

243

the rest of us, and Zohre has no wish to see him. Everyone was hoping that things would work out between her and Bijan. I was hoping myself, until — "

She shrugged again and looked down.

"You seem sad."

"No, I'm not sad," she looked up, lips quivering. "I'm happy. Not sad."

She glanced at Moni. Then, suddenly, the two of them burst into tears.

It was a short summer shower. In a moment, it was over. They blinked and patted their eyes with my handkerchief.

I was bewildered.

What was this uncanny ability I had of prompting these Karimzadeh women to cry? Years ago, it had been Zohre — that, too, during a walk and after some harmless questioning. And now it was Mahin and her friend.

We walked back to the terrace in silence.

More company had shown up. Mahin and Moni, rather than face them immediately, went into the house.

My parents and I didn't stay long afterward.

In the car, my mother gave vent to her feelings. How could the Karimzadehs have agreed to such a mismatch? Mahin was one type of person, and Bijan clearly another. She was intelligent and well brought up, whereas he was untutored and wild. Moreover, she was from a good business family — which was simply wasted on him. She was developing very nicely. Why marry her off? But if marry she had to, then why not to someone more eligible?

My father didn't respond to this line of questioning. Instead, he said something which made my mother and me look at one another in wonder.

"Kemali," he said, with a faraway gaze, which is dangerous when driving, "is going to run for the vacancy on the Chamber of Commerce."

Mahin's flight to Hamburg was scheduled to leave around one in the afternoon, so that seeing her off turned out to be a preluncheon social occasion. My father and I left the office early, picked up my mother, then drove on to Mehrabad Airport.

It was the last week of summer, and the heat had not yet abated.

A largish crowd had gathered around the airline counter — mostly friends and relatives of the Karimzadehs'. The Karimzadehs themselves had not yet arrived. We spotted the Kemalis and chatted with them. Their daughter, they said, had opted to ride with Mahin.

My father and Kemali talked about business.

I went over to the portico, where there was a breeze.

There I found the Karimzadehs, standing in front of their Mercedes. Porters in gray uniforms were taking luggage out of the car. Pulling up behind was a long, sky-blue, chauffeur-driven Lincoln Continental. A porter rushed to open the door.

Gloria stepped out.

She had on a sleeveless white dress, with matching red handbag and shoes — stark colors against her flow of blond hair. Getting out after her, in pallid green, was a magnificently somber Zohre — reconciled, apparently, to the inevitable and now keeping to form. In the vestibule, she and my mother kissed as though they had met at a funeral.

"Don't go away," Gloria addressed me in English. "I want to talk to you, but first I've got some formalities to see to."

She joined the Karimzadehs, who were engulfed by their relatives. She waited her turn, then spoke a few words to Mahin, opened her red bag, and took out a gift. The two of them kissed.

Only then did I notice Bijan in the background.

Still wearing an eye patch. Tall and lean. Dressed in a blue uniform, with a white shirt and black tie.

He was waving the suitcases through customs. Then he crossed the barrier himself. The customs officer saluted. A brief exchange followed, after which the suitcases were marked with chalk and put on a trolley unopened.

Mina Karimzadeh approached us through the crowd.

"Well, she is going," she smiled sadly. "What can we do?"

"It won't be long before we see her again," my mother said reassuringly. "When will she be returning?"

"*Inshallah* in *décembre*."

245

Mahin broke away from her group and moved toward ours.

"Did your father get you the caviar?" Her mother looked about.

"He is getting it now." Mahin put her arm through her mother's.

It was almost a national tradition that, when leaving the country, one took along a tin or two of caviar, purchased from the government store at the airport.

Then she turned to each person and said a few words of farewell. Her eyes were excited, but otherwise she was calm. Even cool, in her beige suede dress, which was more suited to the climate of Hamburg. Above her breast, she wore a peacock pin, made of turquoise embossed in silver — a gift from Bijan.

Mahin's flight was announced.

A throng immediately surrounded her. She kissed each person in turn — Zohre, too, automatically.

"Goodbye, Firuz. Thank you for coming." We shook hands. "I'll send you a postcard from Switzerland."

(She never did. I doubt that she even had my address. All the same, it made for a warmer parting.)

When she finished with her friends and relatives, she walked with her parents toward the passport line. They kissed and held each other long.

On the other side of the barrier was Bijan: the one nonpassenger or airport official allowed across the line.

The group then went up to the terrace to see her plane take off (it being considered impolite not to stay until the passenger's moment of flight). Gloria and I found a niche to ourselves.

"You didn't expect to see me here."

"No, I didn't. How have you been?"

"Just fine — except for this heat," she billowed her dress at the neckline. "It's been one of those summers this country is famous for."

The way she was fanning herself let me see the contours of her breasts.

"At least you live in Shemran," I replied.

"Niavaran," she corrected me.

"That's even cooler."

246

She put a hand on my wrist.

"Well, it may be cool to you, Firuz. You were born in this climate." Her nails had a lavender polish: she was attempting to grow them. On her ring finger, along with her thin wedding band, was an enormous diamond, which seemed incongruously weighty for her childlike hand. "I come from Wisconsin, you know — and that's snow country."

Just then, what popped into my mind was Mrs. Habibi in Hamburg. The first gripe of the foreigner is always the weather: something one can conveniently disparage. With Mrs. Habibi it had been the cold; with Gloria, now, it was the heat. All of which pointed to a broader complaint.

I asked about her husband.

She shook her head. "Parviz is so busy it's amazing. He is completely taken up with his work. He is in business with his stepfather, you know. They're in the process of building a petrochemical plant in Khuzistan. He is down there right now. In this heat. Can you imagine? We were supposed to spend a month on the Caspian, when he broke off his vacation to fly back to work."

"What is he doing there?" I asked.

"Well, that's a big question. But what it all boils down to is that he is thinking of our moving down to Shiraz, so that he can be closer to the construction site."

"Which you don't want."

"Would you?"

"There she goes!" the cry went up from the terrace in Persian. Mahin waved back at the crowd, as she walked toward her plane. Bijan was beside her. Gloria and I joined in the waving, too. At the steps, Bijan handed her a bag, then gave her a kiss. Another shout went up. Mahin climbed the steps and waved again, before entering the plane.

"Do you know about those two?" Gloria cocked her head.

"Do you mean about their getting married?"

"I mean their fling in Ramsar."

"Fling" was not how their romance had been put to me.

"Well, call it what you will." Gloria shrugged and looked away. "The whole thing is ridiculous. I don't know why anyone

247

didn't do anything to stop it. I have nothing against her. She is a very nice person. Intelligent, too. But she is in over her head when it comes to Bijan." She turned back in earnest. "You know what he's like, Firuz. We've discussed this before. No matter what he does, he always hurts someone. He's not going to change. Here he was, practically engaged to Zohre, when he goes and chases Mahin. If there is one thing he's not short on, it's women. Zohre, poor thing, got involved with him more deeply than she should have."

I glanced around.

"Where is she?"

"She is waiting in the car."

The car, of course! I should have know. Zohre's sanctuary.

The plane took off, and we went down the stairs, my parents joining us.

In the vestibule, we came across Bijan. He raised his hat to my mother.

"My apologies for not greeting you earlier. But I had duties to tend to."

Then he saw me.

"Firuz, is that you?" He clasped me by the shoulders. "Well . . . what can I say?" He turned to my mother. "Mrs. Momtaz, I congratulate you on your son." Then he turned back to me. "You rogue, why haven't you been in touch with me?"

"You were up in Ramsar."

He brushed that aside. "That was a long time ago. We'll have to get together." He put an arm around my shoulder. "We have things to talk over, my friend. Lots of things."

He chucked my chin.

Then he herded Gloria and Moni into the Karbalai limousine, which was parked directly in front of the portico.

Before stepping in, he turned to my mother.

"Really, Mrs. Momtaz, it's been too long since we have gotten together. Please forgive me for being so negligent. In the future, I assure you, I shall be more worthy of your esteem."

My mother condescended with a bow.

He turned to my father. "Excellency, my father asked me to convey his regards. He couldn't be here because of the hour and the heat. But he wished me to express his great respect for you."

My father bowed, too, and returned an even more eloquent message.

The Bijan got in beside the chauffeur, and the car drove away.

Returning to our car in the parking lot, my mother linked her arm through mine.

Well." She laughed. "At least he has a great deal of charm!"

27

O ne thing I should say about the climate of Tehran: there are no sudden, dramatic shifts in temperature. One day is much like the next. Major variations take place over a period of time. There are no twenty-four turnabouts. People don't examine the horizon at sunset to see what's in store the next day.

As a matter of fact, I don't think that weather forecasts were regularly featured, back in those days of radio. Likewise the coverage of sports events.

Sports and the weather didn't really become a part of the news until the advent of television.

At any rate, instead of being on the lookout for daily changes, one was attuned to seasonal shifts. Spring, of course, was marked by a universal awakening. Autumn was somewhat different: it came so gradually that, suddenly, one realized that it was no longer hot anymore.

This occurred in October.

On one such day, my father and I set out for a general meeting of the Chamber of Commerce. The guest speaker for the occasion was the Minister of Court, Dr. Hossein Ala.

Dr. Ala had been the Iranian delegate to the United Nations at the time of the Russian occupation of Azerbaijan. He had been the one who had argued the Iranian position, and obtained the General Assembly's support in demanding a total Soviet withdrawal. As such, the man was regarded as one of Iran's foremost diplomats. Later he had been appointed the interim premier, prior to Mossadegh's second government — a position not suited to him. Now, as Minister of Court, one could say he had climbed to the height of his political ladder.

Prime Ministers — back in the early sixties — came and went with a regularity that reflected the instability of their governments. But the Minister of Court was the one constant member of every cabinet: an appointee and spokesman of the king.

In any case, it was ostensibly Dr. Ala whom we were going to hear, but beyond that, my father was putting in an appearance as a candidate for the vacancy on the Chamber of Commerce.

I had just finished teaching a class at Tehran University, when I rushed home to change. My best clothes were laid out for me: a dark summer suit, a silk shirt, and matching pocket handkerchief and tie.

The Chamber of Commerce was located on a small street bearing its name. The building had been the former residence of an old friend of my father. The outer walls and the house were made of yellow brick, and the courtyard, which was largish and bare, was also inlaid with bricks: square ones, like those at our office. A speaker's stand was set up at one end. Facing it were rows of chairs: "American chairs," they were called, because they were made of tubular steel and canvas rather than wood.

Scattered about, groups of smartly dressed businessmen were chatting and greeting one another boisterously. Card holders and members of the Chamber of Commerce.

The "card holders" were the regular merchants, owners of firms who had been issued commercial cards by the government, which allowed them to operate. The "members," on the other hand, were the governing body — a select group of thirty (most of them wealthy), who had been elected by the "card holders" to oversee the activities of the Chamber of Commerce.

Naturally, it was these thirty who made the policy decisions. But, by and large, it was their function to represent the broad interests of the business community.

My father immediately fell in with his peers. The conversations were not the kind which could be kept up for long. People were milling about, constantly moving in and out of groups. Several times my father introduced me as his "business associate." I said little in return: a son's duty being to stand silent — and straight — by his father.

I glanced about and spotted Ashrafi, Karbalai, Karimzadeh — all of them members.

As we moved away from one group, my father lowered his voice and told me in English to "pay homage" to Ashrafi. He was translating literally from Persian. What he meant was that I was to defer to Ashrafi's status on behalf of our family. Since Ashrafi and he had broken off ties, it was incumbent on me to handle the protocol.

He gave me a pat on the shoulder.

I approached Ashrafi through the crowd. Age and illness had visibly affected him. He seemed weary, and his body had entirely given itself over to fat. But he still had his Churchillian bearing.

"I came to pay my respects." I bowed. "My father hopes that you and Mrs. Ashrafi are well."

"Firuz?" he held out his hand, his expression unchanged. "What did you say?"

He leaned his head forward. His touch was clammy and warm.

I repeated the greeting.

He nodded, shrugging it off.

"Have you finished your studies?"

I said yes.

"And gotten your degree?"

I nodded.

"Good. I hear you've gone into business with your father. Is that what you intend to do from now on?"

I told him I had also begun teaching part-time at the university.

He perked up. "Have you spoken to my grandson?"

I told him that I hadn't had the chance.

"I'll take you over to Karbalai." He guided me by the elbow. "The two of you should get together. You will find that you have interests in common. Incidentally," he threw in parenthetically,

251

"tell your father I hold him in great respect. My best wishes to your mother as well."

We were walking slowly, when he stopped and tightened his grip on my elbow.

"It just occurred to me that your grandfather died since the last time I saw you. I should have mentioned it earlier, forgive me. My wife and I were both deeply saddened by the news. I was very fond of the man — may God rest his soul."

We moved on.

Karbalai was standing next to Dr. Ala, who had a circle of listeners around him. He saw us and winked. We waited until the statesman had finished telling his story — at which point a roar of laughter went up. Then Karbalai turned to us.

He was trim in his dark pin-stripe suit — what some women would have called chic and my mother *élégant*. His hair was the same steely gray — no variation in the hairline — and his complexion robust and sunburned. The only eye-catching change I discerned was a small tuft of hair on his nose.

"Do you remember this fellow?" Ashrafi rumbled. His tone indicated an inclination toward levity.

"If I don't, then it's entirely his fault," Karbalai said with a fixed smile. "Is he the one who chooses to stay away from us for so long?" He extended his hand. "Firuz, how are you?"

There followed the usual banter about schooling in America.

Ashrafi was eager somehow to link me up with Parviz.

"Firuz and Parviz should get together. Firuz is teaching at the university. Parviz has talked about doing the same —"

"By all means." Karbalai spread his arms. "I didn't know. How excellent! I thought you were in business with your father."

"I am — "

"But still you manage the two. How excellent! Parviz would be delighted. He is in Khuzistan now. We're doing all sorts of things there. Trying to desalinate the soil — get agriculture going again. Setting up factories. But our major involvement is the petrochemical industry. All the others revolve around that. It's a long-term project. But the potential" — he didn't say profit — "is enormous. Parviz is working very hard with me in that area. Yes, indeed, you will have to get together with him. But when, I don't know." He laughed. "He is almost as much a stranger to Tehran as you are."

"How is Mrs. Karbalai?" I asked.

The question seemed to catch him off guard.

"My wife? She is well, thank you." He paused. "Would you like me to mention that you asked about her?"

A peculiar question in English perhaps, but not so in Persian.

"She sent me a silver cigarette case, when I was in college. I never thanked her. I scarcely know what to say now, since such a long time has elapsed."

"Of course." Karbalai slapped a hand on my shoulder. "That's understandable. I will convey your thanks and make the necessary explanation."

Perhaps he meant well — I don't know. I had intended to say that I wished to get in touch with Nasrin and do the thanking myself.

Ashrafi, in the meantime, had been approached by an associate, and together they had gone off to join Dr. Ala.

My father spotted Karbalai and me by ourselves from the other side of the courtyard. Approaching us, he made a hand-to-heart bow.

"I see your excellency has been talking to my son."

"A very promising fellow." Karbalai winked again. "Just what the country needs."

"You are very kind."

"Not at all. By the way, I've been meaning to congratulate you, Omid, on your establishing your agency. You are representing a very good company. I've been doing business with them for over fifteen years. I hope you understand the circumstances involved, as far as my own organization is concerned: for many years we've had a separate buying agreement, which doesn't involve our going through an agent. All that has been properly explained to you?"

"All that has been made very clear to me." My father smiled. "And I assure you that our agency will in no way interfere with your transactions. If, however, my office can be of any assistance to you, please consider it as being at your disposal. We, too, can act on your behalf, without the agent's commission."

"That is very good of you — most generous. But I don't think that will be necessary."

"But I mean it from my heart."

"In that case, we'll have to create an occasion for it." Karbalai laughed, looking about. It was the kind of remark that would have been appreciated by a larger audience.

"For even though your excellency has been doing business with our principals in Texas for over fifteen years," my father went on — and here he made a tactical error — "please bear in mind that my association with them goes back over thirty."

It was only then that one discerned how much more than money was at stake. My father, at the helm of his new agency, needed some kind of tribute from Karbalai: more than congratulations — a gratuitous offer of mutual support. Something to establish that they were peers in the same world.

The tribute was not forthcoming. Karbalai's eyes flashed with pique.

"Oh, yes." He glanced away. "You bought from them on behalf of the government. One mustn't forget your past services to the government."

Then he excused himself, saying that the proceedings were about to get under way.

My father was pale.

A man stepped up to the microphone and asked everyone to be seated. As it turned out, there were not enough chairs. My father was waved over to an empty seat by a friend. But he declined, and the two of us stood throughout the proceedings.

The sun had gone down some time ago, and the light in the courtyard was a shadowless mauve. The air was seasonably cool.

The man at the microphone talked without the full attention of the audience. He mentioned the upcoming election for a new member of the Chamber of Commerce. He didn't cite the names of any candidates, but asked all those holding commercial cards to turn them in with their votes by a specified date. He was a smallish man, who read from notes, and, I gathered he was the secretary.

I expected Ashrafi, as the president, to speak next. Instead, the Minister of Court was introduced.

Dr. Ala approached the microphone, the audience applauding. He was thin. Distinguished-looking. Bald. In his late sixties, I conjectured. Of medium stature. Wearing rimless glasses.

He spoke with utter precision. In full sentences. Without hesitation or pause. No notes in front of him. Hands clasped behind his back. Standing rigidly — sweeping the audience with a mechanical gaze. Like the side-to-side movement of an electric fan.

What he had to say, one had the feeling, almost everyone present had some foreknowledge of, but needed to have confirmed. Hence, the rapt attention.

Less than two weeks before, the king had voided the national election, which had taken place over the summer. He had done this in response to the public outcry against the enormity of the corruption involved. To have sanctioned the election, under the circumstances, would have been tantamount to condoning the widespread bribery and graft — and leaving himself open to charges of complicity (which some accused him of anyway). As a result, the Prime Minister "elect" had been asked to resign and Parliament had been dissolved.

But in enforcing these measures, the king had also violated constitutional procedure. He had dismissed a Parliament which had come into power — albeit laughingly so — through the electoral process. In its place, he had appointed an interim cabinet government, which had no base of popular support.

In other words, the cabinet government was to function as a healthy head which had been severed from a diseased body. Hardly a situation which could go on for long.

Especially in light of another critical factor: the Prime Minister designate was the same person as before. (Rumor had it, in fact, that he had tendered his resignation one day and been reappointed the next.) Moreover, his cabinet was composed of members who had been "elected" to the previous Parliament.

In any case, the principal task of this interim government was to schedule a new election.

So much for the events of the recent past and the audience's expectation on that score.

With a reassuring calmness in his voice, Dr. Ala announced that a timetable had now been worked out, and that the election would take place in January.

There were a few pats of applause. But not that many. For one thing, there was the sober anticipation of still more news to come. For another, not a few of those present had lost seats themselves in the aftermath of the previous election — substantial investments gone down the drain, unless they could be assured of regaining them.

Following his major announcement, Dr. Ala proceeded methodically — the ideal spokesman — to the next point. The interim government had also been charged with the task of putting together a program of economic reform. Unless certain austerity measures were enacted right away, he warned, no more loans could be expected from the International Monetary Fund. The country had enjoyed six years (he emphasized) of free spending and limited price and import restrictions. But now the time had come to curb inflation and excess spending, before the national economy got out of control. Toward this end, the interim government needed the support of the Chamber of Commerce and the whole business community.

With economic reforms under way and preparations being made for the next national election, a new government could then come into existence, which — with the aid of Parliament (a legitimate one this time) — could legislate the long overdue land-reform program advocated by His Majesty.

This, then, was to be the nation's policy in the months ahead.

Dr. Ala was applauded again — universally, but not zealously.

Not only had some of the businessmen present paid for and lost their seats in the previous election, but many had made enormous profits through the very lack of restraints which the government was now attacking.

In fact, it was on this second issue that rumors had circulated about the possibility of Ashrafi's resignation. It was well known that his views were antithetical, in many ways, to those of the government.

But then, the government in power had hardly the base of support to exercise any radical change in direction. Any major shift would have to be undertaken by the next elected body.

(Or so it was thought at the time.)

In any case, it is somewhat ironic to contemplate that the loss of seats in Parliament for the many might have saved for Ashrafi his position on the Chamber of Commerce.

Ashrafi got up as the applause died down. He had been sitting directly in front of the speaker's stand. Without going up to the microphone, he offered his thanks and support, on behalf of the Chamber. His voice was barely audible.

Another small round of applause followed, and the audience dispersed. A good number went up to the Minister of Court to shake hands.

My father was headed there as well, when he was intercepted by Ahmad Karimzadeh.

The two of them sat amid rows of empty chairs and conversed privately — my father nodding, and Karimzadeh doing most of the talking, it seemed.

When they stood up again, Karimzadeh put a hand on my father's shoulder. My father backed away.

They parted bowing, but not shaking hands. Karimzadeh joined the Minister's circle, and my father — lost for a moment — turned around and walked back.

His face was ashen and bore a pasted smile.

"Let's go," he muttered, striding past me.

Outside, in the street, he waved to people he knew. Still smiling, until we got into the car.

"What's the matter?" I asked.

He deliberated the question, then let out one of his philosophical laughs.

"In a world full of wrong, something is always the matter."

I waited for him to go on.

"Karimzadeh has asked me not to run for the Chamber of Commerce."

I, too — like the audience — had had a sense of foreboding.

"But wasn't he the one who encouraged you to run?"

"Words. Those were words."

"What of his promise to back you?"

257

"An empty promise."

"From a friend?"

A ridiculous question, but I, too, was seething with anger.

"It's not a matter of friendship," my father shook his head. "It's a matter of *partie*." Another French term which had found its way into the language — meaning, basically, power based on pull.

My father bunched his fingers at the tips, throwing me a glance as often as his driving would allow.

"You see, they're a group. Together they form a unit. They make the decisions. They decide who is in and who is out. It's as simple as that. In my case, they decided that I was out. I knocked on their door. Their servant showed me into the hall. Then he consulted his master, who told him to show me out."

He laughed at his allegorical construction.

"And who is the one they asked to step in?" I was wary of questioning him too far.

"Kemali," he replied, then let out a laugh which was alarming.

When we got to our house, he was positively jovial. He was jovial the next day, too. It wasn't until the Friday of that week that the gloom set in. And when it did, it didn't rise easily.

It was ever to be there, threatening to move in — like the winter fog in England.

It was back in September, shortly after Mahin's departure, that I had been interviewed for the teaching position. A week later, I was once again in another academic setting.

As I mentioned, Tehran University was located just north of our street: a convenient five-minute walk from our door to the main gate on Shah Reza Avenue. Its compound covered a square area roughly the size of four city blocks, and was surrounded by a tall iron-bar fence, with seven separate gates (most of which were either guarded or locked). These were meant to symbolize — or so I was told — the seven hills of Rome.

Eight faculty buildings — including one under construction — were arranged in a U-shape around a sunken playing field: one part, surfaced with thick grass, for soccer, and the other, with red clay, for tennis. Between the playing field and the driveway circling it above were rows of maple trees and bushes. Around the faculty buildings and lining the paths were beds of flowers — mostly geraniums. All the buildings, save the one under contruction, were off-white and had been built in the thirties, during the reign of the old king.

The Faculty of Letters was the second up the driveway on the right. The building had several entrances, and one, at the far end, exclusively for the faculty. Beside it was a small parking area for the Dean and his staff. (With a few notable exceptions, cars were not allowed inside the compound.)

Stationed at this entrance was an attendant with a blue uniform and mustache, who opened the door and addressed one as "Doctor."

Beyond was a hall, carpeted with a long red runner. On either side were administrative offices: all the doors being open but one, the largest, which bore the brass name plate of the Dean.

Upstairs was the domain of the English Department, which consisted of several large classrooms and an English Faculty Room, with a window overlooking the Alborz Mountains and a large table in the middle, with chairs arranged neatly around.

Here, too, one encountered another attendant — scruffier-looking, but with the same faded blue clothes. He had sad eyes and an expression that never changed in all the time I knew him.

This was Akbar A'a (no last name as usual), our all-round utility man. He had a perpetual three-day growth of beard, albeit his black mustache was ever radiantly trim. His features, along with the stiff brushlike hair, were the same as those of Golayat — and, like Golayat, he was constantly fetching tea.

This was the world I entered three days a week, from three until five. Within it, though, was another one.

Most of the Iranian professors preferred to teach in the mornings — the earlier the better. Some of them managed to get off before noon.

This left the afternoon session, by and large, in the hands of the people from the British Council: the lot I fell in with — men in their late twenties and thirties, who had public or grammar school backgrounds, and who came to regard me as being one of their kind, namely, a foreigner abroad.

Actually, this was another twist of the distinction between Felix and Firuz. In the office and at home, I was Firuz Khan, as always; in the English Department, I came to be "good old Felix."

After classes "the English set," as we came to be called, would stroll over the grounds and have a few drinks, for want of a pub, at the university pavilion.

This place was located on the southwestern tip of the compound, on the corner adjacent to our street. It too had been built in the thirties, and had been intended, originally, for social occasions. Later it had been turned into living quarters for foreign visitors; with a dining room on the first floor — overlooking a garden and, beyond that, the playing field — and private rooms above.

It was, in that respect, a self-contained world: a concrete block reserved for outsiders, who would not have to venture beyond the purlieus of the compound. Moreover, it was a distinctly male domain. The only exceptions being those social occasions, when the university would take over the downstairs for banquets or high-level gatherings. Even then, women were confined to the first floor.

Behind the building was a small gate — one of the seven — which led to the street. Guarding it was the usual blue-clad, mustachioed attendant. Cerebus we called him, for his brusqueness and ability to keep nonresidents out.

A person could actually live there without setting foot in the rest of the city: sleeping, eating, drinking, teaching.

Such a person was E. V. H. Wedge, Visiting Professor of Biology from Cambridge University — provided one made generous allowances for drinking. It was said of him that the only reason he would venture outside would be to go to the British embassy to pick up his weekly supply of gin and down to the store on our street to pick up his daily supply of *arak*.

Naturally, given this rate of alcoholic consumption, he was the center of social life at the pavilion — which came to be known as "the Breakfast Club"; so-called because it was also said of him that he opened his first bottle of gin before most people had their morning coffee or tea.

Invariably we went straight to his room, where the door was ever open. The drinking was so heavy and constant that if one arrived, say, around, six, one would be sure to be tipsy by seven. There was never anything to eat, to take the edge off the drinking.

And this would apply to all but Wedge himself, who was always seemingly sober, seated comfortably in the sole armchair in his room, casting a benevolent eye around, and sipping at a steady pace which kept him smiling and "elevated."

In this pleasantly inebriated condition, Teddy Wedge — or Daddy Wedge, as we called him — held the world at a suitable distance.

Balding (although he claimed to have more hair than his father had), jovial, with clever, piercing eyes and a great memory for limericks (dirty ones usually), he would sit in his barren quarters, with his pale, thin legs tightly crossed, a glass in hand, drinking. Behind him, on a shelf, in lieu of books, was a row of full bottles. Across from him, by the door, was a row of empty ones — periodically picked up by the servant who did the cleaning (a form of tipping, since these could be sold for one rial apiece). He claimed that he never slept for more than four hours. He "read late" — whatever that meant — and got up early to "see to" his correspondence (written in ink on air letters). In the afternoons he "worked on" his book, correcting proof sent by the Cambridge University Press, even while we were talking. He was always open to visitors. He never turned anyone away. He simply went about his chores and drank in the process, and never quite acknowledged a person's presence, unless that person were drinking, too.

He talked about sex constantly, but in a way which exposed a mind arrested at puberty. None of us could ever imagine him with a woman. A clergyman's son, with an aversion to the church. A college in Cambridge, which he had been bridled to

261

ever since going there as a student. And a cottage in Somerset, inhabited by his mother — the daughter of a family who had sent generations of officers to India.

Back to Clyde, we teased him.

He liked me. He called me "the only damned civilized Persian since Omar Khayyám" — who likewise cherished his booze and had been Anglicized, thanks to FitzGerald.

I liked him, too — though I had to ignore his incessant criticism of Iran.

"Daddy" we called him, more often than Teddy. No one ever used Edward, which he hated — Edward being his father's name, too. "Daddy" had evolved from Teddy, owing to an Indian professor down the hall, who pronounced his T's as D's.

In any case, Daddy Wedge was my mentor in drink. Mentor not only in introducing me to the stuff in such heavy doses, but as a living example of what to avoid. When he left Iran two years later, it was to go to a hospital. He had been dried out three times before, it turned out. If you looked closely at his flesh, you could see it quiver. Quiver constantly. As constantly as his drinking.

At any rate, returning home after these afternoon bouts turned out to be a problem. I had to camouflage my breath in front of my parents.

Felix drank, but Firuz wasn't supposed to.

Tehran University operates on a semester system, with a midyear break falling in January. All the faculties subscribe to one schedule: classes begin and end the same day, and exams take place over the same period.

On paper, the academic calendar looks as balanced and organized as a quality menu.

In actuality, however, the whole thing depends on the pervasive political climate — much in the same way that a one-room school in northern Vermont, say, stays open or shut depending on snow conditions.

The university, at that time, was one of the few arenas of public dissent. This was the case not only because of the intellectuals involved, but also because of the protection it offered to political activists.

The place was literally a sanctuary. Which is to say that neither the police nor any of the armed forces could break into the compound, without the authorized consent of the Chancellor himself. And this meant, basically, freedom from arrest for those disagreeing with or demonstrating against the government.

The same immunities applied to mosques and to Parliament. For a political dissenter to be arrested, he had to be drawn out into the street.

As a result, political activists were in the habit of either enrolling as students or obtaining student identity cards — not just to foment unrest, but to have protection in times of trouble.

Hence the infiltration of the university by agents of the secret police. Or SAVAK, as it was called: the Organization for National Security and Intelligence.

In fact, it was one of the faculty guessing games to determine who was who in one's classes: who the dissenter, who the agent, who the dissenter posing as student, who the agent posing as dissenter or student, and who the genuine student.

At any rate, the major threat of disruption to the university curriculum came from student demonstrations.

How these started was always a puzzle. Students would gather on the steps of one of the faculty buildings — usually the Faculty of Law. There would be shouting. One could hear it distantly from one's classroom. Then there would be a general movement to the next faculty building. Others would join in. From there, the group would move on. Gradually, there would be a chanting crowd outside the Faculty of Letters. By that time, depending on the size of the crowd and the intensity of the chanting, classes would either empty or be temporarily disrupted.

That, by the way, was one way of determining a teacher's political position: if he let out his students automatically, he was labeled a radical. If he kept them behind, he was conservative and progovernment.

263

My way was simply to go to the window to see what was what and dismiss those who wished to go "because of the noise."

At this point, if the crowd was large enough, a ring of police would surround the compound. Thereafter, things would either die down, people returning to classes, or word would come from below (the Dean's office) that classes were canceled for the day.

At worst, a few students, upon leaving the compound, would be apprehended "for questioning." In which case, further, larger demonstrations would be held the next day to demand their release. Which had to come quickly, if matters were not to get out of hand.

This sort of thing happened several times during my first semester of teaching.

January was the month the government had scheduled for the national election. This, it was feared, would set off another wave of large-scale demonstrations. As a preventive measure, the Chancellor had ordered the university to stay closed, even after the midyear break. Classes were to resume sometime after the election results were announced.

When exactly that would be, was not given out. The authorities had no wish to give dissidents a timetable for staging their rallies. Nor did any notice appear in the papers until the very day the gates were reopened.

As a result, the only means of being in touch with the Chancellor's office was via the phone in the English Department — which meant Akbar A'a. No wonder some people suspected him of being an employee of SAVAK.

(Which was not that unusual. We all came under suspicion: especially the faculty from abroad, who were almost universally regarded — and pathologically, they claimed — as being foreign agents.)

One cold January morning, while I was having breakfast, Akbar A'a called to say that classes would resume the following day. I told him I would be over, before going to the office — my class assignments being there, and business being slow that time of year, anyway.

I trudged over a wet layer of snow, dissolving quickly under a steady drizzle. The mountains in the distance could hardly be seen, but they were white from top to bottom.

At the main entrance the guard, who knew me by now, gave an unmilitary salute. The poor fellow was shivering in a thin overcoat and scarf. A heftier man, more warmly clad, asked for my faculty card, which he turned over in his gloves. Then he, too, saluted and waved me through.

Closed gates and double guards were customary sights during times of trouble. No one was allowed in, aside from authorized personnel, which included the faculty.

Hence, my surprise at seeing the Karbalai limousine — the azure-blue Lincoln — parked in front of the Faulty of Letters, alongside the Dean's black Opel Kapitän. As I walked up the steps, the driver and I exchanged glances, nodding automatically: he was leafing through an issue of *Vogue*.

Upstairs, Akbar A'a had a message for me.

The Dean's office had called and, learning that I was coming that morning, asked me to wait for a certain lady who wanted to see me.

"Did they mention a name?"

"Mrs. Amuzegar."

My first reaction was that this was Nasrin. But then I reconsidered: the only Mrs. Amuzegar I knew now was Gloria. What was she doing there, and what did she want to see me about?

I drank tea and shuffled papers, until the telephone rang. Mrs. Amuzegar would be up right away.

A few minutes later, the door opened and Dr. Haeri, the Dean's assistant, bowed Gloria in.

"I hope I'm not intruding." Gloria beamed. "I heard you were teaching at the university, Firuz. So when I dropped by this morning, I asked about you, and they told me that you'd be coming in, too."

She threw open her beige coat, with a brown mink collar — the gesture of a model — then acknowledged Dr. Haeri in the manner that Iranian women do: with a slow and tilting nod of the head.

"Dr. Haeri was kind enough to drive in with me. He also

graciously introduced me to the Dean, and insisted on showing me the way to your office."

"Mrs. Amuzegar will be taking my course in Persian literature for foreign students," Dr. Haeri explained, by way of clarifying matters, then turned to Gloria. "The pleasure was entirely mine."

The two of them were speaking in English, but with a formality that made it seem as though they were translating from Persian.

Gloria was picking up Iranian ways.

"And it will be an even greater pleasure," Dr. Haeri went on, addressing both of us, "to have Mrs. Amuzegar in my class. Most of my students know so little about our culture and customs. But Mrs. Amuzegar . . ."

There followed the usual accolade, which Gloria insistently denied as being her due — until Dr. Haeri, conquered by form, finally broke off.

"You will excuse me, then, if I return to my office. I shall be there, should you need me."

Gloria thanked him again. We all bowed, and he left.

The door closed, Gloria came forward and put her handbag and gloves on the table.

"So you're a lofty professor now!"

"Hardly that." I pulled out a chair for her. "I teach English part-time."

"All the same" — she sat down — "that's what they called you downstairs. Meanwhile" — she threaded her fingers — "I'm still a student."

With that, she became suddenly shy, smiling uneasily and looking about.

"How did you find out I was teaching here?" I asked, trying to put her at ease.

"Oh, that was long ago." She draped her coat over the back of her chair.

She had on a turtleneck cashmere sweater, which outlined her bosom, and a light brown tweed skirt, which looked matronly. The two clashed. Yet the colors were soft. The sweater was off-white, and about her neck was a gold chain, with a gold heart-shaped pendant.

266

She crossed her legs, softly kicking the air, then all became of a piece.

"Hassan mentioned it, after seeing you at the Chamber of Commerce."

It was jarring to hear Karbalai referred to by his first name. As a rule, daughters by marriage were not on such familiar terms with their elders.

"We were all very pleased," she went on. "Parviz especially wanted to know about you. He sends his regards."

I thanked her.

"How is he?"

"Fine."

"Is he still in Shiraz?"

"No, back in Tehran."

"But still hard at work?"

"Of course." Gloria shrugged lightly. "In a way, that's why I'm taking this course at the university. It meets once a week and gives me some reading to do. I need to know more about the basics of this culture. As you know, being married to an Iranian, you can never know enough."

This was oddly put. All the same, it underscored the grounds of our relationship: I was required to see things from her viewpoint. But what precisely was it: the foreigner's or the woman's?

"In any case," she continued, "this Dr. Haeri is going to be good. Parviz has been after me to take his course, ever since we arrived. We knew him slightly, back in the States. He was all wrapped up in his dissertation then. He's a bit stuffy — still, he's dynamic and intelligent."

I nodded: three qualifiers I, too, would have used.

"Now, what about you?" She looked me over and smiled. "Tell me how you got here."

I was about to do so, when Akbar A'a brought in the inevitable tea tray.

"Oh, God, no more of that stuff!" Gloria shaded her eyes. "I had two glasses downstairs out of form. Haven't they got any coffee?"

"Why don't we go to the Wimpy Bar across the street?" I suggested.

Gloria was hesitant. "What sort of place is it?"

I was surprised she didn't know. It was known to most foreigners, being fashioned after the London chain. But then, it occurred to me that this was not the sort of place that she or her set would be likely to frequent.

"It's a corner café where they serve snacks and soft drinks," I explained. "A student hangout. A sort of Hayes-Bick off Shah Reza Avenue."

This made her laugh. "Oh, well, how can I pass up such an invitation? All right," she said, then consulted her watch, "but I'll have to be back in an hour."

I helped her on with her coat, and we left Akbar A'a still holding his tea tray.

On the way down, Gloria asked if we could use another exit.

"I don't want the driver to see us," she added confidingly.

I indicated the door at the far end of the building.

As we stepped outside, I put up my umbrella.

"Are you happier now that the weather has turned cold?" I asked, alluding to her complaint at the airport.

Gloria remembered. She pinned herself against me to give both of us protection from the drizzle.

"I like the cold, yes — but the kind that brings snow. Not when it's raining."

Out in the street, Gloria took my arm. We crossed over to the other side, then, passing a bookstore and bindery, came to the Wimpy Bar.

Gloria stopped before going in.

The place had large windows on both sides of the corner. Inside, there were small tables and chairs, jammed against each other, like those in French sidewalk cafés. Only a few of them were occupied, all by men, who turned around as soon as Gloria walked in. They eyed her with unabashed interest, as she made her way, eyes down, to a table at the back.

It occurred to me that this was precisely what Gloria had wanted to avoid: a place where we could be publicly seen.

"If you're uncomfortable here," I suggested, "we could go."

But go where? I had no alternative in mind.

"No, this will do," she said, pulling off her gloves and accepting the situation. She even managed a bit of humor. "You're right. The place is a sort of Hayes-Bick, except for the glares."

The waiter approached us, and I ordered two American coffees.

Gloria glanced about, as though the place reflected a way of life she had parted with long ago.

It was up to me to keep the conversation going.

"I'm very glad you dropped by." I folded my arms on the table. "I don't see much of old friends. The fact is, I've been rather isolated since the last time I saw you."

Gloria smiled and rubbed the back of my hand with her finger. "You look older."

"Older?" The comment startled me — and I thought of my hairline.

She shook her head. "By that I mean sexier."

Then she leaned back and viewed me from afar.

"Come on now, Firuz. You're not that isolated. You must have a girl friend."

I shrugged. I had my eyes on certain girls, yes, but no girl friend.

The waiter brought the coffee.

She sipped it and put it down.

"I hate to tell you this, but this is even worse than the tea."

"There's no pleasing you."

"Oh, yes, there is," she shot back, as though defensive about the subject. "There's a way of pleasing every woman. You just have to know how."

I nodded noncommittally. "Would you care to elaborate?"

"No, thank you," she murmured. "I'm not your older sister, Firuz. Besides, we haven't much time, and there are other things I want to talk over with you."

Gloria slipped off her coat and draped it over her shoulders.

"Have you heard anything at all about Bijan and Mahin?"

I said no and asked why.

"I assumed you would have heard through their parents. Aren't your families supposed to be close?"

"Well, they are." I glided over the issue. "But they're not always in touch. Why, what's up?"

Gloria looked at me fixedly, then shrugged.

"Well, it's going to make the rounds anyway. They're not getting married. The whole thing is off. Her father stepped in and put an end to it — not that anyone can blame him. Naturally, Bijan was at fault. As I told you before, it's just folly to trust him."

"But what happened?"

"What happened" — Gloria stirred her coffee with a spoon, although she had put nothing in — "was that Bijan Khan — Mr. Casanova of Tehran — got someone pregnant in the meantime."

"While Mahin was away?"

She nodded. "You saw the girl, too. It was that friend of hers — the one who came to the airport."

"Moni Kemali?"

She nodded again.

I envisaged the moon-faced girl, with the large eyes and voluptuous lips, laughing beside Mahin and me, as we walked. As she stepped out of the car with Mahin at the airport.

"A fine, upright sort of fellow, isn't he?" Gloria went on. "First, he drops Zohre for Mahin. Then, when he's got Mahin ready to marry him — and she's worth going after, you know — he has an affair with her best friend, behind her back." She shook her head ruefully. "And what's amazing is that he keeps getting away with these things."

Gloria narrowed her eyes. "This time, at any rate, Bijan Khan didn't get everything he bargained for. When Mahin found out what he was doing, she dropped him."

"How did that happen?"

"Well, her friend — the poor girl — was in hysterics. She couldn't be controlled. Her family discovered that she was pregnant, and got her to say who she'd been with. Then they went to see Mahin's father."

Not Ashrafi? That I found strange.

"Naturally, when Mahin's father found out, he hit the ceiling and demanded an explanation from Bijan. When Bijan couldn't clear himself, her father broke off the engagement. Then he flew to Switzerland to break the news to Mahin."

"When did all this take place?" I lacked a chronological sequence. All this was happening in limbo.

"About a month ago — back in December. Maybe earlier."
Gloria shrugged, then patted my wrist again. "Anyway, that
isn't everything. Bijan isn't satisfied with the response he gets
from Mahin's father. So he flies to Switzerland to talk to Mahin
himself. The father is already there with his daughter. The three
of them then have some kind of summit conference. And do you
know what Bijan expects of her? He wants Mahin to go ahead
with the marriage plans anyway. As though nothing had happened. That's what he told Parviz before leaving — and that,
apparently, is what he told her, too."

Parviz, up till then, had been out of the picture. But I
gathered, from this, that her principal source of information was
her husband. Bijan had ever had his nephew as his confidant.

"Well, Mahin doesn't go for it!" Gloria exclaimed, with obvious relish. There was no question which side she was on:
not just Mahin's, but *the woman's*. In her view, Bijan was a
sort of plague to her sex. "She tells him instead that he has
got to do the right thing. He has got to marry the girl he got
pregnant."

"She takes after her father," I mumbled.

That seemed plausible. Ahmad Karimzadeh had broken off
the engagement to safeguard his daughter's interest: Mahin had
confirmed it in order to safeguard that of her friend. Both were
applying their moral judgment.

"Bijan wrote a very teary letter from Switzerland," Gloria ran
on. "Not to me — to Parviz. Apparently, he tried everything in
his power to make Mahin change her mind. But she was adamant — even though, according to him, she still loved him. Of
course, that's just the sort of thing Bijan *would* write. But even if
it's true, there's no question that she made the right decision.
Even Parviz agrees — and you know how partial he is to Bijan."

I nodded.

"So where does this leave things? Is Bijan back in Tehran?"

Gloria shook her head gravely, indicating that there was more
to the matter.

"No, he's still in Europe, as far as we know. He has taken a
sick leave from the army."

"He's not really ill, is he?"

"Of course not. He's just taking time off. But that's what I wanted to talk to you about. The last time we heard from him was about two weeks ago. He was in France with Zohre."

This piece of news surprised me more than all the rest.

What was Zohre doing in France? And what was Bijan doing, back with Zohre?

"I thought Bijan and Zohre had ended their relationship," I declared. "Only a few months ago . . ."

"They had," she cut me off. "Or maybe it's changed. I don't know. I'm rather removed from what's going on between them. But I can guess. You see, after Bijan started chasing Mahin, Zohre came to live with us. That is, she came back to live with Nasrin — to put it more accurately. You do know that she had been staying at the Karimzadehs' before then, don't you?"

I said yes.

"Well, the poor girl in a way is like flotsam and jetsam. She left Germany to come back to Iran to live with Nasrin. Then, when her uncle and aunt returned from Germany, she went to live with them . . ."

"Any reason?" I broke in.

Gloria tossed back her hair.

"Well, for one thing, they had been living together in the past. And when her uncle and aunt moved back to Iran, it seemed only natural for them to be together again."

"I mean, aside from that."

"Well, for heaven's sake, Firuz! Be a little clairvoyant. When Parviz and I got back to Tehran, we moved in with Hassan and Nasrin. Zohre couldn't very well stay there with two married couples. It would have meant —"

She struggled for words.

A *"ménage à cinq?"* I threw in.

She eyed me steadfastly.

"I wasn't jealous of her, if that's what you mean. Parviz just isn't that sort of person. No, I think it was just a matter of circumstances — time for a change. Besides " — she looked down at her cup — "I'm not sure that she was getting along all that well with Nasrin. I mean, by the time we arrived, Bijan was hot after her — and there were all kinds of speculations going around the house. The situation became awkward."

"So the Karimzadehs had their niece back to protect her."

Gloria looked up. "Let's just say that with Zohre staying at the Karimzadehs', it was easier to control her relationship with Bijan." She waved a hand. "Anyway, to get back to the point: after Mahin left for Switzerland, Zohre found that she couldn't return to the Karimzadehs' — nor could she go on indefinitely living with us."

"The situation must have been awkward for her."

I was seeing Zohre's position more clearly than ever, thanks to this foreigner's openness.

"Well, that's when I really came to know her. You saw us at the airport."

I nodded.

"Afterward we talked — and that wasn't easy, because we could communicate only in Persian — and I found that she was a very nice person. But hurt. She's been hurt so much in her life that I wonder if she will ever be really happy. Still" — Gloria arched her back — "sometimes good things come out of things that go bad. Since she couldn't stay with her uncle, and she couldn't stay with us — she went back to her father."

This stunned me.

No doubt, it explained why she was in France. But still, what kind of foothold was that for a person perpetually sliding?

Gloria continued. "Somehow her father found out about her situation and asked her to join him in France. He is living in Nice, you know."

I acknowledged that I was aware of that.

"I gather he is squatting on a good part of the family fortune — which puts Zohre in line for a tidy inheritance."

"How did she respond to his offer?" I asked.

"She burst into tears. I was there when the letter came. She just held onto me and cried like a child. She must have cried in my arms for hours. Honestly, I had to change my dress afterward."

Gloria, in spite of herself, had to laugh.

I recalled the Zohre of yore, who had done the same in the arms of the Consul General's wife.

"What happened then?"

273

"Well, her father sent her a plane ticket. She packed two suitcases and joined him in Nice. He is living with his wife, who is German, and has two stepchildren in school in Germany."

"When was that?"

"You're always asking when." Gloria puckered her brows. "Back in October. The middle of October. Nasrin, Hassan, and I saw her off at the airport. She didn't want her uncle and aunt to be there. Nasrin thought otherwise — and so, the two of them had a small row before she left. At any rate, she got her way and had a private departure."

"And she's been in Nice ever since then?" I queried.

"Apparently." Gloria tossed back her hair again. "We've had only two letters from her since she left. One was addressed to me — but it was written in Persian, so Nasrin got to read it anyway. You'd think she'd write more often, considering how much Nasrin and Hassan have done for her. But then —" Gloria hesitated, "who know what kinds of problems she's going through? She's been hurt."

"So that's where Bijan is, too." I leaned back. "With Zohre in Nice."

"As far as I know." Gloria shook her head. "Apparently, he went there straight from Switzerland." At the mention of this, her anger flared up again. "Can you imagine the gall of the guy? He goes to Switzerland to patch up things with Mahin, then when she breaks off with him so that he can marry the girl he got pregnant, he flies instead to France to do God knows what with the girl he ditched for Mahin in the first place!"

She let out a huff of protest.

"Does his father know about this?"

"I should think he does. He's footing the bills."

"And Mahin's parents?"

Gloria shrugged. "What can they do? They've done the best they can by getting their daughter off the hook."

"And Moni Kemali?"

Gloria sighed. "I imagine her father is busy looking for a husband." Then she eyed me sheepishly and grinned. "What about you, Firuz? Like to come into a small fortune quickly?"

I was surprised — and she took this to mean that I was offended.

274

"Of course not." She glanced down, taking her gloves. "You were brought up in New England. When you marry, it will be strictly out of honorable motives, won't it?" Then she glanced at her watch. "I've got to be going, Firuz. Walk me back the way we came."

Outside, in the street, I put up my umbrella, and she took my arm again.

"That was an unnecessary thing for me to say."

I told her not to worry. We crossed the street and passed through the gate again.

"The point is" — she tugged at my arm, slowing our pace — "it's not Bijan or Mahin I'm so concerned about. They can fend for themselves. Mahin is a sensible person. Besides, she has the support of her whole family and a full life ahead of her. As for Bijan — well, he's going to do all right for himself anyway. It's Zohre that worries me."

"Zohre is everyone's worry," I muttered.

"Well, of course!" Gloria shot back, almost rebukingly. "Consider the unfortunate life the poor girl has led."

The "poor girl" she was talking about was older than she was. Moreover, had Zohre's life been all that unfortunate? Or had her misfortunes been continuously exaggerated? After all, given her frame of mind, which, I gathered, had been fixed since her mother's death (if not earlier), couldn't one more or less expect her to tumble from one set of unhappy circumstances into another?

It occurred to me then that I had never been her friend. Or possibly I was still smarting from the fact that, at one point, I could have been, but had been spurned.

At any rate, I was not half as easily moved on her behalf as others were. Notably, her female protectors — of whom I surmised Gloria to be the latest.

"I'm concerned about her, Firuz — I really am," Gloria reiterated with insistence. "That girl has the most tenuous ties with the people she loves. She's not on sure ground with anyone. Her father takes off and leaves her. She is forced into living with relatives and friends. Then Bijan flashes into her life as some ray of hope. When he drops her, that makes her feel even more desperate. Finally, when her father shows enough sense to drag her out of that mess — well" — she paused and spat out her words — "Bijan crops up on the scene again! That could lead to disaster, you know."

I nodded, wondering what sort of disaster.

"If Bijan gets it into his mind that he wants to take advantage of Zohre, he'll do it."

"What sort of advantage?"

"Marriage!" she snapped. "He could get himself off the hook with the other girl by marrying her. Zohre may not even know of what's been happening, and Bijan has a way of spinning a very fetching yarn. What do you think?"

I was wondering how Gloria, who was so sympathetic toward Zohre's plight, showed almost no concern for that of Moni Kemali.

"Zohre would go along with it, too," Gloria added emphatically. "I know how she feels about him. What do you think?" she asked again. "You know him. In a way, you know him better than I do. You grew up with him."

That refrain was familiar.

"So did Parviz," I reminded her.

She shook her head and let out a frustrated laugh.

"Parviz is always on his side."

That seemed to explain everything.

We stopped at the door we had come through before. Gloria faced me squarely.

"Am I making any sense, or do you think all this is just foolish conjecture?"

"No, you're making sense." I opened the door. "But I don't think that Bijan would go after Zohre simply to get himself off the hook with a girl he got pregnant. There are other ways of handling those things."

"Well" — she stepped in ahead of me — "what's he doing in France, then?"

"He could be there because he is genuinely fond of her."

Gloria turned around and looked at me incredulously.

"After all," I continued, theorizing, "rejection has a way of warming the heart."

"Bullshit!" she sneered.

I shook my umbrella and closed it. "Or he could be there for revenge."

Gloria blinked and nodded, as though this was what she had been waiting to hear.

"You mean, to get even with Mahin?"

I shrugged evasively — I had extended my limits as a seer. After all, how much could I say about Bijan or his motives over a gulf of so many years?

"Yes, well, I hope Zohre doesn't do anything foolish," Gloria added, as a finishing touch to our tête-à-tête. Then she smiled and resumed the formal air she had begun with. "I'd better go now. Don't bother walking farther with me. Give my regards to your father and mother. And give me a call sometime, will you?"

She walked down the hall and turned the corner. Minutes later, I saw the Karbalai limousine pull out of the driveway and pass through the gate.

On March 21 — Now Ruz Day — 1961, Bijan and Zohre exchanged vows before a mullah in Nice. Their marriage was duly recorded at the Iranian embassy in Paris. Two weeks later they returned to Tehran, where a formal reception was held for them at Ashrafi's house in the city.

My parents and I received a printed invitation.

There was no question, of course, of my father attending. The rift between him and Ashrafi was too deep to be bridged — even by the marriage of his son.

Our family, however, was expected to put in an appearance, and so my mother and I were to go by ourselves.

Just before the occasion, though, I came down with the flu. So my mother phoned her brother, the one who had driven the borrowed car from the airport, and asked him to accompany her in my place.

After making her call, I remember my mother coming into my room. She took out a large suitcase from my closet, which she used for storing small treasures. She went through several items, which she unwrapped and wrapped again, until she came to one which she held up for my approval.

It was a silver picture frame, with an oval shape and a floral design.

This was our wedding gift to Zohre and Bijan Ashrafi.

My uncle showed up around four in the afternoon. I got out of bed to stretch my legs and went down to the living room to greet him. He was wearing his best dark suit — his hair slicked down, and his shoes shining like ebony. Across from him sat my father, in slippers and bathrobe. He had just woken up from a nap and had been going through the paper. Between them was the stove, which hadn't been taken down because of the cold that year. Usually, stoves were dismantled before the Now Ruz celebrations.

The three of us chatted and drank tea, until my mother came down, some half an hour later — ready to rush out the door that instant. They were late, she claimed, and told me to get back into bed immediately.

She had on a new dress and a display of rings, which she wore only on special occasions.

She kissed my father and me, and said that she would be back by eight at the latest. My father handed my uncle the car keys and accompanied them to the car. I returned upstairs and went to sleep.

When I woke up, I was hot and achy. It was dark.

My father came in with a bowl of *aash* — the thick vegetable broth one has when one is sick. He had not stirred in the yogurt, lest it "encourage the fever."

I asked him for the time.

"Half-past eight," he said surlily.

He had sunk into one of his moods. He was still in his bedclothes, so I gathered that he hadn't returned to the office.

At nine, he came back up again to take my temperature. He felt my forehead and examined my pulse like a doctor. Then he patted my cheek and went down again, taking the bowl.

I was drifting off again, when sounds came from below.

"It's past ten!" I heard my father bawl.

278

Then everyone came up to my room. My mother sat on my bed, while my father and uncle looked from the doorway. She was excited and cold. As she put her hand to my forehead, I felt the coldness of her rings.

"He has fever," she announced, then shook the thermometer on my bedstand and slipped it under my tongue.

That done, she took my hand in both of hers and beamed irrepressibly.

"What a pity you weren't there! What a splendid occasion it was. Zohre was beautiful. Bijan was handsome. They both asked about you. But the gifts!" She gave my hand a squeeze. "You wouldn't believe how many there were! Isn't that right?" She turned around to her brother for confirmation.

He let out a whistle and smiled.

"Omid, do you know who was there?" She addressed my father more seriously, then went through a list of names. The Karbalais. The Amuzegars. *Not* the Karimzadehs! But people in banking. People in business. Army people. Two cabinet ministers. And who would have guessed it? My father's brother — the one he had quarreled with.

That was that.

My father blew up.

"I don't want to hear any more! I told you never to mention that man's name again. Never! Not in this house!"

My mother tried to interject, but my father was in full sway.

"Not one more word! About the wedding, or who was at the wedding, or Bijan, or Zohre, or anyone. Not in my house."

With that, he stalked downstairs and called my uncle.

"Where are you going?" my mother yelled from my bed.

"I'm going to drive your brother home!" came back the answer from below. "Someone has to drive your brother home!"

Then there was a slam of the door.

That night my father was so angry, he actually drove my uncle home in his bathrobe and slippers!

28

𝒥 was in bed with the flu for almost two weeks, one part of my body coming under attack after the other: the head, the throat, the lungs, and finally the bowels. Around the middle of April, I got up and, still feeling wobbly, made it to the office. I didn't go back to the university for another two weeks — my mother being adamant about my taking afternoon naps until I had fully recovered.

Meanwhile, the work load at the office had been piling up. The active time of year for spare parts was from the beginning of April till the start of the ginning season, early in September. After the Now Ruz holidays, orders would start coming in on a regular basis — usually by mail, but also sometimes by courier.

My task was to oversee the handling of these goods from start to finish. Which meant placing the orders — that is, checking through company catalogs, making proforma invoices, keeping records, and so on — and then notifying our customers of the arrival of the parts in Tehran. Technically, my duties ended at that point. As it later turned out, not all our customers were able to take delivery of their goods. In which case, I had to act on their behalf — clearing the goods through customs and forwarding them, with the help of Golayat.

At any rate, by May, when the warmth of spring had pried open buds, and leaves had acquired a pale green luster, I was up and about, my usual self, more or less; except for an occasional spell of dizziness and sweating, and an ongoing bout of postillness depression.

That month we had two visitors from Texas.

The first was a short, wiry man in his sixties, with an outdoor complexion: a genuine Texan, born and bred, so he claimed, not far from the Alamo. He worked for our manufacturers on a contractual basis, and had been sent to install two ginning plants, which my father had sold back in February. Both plants were located in Gombad Kavus, and were scheduled to begin operating in September.

The second was our manufacturers' representative: the special agent we had all along been dealing with. He, too, labeled himself a Texan — though he had come by that identity in a roundabout way. He had emigrated to America via Bulgaria, Turkey, and Lebanon — his parents were Russian. He spoke eight languages, he said — yet he was also pleased to point out that his children in Dallas knew only English. For him we rolled out the proverbial red carpet. We reserved a room at the Park Hotel — the best in the city in those days — and wined and dined him at home .

He stayed for a week, and most of that time was spent in discussing ways of dealing with the growing competition from two other companies.

Up until a year or so before, there had been no question that our firm was the major dealer of cotton-ginning machinery in the market. Our only competitor was a manufacturer in Louisiana, which had set up a fairly new agency. But now, yet another — and much more aggressive — manufacturer had entered the picture. It had not yet appointed its agent in Iran, but was doing business through its own sales representative. This meant that, as a special attraction, it was eliminating the commission which would have gone to the middleman, thereby reducing prices for the customer. On the whole, the reduction came to some 10 percent below the figures we offered.

We considered a number of ways of dealing with this problem: setting up a small factory locally to produce simple parts, such as piping, was one. But that required an outlay of a good bit of capital, and so was set aside. The manufacturers' agent asked my father to reduce his commission — temporarily. But that, too, was unfeasible — and a dangerous precedent from our standpoint. Finally, we agreed to make our bids more attractive by offering better financing: longer terms at the same rate of interest.

That issue settled, we turned to spare parts. Since our competitors were providing better conditions there as well, we had to be sure that we didn't lose our own customers. It was decided that I should take a trip north and visit as many of their ginning plants as possible.

This did not include, of course, the half dozen or so plants belonging to the Karbalai corporation. Karbalai, as ever, had maintained separate dealings with our manufacturers. Nor would there have been a need, anyway, for his ginning plants were the most efficient in Iran. In fact, it was a source of irritation to my father and me that we were constantly being goaded by our principals in Texas to bring the other plants up to the standards of his.

Along with the decision to make a trip north, I was advised to take along someone with technical know-how. We turned to a man who had done occasional work for us before: a degreeless Armenian "engineer" named Mirzayan. Our manufacturers' agent wanted the two of us to set out right away, since there was still time to take orders for the coming ginning season. But this was not possible. My work at the university, for one thing, carried into June. After that, there were the shipments arriving from Texas to be cleared through customs. Aside from which, Mirzayan's wife, it turned out, was ill and needed the care of her husband.

Our manufacturers' agent was disgruntled: it was evident that our office was short of qualified help and that we were operating on a minimal budget.

On the eve of his departure, my mother laid out a banquet, and there was much laughter and toasting. All the same, we were glad to see the man gone. My father especially. It was one thing to do business under stringent conditions — he was used to that — but quite another to have one's methods constantly questioned: to be pressured, as it were, from somewhere insubstantially "above."

Eventually, Mirzayan's wife showed signs of recovery and we were off: one morning before dawn, early in August, in Mirzayan's old Borgward, which he had never had the temerity to drive outside the city.

We took the road east — known as the Firuzkuh Road. We had resolved to go directly to Gombad Kavus — the furthest point on our trip — before stopping off at various ginning plants on the way back.

By sunrise, we were out in the desert. A few hours later, we caught sight of Mount Demavand and its snowy crest rising over the Alborz range. Later we arrived at Firuzkuh itself: a village nestled in a valley with tall, thin trees, below the rock after which the area was named. Then we headed north, into the mountains, and the condition of the road deteriorated rapidly. Not only was our progress slow — sometimes no faster than walking pace — but the way became increasingly rocky. Before long, we had a flat tire. Our first of eleven on the trip. Poor Mirzayan! To be burdened first with a sick wife, only to be driven wild afterward by what happened to his car.

We reached Sari by nightfall, exhausted — disgust written all over Mirzayan's face — and shared a room in a small, sparsely furnished hotel.

The next morning, we literally sped to Gorgan: the road linking towns near the sea being considerably better than the one through the mountains. There we stopped for extra springs, then headed northeast again — across arid plains — where we encountered not hard riding, but dust.

At Gombad Kavus, we dropped off supplies and looked over the construction sites. Two days later, the car cleaned — both inside and out — we set off again.

Thereafter, it was a matter of stopping at one ginning plant after another. From Gorgan we went on to Behshahr, Neka, Sari, Shahi, Babol, and Amol, before heading north again toward Nowshahr and the Caspian coast.

Each stop took a day, with a morning's or afternoon's travel in between. When we reached Babol, I wanted to see the plants belonging to Karbalai. After all, I had been aware of their existence since childhood. But then, I thought no. What was the use? It wouldn't have brought us any business — and we were up there purportedly for that.

By the time we got to Nowshahr, I was ready for a vacation. There we finished inspecting our last plant, and I gazed longingly at the sea. The weather was perfect, and so was the water. I suggested to Mirzayan that we head up the coast to Ramsar.

No one, I argued, would miss us if we stayed on an extra day or two.

But Mirzayan was worried about his wife. And so — after barely a day and a half on the coast, and no more than one dip in the Caspian — we turned back to face the stifling mid-August heat of Tehran.

As we left the coast, taking the Chalus road, I vowed that I'd be back within a week.

We made good time and arrived at our house by early afternoon. My parents had already eaten and were resting. The food was warmed up and Mirzayan invited to stay for lunch. But he was tired and dusty and anxious to get back to his wife. He downed a glass of vodka and was off — his car rattling in a way I hadn't been so aware of before.

Over the meal, I recounted our exploits.

The trip had been a success. From my standpoint, it had been enormously informative. Moreover, it had netted our agency some $2000 in commissions (excluding the money which had to be deducted to offset the damages done to Mirzayan's car).

Beyond which, I was in the peak of health and good spirits. I was five feet, nine inches, lean and wiry, weighing 135 pounds, and "brown as a nut," as my father put it.

I told my parents I wished to return to the north.

My mother informed me that the chairman of the English Department had called. He wanted me to supervise the entrance exams, which were due to take place in the first week of September; this was the price I had to pay for being ill back in April.

But that still left me time. A week or so by the Caspian was all that I needed.

"I'm afraid we have another obligation."

My mother's tone of voice irritated me. Why? What could there be to offset a brief trip and a well-earned break?

"Tell him after he finishes his meal," my father counseled.

But my curiosity was up. I wanted to know then.

My mother put some dishes aside.

"Your friend Parviz has just returned from Switzerland. We have to go and see him. He has undergone a serious operation. They had to cut off his leg. He has cancer of the bone. "

My father was right: I should have been told after I had finished eating.

That Friday afternoon, my mother and I drove up to Niavaran. My father stayed behind in his slippers and bedclothes, reading the newspaper and sipping tea. He did not want to take the chance of meeting Ashrafi.

The car had been washed and waxed for the occasion. On the way up, we stopped to buy flowers. The streets were still relatively quiet and free of traffic, due to the heat. Once we reached Shemran, though, we encountered a throng of pedestrians, cars, horse-drawn carts, and donkeys laden with vegetables and fruit.

We made our way across Tajrish Square to the narrow, winding road to Niavaran: the same one which led to the Karimzadehs' and, farther along, to the Ashrafi estate. Midway between the two — perched on the slope of a foothill — was the Karbalai mansion.

It was a mansion in the Iranian sense: new, squarish, with large windows facing one way, overlooking the city, and garishly opulent in being that size without adhering to any definable design. The product of an architect's fancy — welded to the taste of a man whose plenty had clearly to be shown.

I mentioned as much to my mother, who told me not to be so judgmental.

I couldn't really tell whether she approved of it or not. She had been there before. Moreover, she had a kind of awe for the Karbalais, which quashed any critical tendency.

At the gate, we were approached by a man in a dark suit and tie. He asked for our names, then actually went back to a telephone. When he returned, he announced — very politely — that we could pass through.

In a way, it was like a brief border crossing.

On the other side, a more familiar type — with pajamalike trousers and a sunburned face, deeply lined — held the gate open.

I spotted the light blue Lincoln Continental.

Suddenly I recognized the man who had approached us. He was Karbalai's chauffeur. But not just chauffeur, I then gleaned. Obviously, he functioned in other capacities as well.

As we walked up the pebbled path, my mother took my arm and urged me to be "kind" to Parviz.

"He has been through a great deal, you know. Be polite to Mrs. Karbalai, too. She, too, has suffered more than her share."

As though I would have done otherwise!

My mother and I were wide apart in our feelings then. Arms linked, we could have been strangers.

In the middle of the garden was a pool. The path led up to and around it, with flower beds on each side, and beyond them, saplings tied to poles.

In front of the house was a long, elevated terrace – bare but for the small company seated around a table. On the table was a large heap of fruit.

We waved from the path, and my mother hallooed with a smile.

Salaams came back, and two men stood up. One was portly and bald. The other, Parviz, gripped the arms of his chair and took a cane.

My mother preceded me up the steps and embraced Nasrin, who remained seated. They kissed one another lightly on both cheeks. Then she turned to Parviz, pressing him longer and tighter, and delivering a personal message into his ear.

Nasrin held out her arms.

"How long it's been, Firuz. You've grown into a man."

I bent down and kissed her cheek, smelling the familiar mixture of cosmetics and perfume. The beauty of her face was constant, though marred by an expression of tension. There were lines around the mouth. The eyes seemed sunken. These were features I had associated with her laughter, which now seemed gone.

I tried not to scrutinize.

Parviz gave my hand a hard squeeze. If he smiled, he must have done so under a kind of duress which cloaked it.

"We've lost touch," he said in English. "It's good to see you again. Why didn't you come up sooner?"

286

"I tried to," I said, conscious of being on the defensive. "I phoned several times. But you were either out of the city or else occupied."

"That's true." He shifted the weight on his leg. "I do have a way of getting caught up in things. Let me introduce you to my mother's uncle and his wife."

Ashrafi's brother. I had not known he had one.

We shook hands, mumbling the usual greetings, after which the two of them fell silent, while the rest of us talked.

The man was wearing a suit, which, despite his portliness, was too large for him. He also had on a white shirt, buttoned to the neck, without a tie. The woman, on the other hand, was bulging at the seams. Both looked uncomfortable in their clothes. The man, I judged, was at least some twenty years older than his wife. They had come from Khoy to visit Parviz.

So this is what Ashrafi would have looked like, it flashed through my mind, if he hadn't left for the city.

As soon as there was a break in the conversation, I turned to Nasrin.

"I have to thank you for the cigarette case you sent me."

I wanted to say more — to mention that I was sorry for not writing. But she leaned forward and checked me.

"I know your parents don't approve of smoking. Nor do I, when it becomes an addiction. But smoking, every once in a while, is not a bad thing. A young man should know how to smoke on occasions. The cigarette case was meant for occasions." She glanced at my mother. "I hope you don't disapprove."

"Not at all," my mother protested. "It was a beautiful gift, and I don't know why Firuz didn't thank you sooner."

Parviz nudged my arm.

"You haven't seen the house." He spoke in English again. "Why don't I show you around?"

He pushed himself up again and took his cane. As he did so, all eyed him silently. My own impulse was to reach out and help him. But he exuded an almost militant air of self-sufficiency.

He hobbled over to the sliding glass door and stepped over its frame.

287

"Be careful of that." He pointed down. "I always tripped over it, even when I had the use of both legs."

The ice was broken.

"I was very sorry to hear about your operation," I said, joining him in the living room. We were by ourselves now. "My mother told me about it, but didn't go into details. I was up north until a few days ago."

"Vacationing at Ramsar?" He leaned against the back of the sofa.

"No. Just running about, doing business for my father."

He nodded.

I shouldn't have said running, I chided myself.

Parviz must have sensed my uneasiness and let out a sigh — anxious to have done with going over the sad facts of his plight.

"Well, it was all very strange and came very quickly. Last spring I was south, playing soccer with the boys. We have a plant near Shiraz, and I like to mingle with the workers. I got kicked in the shin, and that's how it started. It developed into a lump the size of a golf ball. We had it diagnosed and found it was cancerous. I flew up to Switzerland, and that was more or less that. The leg had to be cut off here."

He drew a line two-thirds the way up his left thigh.

"Then came the radiation therapy. We had to be sure the damned stuff was burned out." He shook his head and snorted. "It was a hell of a way to spend the summer."

"Did the treatment succeed?" I sensed that we'd be off the subject soon.

Parviz shrugged. "So far it has. One has to be grateful for that. But who knows how far the damn thing has gone? We ought to have signs before long. The longer I remain the way I am, the better for me."

Parviz slapped the back of the sofa.

"How about a drink?" he said, with a change of expression and tone. "If we're going to talk about morbid matters, we might as well get some satisfaction out of it. Why not move to my room? We're not going to find any booze here."

Is that why we had left the group on the terrace? I wondered. Tea had been brought out almost as soon as we arrived.

"I've moved downstairs now." Parviz crossed the living room. "There are too many steps to manage a flight."

He walked ahead, and I glanced around.

The furniture was upholstered in a soft and matching creamy-white velvet. The carpets were magnificent: two floral Kashans, with backgrounds of deep blue. There was a large bouquet of flowers on the coffee table. On the wall, in a gold baroque frame, was a portrait of Nasrin — done in oil — as she must have looked in her early twenties. Before I had known her. It was Nasrin, to be sure. But the face was thinner — poised and bloodless. Almost, in fact, like that of Zohre.

"In here." Parviz threw open a door. "My bedroom, sitting room, office, and bar — all rolled into one. What can I get you?"

He lowered the hatch of a liquor cabinet.

"What are you having?"

"Martini with olives — very dry and no ice."

"I'll have the same," I replied, and took a chair by the wall. "Do you remember the last time we had drinks? I got smashed."

That little remark made Parviz gurgle with laughter.

"Yes, you were pretty shaky, all right. You could hardly stand on your feet."

Feet again.

He went on, mixing the drinks. "I remember you reeling and trying to get your words out straight — especially when you were leaving. You were trying so desperately to be proper."

He laughed again and held out a glass. "I seem to recall we played a game of chess, and you lost pretty badly."

"I lost twice pretty badly." I accepted the drink.

He stirred his own cocktail with a spoon.

"Are you sure you don't want any ice? I'm going to the kitchen for olives anyway."

I said no.

"You stay here, then, and I'll be back soon."

The room was comfortably furnished, but Spartan. Apparently, it had been used before as a study. There was a couch by the wall, and below it some bookshelves. An armchair. A desk, with a long fluorescent lamp.

I thought of Cyrus's room in Hamburg. It was not so much because of the basic similarities, as a general feeling.

It seemed cloistered. Boyish.

The desk looked over the eastern range of mountains — the way I had taken to Gombad Kavus. On it were papers with mathematical equations — pads and a box of pencils. I almost expected to see an exercise book.

The carpet was of a lower quality than the Kashans in the living room — a mixture of dull blues and reds. Also there were photographs on the wall, which I got up to examine. Of Karbalai. Bijan and Amuzegar, both in uniform. Of Parviz in front of a petrochemical plant. Other people I didn't recognize.

The royal family.

None of Nasrin — which struck me as odd.

Parviz's diplomas. Certificates of merit.

A color photo of Parviz and Gloria.

I glanced at the couch.

Where was she, and how did she fit into the room?

She didn't.

I had the eerie feeling, in that room, that Parviz and marriage were apart. Severed from each other — like his leg. Something was living, and something was not. Which was which?

Was it the marriage that was dying or dead — or Parviz?

He returned to the room with a jar of green olives.

"I love these things," he muttered. "What a pity we don't grow them in Iran. These are from Greece."

I felt a surge of compassion. Shorn of restraints, I would have buried my face in his shoulder and wept. Instead, I channeled my emotions elsewhere.

"Is there anything wrong?" he queried.

I took a sip from my glass and returned to my chair.

"I was wondering." I sat down. "You must have gone through a great deal of pain. Do you still feel it now?"

He put an olive between his teeth — the way one does with a cube of sugar when drinking tea — and drained his glass in one mouthful.

"Constantly," he said, munching the olive. "I feel pain all the time." He spat out the pit and threw it in the wastebasket. "But pain is a matter of degrees. Sometimes it's only a gnawing sensation. Other times it's so sharp I can't even breathe. When that goes away, I come back to the gnawing with relief. Hold out your glass."

I did so, and he dropped in an olive. Then he fixed himself another drink and lowered himself into the armchair. He propped his wooden leg on a stool beside it — positioning it until he felt comfortable. Then he leaned back and let out a sigh.

"You want to know about pain? Very well." It was as though he were passing from the specific to the general. "It is like other things in life — such as problems. When one lives in the present, one lives with problems. Sometimes big ones. Sometimes small ones. It's only on hindsight that one lives in happy times."

He took another sip from his glass.

" Tell me, were you happy in college?" He stopped me before I answered. "What I mean is, when you look back, do you see clearly the problems you faced? Or perhaps I should go back before then."

"You don't have to," I admitted. "I agree: they tend to blur."

"Precisely." He tapped the arm of his chair. "And that's the case not because your memory is bad, but because you have new ones. I remember specific lessons from my childhood, but not the trouble I had in learning them. The fact is, you are here today because you survived the old problems. Because you survived, they no longer exist. You do. Mind you, I didn't say surmount. Whether you get the better of your problem, or your problem gets the better of you, is another issue altogether — and a secondary one, too, in my opinion. The point is, you are here and you have new ones."

He pointed to the jar in the cabinet.

"Would you put some olives in that ashtray and hand it to me? It's all right. It's never used."

I acquiesced.

As I resumed my seat, he popped an olive into his mouth and raised his eyebrows.

"Do you follow me?"

"I think so."

"Good," he nodded. "Because when you ask about pain, you

shouldn't be confused by the issue. Pain exists in the present, and never in the past or the future."

He spat out the pit and hurled it toward the wastebasket again, missing it.

"It's like one's teeth. One is never really conscious of them until they give one trouble. Then their function seemingly changes — to irritate rather than help one's digestion along. But to think that way is to be gulled by sensation. For when a tooth is decayed, what does one do? One has it extracted and replaced with another one. Is that not the case?"

I nodded somberly.

"Well, then" — he threw out his hands — "that's my point in a nutshell. You have done with one kind of problem, and you march on to the next. It's the same with this." He tapped his wooden limb. "I have it out and go on to the next one. I go on and on and on, and thank my stars that I have another leg to stand on. Do you follow me?"

I nodded again.

"Because to do otherwise would turn me into a bitter person. I could envy you now for having two feet. For being able to run. But I can't afford that. I have to muster all my energies on this other one." He rubbed the live limb. "Why? Because it takes me considerably more effort to get from one place to the next. At first, I couldn't even stand up. Now I do. I couldn't walk from that door to this desk. Now I do. I spent three weeks in a Swiss sanatorium this summer, learning how to walk all over again. And the process was not only awkward, but painful. No child has to put up with pain when it is learning to walk. If it did, it would cry. But adults" — he raised his glass — "can't afford that luxury."

He took another swig and rubbed the wooden limb again.

"No, you can't allow pain to dominate your life. It may have control over your senses, but not over your mind. I learned that as a child, when Bijan was blinded. And now I am going through that same process myself. I don't say this out of maliciousness, but some day so might you. Let's hope not. In any case, you had better prepare yourself."

With that, he let out a short laugh and raised his glass.

292

"Come what may, I drink to your health."

I raised mine in return, then got up to fix us another drink.

Parviz — with two drinks inside him — was feeling better now.

"Tell me," I asked, somewhat lighter myself, "where are things headed from here?"

"Ah, now that's more like it," he smiled, taking the drink I extended. "I'm glad you asked that. From here I go back to Switzerland for more treatment. How long that will last, I'm not sure. Maybe another month. Maybe two. If the disease has been checked, I should be gaining my strength. Then I'll probably come back for a few more months of convalescing and work. By this time next year, I should be off to Cal Tech."

"You've been accepted?"

He nodded, pleased. "I would have gone this year, but for this damn thing," he gave his wooden leg a sharp rap.

"Congratulations!"

"Thank you." He sipped away at his drink.

"I take it that Gloria is happy about all this."

He held his glass in midair — formal again.

"Of course she is," he said, almost castigatingly. "She's my wife. Wherever I go, she goes with me."

Shortly afterward, we heard loud talking from the terrace.

"That will be Gloria." Parviz put his glass on the floor. "She's been playing tennis at the American Club with my stepfather. Let's go out and meet them."

He had trouble getting up.

"Give me a pill from that drawer, will you?" He pointed to his desk.

I went to the kitchen and got him water, then helped him to his feet.

He was too unstable for his cane and asked for his crutches. I got them out of a closet.

Then I watched him carefully pass through the living room and come to the terrace.

When he got there, he was breathing hard.

Everyone must have known we'd been drinking.

Nasrin and my mother looked crestfallen.

"Firuz!" Gloria beamed, and wrapped her arms around my neck. "How nice to see you!"

Then she turned to her husband. "Darling, you look tired."

Parviz stood there on his crutches, eyes glazed and swaying.

Karbalai and I shook hands.

Both he and Gloria were in tennis clothes, he looking dapper in shorts, and she more glamorous than athletic in a V-neck top and short pleated skirt.

"We had better be going." My mother touched Nasrin's arm.

There were remonstrances from all sides, except from Nasrin and Parviz.

"We'll get together again soon." Nasrin wrapped her fingers around my mother's.

Then she looked at me.

"My son and I both thank you for coming."

We shook hands and parted.

Karbalai walked us down the path to our car. He was jovial, as usual. Sunburned and cordial.

As he opened the door for my mother, he raised her hand to his lips.

"Please give my best wishes to Omid."

My mother expected to hear from Nasrin. She had hopes, I suppose, that our visit would lead to reestablishing old ties. It didn't.

Weeks went by without any response.

My mother wanted to telephone. Yet she was also reluctant to make any more overtures. She turned instead to Mrs. Karimzadeh.

The Karimzadehs had just returned from Switzerland. Both husband and wife had undergone checkups — the wife getting additional treatment for her backache.

Mrs. Karimzadeh, by now, was almost addicted to talking about personal ailments — so much so that she even glossed over reports about her children. All except Matin, perhaps, who was the sickly one.

Appropriately enough, it was through her that we received the next piece of news.

Parviz had gone back to Switzerland, accompanied by Nasrin and Gloria. The Karimzadehs had seen the three of them, just before leaving their hospital.

Did this mean, my mother asked, a turn for the worse?

Not at all, was the reply. He looked better than ever.

Had the disease, then, been checked?

Apparently so. At least, there was no cause for alarm for the present. Gloria, in fact, was due to return any day on account of her studies. Parviz was adamant about life going on as normally as possible.

What about Nasrin?

Nasrin was staying on — as a good mother ought.

That was her interjection, not my mother's. Apparently, wives, in Mrs. Karimzadeh's estimation, could come and go more freely than mothers. Possibly the distinction — in her view — was underlined by the fact that Gloria was American.

At any rate, a week or so later — at my mother's instigation — I called Gloria. As usual, I had to try several times before getting through.

I asked about Parviz.

He was fine. Just fine. No cause for alarm — although she was still keeping her fingers crossed.

She sounded unchanged.

When would he be returning?

She was uncertain of that. In a few weeks perhaps. The middle of October. By then, she sighed, they should know.

In November Mrs. Karimzadeh passed along the news to us: The cancer had metastasized, reaching one lung and threatening the other. The doctors were trying to combat it with heavy doses of radium.

Gloria had dropped her course work and flown back to Switzerland.

By December it was clear that Parviz had no more than a few weeks to live. He returned to Iran, ostensibly for a rest from his treatment, but, in fact, we all knew, to be buried.

My mother urged me to visit him.

She had still not heard from Nasrin, and despite the deep empathy she had for her and her son, she couldn't help feeling slighted at this. Disappointed at not being turned to for support. To her, this amounted to rejection — putting her in the frustrating position of not being able to respond, unless specifically asked.

With me, though, it was presumably different. None of this applied, since I was Parviz's childhood friend and — so my mother liked to think — his college companion. Together these amounted to a passport and visa. For me the doors would be open, and I was at liberty to march right in.

In fact, it was my duty to march in — the dying having certain claims on the living.

I thought I ought to go, too, but for other reasons.

I called the Karbalai mansion. A servant answered and said that "Parviz *aqa* " and the *"khanum"* were staying at the Ashrafi home in Niavaran.

Who the *"khanum"* was, he didn't say: I gathered Gloria.

At any rate, this was odd. Why should he be staying at his grandparents'? And why the house in Niavaran? They had one in Tehran. People with villas in the foothills usually moved back to the city once the weather turned cool. Now it was cold. It was winter. Most of the villas did not have adequate heating.

Had Parviz decided to spend his last days in the house he had once romped in, and been happy — the thought occurred to me — as a child? That presupposed that he knew he was dying. Did he know that?

My mother maintained he did not. The doctors' prognosis had been withheld from him.

I dialed Ashrafi's number.

The old man answered himself. The connection was bad, and his voice sounded weak — coming over a great distance, it seemed, and through a roar. He had trouble identifying me and asked me to talk louder.

I spoke on behalf of my family — conveying our sympathy. Then I asked if I could speak to or visit Parviz. He told me to wait a moment, then returned to the phone. I could come up any afternoon other than a Friday. I didn't have to call in advance. But he preferred that I limit my visit to an hour. Any longer would tire his "child."

That's how he referred to him: not as *naveh*, "grandson" —
but *batcheh*, "child." Apparently, to Ashrafi, where offspring
were concerned, one didn't have to make distinctions between
children and grandchildren.

He hung up the phone without suggesting that either of my
parents come along.

The afternoon I paid my visit was a cold one. There had been a
light flurry of snow in the morning — not enough to cover the
streets of Tehran. The sky was a monotone gray, and, in the distance, through the wintry haze, one could detect the snow-
capped mountains.

In Shemran, though, the ground was covered with snow. The
streets were lined with muddy, white banks.

The road to Niavaran — which hadn't been shoveled —
looked like a cart track, with grooves for single-lane traffic. If
one encountered a car, one pulled to the side — into an embankment or puddle — as it went splashing by.

I passed the Karbalai mansion, embedded, it almost seemed,
in the mountains, surrounded by boulders topped with snow. It
appeared curiously abandoned.

Further along, there was a fork in the road, and conditions
were better. One branch led up to the king's new palace, the
other down to Ashrafi's estate.

An estate no longer, I gathered, as I glanced at the houses beside it.

The gate was the same as before, as was the condition of the
wall. But the lot had been subdivided on either side.

The road, moreover, no longer led up to the gate, but sloped
down — asphalted and broad — to Tehran.

I honked at the gate, and a man wearing several sweaters let
me through.

Inside the compound, I was shocked at the size of the place.

First of all, I could actually see the four walls. Secondly, the
upper pool, with the floating watermelons, was gone. The huge
oak tree was the same — as was the house. But one was barren,
and the other looked older. Smaller, too, than I had remembered.

The place, in fact, had been reduced from an estate to a house
with no more than a large garden.

I parked the car under the oak tree, walked up to the door, and knocked.

The door opened, and a woman peered out. A white scarf about her head. She, too, had on several sweaters. Apparently, the servants wore the same clothing both indoors and out. She was thin, old, and bent — a long-time servant, no doubt, though I didn't recall her. With a thick Turkish accent she told me to come in.

Inside, I smelled the familiar odor of food — rice and *khoresht*.

The hall was dark, bare — as before — and chilly. The old woman took my coat and scarf, hanging them up on a wooden rack with a mirror.

"The *aqa* and *khanum* are having tea in the living room," she said, then walked ahead of me.

As we entered the living room, I immediately recognized the furniture and the rug. The one conspicuous addition was the stove at the far end. On either side of it, seated in armchairs, were Mr. and Mrs. Ashrafi. In front of them was a low table with a tea tray.

I took a few steps and bowed.

Ashrafi screwed his eyes before speaking.

"Come in, Firuz. It's good of you to visit us. Sit over there." He pointed to a chair across from him.

Then he turned to the maid. "Bring some more tea and some biscuits. And when you've done that, tell my daughter that we have a visitor."

She was about to leave, when he added: "Tell her it's Firuz Khan."

I sat down without shaking hands. Mrs. Ashrafi asked about my parents.

"They are fine," I replied. "They told me to send you their regards. They wished to come and see you as well, but didn't want to inconvenience you now. They asked me to tell you that, they hope, when Parviz is better . . ."

Both nodded.

Ashrafi hadn't changed since the last time I'd seen him — which had been at the Chamber of Commerce meeting over a year ago. But his corpulence was more pronounced in his casual clothes. He had on his usual open-neck shirt, a sweater buttoned at the chest, but open below, which allowed his stomach to protrude. His feet were cozily slippered.

His wife was wearing her usual drab dress, and a long, green sweater, with a handkerchief sticking out of one pocket.

The room was in semidarkness: no light being on, and the late afternoon glow coming in through the veiled windows.

I asked about Parviz.

Ashrafi gave a concise, unclinical account of his condition — stressing how he felt, rather than going into the details of the disease.

"He gets tired very quickly. He has been through a great deal. The treatment has weakened him. But it is also the drugs he is taking. They put him to sleep." He lifted his glass. "When did you see him last?"

"The end of August," I said. "Before he went back to Switzerland."

He finished the rest of his tea and put it down again. "Don't expect to see the same person. What this boy has gone through, not many can match and come out alive."

The door opened, and the old woman came in with the tea.

Ashrafi sighed, dismissing the subject.

"At any rate, one has to bear with these things as one can. We are all in God's hands."

"God is compassionate," the old woman said, putting down a glass in front of me. She wasn't responding to the conversation, but rather to the mention of the deity by name.

"God is great," Mrs. Ashrafi added. Then she pulled out her handkerchief and put it to her nose — swaying gently back and forth. I couldn't tell whether she was inwardly crying or praying.

"But now, what about you?" Ashrafi turned away from the women. "How is your work coming along? I don't mean business. I mean the university."

I gave him a summarized account of my activities of the past year or so. He listened intently, nodding, pushing me along with affirmative remarks.

"Good, good. I'm glad to hear that."

It was somewhat like being a schoolboy again: home on vacation and reporting on my academic progress.

But it was also more than that: the schoolboy had a respectful audience. Ashrafi's attention was riveted on something he valued. Something he himself didn't have. The listener, in this case, looked decidedly *up*. Not just at me, but at the whole process I was talking about. A mysterious entity — experience — which had bypassed him.

"You must go on." He waved his hand, not horizontally, as Americans do, but vertically. " You must get your doctorate. It doesn't matter in what field. One can always worry about money later. One has a whole lifetime to take care of that. But not education. There your time is limited. There your true money is youth. Provided you have the brains," he tapped his temple. "If you have the ability to go on, then you should. Take advantage of it. Do it!"

Nasrin walked in.

I didn't recognize her at first. In fact, I thought it was the maid again. I got up.

Her hair was pulled back. Straight — without waves. Austere. Nothing glamorous about her — except, oddly enough, her sadness. Paleness. Tautness of skin — which I noticed when she came closer.

She had no makeup on.

She walked with her hands folded in front of her. About her shoulders a dark shawl, which she took off and draped over a chair.

Rembrandt colors and subject.

"Please sit down," she said, with a formality that seemed strangely impersonal.

For a moment, I wondered whether she, too, had trouble making me out. The light in the room cast people in shadows.

Not objects, though.

The tea set, for example, was startlingly clear. As was the lace tablecloth.

She took a chair next to her father and gave me a smile — which settled the issue.

"It was good of you to come, Firuz." She rested her hand on

her father's. Then she glanced at her mother. "He is awake now. He'll be in soon." Then she looked back at me. "My son will be glad to see you, Firuz. You know how fond he is of you."

It was as though she were speaking of the Parviz of years ago.

Ashrafi gazed up at his daughter. "Is he better now?"

She rubbed the back of his hand. "The nap has helped him." She turned back to me. "My son has had a very bad night. He was restless all morning. After lunch, we put him to bed."

Again the reference to Parviz as a child.

"But now" — another quick smile — "I think he is in the mood for a little company."

She let go her father's hand and adjusted the band at the back of her head. "How is your mother?"

The conversation became conventional. It could have taken place anywhere, at any moment, regardless of circumstance. I took it as a ploy to get off a painful subject. A cloak or a screen to cover up the real thing.

Parviz dying — as everyone knew, without mentioning.

Why? Out of politeness, or what?

Then it occurred to me, as we spoke. Not an astute observation. All the same, one that modified things.

This was control.

A way of coping with the horror of death. Seeing and living with a loved one dying.

It wasn't so much a cover-up, as a matter of bearing with. As Ashrafi had mentioned.

Nasrin, in that room, seated with her parents and talking about mine, was bearing her grief.

The distinction, as I say, between "bearing" and "covering" was not a particularly astute one. Nonetheless, it altered my feeling.

I relaxed.

Nasrin saw this and smiled differently. She put some dried fruit on a dish and passed it around.

It was like a small break in an otherwise overcast sky.

Thereafter, we spoke briefly as old friends. Not just Nasrin and I — but, oddly enough, all four of us.

Then the door opened again, and the old woman stepped in — holding it back.

Parviz appeared in a wheelchair — one leg down, the stump of the other with the trouser leg tucked under it.

Behind him — I almost jumped up — was Musa! Older, with deeper furrows about his face. But robust. Still the same man, with the identifiably close-cropped hair and wrestler's physique.

I felt the tug of opposite emotions: joy at unexpectedly seeing the one, and distress — actually a sort of horror — at confronting the other.

Musa wheeled Parviz toward our group. Parviz gazed about distractedly. His eyes were glowy. His skin was like wax. I was about to get up, when he spoke.

"It's hot in here. There's not enough air,"

His voice was high-pitched and peevish. It also came with a wheeze.

"Open the window," Mrs. Ashrafi ordered the old woman by the door in Turkish.

A window at the far end of the room was unlatched, and a gust of air billowed the curtain.

"Not that much!" Mrs. Ashrafi fairly shouted.

Ashrafi leaned forward in his chair.

"How are you, my boy? Did you sleep well?"

Parviz looked at him vacantly. "It's hot in here."

"Move him over here," Mrs. Ashrafi beckoned to Musa — indicating the space between herself and me. "That way he'll be out of the draft." Then she turned to me. "Would you change places with my daughter?"

"Of course." I got up.

Nasrin rose, too, and smiled at Parviz. "Your friend is here. He's been waiting to see you."

Parviz looked up. His eyes, I could see now, were feverish. It was as though some giant had picked him up and wrung him out like a cloth.

"Thank you for coming," he mumbled in Persian.

We shook hands. His grip was bony and weak — hardly a grip at all, except for the curve of the fingers.

302

I glanced at Musa. He was still taller than me.

"Do you remember me?" I asked.

He put a hand to his heart and spoke solemnly. "Your servant, Firuz Khan. I was told you were coming."

That was as much as we could say, under the circumstances. I took my seat beside Ashrafi, and Musa, having positioned Parviz between his mother and grandmother, softly left the room.

Ashrafi turned to his daughter. "Has he had any tea?"

Nasrin nodded.

"Would you like another glass?" he inquired of his grandson.

Parviz shook his head. "Only water."

Hearing this, the old woman went out to fetch it.

Parviz was being catered to. But in a way which made him seem not only cared for, but trapped.

Lacking air, as he himself put it.

Was this the way to go, with so little time left? Was there any alternative?

The old woman returned with the water, and the picture became clearer.

He was surrounded by women: the servant, his mother, his grandmother. All smothering him with attention.

Where was Gloria? Why wasn't she there? Would her presence have made any difference?

A glance at Ashrafi put the whole thing into focus: it was like an old family photograph — in sepia, to boot. On one side, the father and mother, with the stove between them; on the other, the daughter and nanny; in the middle — still helpless — the infant. The four figures formed a sort of square — a human prison — inside which the infant was locked.

Looking directly across at me, the infant started babbling. His gaze was wild and his talk fantastical. It was about a form of escape which he alone could envision.

"In another week or so, I'll be off to Switzerland. This time I'll stay there until the cure is complete. By spring I want to be back to finish work on a project. That's when our new plant is scheduled to open."

Which plant, I didn't ask.

"I've done a lot of the planning you know. Hired the engineers. Gone over all the blueprints. I want to be there when we start operating. It's the first plant of its kind in the country."

I was reminded of the boy who had run after the horse — leaving his construction behind, unfinished.

Ashrafi turned to me. "Parviz has a great mind for industry."

He said this reassuringly, for Parviz's sake. As though to indulge in delusion were his prerogative. Again I thought of children — the games one played with them. One entered their fantasy world without interfering, because to do otherwise would have shattering consequences. From Ashrafi's standpoint, no doubt this, too, was coping.

But, to me, Parviz's words conveyed a different message: because they were directed to me — and because I was the one person outside his group.

"Once the plant is in full operation," he went on, "I'll be free."

Free, I took him to mean, not of the disease, but of a certain mental restriction.

"Then I'll go back to America and work on my doctorate. There's nothing to hold me back any longer. I have to be in good shape for the fall."

With that, he let out a huge, unearthly sigh and sagged in his chair.

That frightened the women.

It was as though the air had suddenly gone out of a balloon. Empty. For a short while, his mind had managed to separate itself from the body. But now it was back in it again. His breathing came heavier, and his gaze went blank as before.

"Tell Musa to come. I want to go."

Mrs. Ashrafi leaned over to feel his forehead. "Do you have a temperature, my love?"

"It's not that!" Parviz pulled away. Behind him, the old woman was biting her forefinger. "I tell you, it's hot in here. I can't breathe. Tell Musa to come. I have to go."

"You have to go?" Ashrafi looked puzzled. Then he turned to his daughter and murmured, "He wishes to go to the bathroom?"

Parviz rolled his head, unable to bear his predicament.

"I have to go. Tell Musa to come."

The old woman had rushed out, in her crablike way.

When Musa showed up, he went straight to Parviz and wheeled him about.

Then the two of them left, as they had come in, without a word. Parviz's face was beaded with sweat.

Mrs. Ashrafi started to cry. Nasrin went over to comfort her. Ashrafi and I peered at the floor in silence. I felt I ought to be leaving, but the occasion wasn't right.

Shortly thereafter, Musa reappeared and said that Parviz Khan was resting in his room.

That caused further consternation.

"Does he have a temperature?" Mrs. Ashrafi asked, as though that were the telling factor in her grandson's case.

Musa mumbled something at the door. At which both mother and daughter got up to find out for themselves.

Ashrafi and I got up after them. It was a good moment now, I thought, to be gone. I had paid my visit. The longer I stayed, the more of an imposition my presence would be.

But Ashrafi detained me.

"No, you sit here until my daughter returns." He pushed away my extended hand. "She will want to thank you for coming herself. I will go and tell her that you are waiting. As for us old people" — he patted my shoulder — "you'll have to excuse us. But age, too, has its prerogatives."

With that, he shuffled out of the room in his slippers, and I was left alone.

I sat down and waited.

I stared at the space across from me, where Parviz had been sitting. Viewed from that angle, the space was the center — the chairs grouped around it. Parviz had sat there, with his family about him.

As I shifted my gaze, the space — as the center — suddenly vanished. In peripheral vision, it became merely a gap between chairs.

Where was the center now? I tried to recapture the original impression. No use. The space was no longer the center. The stove? The coffee table? Those were only objects. Pieces of furniture.

The center had to be humanized.

Me! I was the center! Where I was sitting. The one place I couldn't see.

The association struck me with a mute kind of horror.

I didn't want it to be me. Not at the center of things. Not when the center was vacuous. No trace of Parviz or the chair he'd been sitting in.

I wanted to be gone. My mind was beginning to work in strange ways. I didn't want those ways to take over. Couldn't I just leave word with the old woman?

Out of the question. I was rooted to the spot by some kind of convention. I couldn't move until someone freed me.

Nasrin.

The thought of her angered me. Which surprised me.

Why the anger, and why Nasrin?

Was it because of the etiquette that trapped me? Was it in response to seeing Parviz — trapped as a child again? As helpless in dying as he had been as an infant?

Did I expect his mother somehow to work miracles -- releasing him, as she soon would me?

I was conscious of nodding. The kind of nodding one does when angry and latching on to implausible thoughts.

Implausible that Nasrin could do anything to save him — yet quite plausible from the standpoint of feeling.

Just what did I want her to do? Moreover, did that mysterious want pertain to Parviz or me?

I got up and walked to the window. The light was fast fading, and there was a bluish tint to the snow. A draft came in through the clefts. The pane was cold.

At an immeasurable distance was the swimming pool we had swum in as children. The water had been drained, and it was cemented now.

Then Nasrin walked into the room.

"My father tells me you wish to be going," she said, advancing. "Won't you sit down a few minutes first? I've hardly had a chance to talk to you."

She was polite as before — though not distant. Rather her formality served to camouflage her feelings. Her fatigue. It was evident from her eyes that she hadn't been sleeping well.

Again, I thought, the beauty of that face was marred by suffering. This time, though, it had a more permanent look.

She pointed to the two armchairs her parents had occupied. We sat down.

"I must ask you to convey my apologies to your mother." She locked her fingers. "I should have called her long ago — or written. But the truth of the matter is that I found that impossible. It's not that I wish to be aloof or unsociable. But for the time being, I'm afraid, there is no other course I can take. You saw the condition my son is in..."

"I understand." I wanted to cut her apologies short. "So does my mother. She is quite aware of the pressures you are under. Please accept our family's sympathy."

I, too, was responding to form. But this was the message I had been entrusted to deliver.

"That's kind of you." Nasrin nodded. "Those are comforting words. In such times, one needs the assurance of friends. Even though one can't see them. That's what I want to talk to you about."

Apparently, she couldn't bring herself to communicate with my mother — and I was to be her intermediary.

"My son is dying, you see." A crack slipped into her voice, and she cleared her throat. "It is very important that I make the rest of his days as bearable as possible. He lives in such pain. Both physical and mental. I don't know which kind is worse. At any rate, it is essential for me to minimize his pain. And that means, unfortunately, limiting our contact with others. That may sound strange to you. But I assure you, there is a reason."

She checked herself from going further — then chose her words carefully.

"You see, a mother has to take every factor into account. I assure you, it is my son's interest that is uppermost in my mind."

Her voice was beginning to tremble.

It struck me that I was witness again to this woman's misfortune. But more than that: the issue went deeper. There were factors involved. A "reason" too personal to disclose.

There was more to her agony than her son's dying.

"That is the message I would like you to convey to your mother."

She unlocked her fingers and pushed forward the plate of dried fruit.

Again the rings were gone.

"As for the rest, I speak to you as Parviz's friend. Confidentially. We have moved him here because the situation is, frankly, more comfortable. The poor boy has seen too much of hospitals. He needs to be in an environment now which is full of love and affection."

She broke off as before

Clearly the subject was not one she could talk about openly.

"In any case, this is not the time or the place to go into details. The point is, my son has to be happy. And I think he is happier here than anywhere else."

In his grandfather's house, rather than hers.

"Tell me the truth," she eyed me squarely for the first time. "Did you not wonder about this? About why he was here?"

I had to admit that I did.

"Well, then." She nodded again. "That's why we've had to cut out all company. There would be too many questions — too many speculations of a troubling nature. I want my son to have peace. Here he can be in the midst of his immediate family. In the care of his mother and grandparents. I doubt very much whether others would understand."

Then, she uttered the words so quietly I had to reach for them.

"Therefore, I ask you not to say anything about this."

So that was it. I had seen things — just by being there — that were meant to be concealed. Never mind what or how much I knew, I had pried into something which had to stay hidden.

Henceforward my lips were to be sealed.

I had a message to deliver to my mother — and the rest was between us.

No wonder Ashrafi had wanted me to wait for his daughter.

But what had I seen?

Only this: the full weight of the burden was actually on Nasrin. It was her agony that penetrated the deepest. Deeper even than her son's.

The living had more to suffer than the dying.

Curiously, I felt a sense of relief at this.

"What about you?" I asked.

"Me?" She looked startled.

"Is there no one to comfort you?"

I had presumed too far. She drew back.

"Being with my own son is comfort enough."

She was distant now, as I hadn't seen her before. I had the optical sensation, in fact, that she was receding.

"But thank you for thinking of me."

She receded even further.

It was not coldness I sensed, but a petrification. It was as though she were turning into an inanimate object.

I gathered, from the long pause, that I was to leave.

I got up, she followed suit, and we walked to the door.

"Again, thank you for coming."

In the hall, I put on my coat and turned to her. "I wish I could do something to help."

She smiled and patted my cheek.

"Be discreet."

Then she lowered her eyes and opened the door. "Thank you for coming."

The repetition was almost a push to be gone.

Two weeks later, Parviz was buried. There was a notice in the papers. His wife was mentioned. His parents and grandparents. Bijan. No mention of Karbalai. On the other hand, there was a long column about his accomplishments and the contributions he had made to the petrochemical industry.

For a person so young — twenty-five — these were impressive indeed.

29

One morning, toward the end of that month — January 1962 — I received a call from Akbar A'a. I was at the office, and he was using the phone in the English Faculty Room. He said there was trouble at the university and advised me not to come.

What kind of trouble, I asked.

The usual kind, was his bland reply. Students were organizing a strike. They were marching around the compound, making speeches — urging people to walk out of classes. Most of the teachers, he added, had already left.

The news didn't surprise me. A demonstration of this sort had been a long time in coming. All through the fall, as with the one before, there had been miniature uprisings. Harangues outside one's classroom windows. Nothing seriously disruptive — but, cumulatively, building up a charged atmosphere. No longer was it a matter of whether or not there would be agitations — rather it was a matter of determining when.

There was good reason for expecting this. The country had gone through two elections, by now, without coming up with a parliament. Both elections had been declared void, on account of the widespread corruption. No one could have any more confidence in a government which was, so to speak, "popularly elected." The king, in response to this, had given emergency powers to yet another interim government. The task of this government was to bring about immediate reforms: the most important and controversial one being land reform. The king was intent on breaking the power of the traditional aristocracy — the great landowning families — by forcing them to give up their land. That is, requiring them, by law, to sell their land to the government, so that the government could turn around and sell it back piecemeal to the people who worked it: the traditional peasantry. The aim of this measure was to free the country economically, though not necessarily politically, from the strictures of feudalism: by releasing the peasants from their contractual obligations to their landlords, and by encouraging the landlords, in turn, to reinvest the capital gained by the sale of their land in industry. Thus, the land barons could be turned into industrial barons, the economy could be shifted, a new class of peasant farmers and industrialists could come into being, and Iran could enter into the spirit of the twentieth century without recourse to violence. Without upsetting the government or the monarchy.

Needless to say, this approach to dealing with progress had the blessings of Washington.

But violence — or a violent reaction — was bound to ensue sooner or later. For one thing, there were too many disgruntled people — and they were forming into factions. The landowners were upset about having to lose their land. The clergy were behind them, because such a move threatened to alter the basic fabric of society — and wherever that happened, as had been their experience in the past, they tended to lose power and influence. These two groups — hitherto suspicious of each other and with different interests to protect — formed the right wing. The reactionary front.

But, at the other extreme, there was the dissident one — the National Front, which had been out of power and in steady decline ever since the demise of Mossadegh. This was the faction that claimed to speak for the majority of the people — not just the religious zealots and wealthy, but the nation at large. Two fraudulent elections had shown them how they had been prevented from assuming power through the ballot box. Twice they had been frustrated in their attempts to gain control of Parliament. Furthermore, this faction had views of its own as to how to go about implementing land reform: no concrete or well-defined proposals, such as the government had come up with, but, rather, various differing theoretical and ideological approaches. It was argued that once this faction assumed power, it could then thrash out the issues more specifically.

The problem here, though, was that this faction, too, had its splinter groups to contend with. The National Front was a front

311

in name alone. More accurately, it consisted of a body of people — largely carry-overs from the Mossadegh era — who had gone their separate ways and formed small parties of their own. The leader of one party would blame the leaders of others for mistakes of the past. By and large, these were backward- rather than forward-looking people. I attended a few of their meetings. Mingled with protests against widespread corruption and cries for government reform was a curious air of nostalgia — as though those were the issues which could have been dealt with more effectively in the past, but that somehow they hadn't been, and that there was even less point in trying to deal with them now.

Faced with such a volatile situation — a country without a parliament, a disgruntled aristocracy, clergy, and intelligentsia, all of whom combined could whip up the masses to fury again from both left and right — the king had appointed as Prime Minister a man who was declaredly divorced from politics altogether and committed only to reform.

This was Dr. Ali Amini. A well-to-do landowner himself. A former ambassador to Washington. An economist pledged to economic reform — and a person so disinterested in other people's opinion that he was famed for his arrogance. The model patrician who could single-handedly remove the country's ills from above.

He had very little popular support. The small backing he did have came from the mercantile class and those few landowners who chose to go along with government measures rather than put up any time-wasting opposition.

People like my father, in other words, who had businesses to run, and who were disenchanted with the politics of the past.

Amini's major opponent — some claimed personal enemy — was a General Teymour Bakhtiar. Bakhtiar was from an equally large and well-known landowning family (a relative, in fact, of Mrs. Karimzadeh). He had made a career of the army and a name for himself in setting up SAVAK. Bakhtiar was not in favor of these reforms and was said to be plotting the downfall of Amini. Rumor had it that his plotting went further and included even the king. His ambition was boundless.

In any case, when government measures were ready for enforcement, Amini threatened to jail Bakhtiar, if his opposition continued. That is, if he tried to thwart matters by heading an opposition group, comprising landowners and clergy. The king, who, it was further said, did not wish to see things come to this point, apparently asked Bakhtiar to leave the country. The newspapers announced the General's departure for Switzerland. With Bakhtiar out of the way, land reform could proceed under Amini's resolute leadership.

That issue, in itself, was one of the sparks that touched off what turned out to be the Tehran University riot. At least, that is how people interpreted the situation at the time. Later I read a *Time* magazine account, which reported that the trouble had been started by the firing of five high school teachers for allegedly drawing whiskers on pictures of the king. These teachers, according to the report, had been branded as ringleaders of the banned Tudeh party. Which may have been the case — I don't know. All I know is that *that* version of the cause was not the one which reached my ears. Nor was it one which was widely circulated.

Whatever the cause, an implausible mingling of leftists and rightists — supporters of the National Front, the clergy, and what was popularly referred to as the stooges of the aristocracy — coalesced momentarily to form an unhappy union of dissidents: crying out against all the ills in the country. Demanding the removal of Amini. Some shouting for Parliament. Others for the country. And finally the drowning cry of all — the chant of unity in dissent:

"Mo-ssa-degh! Mo-ssa-degh! Mo-ssa-degh!"

That's what I heard, as I stepped out of the taxi on Shah Reza Avenue. Across the corner from the Wimpy Bar.

I had left the office to go to the bank and told my father that I would see him at home for lunch.

A policeman was waving the traffic south, away from the compound. The corner at my end was lined with trucks. Inside, seated facing each other, were youths in light blue uniforms. Police cadets. One student force brought in to counter the other. I had never seen the two in conflict — and if the cadets had

313

weapons, I couldn't spot them. They were there, I surmised, as a show of strength. As a psychological means of containment.

At the far end of the street, on the other hand — rounding the corner near the university pavilion — were army trucks. About a dozen — full of troops, with helmets and rifles. A sufficient force to contain a small riot.

Milling about between these two groups were clusters of police. Parked in front of the main gate — right on the sidewalk — were several closed jeeps.

It was difficult to estimate the size of the crowd in the compound. The demonstrators were filing past in irregular batches — chanting and waving their fists.

In a way, it was like watching a tiger circling its cage, with armed attendants looking on.

There was no sign of violence. Nonetheless, the two forces were clearly arrayed.

I crossed the street to get a closer look. A policeman approached me.

"You cannot go farther."

I showed him my faculty card.

"Has the university been officially closed?"

He examined it carefully. "No, excellency."

"Then please let me through."

"You'll have to speak to the chief officer at the gate." He returned the card and escorted me.

The chief officer at the gate was clad in a dark blue uniform, a matching hat and open overcoat, and shiny, black leather boots. Attached to one sleeve of the overcoat was a black arm band.

He was pacing up and down in front of the main gate, beating a small whip against the palm of his gloved hand.

He stopped and watched us. Plainly, the sight of a man in civilian clothes infuriated him.

"Get that man off the street!" he shouted.

The policeman held a hand across my chest.

"He has a valid faculty card, excellency."

Captain Ashrafi advanced toward us, then suddenly recognized me.

"Firuz! Is that you?" He snatched off his glove and extended his hand. "What are you doing here?"

314

"I heard there was trouble." We shook hands. His grip was firm. "I came to see what was happening."

"Of course! You teach here." He tapped his brow, then grasped my shoulders. "Old friend, where have you been? At one time, we were inseparable. Where have you been hiding yourself?"

It was typical of Bijan to take the offensive.

He turned to his cohorts. "Gentlemen, allow me to present to you his excellency, Dr. Momtaz — one of our most brilliant professors at the university."

The two men saluted and offered their hands, as Bijan introduced them.

"Lieutenant Taheri. Lieutenant Nosratian."

Both were of medium height — one on the stout side, the other on the slim — with faces of a military cast: unquestioning eyes and long, thin mustaches, which the young officers usually wore. Bijan — their superior — was clean-shaven.

All three, though, looked of a piece — as though they had been born to wear uniforms.

I turned to Bijan. "I was very sorry to hear about the death of Parviz. Please accept my condolences."

He nodded and patted my back. Always touching.

"Thank you, Firuz. It was a great loss to all of us. For me, it was a double loss. He was both brother and nephew. For our country, though" — he paused and shook his head —"it was a tragedy. What a brilliant scientist he was! What an intellect! How often does this poor land come up with someone like him? Why do such people have to go, eh Firuz?" He shook his head again. "Why those? Why not this kind?" He waved a hand at the crowd of demonstrators.

"I'm sorry that I wasn't at the funeral," I said. "I didn't wish to impose on your family."

"You needn't apologize," he gave my back another pat. "It was a very simple burial. A Moslem doesn't need more than to be returned to the soil. It comes to all of us. God is great." He let out a sigh, then scrutinized me. "But, tell me, what is it exactly that you're doing here?"

"I thought I would try to see if I could get into the university." I measured my words.

"But didn't anyone get in touch with you? Weren't you told that classes were canceled?"

I said yes.

"Well, then." He flushed. "What's the point of going inside? You see what chaos the place is in." Bijan walked ahead of me, waving at the demonstrators. "These fools have been marching around like that the whole morning. Making speeches. Shouting. They have nothing better to do." He shook his head and glanced back at me. "They call themselves students. But they're not students. Most of those creatures you see are riffraff with forged identity cards. I know them. We've picked them up countless times. On charges of disturbing the peace. Yes" — he nodded emphatically —"not just here, but all over Tehran. They make a parade of their ill feelings everywhere. That's because they're paid. They are professional agitators. Political prostitutes. As for the others" — he brushed them off with a sneer —"they are merely puppets in their hands. So much clay to be molded. They are in there shouting, because they are easily led and have nothing better to do." He turned to me full face. "Don't talk about going in. Because, frankly, I can't let you. You're one sort of person, and they are another. Don't you see? You are educated and intelligent. They are only fools who would try to take advantage of you. These aren't your students." He pointed again. "Your students have gone home long ago. Many of them didn't even show up, when they heard about the trouble. I assure you, this is true. By the time I arrived here, the real students were pouring out — glad to be gone. I should know. My men checked their cards." He waved at his cohorts. "Taheri, here — Nosratian."

Both nodded, agreeing with their chief.

"You see — all that remains here is the riffraff. They march around and make a lot of noise. Why? Because they have nothing better to do. Most of them are political prostitutes."

He glanced at his watch. "I'll tell you what. It's past noon. I'm tired of all this. This business is going to go on for some time. Why don't we go to my house for lunch?"

I tried to back out: my parents were expecting me — I had to return to the office.

316

But he was adamant. "No use, my friend. You can call your parents from my house. I'm sure they can spare you for one meal. As for the office, we can drive you there afterward."

I continued to resist, making *taarof*, as we call it in Persian: that is, deferring out of form.

Then came the clincher.

"But what will Zohre say, when I tell her I saw you? She'll ask me why I couldn't convince you. You don't want me to disappoint her, do you? I can't lie. I tell you, if you don't come, I may have to eat alone."

That touched off a trio of laughter.

"Come, my friend." Bijan put his arm around me. "Believe me, it is never wise to resist our police. If you don't accept my invitation, we'll have no choice but to handcuff you."

More laughter. I complied.

Bijan motioned to a jeep with a driver. Then he turned to his twosome.

"Stay here until I have you relieved. You can send out for rice and *kabab*. If anything happens — if so much as one stone is thrown — I want you to phone me immediately. In the meantime, no one goes in or comes out. If any of the riffraff try to break out, arrest them!"

Both men saluted and held the doors open. I sat in the back.

On the way, I asked Bijan about his orders.

"Why won't you let the demonstrators out? If they break up and go home, that could be the end of the trouble."

"They won't go home." He glanced over his shoulder. "The real rabble-rousers will try to stir up trouble elsewhere. The bazaar. In front of Parliament. They'll leave enough of their people behind to keep up the shouting. Meanwhile, they'll try to spread the confusion. No, it's better to have them stay where they are. This way, they're contained. We can't go into the compound, because we haven't the Chancellor's permission. The Chancellor won't act, unless he is authorized by the Prime Minister. The demonstrators know that, so they feel safe. Let them feel safe. But they can't go on marching and shouting forever. Sooner or later, they will have to come out. Otherwise, they are merely demonstrating inside a prison."

317

"And when they do?" I leaned forward to listen.

"It will be the same procedure as always," Bijan smiled. "We'll get their numbers. We'll sift out the agitators from the students."

"And what will you do, when you've done that?"

He turned around fully and grinned. "Ever the same inquisitive fellow. One question after another. Is that how you got to be a professor so young?"

The word he used was *ostad*, which means master, in the traditional sense, as well as professor. Any person with a certain claim to knowledge could be referred to as *ostad*: it was a term of respect.

"I'm hardly that," I protested, trying to inject some levity into my voice. "I merely teach English part-time."

"To us, my dear fellow, that means a professor." He glanced at the driver. "Isn't that so?" "To us, yes, excellency," came back the inevitable reply.

Bijan nodded, then peered at me.

"You have to get used to the way we say things. Or have you forgotten your mother tongue?"

That was a challenge. It demanded a retort.

"If I have" — I shrugged debonairly — "then my tongue is at odds with the one we're speaking."

It was a poor pun, even in Persian. But it served its purpose. All three of us laughed, and the air was clear again.

The jeep pulled into a narrow street — newly paved and with new houses around — and stopped in front of a wrought-iron gate. We were at the northern edge of the city.

Bijan turned to the driver.

"Come into the kitchen and have some food. There's no point in sitting in the cold. Wait there until I send for you."

The driver bowed with a hand to his heart — the gesture of a servant.

Bijan and I then got out and walked through the yard. It was barren and treeless, and the small circular pool in the middle had been drained. As we climbed the steps to the house, another man in uniform — this one in army green — opened the door.

Bijan held out his hat, gloves, and whip, then whirled around to have his coat taken.

"Is Mrs. Ashrafi presentable?"

"She is upstairs resting, excellency." The batman draped the coat over his arm.

"Tell her we have a guest. Dr. Momtaz," he enunciated, rubbing his hands. "Be sure to give her the name. Then go tell the cook to have lunch ready as soon as possible."

"Yes, excellency." The batman stood poised to take my coat.

"I'll see to that." Bijan waved him off. "You do as you're told. And tell the cook to feed the driver as well."

The batman hung up Bijan's hat and coat, and scurried upstairs.

"My wife is one of those fashionable women who stays in bed until noon. I hope she will favor us with her company. But then, she says she has a cold. So who knows if we'll be favored or not?" He hung up my coat on the peg beside his and guided me by the arm. "In any case, here is the telephone, and there is the door to the living room. Please go in when you've finished. I'll be with you in a moment. In the meantime, I beg you not to stand on ceremony. Consider this your home."

He disappeared down the hall, and I picked up the receiver.

My mother answered and registered her surprise at my being there — plying me with questions. Her reaction, in fact, made me all the more aware of the strangeness of the situation. Here I was, where I least expected to be — in Bijan's house. My father hadn't come home yet, and I asked my mother to tell him that I'd be going straight back to the office.

I put down the receiver and entered the living room.

The area was spacious, with high windows and ceiling. Suspended in the middle was a thick crystal chandelier. The floor was marbled and carpeted with light blue matching Kashans. The furniture was of a piece — in bleached wood and upholstered in silvery blue velvet and satin. The walls were white — which, along with the glare from the windows, gave the room a stark, cold aura.

The overall effect was that of a sort of belabored, shining elegance.

In contrast with this — almost at odds with the rest — were the paintings: irregularly spaced, hung above eye level, and gaudy in color, depicting romanticized scenes of the desert. A string of camels crossing over dunes in the moonlight.

At the far end of the room, next to the stove, was a handsome piano. A baby grand. Also white. With the lid down and a dazzling piece of tapestry draped over it. On top of that, I was surprised to see, was the silver frame my mother had given as our wedding gift.

I went over to examine it.

Inside was a black and white photograph of Mahin! In her riding clothes. Her blouse open to her cleavage. Not quite in focus. But the light accentuating her features. Not just smiling, but radiating a glow.

"You recognize your gift?" Bijan closed the door behind him.

"And the picture as well." I turned about. "I was admiring your furnishing. My compliments on your home."

"You are too kind. It is merely the house of an officer." He sauntered over to the piano and picked up the frame. "It's a fine piece of workmanship. Your mother tells me it's from Isfahan."

I nodded, not aware of where it was from.

"One can find this kind of silverwork only in Iran. I came by this bit of cloth," he fingered the tapestry, "when I was in Italy. It's a nice piece of artistry, but it doesn't compare with our carpets." He gazed at the photograph. "As for the woman, she is matchless as well — don't you think?"

What could I say? I was still at a loss as to what it was doing there. I concurred, then commented on the beauty of the piano. "Who plays it?" I asked.

"No one. It hides the stove." He traced the features with a finger. "What do you think of that face?"

"Mahin's?" I looked again. "I agree, it's very attractive. It has a loveliness enhanced by intelligence. A quality that makes her distinctive."

"She is the most beautiful woman I have known." He set the frame down.

Words my mother would have used.

"I took the photograph myself the summer before last in Ramsar. It was an exceptional time for both of us. But that face" — he waved the finger again — "I tell you, it belongs in that frame.

Combine the two, and you have something distilled. She is the perfect Iranian woman. Have you ever felt that way toward anyone?"

I thought of his sister, Nasrin. But as I had seen her as a child. Surely, there had been something complete about her as well. But seeing, then, had meant looking up. At an older woman. Married and always at a distance — despite the feeling of closeness. And certainly nothing so acutely defined as a photograph in an embellished frame.

He unbuttoned his tunic and walked over to the sofa.

"You know, of course, about our being in love — our intentions of marrying. That story made the rounds. But do you know how we came to break up?" He sank into the cushions. "Did you hear about that?"

"I heard something from Gloria. We ran into each other at the university."

"Oh, Gloria! The university!" He threw up a hand, then loosened his tie. "You can put aside whatever that woman told you. She is one half ignorance and the other half I won't say what, because I am too conscious of being a host. What would she know about this anyway? No, the truth of the matter is that Mahin and I were in love when we parted. We still are. Feelings don't change because certain things happen. If her parents hadn't interfered, we might have been married. But then, we might not. Parents aren't everything. In any case, the real issue goes deeper."

He heaved a sigh and pointed to a chair across from him.

"Why don't you sit there, my dear fellow? We can't have a serious talk with you standing up."

I went over and sat down.

"That's better," he smiled. "Now we're eyeball to eyeball. I'll tell you why we didn't — or couldn't — marry. I'll give you the truth in a nutshell." He leaned forward and lowered his voice. "It was because she was *too* perfect a woman!" He nodded confirmingly. "If I had married her, I would have had to become a different person — and that, you see, is something I can never be. Not even for love."

He leaned back again.

"There's more to the story, of course. But what I have given you is the gist. The substance. The rest is just details. Things people like Gloria make a pastime of twisting." He folded his arms. "There was a girl who got pregnant. A friend of Mahin. When all the parents found out, they thought I had done a terrible deed. The truth of the matter was that the girl couldn't wait until Mahin was out of the way, so she could go after me. So who seduced whom? Naturally, when it comes to these things, everyone points the accusing finger at me. Why not? I'm the perfect target. I'm the one with the notorious history with women. But I assure you, in this case, the matter was different. It was the girl who pursued — not the other way round. And do you know why? Because she was jealous of Mahin."

He let out a short laugh.

"That's what's ironic. I never laid a hand on Mahin. I swear by the Koran, that whole summer I courted her, I never even fondled her."

That I found a little hard to believe.

"But you were both strongly attracted to each other . . ."

"No, my friend." Bijan shook his head — confidingly low-voiced again. "Not with that woman. You see, her values were different, and I wanted to make her my wife. To have touched her before we had gotten married would have been like defacing that picture."

Just then the door opened, and Zohre walked in. Dressed in black again. In mourning for yet another death in the family. But this time more filled out. With womanly curves.

As she approached, I noted the lines around the eyes. She was prematurely reaching into her thirties.

"Firuz!" She leaned on my name, her arms outstretched. "It is good to see you again. How long it has been."

I got up to shake hands. She covered mine with cold fingers, actually squeezing it.

"I would kiss you, but I have a cold."

Zohre true to form. But not the one of yore. True, she was still holding back, but in a way which was different.

"Please be seated," she went on somewhat flustered. "I'm so glad you came by. How is your dear mother? How is your father?"

322

"Sit over here." Her husband patted the cushion beside him. She complied, sitting bolt upright and going on with her questions.

There followed a brief and formal exchange. Then her husband broke in again.

"Your old friend and I were having a heart-to-heart talk. You can catch up on one another later." He gripped her hand. "How are you feeling?"

"Better." She smiled quickly.

"And how long will lunch be?"

"Very soon."

"Good. In that case" — he glanced at me — "let's continue."

Were we to go on talking about Bijan's former love in front of his wife?

"I was telling Firuz about Mahin. Firuz wants to know why we didn't get married, and I was in the process of telling him, when you joined us."

I stared at Zohre, trying to communicate my outrage. She gave another quick smile and looked down.

"The fact of the matter is this, Firuz," he declared — always getting down to brass tacks. "You yourself have never been married, so let me give you some friendly advice. Never go after the perfect woman. That kind will only try to straighten out the warps in your personality. The trouble is, without warps, your personality comes crashing down — like a pile of bricks without mortar. That some women find hard to grasp. Mahin is one of them. Basically, she is a reformer. That's why we got along so famously. She wanted to change me, and, frankly, at the time, I needed her influence."

Bijan stroked his wife's hand and smiled.

"You see, Zohre and I had been intimate so long that we weren't getting anywhere. We had talked of marriage many times. She, I confess, had the more serious attitude. But I wasn't ready. My mind was on other things."

"Bijan, please." His wife nudged him. "Let's not trouble Firuz with these details."

"Why not, my dear?" He chucked her under the chin. Then he turned to me with a blameless expression. "Does any of this trouble you?"

I crossed my legs. "I see that it's making your wife uncomfortable."

He slipped his arm around Zohre's shoulder and gave her a hug. "My wife is used to discomforts. She has so many, she can't keep track of them. Like an old hypochondriac." He planted a kiss on her forehead.

Was he putting her through some kind of ordeal, I wondered, or was he speaking to some ulterior issue?

"Besides, what I have to say," he went on, "can only reflect well on my wife. You see, ultimately, the relationship between me and Mahin couldn't stand up to our differences. Had we married immediately, she would have been committed to me in a way that was fixed. That, in itself, would have made her absorb the nature of my character. As it was, all she saw was a chivalrous suitor."

I thought of Nasrin again. As she would have been at the time of her marriage to Amuzegar.

"The suitor laid open all his foibles and follies — in the same breath that he was exposing his love. He did this in the hope of winning her love. Which he did. Because the two make a powerful combination. But what did that mean? What can any number of words mean? The point is, our relationship had yet to be tested. Along came the test."

He turned to his wife. "She was a friend of yours, too."

"I didn't know her that well." Zohre rejected the association. She looked like a sulking child, but this time, she couldn't be blamed.

" Well, that affair was the test," Bijan stated flatly. "As I told you before Zohre came in, it was the girl who pursued me — not the other way round. But then, there is another side to the story. I was a man who had lived on nothing but tender glances and words for months. I had forsworn all bodily contact until the holy occasion of matrimonial bliss. Even in Ramazan, as they say, people have something to eat after the sun goes down. But never mind. That was expected of me — I even expected it of myself — and I complied. But something in me wanted to defy all that nonsense. After all, I was not preparing myself for entry into paradise. The girl could have been anyone. But the fact that she was Mahin's friend made her somehow even more desirable."

Zohre turned away.

"My wife doesn't like to hear this part of the story, but I have my reasons for telling it. I turned on that girl the way a hungry bear digs into honey. No wonder she got pregnant! It was my intention, of course, to tell Mahin everything. I *wanted* to tell her, in fact. I wanted to nail into that innocent, educated head of hers that I was a man as well as a suitor. Her *fiancé* — that wretched word which has crept into our language through affectation. But then, the whole thing became a scandal — it made everything seem sordid. I, the *fiancé*, who had taken the oath of chastity and loyalty, was cast in the role of a villain. A debauchee. A scoundrel. Someone an immaculate woman, with all her good upbringing and schooling, was well to be rid of. All her family — father, mother, brothers, and the rest — came together as one tribe and painted me in that light. So I flew up to Switzerland to make a distinction between me and the stories. I made a clean breast of everything. I told her how it happened, why it happened, and how it might come to happen again. Marriage to me, you see, is not a straitjacket. Nor is a woman a straitjacket to be put over a man. Either I am free to be the way I am, or I am not myself anymore. Can anything be plainer than that? So I asked her to consider me on that basis: to accept or reject me as I was. Do you know what her answer was?"

I glanced at Zohre.

Both of us, in a way, were like hostages: she, sitting next to Bijan, looking almost chained, with her hand locked in his. Me, directly across and no more able to move than if I had been tied to the chair.

"She didn't say: no, I don't want you, you wretch — go! She said something else. She said: I still love you, Bijan — nothing can change that. But you have a duty now, and so have I. My duty is to renounce all claims on you, and yours is to marry that girl. Her friend. In other words, we both had obligations of a higher nature to submit to. Just at the moment I was declaring my love and asking her to acknowledge my flaws, she turned around and wanted to redeem me. Save me from myself by freeing me to marry the girl who had forced herself upon me and betrayed her. Wasn't that noble?"

He let out another short laugh.

"Let me go and check on the lunch," Zohre murmured.

"When lunch is ready, the man will inform us," Bijan countered automatically, then turned to his wife. "Besides, I have yet to bring you into the picture, my love." He gazed back at me. "That, my dear Firuz, is when the so-called scales fell from my eyes. Everything fell into place. I knew the woman for me was the one who could accept me totally as I was. You see, by then I was ready for marriage. I had made up my mind. Zohre was in France at the time. I immediately went to her, and put the same question. Only to her, I added something more: I told her I was in love with Mahin. Could she accept a man who refused to be bound by the restrictions of marriage and who was, furthermore, bound heart and mind to another woman who couldn't accept him?" He beamed a tender glance at his wife. "Unhesitatingly, she said yes. She didn't even want to wait for us to be married in Iran. We were married right there in France."

Zohre never raised her eyes from the floor.

"You see" — Bijan nodded with a smile — "she is the perfect *wife*. She wants a husband so badly — which is to say not any husband, but me — that she will put up with anything. That is a wife. She does not have to be young. Or intelligent. Or even beautiful anymore. Nor does she have to have taste." He pointed to the paintings on the walls. "I gave her five thousand tomans to decorate this room, and she came back with those." He shrugged and shook his head lamentingly. "Here is a girl who was brought up in Germany, surrounded by the best that money could buy. The rest that you see here — including the piano — is all my own choice. But that, you see, is one of the redeeming features of marriage." He blinked knowingly. "She tolerates my faults, and I tolerate hers."

The door opened, and the batman announced that lunch was ready to be served. Zohre got up immediately and excused herself — blowing her nose as she went out of the room.

Bijan and I responded more slowly, rising after her. Then Bijan walked over to the piano and beckoned me to join him.

"As for this woman" — he picked up the frame again — "some day she will make an excellent goddess. I would offer her to you, but I doubt she will marry." He gazed fondly at the photograph. "I can see her behind a desk, or at the head of some function. But not with a husband." He put down the frame and looked at me. "Besides, she is the one woman I have loved."

With his arm around my shoulder, we passed into the dining room.

It was small — almost intimate — by contrast. With a glass cabinet against the wall.

Zohre was standing, taking dishes from the batman, who, at her bidding, stole away as we entered.

She indicated our places on either side of her.

There was a gaunt look about her, despite the weight she had put on. A thin face over a heavier body.

She served the rice in large mounds and left us to apply our own helping of sauce. Then, serving her own portion, which was meager, she sat down.

The plates were gold-rimmed, and the glasses crystal. The tablecloth and napkins were damask. Overhead was another, smaller chandelier.

Bijan tasted the rice before adding the sauce.

I complimented Zohre on the cooking and attempted to turn the conversation around.

"My mother told me about your wedding reception. She was quite ecstatic about it. I was sorry I missed it."

"Thank you." Zohre smiled faintly. "Your mother is a very dear person. I am sorry I haven't been able to see more of her. The fact is, it was shortly after our wedding that Parviz fell ill."

"We don't have to make an issue of that," Bijan said tartly. He forked a cut of meat, then sliced it. "We have other excuses. Buying and furnishing this place. Entertaining people we scarcely see. Trying to straighten out family problems."

He put a slice on my plate. I thanked him.

"There were plenty of those," he went on. "There still are. At least, Parviz — God rest his soul — is spared the worst."

Zohre looked startled.

"Don't worry, my dear," Bijan reassured her. "I won't go into

327

the business about your dowry." He turned back to me. "Suffice it to say that my father took care of the details. He worked out an agreement with her father, so that the money coming to her didn't revert to the other side of her family. Her uncle wasn't too pleased. But then, what could he do? If he wanted our money, he could have tried to work out something between his daughter and me. As it is, his brother's share of their estate comes to us through Zohre. It's a good arrangement. It has paid for this house."

He applied a napkin to his lips, then sipped some water.

"By the way, do you know who was the first to suggest that I marry into that family?"

He waited for an answer.

"Your sister?" I ventured a guess.

He shook his head.

"Nasrin's approval came later — when she came to know about Zohre and me. No, my father. At last I can say that I have done something to please him. I slipped into that house through one door or another."

He resumed eating.

I smiled at Zohre.

She smiled back, then nibbled at her food.

So here she was, finally settled in her own home. At the head of her own table — with her husband beside her. Was she any the happier? Basically, it seemed to me, yes. But what a price to pay for removing such deep-seated unrest.

She glanced up again, smiling.

"Bijan's sister has been like a mother to me. She helped me over a trying period; providing me with a home and a fresh start. Without her friendship and guidance, I don't know what I would have done."

"Thrown yourself into another canal."

Zohre gasped. "Bijan! Why do you say such things? Have I said or done anything to displease you? Should the food be returned to the kitchen?"

He put a hand over hers, gently placating her.

"Don't take my comments so personally. Those words come out because there is a great pain in my heart. You mentioned

Parviz, and it opened a wound. You shouldn't have used his death as an excuse."

"Forgive me." She swallowed.

Bijan turned to me.

"I understand that you went to see him before he died."

I acknowledged that I had.

"Then you know what misery he went through before he died."

I nodded. It was awkward to continue eating at that point.

"But there is misery in living as well. Misery of the heart. You saw my sister, too. Did you talk to her?"

"Briefly."

"What about?"

"Parviz. His need for privacy. She wanted to apologize for not contacting my mother. I didn't stay long. I intend, of course, to visit her again — to convey my condolence. To Gloria, too. I didn't see her then."

He shook his head. "No, you wouldn't have. You won't see her now either. She has gone back to America. She left after the funeral — which is just as well. There's enough trash in this country."

"Bijan — " his wife tried to break in, but he continued regardless.

"At least, she won't be able to put a finger on his money. Every rial of his stays in the family. For which, God be praised. Not that she is lacking for support. For the present, at any rate, she lives like a queen."

"Bijan, please!" Zohre was aroused to genuine alarm. "There is no reason to go into all this. I am sure we have other things to talk about."

"You're not eating, my dear." Bijan helped himself to more sauce. "To get over your cold, you should eat."

Zohre appealed to me. "Don't listen to him, Firuz. I know why he is doing this. He is still angry with me. He is saying all this to torture me."

"Torture you?" Bijan pushed the dish of sauce toward me. "Why should I want to do that? Why should I choose such a method? No, what I say is intended strictly for the ears of my old friend, Firuz. He has known our family a long time. In a sense, he is more than a friend. He is an intimate companion, a confidant. For one thing" — he pointed to his blind eye — "he saw how this happened. He knows what came of it. That gives him a privileged position in our lives. For another" — he looked back at me — "he has seen the two people closest to me suffer. He feels close to them, too, and wishes to know more of their suffering. Is that not so?"

It was true But he had anticipated me in a way which I, myself, had been striving to deny. I did feel a sense of kinship with them — and the rest simply followed.

Zohre placed her knife and fork side by side on her plate.

"In that case, if you will excuse me, I will return to my room."

"I would rather you stayed," Bijan said quietly.

"But I don't wish to hear this."

"Then stay for my sake."

"Why?"

There was a steady defiance about her, which, despite her mellowness, I thought, would bring out his anger.

But it didn't. He was even more gentle.

"Because you are my wife. Because we have a guest."

Zohre submitted, in spite of herself.

Bijan turned to me full face again.

"My dear Firuz, when you went to my father's house, you saw the pitiful condition my nephew was in. You saw the suffering he went through. What the naked eye grasps does not require any further explanation. But then, there is another kind of suffering: the kind we don't know about or talk about, because it is hidden. We say that one kind is worse, because it is out in the open, and we know what the end is. There is no arguing with death. But the other kind can lead to suicide. So we mustn't judge things from the standpoint of death. Death comes to all of us. God is merciful. But *willing* your own death — getting to that point — is that not a greater misery than trying to avoid it?"

He poured water into his glass from a bowl-shaped pitcher.

"If my nephew found any solace in life toward the end, it was due to my sister, Nasrin. She gave him the comfort and love that he needed — and protected him. You may think that this is only to be expected of a mother. But how far can a mother's love be stretched, before it exposes her pain? Her own personal sorrow? Parviz never saw that side of my sister. Much to her credit, I can tell you that, given the circumstances, he died as peaceful a death as any of us would wish for. When our time comes, may we be that fortunate."

He raised his glass — as though making a toast — then drank.

"But the cost to herself was enormous. There was no measure of that, until after the funeral. It was a good thing that you didn't come, because something in her broke. I had no notion of what, until I had fathomed the nightmare she had been through. My dear fellow, that woman's misery didn't end with the dying of her son. It began there. Cooped up in that house of hers, she had another horror to live through. Her son's wife was taking her place in her husband's bed. Time and again. Under the same roof. In one room this. In the other room that. Can you imagine the agony she had to endure? She couldn't tell anyone. She couldn't even leave. Any sort of disclosure might get to her son. So she bore all in silence. No one knew. When they got back from Switzerland, she saw her chance and moved her son to my father's house. She moved him there to protect him. The wife and husband came and went as usual. All looked normal. But the strain on her was enormous. So great that, when her son died, at the funeral — can you believe this — I sensed her relief!"

He shook his head.

I was numb. It was like seeing things merge in two-dimensional perspective: what was graphic was also unreal.

"How long had this been going on?" I managed to blurt out.

Bijan shrugged.

"My sister is a very patient and long-suffering woman."

"But how do you know this?"

"How do I know what my sister was going through? Believe me, I know. I would have thought you'd be aware of that."

"I have a headache," Zohre whimpered.

Bijan gave her a nod.

"My wife has gone through a similar experience. Yet, she, too, finds this hard to believe."

"She hasn't talked to Nasrin?"

331

I was conscious only after the fact of referring to Zohre in the third person.

Bijan shook his head again.

"My sister refuses to see anyone. That is, anyone outside the immediate family — my poor parents and me. Can you blame her? She has aged more in a year than she would have in a decade. She lives apart from her husband. He, too, for the present, is out of the country. In another few months, the separation becomes permanent. What comfort could there be in facing others? Having others torment her with looks and questions? She is too distressed, as it is, to set eyes on my wife."

"I beg you to excuse me," Zohre mumbled — so feebly, I wondered whether her husband heard.

"I tell you this, Firuz, because, quite frankly, there's no point in your trying to visit her. At times, it is best to leave a person alone. To allow the process of recovery to take its own course. But I also go into this to give you a grasp of things. Soon there will have to be another divorce. A second divorce will damage her. There will be stories in the streets. Like the stories about me. But you — our friend — should be privy to better knowledge than that."

He rounded his fingers, as though gripping a ball.

"You see, there is a putrid odor to all this. And it can't be denied by just turning one's nose away. My wife has a cold. So she can be excused. Her nose is stuffed up. But you, my friend, are able to breathe. When you breathe, you are also able to smell. Is that not so? What's the use of breathing, if you refuse to acknowledge the stench that goes with it? Do you follow me? That's what I'm asking you to do — acknowledge the stench, rather than go by the words you will hear."

He released the invisible ball and turned to his wife.

"If you take the pills the pharmacist gave you and get some sleep, you should feel better by supper."

Zohre responded to the cue, getting up slowly.

"Firuz, excuse me. My headache prevents me from staying any longer. I have to lie down. It was good of you to come. Please give my best wishes to your parents."

I got up and bowed.

Then she glanced at her husband. "I will try to feel better by supper."

As though trying could do it.

One last smile, and she swished out of the room.

With Zohre gone, there was suddenly an uncomfortable void. I was alone with Bijan in a way I did not wish to be.

"Perhaps I should be leaving, too. I appreciate the confidence you have shown in me. I assure you, what you have said will remain between us . . ."

"Sit down," he replied. "We haven't finished talking yet. That subject is closed. But another has still to be opened. We haven't come to you yet. Do you drink Turkish coffee?"

I said yes.

"Then allow me to finish eating. We'll have coffee in the living room."

He called to the batman — who promptly appeared — and gave him instructions.

After which, he returned to his food, eating quickly. In silence. Using a morsel of bread to counter his fork.

Solo, concentrated eating.

But not the kind that registers feeling. As in eating with gusto. But rather a mood. A brooding intensity, which captured the face muscles at work. Doing what they were primordially meant to do.

The human animal eating, I found myself pondering.

I felt a tingle of panic.

This wasn't a plain visit. A luncheon encounter. It was an ordeal.

And clearly the ordeal wasn't over yet.

Why? Was there something else to be unraveled or fathomed? Involving me?

Why me? Because I was a friend? What had I done to warrant such friendship?

Then it sank into me — what Bijan had said.

We were more than friends. We were "intimate." Our lives had intersected at so many points that we were parts of one process, inhabiting the same world.

Which is not the same thing as being friends. One is free to choose one's own friends. One has a separate identity apart from them.

But we don't choose those with whom our lives are bound up. We are simply linked to them.

Bijan and I — through our past and family ties — were entangled in the same human meshwork.

In that sense — and no other — were we "close."

But then, that is also like saying that two threads interwoven are really apart, provided the weave weren't there.

"Have you had enough to eat?" He wiped his lips with his napkin.

"Plenty, thank you."

"Then shall we rise from the table?"

He indicated with his arm that I should go ahead of him, and we returned to the living room.

The batman followed almost on our heels — with a tray and two small cups of coffee. He set the tray down on the low table in front of the sofa, then asked if we cared for some dried fruit. We said no, and he crept out of the room.

Automatically, we resumed our former places. Bijan leaned forward and handed me my cup.

"Now, tell me about you. I have only heard about you in bits and pieces. What have you been doing since your return from America?"

I launched into what had come to be my usual narrative. Going over the same facts and details I had given out countless times. My reactions upon returning. My job at the office. My work at the university. I was conscious of using the same phrases and sentences.

Bijan listened intently, stopping me occasionally to clarify matters. And sipping his coffee so slowly that he evidently savored the taste.

Then the topic expanded to my growing involvement with teaching — which necessitated a decision, on my part, as to which way to go. That worked its way around to future plans.

"I have one question to ask you." Bijan put down his coffee cup. "Do you intend to go on to your doctorate?"

"I'm thinking of it."

He nodded. "My nephew was intending to go after it as well." That suggested a parallel. "In what field?"

"Literature."

He nodded again. "And where do you intend to get your degree?"

"I don't know yet." I finished the thick brew and put the cup and saucer down on the low table. "It's still too early to say — probably America."

"Why America? You've just come back from America. Why not here?"

The thought hadn't even occurred to me.

"They don't offer a doctorate in my field here."

"Then why not change fields?"

I gazed at him in surprise, unable to answer such an unexpected response.

"I am serious," he nodded vehemently. "What is so special about your field? You have spent most of your life studying abroad. Why don't you study something now that will keep you here?"

"I plan to come back," I assured him.

"That may be. But meanwhile you're ignoring your country. We have some of the best literature in the world. Why don't you study that here? If you want a doctorate in that field, our university will give you a doctorate."

"That's true as far as our own literature goes," I replied, trying to make a case for myself, "but in other literatures, I'm afraid, we are weak."

"In other words, one has to go abroad for an education. One has to go to places like America. Is that right?"

I shrugged. "It's simply a matter of what area one wants to study. In some cases, their programs are better."

"Better than ours, you mean. Always what the outsider has is better than ours. So why not spend one's whole lifetime abroad? Why come back to Iran? Why delay the process until the end of one's education? Why come back at all?"

His inquisitiveness had turned into belligerence.

"You see, my friend, I want to warn you of a danger: as soon as one acquires an education — becomes intelligent, as they say

— one becomes negative and critical. Who needs it? Perhaps you do." He smiled. "Do you? Why? To make yourself look good? Look proud? Be different? Be European? Be American? Be Western? Is being Iranian the same thing as being stupid to you?"

"Of course not . . ."

"Then why do you go away to America? Why? What do you gain by going away to America? An education? No, not an education. You can get an education here. There are educated men in this poor country as well. Yes, very well educated men. I ought to know. Not that I am educated myself, or wise. No, I never admit to such things — such pretensions. I only say this because I have been educated here."

He rapped the table with his forefinger — which made the coffee cups jump.

"Here. Not America or England. I ought to know, when I say we have good teachers and professors. They are loyal countrymen, too. They love their land and their people. They don't turn their backs on them. So I ask you: why do you intelligent and foreign-educated and critical people want to go back abroad? Do you wish to say, or do you want me to tell you?"

I was silent a moment, then signaled him to proceed.

"You don't say, because your only answer is for more education. But I'll tell you the real reason. The real reason is that you people seek escape."

He glared at me, constantly nodding.

"You're afraid of us. You're afraid of your own culture and your own kind. Those foreigners, they've taught you to hate us. You don't see that, because they have taught you to see things their way. The foreigner has taught you that what is Iranian is bad. And those who believe him are not only fools, they are worse — they are traitors."

He leaned back against the cushion, crossing his arms. Legs crossed, and eyeing me fixedly.

"Take a look at yourself. How well do you know your own language? Can you quote a line from Hafez? Go on, quote a line from Hafez. You don't know any Hafez? You don't know your own country's poets by heart? Very well, then. Tell me what this means."

336

He quoted a couplet, two or three words of which made any sense to me.

"You don't know the meaning of it, do you? No, you don't. You're so busy reading Shakespeare— that pig of a Russian, Tolstoi. I bet you could quote me some Shakespeare and that pig of a Russian, couldn't you?"

He was right. I could have.

He laughed. "You think I'm dense, but I know you. Oh yes, I know all about you. You can't keep any secrets from me. You think I'm dense because I'm in uniform. All of us uniformed people are stupid. Look about you, O intelligent one. Nine tenths of the world is ruled by uniformed people. The other tenth is ruled by the rich, who don't have to wear uniforms."

He paused and nodded to let that register.

"Where does the so-called intelligentsia rule? Tell me, where? Tell me one spot, and I'll pick up the telephone and have their man shot. I could have you shot, too. Yes, I could. You people don't seem to understand that. I could shoot you right here with my pistol and get away with it. And do you know why? The answer is simple."

He paused again — not to elicit a comment, but to dramatize his point.

"Because I have the license to kill. This thing — this uniform — gives me the right to kill you. What can you do about that?"

A strange silence followed. Not a long, but a restive one — which had the same impact.

"But I don't. And I won't. And I never will, unless I am given absolutely no choice. And I want you to understand why."

His voice became calm. Instructive.

"Consider your clothes. Where does your shirt come from — England?"

"America," I replied.

"England, America — it's all the same to me. Your shoes come from Italy, your suit from England. Your cuff links from France. As opposed to what I wear. This poor uniform was made in Iran. But back to you. Every part of your clothing is made elsewhere, is that not so? Now, how about this?"

Suddenly he squeezed the flesh on my wrist, pulling the hairs.

"Your skin, your flesh, your hair — your bones beneath all those. *They* are Iranian. As is all this!"

And he grabbed my hand and slapped it against his forearm.

"That's why I would never kill you or harm you. I would slit the throats of a hundred foreigners first — be they Moslem or Christian. Armenians or Arabs."

He laughed.

"If they're English or Russian, I would gladly slit one thousand. Two thousand. I'd wipe the whole lot of them off the face of the earth. Like Genghis Khan."

He was laughing at that conception of himself.

"Yes, Genghis Khan still lives today."

He leaned forward to talk more intimately.

"You, to me, are like a brother. A younger brother — like Parviz . . ."

At that point, the phone in the hall rang. Then the batman knocked and entered, announcing that "his excellency" was wanted.

Bijan got up and left, then returned within minutes, straightening his tie.

"It's the university again." He went over to the sofa and picked up his tunic belt. "They're starting to throw rocks."

I got up, too. "What are you going to do?"

He shrugged. "When things get to that point, we have to flex our muscles."

"You're going to use force?"

"No, my dear fellow." He buttoned his tunic, then strapped his pistol and holder to his belt. "We're not going to use force. I'm going there to prevent a fight, not to start one."

Then he came over to me and placed both hands on my shoulder.

"Look, my dear fellow, I'm sorry if I've been a little hard on you. But it was meant for your own good. I tell you, too much education abroad can be a bad thing for person. I'm speaking of Iranians. Look at Parviz. Look at Mahin. Consider how it affected their judgment. One married a whore, and the other got

338

carried away by beautiful ideas. I loved them both. I don't want the same thing to happen to you. I'm cautioning you not to fall into their trap. You want to return to America to complete your education. Good. But don't do anything more. Don't lose your Iranian identity. Don't adulterate yourself in the process. Get your degree and come back. Right away. Without looking behind. Without thinking twice. Remember, this is your home. Here."

He waved a hand around the room.

"See what a nice home it is? Here you are the master in your home. Anywhere else, you are this."

He joined his middle finger and thumb.

"A zero. A nothing. A mere statistic."

We walked out of the room with his arm around my shoulder.

"What are people in America anyway? What are they? I've been there myself, so I can say. They are merely pebbles on a beach. So many grains of sand and nothing more. One indistinguishable from another. But here" — he gave my shoulder a squeeze — "you have your own imprint. Here you are the master of your house. Do you follow me?"

We put on our overcoats and walked out the door into the courtyard. A sudden gust of cold made me turn up my collar.

"Can I drop you off home?" he said, putting on his gloves.

"Thank you, no. I'm going to the office, and that's out of your way. I'll take a taxi."

"As you wish."

We stepped out into the street, where the jeep was waiting — motor running.

"By the way," he said, "the policeman told me you have a faculty card. May I see it?"

I dug into my breast pocket and brought out the card.

He took it, examined it, then tore it in two.

"You won't need that anymore." He flung the pieces in the gutter. "The only way to get into the university is with my personal permission."

He clapped both gloved hands on my shoulders and peered into my eyes.

"Now do you know the meaning of power?"

339

I nodded.

"Good, we're still friends."

He patted my cheek, then climbed into the jeep. The driver was about to close the door on him, when he held it back.

"Don't worry, my friend. We're not going to do anything to your precious students. Their safety is as much our concern as yours."

He blinked and smiled reassuringly.

"As for your card, I'll get you another one. But first, you'll have to ask me."

A last wave. The driver shut the door. And they were off.

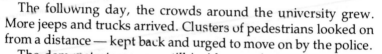

The following day, the crowds around the university grew. More jeeps and trucks arrived. Clusters of pedestrians looked on from a distance — kept back and urged to move on by the police.

The demonstrators were still inside — refusing to come out. Still chanting. This time, calling for a change in government.

Rumor had it that food and supplies had been slipped through to them during the night. By the very people who were guarding them, to boot — either because they were sympathetic to their cause, or because they were bribed by sympathizers outside.

Our servant claimed he had seen someone up the street throw a bundle of bread over the railing — and then get beaten for it by a policeman. But when we questioned him further, he corrected his story: it so happened that *someone* had seen a man throw a bundle of bread over the railing . . . etc. That someone being a neighborhood raconteur who held forth in the tea house next door.

The same kind of stories circulated around the bazaar. Everyone there knew about the university's being surrounded and the demonstrations going on. The question there was, where would the demonstrations spread to next? Which area of town? Or rather, gathering place?

In the years before and shortly after the Mossadegh government, Parliament Square had been the favorite rallying point of protestors. But that was at a time when the country still had a functioning parliament.

The next area had been the bazaar.

Rumor had it that machine guns were being set up atop buildings in both areas to prevent any further demonstrations from breaking out.

It was Golayat who brought me that story. I remember the two of us standing at the window, scanning the roof tops across from us, trying to spot nests. We saw nothing.

All the same, not seeing anything did not necessarily mean that nothing was happening. Something *had* to be happening. There were army trucks all over the place — either parked or in passing. If one headed up anywhere near the king's palace in the city — which was, after all, in a central location — one was directed away by helmeted guards.

Furthermore, there was no official news to be had — either from the papers or over the radio. One read about the mild winter we were having — as opposed to its frosty start — and what that would augur for the crops. One read about President Kennedy and the Alliance for Progress. The newly initiated Peace Corps program. Queen Elizabeth's intended visit in the spring — the first British monarch to set foot in Iran.

Nothing about what was going on in the streets. Demonstrators. Students. Troop movements. Things one could see with one's eyes.

The demonstration at the university ran into the third day and fourth. There was a sort of armistice in between to observe a religious holiday. And I believe that food was allowed to pass through for that reason. But that, too, may have been just another story.

In the meantime — after four such days of unbroken protest — a genuine sense of ferment began to take hold. It was felt in an undefinable way. But it paralleled the feeling of the early fifties: a general, though vague, coming together of popular sentiment in support of a cause.

Outwardly, there were several signs, too. Some shops closed down. Fewer cars were on the street. Fewer pedestrians. Some hard-working businessmen in our office building didn't show up for work.

It was strange. If such a thing could have been smelled, the air was tinged with the odor of anticipation.

Then it came.

Another phone call from Akbar A'a: police and soldiers had broken into the compound. There was fighting going on. He had been directed to tell me that I was on no account to come near the university. He didn't say where he was calling from — and it slipped my mind to ask.

I hung up, then told Golayat to give my father the news — he had gone out on business — and then to lock up and go home for the day.

There was no telling how far the rioting would spread.

Then I took a taxi to our house. The streets along the way were still open. As I got out of the car, I heard the din in the distance. It was somewhat like the roar of a crowd at a stadium — only harsher, without the even swells of voices in unison.

I had never heard such a sound before. Simultaneously chilling and mesmerizing, it made you want to run for cover, yet drew you out.

It is hard to dissociate the noise from its effect. In a sense, the two became one. I was hypnotized, if you will. Maybe not literally or clinically, but in a way which nevertheless incapacitated my will.

From that point on, I was drawn. Walking toward some invisible center — some dark focal point of human history. Of which I was a part, but no longer the center. The center was outside me — drawing me.

The odd thing was, walking toward it — passing from sound to sight, coming closer to the event — the whole thing turned into a dreamlike sequence.

It couldn't be happening!

Shah Reza Avenue — the scene of a blood bath. People pummeling each other. The asphalt torn up. Windows broken. Glass and blood sprayed on the pavement. A yellow haze — of dust or what, I couldn't tell — standing over everything.

342

All my senses told me this was real. Yet my mind couldn't accept it. No wonder people doubt history.

My eyes focused on individual occurrences — as though to come up with proof. More proof. Specific proof.

An armored truck, with bars on the rear windows. Several policemen clubbing a victim and throwing him in. A rock, the size of an orange, smashing into the face of a soldier.

Screaming — as though one's bowels were ripped out.

Then the sight of a man literally hurling another one around — off the ground — by the hair. Neither in uniform.

From the distance — in the compound — incredible: still remnants of chanting.

Suddenly my eyes shifted to the side gate leading to the university pavilion. It was open. Unguarded. Nothing was happening there.

I crossed the street — on the far side of a line of parked trucks. Between one truck and the next, I caught sight of two men in dark blue uniforms — waving their arms, as though they were directing traffic.

Taheri and Nosratian.

I walked through the gate. I was inside the compound. From there, it was a few steps to the door of the pavilion.

Then I heard shouting and screaming from within.

Soldiers were running up the stairs. Paratroopers in black berets and multicolored green uniforms — with sten guns strapped to their shoulders. What were they doing there?

I waited until they had all gone up, then walked in.

The noise was from above. The rooms and the corridor. I went up the steps.

"I'm a foreigner! I'm a foreigner!"

The man's head was bashed against the wall. His camera smashed. His typewriter thrown out the window. The clothes in his closet methodically ripped apart. He slumped to the floor — eyes glazed and bleeding.

The soldiers were going down the hall — ransacking the rooms dispassionately, one by one. Licensed to act. Indiscriminate. Eager. Victors from start to finish. Without armed resistance. Smashing furniture. Butting ribs. Kicking groins. Breaking things — animate, inanimate.

Methodically, they went down the hall.

Had one of them turned around and seen me whole — in one piece — I, too, would have been victimized.

But no one did. They were all so efficient and methodical. Going down the hall. Tearing into people and things.

When the last of them was gone, disappearing down the stairs at the other end of the corridor, a man stepped out of a room.

Teddy Wedge in a nightgown.

Had he been ill? Sleeping — when yanked out of bed?

His face was contorted with fury.

"Bloody bastards!" he shouted.

I went over. To put a hand on his shoulder. But he wrenched away, drew back to his room — which was in a shambles.

The desk upturned. The liquor bottles smashed. The room reeking of alcohol. The floor wet and spattered with glass. His papers flung about — ink running and the writing illegible.

Wide-eyed and trembling, he stared at me.

"Bloody . . . bloody barbarians!"

Pale blue eyes in a flushed pink face. It was only then I realized that he was lumping me with the others.

30

I do not know how many people were killed. Some said a dozen, others a hundred. *Time*, I recall, reported two — *Newsweek* only one. But then, both got their figures from government sources. Both agreed, though, that 6000 demonstrators were involved. *Time*, I remember, stated that about 500 were injured — about four students to each soldier. *Newsweek's* estimate was less than half. There was no telling how many were arrested. Figures ran anywhere from 300 to 3000. American papers played things down. Iranian rumors ran things up.

At any rate, that riot and its outcome were to mark a new era in Iranian politics. The forces behind Mossadegh were routed forever. Amini's government remained in power, but only for a while. From that point on, it was evident that if anyone was to rule it was the king. Land reform went into effect as scheduled. A new government was set up with the sole purpose of implementing the king's policies and programs. That was the beginning of the much publicized White Revolution: a revolution from above to prevent the kind from below.

Parliament, in the process, became a quiescent body: passive and easily disposed of if it didn't behave properly — that is, carry out the programs assigned to it. The country thereafter was to be led by one man. The son had followed in the steps of his father — and in doing so, had measured up to his stature.

When the university reopened — in April, I think — the place seemed deserted. About half the students in my classes showed up to take their final exams: most of them women.

⁂

My memory of that period is largely a blur. That spring I took up climbing in the Alborz Mountains. Not climbing in the sense of tackling a peak with crampons and rope, but rather walking indiscriminately up in boots and carrying a light knapsack. I did this on Fridays. I would set out in the morning, have lunch on some frosty slope, amid patches of snow with deep fields up above, then head back in the late afternoon haze: muscle-weary, sunburned, wet, and all aglow from energy spent. In the villages above Shemran, I would stop and bolt down goblets of tea and mounds of honey on wafer-thin bread. Then at night, at home, I would lie in a hot bath and listen to music.

Invariably I went out alone, courting small dangers the higher I reached — the more proficient I became at picking my way through the labyrinthine range. A few times I tried climbing with others, but not with success. Either the pace was too slow or I found myself unwillingly driven to capture a peak.

Actually, it was not a summit I was reaching for, but solitude: the kind that surrounds you with its awesome silence — the

345

only response to which is to trudge on. Week after week. Losing oneself through physical exertion in the scenery. One can whistle or sing — and I did both — but not think.

I also took photographs. Rolls of them — one for each mountain I climbed. From all sides. Front face. Rear face. Looking down. As though I were piecing together facets of a huge, ungainly, orderless mass.

On one of those outings, viewing a sheer drop through the eye of my camera, it dawned on me that I would have to be gone. Leave the country again while there was still time.

I clambered down the slopes, wondering where the urge had sprung from.

My parents understood, when I tried to tell them. It was time for me to go on for my doctorate: my education wasn't over until I had "gathered its harvest," as my father expressed it. I could always return to the business and teaching afterward. He stipulated, though, that the expenses would have to fall on my shoulders. He could spare me $1000 to set me off, but no more.

Thereafter, it was a matter of filling out applications and sending a flurry of telegrams, for it was late in the year to be applying. Eventually, an offer came through from the University of Michigan: I was given a teaching fellowship in English for the fall. A final cable on my part concluded the matter: my next destination was to be the Midwest.

Before leaving, I made my usual round of farewells. My father suggested that I see Ashrafi. By then it was September, and Ashrafi had already moved to his house in Tehran. A maid led me into a small sitting room, where he was seated, reading, with spectacles perched below the bridge of his nose.

He had stepped down that winter as president of the Chamber of Commerce, but was still a member of the Senate. As we talked, his wife puttered in and out of the room, bringing in, among other things, a plate of figs which she said were from Tabriz.

Ashrafi was eager to talk about education. A "semi-invalid in semi-retirement," as he put it, he was turning his energies to what he claimed he always wanted to do: set up a foundation which would provide rotating funds for needy students. He went on to explain. Students could apply for funds as long as they were studying. Once their studies were over, they would be obligated to return the full amount taken over a period of five years at the rate of one percent per annum. After that period, the interest rate would be raised to twelve.

He said that the funds were to be subsidized by the Chamber of Commerce and that he himself had created a scholarship in the name of Parviz. He asked me to help him by soliciting funds, when I got to America, from the Rockefeller Foundation.

He was so fervent about this that he got up and fetched me a packet of brochures to be distributed among "the Rockefeller people." These I later forwarded on his behalf, along with a covering letter asking for support, which was promptly rejected.

He also handed me a thin paperback book, which he wanted to give to my father. On its cover, in Persian, were the words: "*Money* by Amin Ashrafi." It took my breath away to think of Ashrafi as an author. Still, there it was, plainly in print, a publication of the National Bank of Iran.

At the door, I inquired about Nasrin. She was still living in Niavaran, he said, but he counseled me against going to see her. He alluded broadly to her desire for seclusion and urged me instead to visit Bijan.

Which I could not, in all candor, bring myself to do. Nor did I see the Karimzadehs, despite my mother's prompting. There simply wasn't time.

The last Friday before my departure, my parents and I went to my grandmother's house, where there was a largish gathering of relatives. We went in the morning and stayed for lunch, after which I took photographs. In the midafternoon, when people were either napping or playing backgammon, I felt the urge to get away and be by myself. I took my father's car keys and drove up Pahlavi Avenue.

It wasn't until I was well on my way that I realized I was actually going to see Nasrin.

I turned off on the familiar road which led to the Ashrafi house in Niavaran. At the gate, I sounded the horn and an old gardener stepped out. He stood squarely in front of the car and apologized profusely for not letting me in. When I pressed him for reasons, he shrugged and asked me to wait while he went back inside. He closed the gate, and I turned off the motor. Then

347

Musa came out, touching his forehead, bowing and smiling as usual. He, too, was sorry that he couldn't let me in.

Why, I asked, was the lady not feeling well?

He nodded: in her condition, she was not ready to receive visitors — even friends.

I told him that I would be leaving within the week.

He nodded again: she had heard — she had told him to give me her warmest regards and best wishes for the future. Did I have any message in return?

I was in a curious sort of limbo and not able to answer. Musa understood and changed the subject. We chatted briefly about my trip. He said if he could ever get out of the country, he would like to see Argentina: the land there was fertile and cheap.

I started the car, and we shook hands. Then hastily I reached into my pocket and gave him a ten-toman note, along with one for the gardener. He said he would give my respects to Mrs. Karbalai.

At the top of the road, where it curved, I glanced back and saw Musa shutting the gate behind him. I thought of Queen Victoria tended to by her ever-faithful John Brown.

I didn't know where to go next. It was too early to return to Tehran. So I parked the car and walked up a hill, taking my camera to finish the roll of film. Wending my way up between rocks, in dapper clothes which soon became dirty, I wearied quickly — as though I hadn't done any climbing. At the top of a bluff, I took pictures of the city, gleaming in the distance. The Ashrafi garden was hidden below.

Years later I would return, and the strip of desert above the city would be gone, swallowed up by a network of housing and roads reaching clear up to the foothills. And the Ashrafi garden would be sold and subdivided yet again. I had little notion then of how long the interim would be.

Later that year, Nasrin got her second divorce — she was in the process, in fact, of getting it that summer. She remained in Iran — still sequestered in Niavaran — until her father's death.

After that she left with her mother for Switzerland. Then there appeared — a surprise to everyone who knew her — a volume, in Persian, of her poetry. A second one followed, which established, in a modest way, her reputation as a "poetess of intimate feeling." (I'm quoting as nearly as I can from one review.) Where she is now, I don't know: she leads a private existence.

The opposite is the case with her second husband, about whom one reads in the papers — the Iranian ones, at any rate. Shortly after the divorce, Karbalai and Gloria were married. They keep an apartment in New York — on Park Avenue — and another in the heart of Tehran. They go back and forth, from what I gather, between the two cities. They also have a seven-year-old daughter. Her name is Yasmin — jasmine.

Amuzegar, soon after I left, became Minister of War and then took a tumble. He was accused of embezzling funds from the army — which my parents say isn't true. It was simply that he was getting too powerful. Everyone embezzles, anyway. Ironically, they claim, he was one of the few who didn't. He didn't need to. He gambled like mad, but, apparently, that was as far as things went. His gambling, though, was used as an excuse: his downfall from start to finish. He never remarried, and died in prison — of a heart attack. My parents had gone to see him only two weeks before.

The Karimzadehs, on the other hand, are doing very well. Ahmad Karimzadeh is a senator. He resigned as president of the Chamber of Commerce a few years back, on account of his health. His wife is about the same as ever. Farid is running the family business and doing fabulously, too. I'll mention just one of his coups. While he was still in Hamburg, he managed to buy out my grandfather's store from under my half-uncle. Without Magdalena, apparently, my half-uncle wasn't able to operate the business. So Haus Teheran is now in the hands of the Karimzadehs — and run by Matin. Having set up his brother to manage the German end of the business, Farid returned to Iran to take over from his father. At 38 or so, people are already looking to him as a future Minister of Finance. Like his father, he married a woman of means and has three — I'm quoting my mother — beautiful children.

Mahin returned to Tehran after finishing her studies, and is now teaching at the university. She is also the head of a women's organization, which should put her some day in Parliament. In any case, her career is set. Bijan was right about something else, too: she still hasn't married.

Bijan is now Colonel Ashrafi. He and Zohre are still married, which alternately surprises me and doesn't. It is said that he is high up in the secret police. It is also said that one of the moves that got him there was the information he gathered against General Amuzegar. I have no way, of course, of confirming this.

As for my father's business, two years after I left, the company in Texas canceled its working agreement with him. The agency then became a part of the Karbalai Corporation.

That afternoon up on the hill, after taking pictures of the city, I was about to go down when I noticed a strip of green in the cleft of a gully, some way off and below. It was a small strip, but an oasis of sorts amid all the barrenness, and I felt drawn to it.

When I got there, I saw a tiny stream lining the bottom. The stream was about as narrow as a thick piece of string and dropped over some rocks into a tiny pool. There it stopped and seeped into the earth.

I went over to it and caught a remarkable sight: the trickle of water was making its way through a cobweb, stretched like a sheet over the rocks.

I took a picture of it; when the picture came out, the cobweb was gone.